Moments and Milestones

DIANE GREENWOOD MUIR

Cover Design Photography: Maxim M. Muir

Don't miss any books in Diane Greenwood Muir's

Bellingwood Series

Diane publishes a new book in this series
on the 25th of March, June, September, and December.
Short stories are published between those dates
and vignettes are written and published each month
in the newsletter.

Journals
(Paperback only)
Find Joy — A Gratitude Journal
Books are Life — A Reading Journal
Capture Your Memories — A Journal

Re-told Bible Stories
(Kindle only)
Abiding Love — the story of Ruth
Abiding Grace — the story of the Prodigal Son
Abiding Hope — the story of the Good Samaritan

You can find a list of all published works
at nammynools.com

CONTENTS

ACKNOWLEDGMENTS

What do you do when the crazy outweighs the normal? I write. Thank goodness for the opportunity to tell stories. This last spring has been filled with repair craziness around here. I am so thankful for small towns and the people I can reach out to for help. They are here in a flash and fix me right up.

If I am asked to identify my favorite part of writing this series, every single time I will identify the growing community - mostly on Facebook (facebook.com/pollygiller). You have no idea how much you all mean to me. When I am struggling with anything related to my writing, a few minutes spent with you all reminds me of the joy that comes from sharing these stories.

One thing I continually see you mention is that you'd like to have a Polly in your life … or a Lydia, Beryl, Sylvie, or Andy. My mother wasn't much for wishing and not doing. She would tell us all that to have a Polly in your life, you need to be a Polly. She was right. It's so simple to wish that everyone else would be what we desire them to be and forget that someone might be wishing we would step up and be their friend.

It's not easy, but no matter what the world tries to tell us, people are worth it. You all are proof positive of that in my life. Not a day goes by that someone from the Bellingwood community reaches out to offer a bit of love and joy to me. I am so thankful.

The group that helps me with the Bellingwood series is filled with incredible and brilliant women. I am grateful to them. Thank you to: Diane Wendt, Carol Greenwood, Alice Stewart, Eileen Adickes, Fran Neff, Max Muir, Tracy Simpson, Linda Watson, Nancy Quist, Rebecca Bauman, and Judy Tew.

Spend time with us at facebook.com/pollygiller.

CHAPTER ONE

Polly closed her eyes and leaned back in the rocking chair on the porch outside her office. The sun was on the other side of the house and a breeze licked the heat of the day away. What a wonderful place to spend an hour this afternoon.

Silence. Pure, blessed silence. Well, other than birds singing in the trees. Oh yeah, and Han snoring loudly beside her.

She opened her eyes long enough to pick up a glass of iced coffee. This was one of those perfect days. She loved her back yard, her family was busy with their own activities, things were going well with Sycamore Enterprises, a long holiday weekend was only a few days away, and she had nothing to complain about. She put the coffee back on the table beside her and let her hand drift down to rest on Obiwan's head. Rubbing around his ears, she grinned. "Pretty good moment in time, isn't it, bud?"

Han sat up at her voice. That dog was always ready to go. He stood and shook himself, then bounced on his front paws at Obiwan. The older dog stood and nudged Polly's leg before following Han off the porch. In moments, the two were racing across the yard, yapping and playing.

The hour of peace would soon be up when Cassidy woke from her nap. There were a million things Polly could be doing in her office, but this was worth setting that all aside.

She'd spent the morning with Edna Dahlman at Sycamore House. Mondays were quiet over there. Both Stephanie and Jeff took the day off after working Friday nights and all day on Saturdays. Rachel and her catering crew rarely worked on Mondays either. The newest employee, Scott Luther, came in to work late, but Eliseo could always be found, no matter what day of the week it was.

With Cat at home this summer, Polly had freedom to work outside the house without taking her shadow along. She tried to do most of her work in the mornings since Cat generally took the boys to the swimming pool as soon as it opened in the afternoons.

Cassidy was taking swimming lessons so she'd be comfortable in the pool, but with as busy as the community pool was on these warm days, Cat had enough to do watching four young boys who loved to swim and play with their friends.

While they'd all have preferred Hayden work for Henry this summer, he'd taken a position at a research facility in Ames. He was still home every evening, but Polly hated to admit how much she had looked forward to him being around. She loved having her family close during the summer break.

Rebecca was having a grand time working at Greene Space, Reuben and Judy Greene's studio and gallery down the street from Sweet Beans. Reuben and Judy were early morning people, so they were up and out at the bed and breakfast before Rebecca even recognized the sun had risen. But by ten o'clock every morning, Rebecca had the gallery open and worked alone until noon when one or the other arrived to give her a lunch break. Reuben spent afternoons with her in the gallery. She worked until three, six days a week. Thursdays were her big day out and about. After leaving work, Rebecca headed for Beryl's to spend time with her mentor. Home by five for a quick dinner, she was back at the gallery at six to work until they closed at eight. Polly was glad Rebecca loved her job because she was there all the time.

Since she was finished mid-afternoon every day, Rebecca had plenty of time to spend with her friends. Cilla was working at the quilt shop, Andrew at the grocery store, their friend, Libby, had taken a job at the general store, and Dierdre was working for Elva Johnson at the stables, a twist no one saw coming. The girl most everyone assumed slept in a coffin in her parent's basement loved being outside with the animals Elva continued to acquire. She'd been hired to answer the phone and help with scheduling during the busy summer season, but was soon tending to geese and ducks, goats, and rabbits. There was even a pot-bellied pig whose original owners had no idea how to handle once it got too large for their home.

Elva hadn't intended to become an animal rescue, but she had trouble saying no when Doc Ogden begged her to care for animals that needed a home. They had plenty of land and she loved those beasts, no matter their size or shape.

Henry's aunt and uncle, Betty and Dick Mercer, thought it was wonderful fun. Their farmland surrounded Elva and Eliseo's land, so they carved out a few neighboring acres and the next thing anyone knew, Dick was building shelters and pens to house some of the animals. On any given morning, he could be found playing with the goats or finding a favorite scratching spot on Arnold the pig's back. He didn't particularly care about the horses, but the other animals were fun to play with.

"Mommy, can I be up now?"

Polly jumped out of the rocker and smiled at Cassidy who was standing in the office doorway.

"Of course." Polly opened the door while Cassidy walked past her onto the porch. "Did you fall asleep?"

The answer was in the little girl's eyes. She'd definitely been asleep. Polly reached to caress her daughter's cheek where she could still see the imprint of a wrinkle from a pillow.

"Yes," Cassidy said. "I had a dream." She grinned up at Polly. "About ice cream."

Polly laughed out loud. "Did you, now. What flavor?"

"Vanilla."

"Do you think we should have ice cream today?"

"With chocolate sauce."

"I love you, little girl. Why don't we save that ice cream for after dinner tonight when everyone is home?"

Cassidy had turned five in April. Polly knew better than to think the birthday had anything to do with it, but at some point in the weeks following, Cassidy's voice showed up. Full sentences, interesting commentary, protests when she didn't think her treatment was fair, warnings to her brothers to be nice to her, on and on. It was all there.

The birthday party had been a huge success. As Polly watched Cassidy's awe at the idea a party could be all about her, her heart had nearly broken in two. It wasn't even the gifts. Because so many people had been invited, Polly asked them to not bring anything. Cassidy's immediate family gave her plenty and she needed nothing else. Some couldn't help themselves, but that wasn't what made Cassidy so happy. It was the fact that everyone, from the youngest to the oldest, made time for her that afternoon. She didn't know what to do with the attention. Not only did they wish her happy birthday, but Polly and Henry's friends all seemed to know that taking a few moments to attempt a conversation with the girl was important.

Two weeks later, at Rebecca's sixteenth birthday party, Cassidy watched the same thing happen for her older sister with great interest. It was almost as if she made the connection between a birthday celebration and the fact that she belonged to a family. Soon words flowed from her mouth and they hadn't stopped.

Cassidy didn't act as if anything had changed. She wasn't at all surprised by the sudden transformation and didn't understand why others were so excited to hear her use complete sentences. One other major change had been in her attitude. She still dealt with anger and frustration, but once she was able to express herself, it didn't escalate quite so fast.

"Where are your shoes?" Polly asked.

Cassidy looked down at her feet and then back up at Polly, as if she were surprised not to find them there.

"Are they in the mudroom?"

"Yes!"

"Put them on and come back. We'll play on the swing set."

Cassidy ran off to find her shoes.

Polly had trouble keeping Cassidy active. She preferred to watch television or even sit and watch while her brothers played. More than likely, the little girl had never done anything that felt like play until she came into Polly's house. When asked to roll a ball back and forth across the foyer floor, she would push it and then get distracted by something else. Sometimes she simply laid down on the floor and ignored the ball completely.

On the other hand, her older brothers were learning to wrestle with each other, something *they* had never done before. Now that their lives felt more normal and they were confident that this home was theirs for good, they were ready for nearly anything. Henry had them on the floor in big dogpiles and scrambling back and forth whenever he had time in the evening, to the utter delight of everyone. Those four boys turned into happy mush when Henry took time to play with them. Screams and howls of laughter were often heard coming from the living room. Once it warmed up and the back yard dried out after the long, wet winter, the boys dragged him outside, begging him to chase them. He was never going to be out of shape with those four in his life.

Things were finally getting easier with his business. Gavin Riddle had been a great hire, though it took him a couple of months to learn the ropes. The men learned to trust him and soon allowed him to be Henry's voice in the field. When Heath finished with school mid-May, he and Gavin took more leadership roles together. Gavin was a smart young man and understood that Heath would one day be his boss. With those two working side by side, Henry found he was much less stressed. He still worked too many hours, but a lot of those were spent in the office at home, in the evenings and on weekends. At least when he was home, he found time to play with the kids.

As much time as the boys spent outside, Cassidy wasn't willing to participate in their playtime yet. Even when the neighbor children, Lara and Abby Waters and Rose Bright came over to play, she didn't want to be out with them.

Changing that behavior had been Polly's goal for this summer. When it was just Polly and Cassidy, the little girl loved playing outside. She would swing and run up the steps to slide down the slide. Polly wanted her to be comfortable with balls, which as she observed, was one thing that seemed to terrify her daughter. They played with a soccer ball, kicking it back and forth to each other. They played with brightly colored balls, tossing them across a short space. All Polly wanted her to do was catch it once in a while. So far, Cassidy had trouble finding the ball in the air before it landed in front of her. Not that this was anything new to Polly. She was the last person who should be teaching Cassidy to throw and catch, but if the little girl was going to learn, Polly might as well practice.

Polly made sure they did all of this out of sight of the boys. She didn't think any of them would laugh at Cassidy or tease her, but she knew what it was like to be embarrassed at not having a skill that everyone else seemed to have. There was so much catch-up that needed to be done with this child before she was prepared to go to kindergarten in September.

Cassidy ran back into the room, carrying her shoes.

"Put them on, honey."

Obiwan and Han had come back up onto the porch to see what was going on. When they realized that Cassidy was coming outside with them, their tails wagged with joy. Han yapped, expressing his urgent desire to play.

Cassidy pulled the Velcro tab across the top of her shoe and stood up. She didn't wait for Polly but headed out the back door. Polly just shook her head and followed her daughter down the steps and over to the side yard where Henry had built a swing set. Cassidy laughed as the dogs ran around her, pushing Han away when he got too close. She spent plenty of time falling on her bottom when the dogs got excited and she wasn't paying attention.

"Do you want to swing first?" Polly asked.

She started slowly with Cassidy as the little girl dangled her feet in front of her while holding onto the chains with a death grip. She'd loosen up soon; it just took time.

The dogs ran back and forth in front of Cassidy making her laugh, while Polly looked over at the new house next door which was finally rising above their fence line.

There was a great deal of gossip about the new owners of the newspaper — Lillybeth and Brad Anderson. Nothing had been done yet in the old newspaper office. The doors had never been opened as far as anyone could tell. Henry had received a call in early April to stop all work on their new house, so construction stopped just after the basement walls had gone up. No explanation, just directions to stop. After Memorial Day, out of the blue, Lillybeth had called again, asking him to pick up where he'd left off. He tried to explain that he'd pushed other projects ahead of hers, but she didn't care. She'd pay anything for him to start again. These were definitely going to be interesting neighbors.

Her mother, Elaine Borden, had been in Bellingwood more often than either Lillybeth or her husband. She and Simon Gardner at the antique shop were often seen together, but they weren't saying anything to anyone about what had happened with the house or the newspaper.

They regularly ate lunch at the diner and if anyone could uncover what was happening, it would be her favorite waitress, Lucy Parker. But even she had no idea.

Polly wondered if the Andersons had any idea that living in a small town was quite different than living in a city. People paid attention. If they didn't get the correct information, they were more than happy to make things up. As long as the mystery continued, gossip would spread.

"Higher," Cassidy called out.

Polly stepped to the side and gave her a strong push. "Kick your legs like I taught you. You can make it go as high as you want." She sat in the swing next to Cassidy and pulled her legs up so they could dangle freely. She'd hooked the links up so she could use the swing, but one of the boys had changed the height on them and now she was too close to the ground. They wouldn't be here long enough this afternoon for her to change it again.

"Do you want to throw the ball with me?" Polly asked.

Cassidy shook her head as she kicked her legs. Once she got into the rhythm, she sailed back and forth, a happy grin on her face. "I'm flying!"

"Look at you go, sweetie. Isn't it wonderful?" There was something freeing about a swing set. Polly had forgotten what it felt like until she'd experienced it again as an adult.

"What do you want to do when you grow up?" Polly asked Cassidy.

The little girl quit kicking and allowed her swing to slow. She took a long look at Polly. "I want to be a teacher."

"Like Cat?" She wasn't sure how Cassidy would have any other context. She'd only met her school teacher once at Kindergarten Roundup. She went to Sunday School, but those were the only teachers in her young life so far.

"Like you."

That made Polly smile. The two of them spent a lot of time together these last months as Polly did her best to bring Cassidy to a point where she could attend school with confidence. She'd had no concept of letters or numbers, much less words and sentences when she arrived in the house.

Caleb still read to her whenever Heath was around to encourage him. Since Marie had been working with Molly so much, she'd also drawn Cassidy into the learning. That had been helpful. Polly took Cassidy to the library for story time every week, hoping that she would see how other children interacted with each other as well as with the books they read together. There was so much that Cassidy had missed out on in those first four years when she'd been passed around. She couldn't verbalize any memories of her past, but nightmares and irrational fears pointed out how far she had yet to go.

Once Cassidy came to a full stop, Polly stood. "Let's get a ball."

Balls were stashed in a wooden box on the back porch and Polly stood over the open container. "Pick one out," she said.

Cassidy reached in and took out a red ball the size of her head.

"Okay," Polly said. "I'll go over here and you throw it to me."

With a fling, the ball sailed into the air and dropped about a foot in front of Cassidy.

Fortunately, that was also only about a foot from Polly. She knew better than to put much distance between them. It would get better, but after two months of this, Polly was working hard on her patience.

They played with the ball for a while until Cassidy sat down on the grass, then flopped on her back.

"Are you all done?" Polly asked.

"I don't want no more ball," Cassidy whined.

"Okay. Rebecca should be home soon."

At that, Cassidy jumped up and ran for the door into Polly's office. It was amazing what could stir the little girl into action. The dogs followed them inside.

"Go upstairs and get your doll and two books," Polly said. "I'll read to you while we wait for Rebecca."

Cassidy hesitated. She was more coordinated than she'd been when she first arrived, but her little legs still fought with the big stairs in the foyer. Though it was closer, it would take her much more work, each step requiring at least two steps on Cassidy's part. She made a decision and ran for the kitchen.

Because so many of Rebecca's friends worked downtown, Polly was never quite sure when her older daughter would be home. She took any opportunity to meet up with one or another of her friends to wander through shops or go to the diner or the coffee shop for something to drink, even the General Store for ice cream or the library to find the newest book in a series that she was reading. Rarely did Rebecca come straight home.

It wasn't like Polly couldn't track her down with little effort. One or two phone calls to her own friends who worked downtown and Rebecca's exact location and her companions would be known.

They'd found a used car for her. It wasn't flashy, it wasn't exciting, but it got her around. Polly still had trouble accepting that little Rebecca was driving. Alone. Without adult supervision. The thing was, she was a great driver. But still, how had this happened? She was going to be a junior in high school this fall. There were only two more years left of her childhood. It nearly drove Polly to tears every time she thought about it, though she was proud of the young woman that Rebecca was becoming.

The door to the mud room opened and Rebecca talked to the dogs as she pushed past them. When she got into the kitchen, she slammed her purse down on the counter beside the coffee maker.

Cassidy came running in from the back steps, carrying books and a doll. She dropped them on the floor when she saw Rebecca and ran over with her arms help open wide. "You're home!"

Rebecca looked at Polly over the top of the little girl's head, snarled and then pasted on a smile as she bent down for a hug. "I am home. What did you do today?"

"I want to be a teacher when I grow up."

Rebecca frowned. "A teacher? When did you decide this?"

"Today. I'm going to be a teacher."

"You will be a wonderful teacher." Rebecca stood up and huffed a laugh. "I'm not even sure what I want to be when I grow up. Maybe I'll work at Greene Space for the rest of my life."

"Bad day?" Polly asked.

Rebecca allowed Cassidy to pull her across the room, stopping only when the little girl picked up her books. She handed them one by one to Rebecca, holding tight to her doll.

"Just the last little bit. Work was great. I met this cool couple from Mediapolis. She wanted to see some of Beryl's artwork. So weird. Her sister lives in Portland, Maine and owns one of Beryl's paintings. I called Jeff at Sycamore House and asked if she could go over there to see some of Beryl's other pieces. It was fun talking to them."

"What happened to upset you?"

Rebecca blew out a disgusted breath. "Oh, it's nothing. Just dumb stuff. Not at work. Don't worry about that."

CHAPTER TWO

Rebecca was quiet through dinner, except for brushing off Elijah's attention when he tried to talk to her. When Polly pressed for more information, she got no response. As soon as the dining room was clear and the kitchen was clean, the boys tore for the basement. They'd been playing down there all day and weren't finished building whatever it was they were building.

Rebecca took off for the gazebo in the back yard and soon Cilla, Andrew, and Kayla were all out back with her. Now that Andrew had his driver's license, the four of them spent many evenings hanging out at the Bell House. He'd pick Kayla up from the hotel after dinner and they'd come over together. It was better than having them driving back and forth on the main strip, Polly supposed. That was what she'd done through high school and the memory made her smile. Sometimes the four kids made their way downtown, but tonight they were huddled together, gesturing furiously while they talked.

Polly watched from the kitchen. Rebecca was angry about something. She could tell by the way her daughter used her hands and the fire on her face. The other three listened and responded as if they were trying to come up with ways to help.

"What's going on?" Henry asked.

"Something's up with Rebecca, but she's not talking to me."

He nodded toward the gazebo. "Looks like she's talking to them."

Polly smiled. "I suppose that's the way things will go from now on. I miss being her favorite person, but there isn't anything I can do about it. Her friends will always be her outlet."

"She'll tell you eventually. The girl can't help herself. She tells you everything."

He was right about that. Rebecca might believe she was an independent young woman, but when it came down to it, she needed Polly to know what was going on and either discipline her or approve of her decisions. For the most part, Rebecca made good choices.

"How was your morning with Edna?" he asked, leading her away from the door.

Polly allowed herself to be drawn to the sofas. "I like her. She's so soft-spoken, you don't realize how much depth there is to the woman. And I've never seen anything like it. Edna knows exactly where every penny is, can spit out a report faster than you can imagine and today she told me that in the next six months we'd better add more businesses or she's going to be bored."

He frowned. "Bored?"

"I know. Jeff and Sal meet with her every week about the foundation, too. She's got that thing down to a science. I asked if she'd consider taking on the accounting for Sturtz Construction and the crazy woman's eyes lit up. Like it's a new puzzle she gets to unwrap. I will never understand a mind like that."

"You can do the work; you just don't like it."

"Exactly," Polly said. "When I walk in on Monday mornings, she has reports for every single one of the businesses ready for me. She told me that I didn't have to come in if I didn't want to. She'd be glad to send them to me, but when she said the words, her eyes didn't quite back them up. I think she likes having me spend time with her. I like it too. She's a genuinely nice person."

"Who likes accounting," Henry said, shaking his head.

"She's also helping Kristen in the main office. As good as Kristen is, she didn't come to us with a great deal of office management training. Edna is helping her implement better processes. They're a good team."

"Do you want to give up my accounting to her?" Henry asked.

Polly looked at him sideways.

"Dumb question," he said. "Do what you want with it."

"Not quite yet, but we'll talk about it," she said. "I still like working on things with you."

Henry waggled his eyes. "Me too."

Cassidy came down the steps as fast as her little legs would carry her. "Ice cream?" she asked.

Polly groaned. "I did promise you that we'd have ice cream tonight, didn't I." She turned to Henry. "This one forgets nothing."

"Do we have any?" He stood up to head for the refrigerator.

"When I said something this afternoon, I'd considered making homemade, but in no time, I'd forgotten. I don't even know if we have enough milk and eggs. I'll pick some up tomorrow."

Cassidy stuck her lower lip out in a pout. "But you said …"

"I did. If we have any in the freezer, we'll have ice cream," Polly assured her. "Tomorrow afternoon we'll make our own. That's always better, isn't it?"

"There's nothing in here," Henry said. "Let me check the porch."

"Mommy," Cassidy said, her lip starting to quiver. "You said we'd get ice cream."

Henry came back into the kitchen brandishing an unopened box of ice cream sandwiches. "Look what I found. Mommy's favorites."

"Ah ha ha," Polly said, with a relieved laugh. "Perfect."

But when she bent to help Cassidy up so she could sit at the island, she was met with a full-on pout. "I wanted ice cream with chocolate sauce."

Polly lifted an eyebrow. "We don't have any in the house. You can have an ice cream sandwich or you can have nothing. It's your choice."

13

This was always a delicate moment in Polly's evening. There was no telling which way Cassidy's emotions would take her. She set Cassidy down on one of the seats and sat beside her while Henry opened the box.

Cassidy looked at Polly, then at Henry. Neither of them put up with her temper tantrums, but that didn't stop her from throwing one whenever she felt like it.

Henry took a wrapped sandwich out and handed it across to Polly, then opened the cupboard and took down a plate. He put a second sandwich on the plate and pushed it across to them. "Do you want this, Cassidy?"

She looked at it, then up at him and smiled a radiant smile. "I like ice cream sandwiches," she said.

Polly's phone rang in the charging station and Henry walked over for it while she unwrapped Cassidy's ice cream.

"It's Skylar," he said.

"Why is he calling? Go ahead."

Henry swiped the call open. "Hello, Sky. How are you this evening?" He took the package of ice cream sandwiches to the freezer in the fridge and opened the door. "Sure. We'll be right over. Thanks for calling."

"What's up?" Polly asked.

"Skylar says they found something in one of the rooms. He wants us to come over before he calls Chief Wallers."

"What did he find?" She pursed her lips. "You didn't ask, did you?"

"We're going to be there in ten minutes."

"You're useless. I hope it isn't more gas cans."

"Me too."

She looked down at herself, dressed in shorts and a baggy t-shirt. She hadn't been planning to go anywhere. "I'm going upstairs to change my shirt and ask Cat to keep an eye on things."

"I'll keep working on ice cream. What about yours?"

"Put it in the freezer. I'm not interested." Polly ran to the back steps, paying no attention to Cassidy's protestations. Henry would deal with her.

She knocked on the door to Cat and Hayden's apartment and pushed it open. The long hallway that turned at the end to their bedroom offered them a great deal of privacy.

"Cat? I need to go to the hotel. Can you head downstairs to watch the kids?"

The sound of their television went off and in a second, Cat was in the hallway. "Sure. What's going on?"

"We don't know. Skylar just called and asked us to come over. He says they found something and we need to call the police."

"Not another batch of gas cans."

"Let's hope not. I need to change my clothes. Henry is helping Cassidy eat an ice cream sandwich in the kitchen, the boys are in the basement, and Rebecca is out back with her friends."

"Thanks. We'll be right down."

Cat was on duty all day with the kids. Once school was out, she went back to helping with cleaning and laundry, kid-sitting and transporting them from place to place. Since Hayden was gone during the day, Polly and Henry made sure they had their evenings free unless something came up. The young couple was pretty wonderful about spending time with the family, making it easy for Polly to ask.

She ran to her bedroom, doing her best not to trip over the many animals that wanted to race her down the hall. The cats jumped up on the bed. It might be early, but if they could find the perfect spot before Han and Obiwan landed, they were the winners. A pair of jeans lay over the back of Henry's chair and she slid into them, then snagged a blouse to replace the t-shirt. At least she looked better. Polly checked her hair in the full-length mirror Henry had installed behind the door. She'd become used to the layers and color that Mina had given her and found that it was easy to maintain. Mina and her team were in the new salon now and whenever Polly spent time there, it felt like a party. Everyone that worked there enjoyed the space.

Running back down the hallway, she met Hayden at the door to his apartment's bathroom. He backed up and gestured for her to go first.

"Sorry," she said.

"Never get in the way of a woman in a hurry."

"You're a smart boy." Polly trotted down the steps. Now that she'd dealt with everything here, her mind was working on what might be happening at the hotel. If she'd answered the phone, Skylar would have given her more details. Sometimes Henry was just too pragmatic. Of course, they'd be there soon and would know everything they needed to know. Since they couldn't do anything about it from the house, why worry. She gave Cassidy a quick hug on her way past.

"Call us," Cat said. "Hopefully it's nothing."

Polly stopped in the doorway to the porch. "I hope so. Thank you."

Henry was already in his truck, the windows rolled down and one of his favorite country bands playing on the radio. His musical taste was all over the place, but when he was in his truck, this was his choice. He knew it wasn't her favorite and took every opportunity to make sure it was playing when she rode with him.

"Skylar wouldn't call if it wasn't important," Polly said, reaching to turn down the sound. She wouldn't turn it off, that only made him ornerier. But she always turned it way down. There was nothing worse than trying to talk over music. Especially when she was already stressed.

"He sounded worried," Henry replied.

She snapped her head to him. "Did I take too long changing my clothes?"

"You took no more than five minutes. Since you aren't already there, it's not a dead body. Likely, anything else can wait. If a guest was hurt, he'd have called for a squad first. Stop worrying."

"I can't help it. When Jeff and Adam move to Bellingwood, I'm going to make him be first on the emergency call list."

Henry laughed out loud.

"Why are you laughing?"

"Because it would kill you to not know what was going on." He reached over and took her hand, giving it a gentle squeeze. "It's going to be okay."

"I know. But my stomach is all fluttery with worry right now. Why didn't you ask more questions?"

"Because I'm the worst husband in the world." Henry pulled into a parking space. The hotel was full tonight. She loved seeing that and now dreaded even more what might be coming at her. Nothing like facing down a large group of people if there was a problem.

She didn't see any people milling around outside, but when they got into the lobby, two groups of four guests each were seated at tables.

Skylar looked up from where he was talking to Nick Arthur, Sycamore Inn's night clerk. He came out to greet them. "I'm so glad you're here. I should probably call the police, but I wanted you to know what I was doing first."

"Is anyone hurt?"

"Not physically," he said.

Polly scowled. "What do you mean by that?"

"Come back here. I'll show you." He led the two of them behind the counter and lifted a cardboard box that had been set over a small black rectangular object.

"What's that?" Polly asked.

"It's a digital clock."

She peered at him. "Okay?"

"It isn't one of the digital clocks we provide in the rooms and it has a Wi-Fi camera inside."

Polly stepped back and gulped down a breath. "It has a what?"

"I know." Skylar dropped the box back over the clock. "It was plugged in, but it has a battery backup."

"How did you find this?"

"Nick got a call from the guest that the clock wasn't working and they couldn't set the alarm. He took an extra in to replace it and was startled when he found this. It's like nothing I've seen here. At first, I thought maybe a guest had left theirs behind. Nick looked up the model number and, well, he discovered what it is." Skylar pointed at the computer where Nick was scrolling around on a website.

"This is the one," Nick said, landing on a page.

Henry walked over to look at it. "Nearly two hundred dollars? That's not a cheap item to leave behind in a hotel room."

"Was it left or was it planted?" Polly asked. "We need to find out if any more rooms have these in them."

Skylar nodded. "That's why I wanted you to come over. Should we do it or should we let the police?"

Even while he was still talking, Polly took her phone out. "It's late. Who do I call?"

"Call Bellingwood police," Henry said.

She nodded and swiped the call open. Mindy wouldn't be on duty as dispatcher at this hour. She didn't know the others as well as Mindy, but that didn't matter. Everyone knew Polly Giller.

"Bellingwood Police."

"Hi, this is Polly Giller. I'm at Sycamore Inn and I think we need to have an officer come over. Who's on duty tonight?"

"Hello, Ms. Giller. Officer Bradford is on tonight. He'll be responding. What's the problem?"

"You aren't going to believe this, but someone on staff found a spy camera in one of the rooms."

"Hmmm," he said. "Okay. I'll send Officer Bradford. You're in the lobby?"

"Yes. Thank you."

"Thank you for calling." He ended the call and Polly gave Henry a look.

"What's that look for?"

"Bert's on his way, I wish I knew what this was about." She turned back to Skylar. "Does anyone here know what's going on but us?"

He shook his head. "No. I didn't want to upset anyone. I figure that's the police's job. Do you want to come into the apartment? Stephanie's just watching television. I told her you were coming over."

"I don't want to bother her," Polly said. "The girl needs to relax without us intruding on her evening."

"It's really okay. She said it was."

"You go ahead, Polly," Henry said. "I'll stay out here and wait for Bert."

Skylar opened the door to the apartment. "Steph? Polly's here." He bent down to scoop up an orange tabby cat that tried to scoot past him into the lobby. "I always have to pay attention to this one. He wants to know everything that's going on."

Stephanie limped into the kitchen. She'd always walk with a limp, but everyone was just glad she'd lived through the terrible car accident that she'd been in last year. "Hi, Polly. Wish you wouldn't have had to come. I told Skylar to just call the police, but he wanted you here."

"Have you called Jeff?" Polly asked.

"Texted him. He told me to let him know if he needed to come over. You don't think he does, do you?"

"No. He can deal with whatever the fallout is tomorrow."

She chuckled. "Fallout. I'll tell him you said that. Come on in. I've been so lazy today. I should have been cleaning, but it was nice to just have a whole day off."

Polly followed her into the tidy living room. "I'll have to leave town if I ever want a whole day off."

"You really should," Stephanie said. "Just you and Henry. Go somewhere and do nothing."

"I wouldn't know what to do with myself."

Stephanie laughed. "You never slow down. It's exhausting to watch you sometimes."

"It's all that coffee I drink."

"You and Jeff. That man drinks coffee all day. I can't believe he ever sleeps. If I don't stop drinking it by about four o'clock, I'm awake all night." She smiled at Polly. "Is it weird that we're sitting here having a normal conversation while we're waiting for the police to show up?"

Polly nodded. "Because there was a spy camera in one of the hotel rooms. I swear to you, Stephanie, my life used to be boring. I went to work. I went out with my friends. I went home. That was it. Boring. I moved to Bellingwood and a spy camera shows up in my hotel."

"How many people do you know that own a hotel?" Stephanie asked, a knowing smirk on her face.

"You have me there, but still. Weird things started happening after I came back to Iowa."

"Well, I have to tell you, Polly, it feels like my life got more normal when I moved to Bellingwood. That's because of you. Maybe you had to come to Iowa and start a crazy life so some of the rest of us could have a normal one."

"I like the way you think," Polly said. "Kayla's doing well."

Stephanie nodded and sat back when Flash, the cat, jumped into her lap. She stroked down his back. "She's starting to think about what she wants to do after high school. You know she'd follow Rebecca anywhere."

"Does she want to go to college?"

"It scares her, but she doesn't want to be left out. She's so afraid that if she doesn't go, she'll miss out on something exciting and fun that Rebecca is doing." She shrugged. "Her grades are okay. Not like Rebecca and Andrew's. And she doesn't really love doing anything like they do. I think she'd be happy as a secretary or receptionist and being a mom. I want to tell her that's okay, too."

"It is," Polly said.

"But how do you justify not being motivated to change the world when your best friend is Rebecca?"

Polly laughed out loud. "That would be nearly impossible. I can talk to Rebecca."

"That's not what I'm asking for. Not at all. I'm just thinking out loud. Kayla isn't like me either. She wants things that aren't important to me. I don't want a family. I went through too much. Leslie said that I should be okay with who I am."

Leslie was the counselor Stephanie had been seeing since she got to Bellingwood.

"She's right. Henry and I decided we didn't want children and even though we heard snide comments from people around town, it was the right decision for us. Whatever is the right decision for you is your business, no one else's."

"You have a houseful of kids though."

20

"Yeah, but they came to me. I didn't make them."

"I think that's just as important," Stephanie said.

"The thing is," Polly said, "it was my choice. Well, mine and Henry's. We made it together. It's nobody else's business. You get to do what you want to do with your life. And so does Kayla. She shouldn't feel like she needs to be like Rebecca. One reason Rebecca loves her so much is that she is Kayla. She's perfect for my daughter just the way she is."

"I'd like her to have some college experience. Just so she can get away from me for a while and see what it's like to live on her own. She's always been at home."

"The next two years are going to be over before we know it," Polly said. "At the same time, a million things could happen between now and then."

"No kidding. It's going so fast. I stay awake at night worrying about her, you know."

"About her present or her future?"

"Both," Stephanie said with a shrug. "She's so naïve. I'm glad for that. I really am, but Rebecca and her friends all protect Kayla from so much. Rebecca pushes her to get better grades while Cilla and Dierdre and Libby all are part of the crowd that gets her involved in activities. Andrew treats her like a sister, so she's safe with him. When she went on the few dates she had, they were Andrew's friends. Skylar and I are giving her more responsibility around here and I know she likes working at the front counter."

"She's wonderful with customers," Polly said. "Whenever I'm here, I see how much they like her."

"That's because she's sweet and will do everything she can to please them. I'm trying to teach her how to be frugal and watch her money, but it's hard to deny her something she really wants. She doesn't ask for much from me. I know she should get a car, but we can't afford it right now and having her drive terrifies me. Skylar took her out in his car to teach her. He says she's a good driver, but she isn't ready for that much responsibility. And she's perfectly happy riding with Rebecca. Heck, she'd probably still be happy on the bus."

As glad as Polly was that Stephanie had a good grasp on her sister's personality, it broke Polly's heart to realize that the protection high school offered would soon be gone. Kayla needed to grow up. Cilla and Rebecca were chomping at the bit to be independent. They'd drag their friend with them, but at some point, she needed to make her own way.

"You know," Polly said. "When Heath graduated from high school, he had no idea what he was going to do next. We pushed him to go to college. He went, knowing that the education would be useful to Henry and he'd have a place in the business when he was finished. He wasn't ready to be independent then, but two years later, he's making his own way. Kayla will find it, though it won't be easy for you or Rebecca, or even me, to let her go out there on her own."

"I know she will," Stephanie said. "I just want that part of it to be over so I can quit worrying." She looked up at the sound of the door opening.

"Polly?" Skylar called. "Officer Bradford is here and wants to talk to you."

CHAPTER THREE

"You are always up to something, Polly," Bert Bradford said. He put his hand out as she walked toward him. "Good evening. It sounds like it's been interesting."

"It certainly turned into a strange one," she replied. "I didn't expect to have a spy camera show up in one of my hotel rooms."

He chuckled. "I don't suppose so. I've reached out to the Chief. He's on his way over."

"Okay?"

"We might turn this over to the sheriff's office; they have more tech-savvy people than we do. I didn't even know these types of things were available." Bert huffed a laugh. "Not that I'm surprised, but I would have thought that a spy camera was just like one of those little things you have on the computer. This is some pretty fancy stuff." He turned to Skylar. "You have no idea how long that was in the room?"

Skylar shook his head. "We can talk to Barb and Cindy. They might have noticed. It can't have been too long. Guests use the clocks all the time. Surely someone would have noticed that they couldn't set an alarm before tonight."

Barb and Cindy Evering had been cleaning rooms at Sycamore Inn since it opened. The two were a dynamo and flew through their tasks every day.

"What about the other rooms?" Polly asked.

"We can go through the empty rooms right now," Skylar said. "I wasn't sure what you wanted to do about those that are occupied."

"If there are any more of these in the hotel, I want them out of the rooms," she replied. "I don't care what you tell people. Take new clocks with you and replace them, do whatever you have to do. I'm sick that people's privacy has been messed with."

"You want us to tell them the truth?"

"Not unless we have to."

Skylar nodded before giving a slight shudder. "I'll start on that right now. You have no idea how much I hate knocking on doors in the evening."

"Why's that?"

"What people wear at night in hotel rooms is a little out there. I've seen more naked bodies than a man should ever have to see. Why would you answer the door like that?" He rolled his shoulders and left them to walk over to where Nick was standing at his computer. The two talked for a few minutes, Nick handed over a key card and a piece of paper he'd picked off the printer, and Skylar headed out.

The guests in the lobby had watched much of the activity and Polly was thankful that Ken Wallers came in wearing street clothes rather than his uniform. He smiled warmly at the people who watched his entrance and strode over to Bert, Polly, and Henry. After shaking their hands, he led them behind the counter.

"What do we know?"

"Nothing yet," Bert said, pointing at the brown box that sat atop the clock. "That's the device."

Ken put his hand on the box and looked up with a grin. "Looks like a normal shipping box."

"We don't know if the thing under there is recording," Bert said. "It's a clock."

Ken chuckled and lifted the box, then dropped it back down. "Aren't we a bunch of neophytes. Has anyone thought to take the battery out?"

"I didn't know if you'd want to do that. Would it break the connection with whoever is recording?"

"I'm guessing they've already taken care of that with all the activity it's seen tonight." Ken pushed the box off, lifted the clock and flipped it back and forth. When he found the battery compartment, he opened it, then looked at Bert. "Evidence bag?"

"Oh, yes sir," Bert said and pulled one out of a pocket. He held it open while Ken dropped the two batteries into it.

"Everyone has touched the clock," Ken said. "Only our suspect touched the batteries. We'll see how smart he is."

"Or she," Polly retorted with a grin.

"I can't ever get away with anything." He put his hand out again and Bert handed him another evidence bag, which soon contained the errant clock. "Bert, you speak with Mr. James. Get his statement. I'll assume the Everings aren't behind this, so we'll wait until the morning to speak with them. I take it that you've already set someone to the task of checking the rest of the rooms?"

Bert nodded. "Mr. Morris is doing that right now."

Polly knew that Skylar's last name was Morris; she saw it all the time on various reports, but hearing him called *Mr. Morris* sounded strange and made him seem so much older than he was. She yanked her attention back to Ken and Bert.

"Seems to me we have two possibilities here," Ken said. "If we discover several devices, we likely have a peeping tom. That will require one response. If this is the only device, it could still be a peeping tom, or our suspect could have been spying on a specific guest. Polly, we're going to want your guest list for that room and any others where these devices are found."

She nodded. "Nick can get that for you."

"I'm also reaching out to Sheriff Merritt. I'd like his tech department to take a look at this."

"Anita?" Polly asked with a smile.

Anita Banks was one of her favorite people. A brilliant young woman who was a genius with all things tech, she was also a genius with all things related to Doug Randall. They'd discovered last Christmas that Anita's family was extremely wealthy. Somehow the girl had managed to live in Boone for years without letting anyone know that she came from money. Even her closest friends had been surprised. Whether Doug would ask her to marry him was anyone's guess. He'd handled the news of her family's wealth with equanimity, but then, nothing jarred Doug much these days. Polly had only seen him embarrassed once and that was the day she dumped her laundry down the stairs at Sycamore House and he'd seen her purple panties. But even then, he'd found it more funny than embarrassing.

"If that's who Aaron sends, we'll be lucky," Ken replied. "She's a smart one."

Skylar came back in the front door and headed over to them, shaking his head. "Nothing in any of the empty rooms," he said. "Standard clocks. It's kind of creepy, wondering if our spy has other types of devices installed. There are all sorts of things you can buy on that website. I wouldn't even know what to look for or where to look. Nothing seemed out of place, but who knows."

"Did you check the occupied rooms?" Bert asked him.

"No. I wanted to let you know that I hadn't found anything yet. Didn't want to keep you waiting. I'm going to grab a stack of towels and use that as an excuse to be there. If I see a weird clock, I have a couple with me and will change it out."

"Let me help you," Ken said. "No one need know that I'm not staff. I'm dressed like a concierge, aren't I?" He wore a pair of khakis and a neatly pressed western style plaid shirt. Somehow he still looked like a cop.

Polly laughed. "I should help. This is my hotel."

"Three of us will make this happen in a flash," Ken said.

"Four," Henry replied. "How many rooms are rented tonight?"

"Just seven," Skylar said. "The clock was found in room six." He gestured toward the group in the lobby with his head. "They have four of the rooms along the front. What should I do?"

Ken grinned. "We'll ask them to show us their rooms."

26

Polly's eyes grew big. "That's a little much. You're the police. What if they don't want you in there?"

"Tell them there's a problem with the water line and you want to check the bathroom."

"Maybe you should stay here," Polly said. "I don't want you to have to arrest someone simply because you walk in on them smoking some weed."

Ken laughed out loud. "Point taken. I'll wait here."

She shook her head and walked to the tables. "Excuse me."

Her words weren't really necessary as every eye was on her.

"What's going on?" one of the young women asked. "Is that the police? We've been trying to figure out if there's a raid or what."

Polly nodded, though she was curious as to why the girl's first thought was that there was a raid. "We'd like to check your bathrooms if we could. There has been some vandalism and we're worried about water coming in where it shouldn't be. If we find a problem, we'll move you to another room. Would that be okay?"

One of the young men looked at her. "The cops are coming into our rooms?"

"No. Either myself or the hotel manager will check. Your things are safe," she said with a smile. "Unless you're doing something illegal."

He glanced at the others in the group. "Give me a minute?"

She laughed. "Go on. Skylar or I will be there in a bit. Thank you."

The eight of them took off, leaving a mess on the tables, their chairs pulled out, and even a jacket draped over the back of one. Polly picked it up before heading toward Skylar. She held it out. "They were in a hurry."

He gave her a perplexed look and she grinned at him. "Maybe their rooms aren't quite as clean as they'd like us to believe. I told them we'd had some vandalism and needed to check for water damage in the bathrooms. If you find a device, just make something up and move them to one of the empty rooms. I'll let you take those four rooms and Henry and I will take the other three. Where are we going?"

"Seven, nine and eleven," he said. "Want some towels?"

"That's fine. We'll use the same excuse. Henry, you ready to look at some bathrooms?"

Henry shook his head. "I'll follow you anywhere, my sweet."

Rooms seven, nine, and eleven were on the back corner of the hotel. Alistair Greyson's small skating rink was closed for the summer, the cover pulled tight across its top. Polly hoped to get her boys involved with his program this next winter. He was so good with the kids in town and they already knew and liked him.

Henry stopped in front of room seven. "You're the owner."

She chuckled. "I seem to remember that you bought this piece of property with me." But even as she spoke, she raised her hand to knock and called out, "Management."

Within seconds, she heard the chain move into place. The door was pulled open as far as the chain allowed.

"What?" the man demanded.

Polly held out a business card, glad she carried extras in her pocket. "I'm the owner of the property. We've had some vandalism and are worried about water leaks in the bathroom. I'd like my plumber to check. If there are any problems, we'll move you to another room."

"I don't hear any water running," he said.

"We'd like to check. We'll be in and out in a flash."

"Just a minute," the man said grumpily. He closed the door and she heard the chain again before the door was opened all the way.

"I'm sorry to bother you," Polly continued, stepping into the room. Henry moved past her to the bathroom. She looked around and finally discovered a standard clock where it belonged on a bedside table. She breathed a sigh of relief.

Henry came out of the bathroom. "Everything is fine in this room. Thank you for understanding," he said to the man. "We'll get out of your hair."

The very bald man looked at Henry as if he had lost his mind and walked with them to the door, closing it as soon as they crossed the threshold. They giggled as they heard the sound of the chain snapping into place.

"I'll get out of your hair?" Polly asked in a whisper.

Henry shook his head, then stopped and doubled over in laughter. "As soon as it was out of my mouth, I recognized my mistake, but there was no getting out of it. Hopefully I didn't insult a regular guest."

When he had his laughter under control, they moved to the next room. Neither of the next two rooms had anything other than the hotel's regular clock beside the bed. The guests were understanding, though the couple in room eleven looked as if Polly and Henry had interrupted something intimate.

"I don't know what to think," Polly said as they walked back to the lobby. "We live in Bellingwood. It isn't near a big city; we don't have big city traffic or even big city guests staying at the hotel. Who would be spying on someone in this little place?"

"Maybe it's one of Agnes's assassins," Henry replied.

Agnes Hill had fast become part of Polly's family, her love for young Cassidy knowing no bounds. She spent time several days a week at the Bell House, playing with Cassidy, reading to her, talking to her, helping her negotiate her way around the life of a little girl. She was a wonder with that child and seemed to enjoy the rest of the family just as much.

It was hard for Polly to imagine, now that she had a big family of her own, not having that as she grew older. Agnes never said anything about missing out but took every opportunity to be part of their lives. When spring concerts, recitals, programs and activities occurred, Polly took Cassidy and Agnes to everything. The woman didn't want to miss a single event. If Cassidy got distracted during a long concert, Agnes was right there to keep her quiet and occupied.

Agnes hadn't lost a bit of her snarky, tough mouth and continued to insist that when she wasn't with the Giller-Sturtz family, she was managing teams of assassins around the world. Polly's family didn't quite know what to make of that. Even Polly was having trouble with it. After all this time, she was sure that Agnes would have given up the charade, but every week she was talking about another team who needed her to intervene with an international government official. It had become quite the story around the dinner table.

"That really isn't funny," Polly said. "What if it's true?"

He laughed. "Oh, come on."

They'd had this discussion before. Neither of them wanted to believe it was legitimate, but at the same time, how was the woman able to drag the story out this long?

"If it's true, you and I are going to be embarrassed," she said.

"If it's true, you and I are going to be shocked," he replied. "That old lady is crazy, but she isn't insane."

"I know."

"Woman of mystery," he said, holding the door to the lobby open for her.

Skylar was already back and the lobby was empty of guests, so everyone was seated at the tables out front. Whatever mess the guests had left was now cleaned up. Stephanie had joined them and waved at Polly when they came in.

"Nothing," Henry said.

Skylar shook his head, then asked with a grin, "Me neither. What did you think of Dave Austin back in room seven?"

"He's a regular?" Henry asked.

"Yeah. He sells farm insurance and is in town once a quarter. Stays for a few days and then he moves on. The guy is an old codger. Luckily, June's got his number and doesn't put up with much from him."

"Henry told him we'd get out of his hair," Polly said.

Skylar looked at her husband in shock. "You didn't." Then he turned to Ken and Bert Bradford. "The man is cue-ball bald."

Ken laughed until he snorted.

"Does this mean one of our guests was targeted?" Polly asked, sobering the gathering.

"I suspect so," Ken replied. "I hope Miss Banks will help us pinpoint when the device was installed, though I can't imagine how. Maybe she has several magic tricks up her sleeves."

"If anyone does, it will be Anita," Polly said. "Have you gotten everything you need tonight?"

Bert looked at Ken, who nodded. Bert brandished a piece of paper. "This is a list of the guests who stayed in that room for the last month. If we have to go back further, I'll be in touch."

Bert handed the list to Polly, who scanned it, unsure why she needed to know the information and then handed it back to him with a nod. He folded it in half, then half again and slid it into a pocket.

Henry put his hand on Polly's back. "If you don't need us any longer, I'm taking my wife out for an ice cream sandwich before we go home."

"He's my big spender," Polly said. "Let me know what you find out." She raised her eyebrows at Ken. "Yes?"

"I'll do what I can," he said, his eyes alight with laughter. "If I don't, you'll find out anyway. I know you. I'm just glad you call Aaron when you find the bodies. You can call my office any time for the other stuff. Though I must admit, this is a new one."

"Glad we can keep you on your toes." Polly stepped away from her husband and over to Skylar. "You okay?"

He shrugged. "This one is going into my journal. Every time something new and odd happens around here, I make a note. Someday I'm going to write a bestseller about Bellingwood."

She gave him a quick hug, then touched Stephanie's arm. "Have a good rest of the evening. When do you expect Kayla home?"

"I told her to call me if it was going to be after ten thirty."

"Got it." Polly hooked her arm in Henry's and they left by the front door. He held the door of his truck open for her, then stepped in and kissed her before she pulled the seatbelt on. "What's that for?" she asked.

"I don't know. It's just so nice to be out with you."

"Even if we're in the middle of an investigation into possible spying?"

"Even if. What would we normally be doing right now?"

The sky was still light. It was likely about eight thirty. "You'd be working or playing with the boys and I'd be helping Cassidy get ready for bed."

"And look. Here we are. It's a beautiful evening, the kids are safe at home, and we don't have to be in a hurry. Let's go get an ice cream sandwich."

"If you insist," she said and bent to kiss him again. "Thanks for coming with me."

"If I wasn't so worried that you might find a body, I'd have let you come alone."

"You aren't serious."

He closed her door and walked around to the driver's side. She stared at him as he climbed in and put his seat belt on.

"What?" he asked.

"You aren't serious about the body."

"I'm a little serious. It's been a while. Seems like it's just about time for something to fall apart in our lives. When Skylar called, I didn't know what to expect. This is manageable, though. Let's keep it that way."

"Like I have a choice."

The old convenience store in the middle of town had closed a few weeks ago. The chain was building a bigger and better facility on the west edge of town, past Davey's. Bellingwood couldn't help itself, growth and change kept happening. While change brought more conveniences into town, she wasn't ready for the number of people that moved in at the same time. They were talking about building either a second elementary school or at least a new middle school on the north side of town. That was well into the future, but conversations were already starting.

When she'd purchased the old high school, no one expected to see a surge of growth like they'd experienced over the last five years. But they would never have repurposed Sycamore House into a school again. That would have required too much work. A brand new facility would be built someday. It took her breath away when she thought about it.

Henry drove past Sycamore House. Even on a weeknight, activities were going on in the building. Scott Luther would be on site this evening to ensure that the place was locked up when this evening's classes were finished.

He pulled into a parking space in front of the shiny new convenience store. "Are you coming in with me?"

"Sure," she said. "Let's see what fun things we can find. I'll text Cat and tell her we're going to be just a bit longer. I'm in no hurry."

"Kind of pathetic to be taking you on a date to the convenience store," he said, climbing down out of the truck. "I need to step up my game."

"I like your game just fine."

CHAPTER FOUR

"I believe that Cassidy and I will take a long walk and then a long nap," Agnes said to Polly. "You go on."

Cassidy looked at the older woman with big eyes. She wasn't thrilled with either of those options, but she adored Agnes and would do anything the woman asked of her.

Agnes smiled down at her, then grinned at Polly. "Or we might make some lemonade and sit out on the patio watching the world go by. It depends on how energetic I feel once you drive off."

"It shouldn't be long," Polly said. "Thank you for taking the time with her. I know you're busy."

Patting the phone in a holster on her hip, Agnes smiled. "I can be reached any time, night or day, even if Cassidy is with me. My teams know how to reach me. Never fear. I can care for her and keep up with my busy lifestyle."

Polly had never gotten Agnes to change her tune on managing international assassination teams. No matter what Polly said or how she asked questions, Agnes continued to insist that was her life. After all this time, it was either part of her shtick or it was the truth and Polly had no idea how to discern the difference.

"You're thinking about it again, aren't you?" Agnes asked. "You don't want to hurt those pretty little brain cells. They need to be kept well-oiled and content so you can run your businesses. I'll take care of mine. You take care of yours. And when it works out, I'll take care of your little girl, here. She is a joy."

"I'm glad you think so," Polly said. "She loves you."

Cassidy pulled at Agnes's hand, tugging her toward the front door. The little house was neat and tidy, and the back yard was beautiful. Polly and Henry had been invited over a couple of times to see what Agnes did with her gardens. There wasn't a speck of grass. Walkways traversed lovely gardens made of fruit trees, bushes and flowers; things Polly had never seen before. Very few people would even know it was back there, but it was gorgeous. Even though the yard was small and enclosed by a privacy fence, because of the way Agnes arranged things, it looked much bigger. They'd spent a nice evening on her patio as she told stories of the years she and her husband owned the buffet in Boone. The woman had always known hard work and wasn't afraid of it, even to this day.

"Good-bye, Cassidy," Polly called out. "I love you."

"I love you," Cassidy replied, turning to wave before opening Agnes's front door.

Polly got into Cat's car and headed for Bill Sturtz's shop. After years of waiting and preparation, Len Specek was ready to work on the grand piano that had been in storage. He'd returned from two weeks of training only to realize that wasn't enough and so traveled to Minnesota to take another course and receive certification as a piano technician. She couldn't believe he was taking things that far, but Andy insisted that he was excited about a new career.

While Len was in the middle of training, Bill Sturtz, Henry, and a crew turned the storage area of the shop into a facility ready for his new business.

Today, Polly was meeting two other technicians who were planning to work with Len on her piano. She wasn't in any hurry, but Len was ready to get started.

According to Andy, throughout these last few months, Len had become a different person. He loved traveling to meet other technicians in the area and when it came to working inside the guts of a piano, he spent hours with them, doing everything from tearing apart keybeds to tuning newly strung soundboards. After all these years, he'd found his passion and made friends with others who were just as passionate about caring for pianos.

She pulled into the parking lot in front of the main shop and waved at Marie, who was just walking out the back door.

"Hello, dear," Marie called when Polly got out of the car. "Are you here to see Len this morning?"

Polly smiled. There would never be any secrets around here. Everyone knew everything. "Yeah. He wanted me to meet the other people who would be working with him. Where's Molly?"

"She's at daycare today," Marie said. "I'm about to steal Bill so we can go look at new bedroom furniture."

"For you?" Polly couldn't believe it. Bill was so thrifty he'd never let her spend money on something like that.

Marie chuckled. "No, not for us. Bill is perfectly happy in our room. We're putting new furniture in the guest bedroom and looking for something fun for the third bedroom. Since we have so many grandchildren in our lives, I decided it's time to update those two rooms whether he likes it or not. We've already donated the other furniture. Pastor Dunlap is setting up a family in one of the apartments south of town and they have nothing."

Polly frowned. "Does he need anything else?"

"You might call him. He mentioned something to Bill at coffee last week. As soon as Bill told me about it, I didn't wait another second. I stripped the beds and emptied the drawers. Before my poor husband realized what had happened, I brought helpers in to move everything out and into the shop." She gestured with her head. "Pastor doesn't need them until after the holiday, but I wasn't going to let this one get past me."

"That's wonderful."

Marie gave her a wicked grin. "I also knew that once that furniture was in the shop, Bill wouldn't be able to help himself.

He's been cleaning it up, making sure drawers glide smoothly, and fixing little dents and scratches. If I wasn't so excited about re-doing those rooms, I'd almost ask him to move it all back. But what's done is done and I couldn't be happier."

"I'm surprised Bill isn't building the furniture you want for those rooms," Polly said.

"We'll see," Marie said, her eyes lighting up.

"What have you done?"

"Bill insists he doesn't have time, but I've played this game before. After I drag him to four or five stores today and he's exhausted and frustrated at the poor quality of workmanship, he'll unleash a tirade about how he could make something beautiful. Then I'll take him to his favorite lumberyard, he'll walk through stacks of cherry and walnut, maple and oak, and I'll get exactly what I want."

"You're a horrible woman. I bow to your cunning." Polly dipped her head.

"Let's hope I can hold up my end of the plan," Marie said. "It's been a long time since I've undertaken something so devious with that man."

"If anyone can, it's you." Polly held the door to the shop open and Marie walked in ahead of her.

The sound of drills and saws, sanders and other tools greeted them. Bill, Len, and Henry had hired three more people to work in the shop along with Doug Shaffer. Stan McKellan, a man in his mid-40s, lived in Pilot Mound with his wife and two children. Craig Griffith was in his early twenties and had moved to Bellingwood to live with his girlfriend. Right now, he was nothing more than a glorified go-fer, but he was learning and seemed to be a hard worker. The third new employee, Haley Ferguson, had been hired to assist in both the main shop and to work with Len in the piano shop. If things worked out, she would travel to Minneapolis this fall to take the piano technician course.

Polly hadn't had much opportunity to get to know any of them well, but if they were there long enough, they'd become family.

Bill looked up from his work along the west wall and nodded.

"I guess I'll wait," Marie said. "Look how busy it is. Bill is talking about needing more space. Where will we come up with more space?"

Polly didn't know what to say. She and Henry had discussed this several times. There weren't many options. They either built a new shop outside of town or bought up a couple of the homes next door and pulled them down. Neither was optimal, but something would have to be done if they continued to grow. Henry rented space from Al Dempsey's father, John, to store equipment and didn't want to do that much longer.

Dick and Betty Mercer, Henry's aunt and uncle, had offered to sell him a parcel of land to build his shop and offices. Moving to a permanent location in the country would change things for everyone. There were always so many decisions to be made.

A door at the back of the shop off to the right opened and Len stepped through. He caught Polly's eye and waved.

"I should go," she said to Marie. "I hope you have a successful day."

"Don't worry. I will," Marie said. "Have fun."

Polly made her way around the shop to the back door. When she walked through into the new piano space and Len shut the door, she breathed a sigh of relief at the cessation of sound.

"You really insulated that wall," she said.

"Had to if we wanted to hear what we were doing," Len said. "I'd like you to meet some people. They're going to be instrumental in restoring your piano."

"Instrumental," said the man with a long, gray ponytail. He laughed a booming laugh. "That's funny. I'm Roy Eslick. Nice to meet you."

Polly shook the hand he held out. His long, thin fingers were strong and firm.

"This is Brandon Fortney," Roy said, pointing to the other man in the room. "He's our muscle."

She blinked. The guy was over six-foot-tall and built like a Mack truck. His muscles had muscles. "I guess you work out," she said.

The young man laughed out loud. "Yes, I do. It's my sanity after spending all day putting tiny pieces of a piano key back together. Once I get the first one in place, I get to do it eighty-seven more times. I have to find my balance somewhere."

"And you know Haley," Len said.

The woman smiled shyly at Polly. "I'm glad to have this opportunity," she said.

The piano was already in pieces and Polly slowly turned, looking around the room. "How bad is it?" she asked.

Len shook his head. "We have work ahead of us, but we'll stay within your budget. Have no fear."

"I'm not afraid, but I am curious."

"About what?" Roy Eslick asked. "I'm a veritable fount of knowledge."

"He'll keep telling you that until you believe him," Brandon said. "He's no slouch in the ego area either."

"When you've got it, you flaunt it." Roy took her arm. "Let me introduce you to your piano keybed. Do you realize that most pianists have very little understanding of how their instrument works? Oh, they can tell you that a hammer strikes a string, but they don't ever take the time to learn the intricacies of how or why that happens. Most people believe that the piano is a stringed instrument, but though there are more than 200 strings inside, the sound is actually made when the hammer hits them, making it a percussion instrument. Have you ever seen the way a key works?"

Polly smiled at him. He sounded like an encyclopedia. "I haven't."

"There are many moving parts," he said. "Would you believe that a piano has over twelve thousand parts, ten thousand of which move? So many things happen between the moment your finger touches a key and the hammer strikes the string or strings. And all of them have to be perfectly in sync. We will adjust and readjust this all as we replace the felts and the strings, the bushings and pins. It will be terribly exciting."

"I'm sure it will," Polly said. "I'm glad it's you and not me. Do you play?"

Roy wiggled his fingers. "I'm sorry that I don't have a piano here to play for you. We all play, don't we, fellas?" He gasped and turned to Haley. "And lady? Or woman? Or, oh what am I supposed to call you?"

"Haley is just fine," the woman said. "If I have to answer to fella to keep you happy, I can live with it."

"Let's not make a habit of it." Len stepped forward. "I'm probably the least qualified at the keyboard."

"I didn't even know you played," Polly said. "I just thought you were interested in this because of your background in woodworking."

"Many years ago, I played piano with a wonderful jazz combo. It was a dream," Len said. His eyes closed and he gave his head a quick shake. "But things changed and that career wasn't something that would allow me to raise a family, so I set it aside and moved on. I wouldn't have changed a thing. Everything brought me to this point."

"Does Andy know?"

He frowned as he considered her question. "I'm not sure. It's not anything we ever talked about."

"You've taken on this new career path and she doesn't know that you used to play?"

"Oh, she knows that I used to play, but it's not something I talk about. That was a long time ago."

"What about Ellen? Does she know?" Len's daughter, Ellen, was a wonderful young woman who lived in Barcelona, Spain.

Len shrugged. "I doubt it. Her mother wasn't much for artistic flights of fancy. It never came up." He smiled. "I'm glad you were able to get over to meet everyone. I hope you'll stop in any time you like. It's going to be a fun undertaking."

"What would you think of letting Elijah visit?" Polly asked, still considering the fact that this man had given up his music so many years ago. How could anyone allow their husband to sacrifice something like that? She'd not known his first wife, but this would rock Andy's world.

"Do you think he'd want to?" Len asked.

"He will be the one who brings this piano to life once it ends up in our house. If what Mr. Eslick says is true, that most pianists don't understand their instrument, I'd like Elijah to be one of those who does."

Roy Eslick set down the nearly two-foot key assembly he had in his hand and walked back over to them. "How old is the boy?"

"He's ten," Polly said. Her kids were growing up far too quickly. "All we have right now is a digital keyboard."

The man scowled.

"I know, I know," she said. "I purchased it so he'd have something to use until this was finished. I should probably have purchased a nice upright, but we needed something fast." Then she chuckled at the fact that she was explaining herself to a perfect stranger. "What do you think about him visiting?"

"It would be a perfect opportunity for him to learn about the inside of a piano," Brandon Fortney said. "We'll put him to work whenever he's here. That way he'll know that he had a hand in restoring the instrument he uses every day. It will mean something to him."

She nodded and said to Len, "I'll make sure to check with you first. Will you all be here most of the day today?"

"We're just digging in," Roy said. "It's going to be a long few days while we decide how much work needs to be done."

"Then I will bring him over." Polly turned to head for the door. "It was nice to meet you all. Thanks for being part of this."

Roy and Brandon had already turned back to the keybed and were lifting keys up and off, setting them in line on another table.

"These are your people, aren't they, Len," she said as he walked her to the door. "Maybe you should start a band."

He chuckled. "That would be interesting. Bring Elijah over any time. We'll take good care of him. If he wants to stay, I can drop him off when I head home."

"You know I'm telling Andy about your past, right?"

"As soon as the words were out of my mouth."

"Good. Are you ready to have a piano in your house again? She'll never let you get away with ignoring this once she knows."

He peered at her. "I hadn't considered that."

"Len Specek, you need to speak up for yourself more often."

"I lived without a piano for more than forty years. My life has changed so much these last few years, it never occurred to me that I should go looking for that part of my youth."

Polly shook her head. "You're a good man, Len. I'm glad you are working on my piano. Let me know if I can do anything for you. And by the way, thanks for sticking up for Haley."

"What?"

"You know what I mean. She's working in a man's world. She can do it, but thanks for not letting them be stupid about the way they talk around her."

He looked back at the three working together. "They're good guys."

"You wouldn't have brought them on if they weren't. Thanks for inviting me over."

He pushed the door open and Polly walked out into the main shop, the sounds of machines assaulting her ears. Everyone who worked here wore hearing protection, for which she was thankful. It didn't do anything to help her though as she made her way back through the shop. She waved at Doug Shaffer, who glanced up from running a long piece of board through a machine that was sending sawdust into a collector.

When she got outside, Polly looked over at the house next to Bill and Marie's. They'd tried to purchase the Naylor house, but it had gone to another buyer; a couple who moved in last month. Marie was having the hardest time getting to know them since both worked in Ames and were rarely at home. They had no children and the woman spent no time outside. Marie had stopped over a couple of times with cupcakes or homemade goodies, but after an abrupt thank you both times, she'd given up.

The idea of building a day care for their employees was still something that interested Polly and Henry, but until they found the right spot, it was an idea they'd put on hold.

She wasn't expected to pick up Cassidy until just before lunch. Rebecca was likely still in bed, not having to be at work until just before ten o'clock. Cat and the boys had been outside when she left this morning with Cassidy. She was taking them up to Elva's this afternoon. There were so many things for the kids to do in town, they were never given much time to be bored.

Polly heard other mothers complain about the amount of time their kids spent watching television or playing on tablets or phones and was incredibly grateful for the large group of friends she'd managed to surround herself with. There was always something going on.

She drove past Sycamore House and hesitated, then turned north toward downtown. She was free of responsibility and there was no reason not to make a quick stop at the coffee shop.

CHAPTER FIVE

Not sure how long she'd be, Polly sent a quick text to Cat just to make sure everything was still going smoothly. The boys were much more active this year than they'd been in the past, playing harder with each other inside and outside. JaRon had gotten stitches in his forearm after racing through the basement and falling into an empty crate. It was no one's fault; well, it was someone's fault, but none of the boys were telling on each other. That had made Polly happier than getting her little boy home after a quick trip to see Doctor Mason. They'd been playing hard and though there were some tears, the boys were fascinated with the stitches, the wound and the potential scar.

She and Cat had first aid kits on every level and even one out in the shed over the stairs to the tunnel. They'd patched up more scrapes and cuts than she could have ever imagined. Polly was so thankful for the tetanus vaccine. Noah had been scraped up while working at the barn, the boys found ways to hurt themselves while out at Elva's house riding her horses and playing with the animals, and even when they were playing next door with the Waters' kids, Elijah had managed to get through the locked door to the new construction and tumbled off the deck. She'd given up on the terror and knew that acceptance was the only way to get through her life with four young boys.

Cat wasn't quite there yet, though Polly assured her there wasn't a thing anyone could do to protect them from everything those curious minds found to get into.

She chuckled when she read Cat's response.

"Caleb tripped up the basement steps and has a new bruise on his arm. At least it wasn't his head this time. I'm glad you don't believe that I'm breaking your children. How am I ever going to handle a classroom full of these wild things?"

"You make them sit on the floor," Polly said, adding a smiley face emoji.

"I'm going to buy pillows. Lots of pillows. Noah asked if he could spend the afternoon at the barn with Eliseo rather than go to Elva's. Is that okay with you? Eliseo called him."

Polly frowned, wondering what was up. *"That's always fine. Thanks. Is Rebecca up and moving?"*

"In the shower now. Cilla's mom is taking them to work today."

"Lazy girls," Polly sent back, laughing out loud. *"I had to walk up hill both ways."*

"In eight-foot drifts until the end of April. I know the drill. Okay, I hear yelling. We'll be fine. I promise. We'll be just fine. Hahaha."

Cat wouldn't be student teaching in any of her kids' classrooms this fall. They'd made sure of that. But at least the boys would see her during the day. She was going to make a good teacher. The boys didn't get away with much, but Cat loved them with everything she had. Polly was so thankful to have her in the house and dreaded the day she and Hayden moved out.

Her phone buzzed with another text, this time from Agnes. Polly laughed out loud when she read it.

"If you aren't terribly busy later this morning, Cassidy and I decided we would like to take a drive to Boone. I just got a call that some books are ready for me to pick up at the book shop. I'd take you two out for lunch."

"Bribery?" Polly sent back.

"I'll resort to anything necessary. Am I being a bother?"

"You know you aren't. I've told you over and over that I'm here for you. I'm sitting in front of the coffee shop, but could drive right over if you're ready."

"Go inside and buy yourself some energy. You know how much extra you need when you're with me."

"Can I get anything for you?"

"We made a coffee cake this morning. Our bellies can wait until lunch. Where ya taking us?"

"I thought you were taking me." Polly opened the door of Cat's car and got out. If she had time to go inside and get some coffee, she was taking it. Agnes was right. She did need to have a jug full of energy to deal with that woman.

"Have you been tippling already this morning?" Agnes asked.

"I'll be there in fifteen minutes."

"I got too close to home, eh?"

Polly shook her head and headed in the door, stopping as she did every time to enjoy the moment. The coffee shop had been Sal's idea and it had never occurred to Polly that she would appreciate this place as much as Sal did.

"Hey, Polly," Andrew Donovan said as he came up beside her.

"Andrew, what are you doing here?"

"I don't have to be at work until two. Mom said Camille needed some help, so I'm helping."

"Where is everyone?"

He shrugged. "Who knows? Josie's here, but Camille had to run to Omaha for something with her family and the other girls couldn't work until eleven. I had to be here at five-stinking-thirty this morning. Do you know how wrong that is?"

"They're paying you, right?"

"Yeah, but not overtime." He flattened his lips together and shook his head. "Good thing I need money for a car or Mom would never be able to drag me out of bed at that horrible hour."

"Sure she would," Polly said with a smile. "You're a good kid."

Andrew slapped a wet cloth down on the table. "Don't tell anyone. It's better that they think I'm incorrigible."

"You are that."

Josie Riddle smiled as Polly approached the counter. "Anything special today?"

"Just coffee. Let's make it iced, though. It's warm outside. How are you?"

"I'm good. I thought we'd be able to come to Shelly's celebration at your house, but Gavin and I are heading to Jefferson that day. I was looking forward to seeing what you've done inside that place."

"We should have you over for dinner sometime. I'm sorry I haven't done that yet."

Her husband, Gavin, worked for Sturtz Construction and had taken an immense load off Henry's shoulders. He was just the person Henry was looking for to manage crews on worksites. Henry was still busy, but he was much calmer these days.

"No worries. I still don't feel like we're settled in town yet," Josie said. "We work and spend time with the kids and when we have any free time, we head over to be with Gavin's family. Everything just keeps moving along. Before we know it, Christmas will be here." She handed over Polly's coffee with a grin.

"Well, that was mean," Polly said with a laugh. "I haven't even celebrated Independence Day and now you want me to think about Christmas?"

Josie nodded. "I bought my first Christmas present last weekend. It was just a fancy tape measure for Gavin, but it went into the Christmas box."

"You're the devil."

"Sorry." Josie laughed out loud.

"Andrew said Camille had to run to Omaha. Is everything okay?"

"It was something with her mother. She didn't tell me too much, just asked if I'd be able to keep an eye on things for a couple of days. I think maybe her mother is in the hospital. I should have asked more questions, but she was in a hurry."

"Are you okay being here? Do you have a babysitter?"

Josie heaved a sigh. "Best babysitter ever. It's the same woman that Sal uses. Mrs. Dobley. Whenever I run into trouble, I just call her. No matter what time, she's always available." She chuckled. "Especially if I check with Sal first. When I called this morning, Sal told me to just take her. Tuesday mornings she's usually up here and Mrs. Dobley watches her boys, but, well, this worked out."

"I'm glad you two are sharing Mrs. Dobley. That's awesome," Polly said. "I'll check on Camille. I hope things are okay."

"She's told me a ton of stories about her mother," Josie said. "The woman sounds formidable, but I'd love to meet her."

"She's intimidating, that's for sure."

The bell on the front door clanged and a group of women walked in. Andrew headed back toward the counter and Josie looked past Polly.

"I'll talk to you later," Polly said and walked away. She'd spent more time in here than she expected and would be well past the allotted fifteen minutes. Agnes would have something to say about that.

When she pulled up in front of Agnes's house, Cassidy was sitting on the front stoop. The little girl jumped up, waved at Polly and ran inside. In moments, Agnes came out with Cassidy in tow, carrying an immense tote bag.

"Hello there," Polly said as she got out of the car to put Cassidy into her car seat.

"We wondered if you'd gotten caught by your handsome husband. I didn't want to tell the young ears there that it was too early for a nooner, but when you get the chance, you take it, don't you?"

Polly blinked. "I'm only two minutes late. That isn't enough time."

"Bet me," Agnes said. "If you can't finish in two minutes, what kind of woman are you?"

"Uhh, ummm." Polly had no idea what to say, so she stuck her head inside the car and snuggled Cassidy's cheek while the little girl handed her the belt clasp. "Did you have a fun morning?"

"We went for a walk to see the horses."

"At Sycamore House?"

"Mr. Akee, Aquee," Cassidy stammered.

"Aquila," Polly said. "Like quilt."

"Mr. Aquila." Cassidy rolled the name around a few times. "He gave me a tomato. A little tomato that I ate right there."

Eliseo was growing grape tomatoes this year and they were sweet and wonderful. He sold pints and pints of them at the Farmer's Market they held every Wednesday afternoon at Sycamore House.

"Did you tell him thank you?"

Cassidy nodded. "He's nice."

"Yes, he is. Are you tucked in here? Everything feel good?" Polly brushed her fingers across Cassidy's cheek. She'd come so far these last few months. "I love you, little one."

She got a smile before Cassidy leaned forward. "May I have my doll, please?" she asked Agnes.

Polly blinked. That was a perfect sentence. Even using the word *may* instead of *can*.

"You certainly may," Agnes said, pulling Cassidy's favorite doll from her tote bag. "We've been working on the proper way to ask for things. Impressive, isn't it?"

"Very," Polly said. "I'm so proud of you, Cassidy."

"What about me?" Agnes asked. "I'm doing all the work."

"I'm grateful for you. How's that?" Polly closed Cassidy's door and sat down in the driver's seat. "You're kind of a brat. Have I ever used those words to describe you?"

"Every time you see me," Agnes said. "But I still love you."

"What you've done with Cassidy is nothing short of amazing. Thank you."

"You're a good girl." Agnes dug down into her tote bag and drew out a tootsie pop. "For that you get a sucker."

"I want a sucker," Cassidy said from the back seat.

Agnes turned. "Have you already had one this morning?"

"Yes," Cassidy said, sounding dismayed.

"What did we talk about before coming out to the car?"

"That Polly should have a sucker, too."

"Why should she get a sucker?"

"Because she's a good mommy."

Agnes reached back and rubbed Cassidy's knee. "You are such a good girl." Then she pointed out the front window. "Onward, Jeeves. I have books to pick up. Cassidy and I discussed where we should have lunch. She thought McDonald's would do, but I've convinced her that we want to eat at a real restaurant where waitresses bring us our food. How does that sound to you?"

"Do you have a preference?" Polly asked.

"Have the Chippendales opened a restaurant in Boone lately?"

"I don't think so."

"Then no preference." Agnes grinned at her. "It is so difficult to come up with phrases that little ears won't understand. It's good practice."

"Practice for what?"

"What ails ya."

Polly laughed. "Sometimes I have no idea what you are saying."

"Sometimes I have no idea what I'm saying. It's more fun that way, don't you think?"

The trip to Boone only took fifteen minutes and Polly pointed to the clock. "I don't think the bookstore is open yet. Is there anything else you'd like to do while we're in town?"

"I'm still hoping for Chippendales."

"Something other than that."

"Your mommy is a fuddy duddy, Miss Cassidy."

When there was no response, Agnes turned to look in the back seat. "Out like a light. It will only be a ten-minute wait, let's drive over and look at the old trains."

"How long has it been since you've ridden on the train?" Polly asked. "The boys love this trip. We haven't taken Cassidy yet."

"It's been years and years."

"One of these days we'll make another trek down here. Would you come with us?"

"You're such a sweet girl. I'm an old biddy and you make me feel like I'm part of your family."

"You *are* part of the family. Cassidy adores you and you've given her so much confidence when it comes to speaking and interacting with people. The boys think you're a hoot. Henry isn't sure what to make of you and I'm afraid that poor Rebecca might actually believe you manage teams of spies and assassins around the world."

"She's the smartest one of you all," Agnes said.

"Do you want to see the trains, Cassidy?" Polly asked loudly.

"Trains?" Cassidy asked. "Where?"

"Open your eyes and look around," Agnes said.

Polly turned into a parking space. There weren't many other cars here. The museum didn't open until ten o'clock, and the first train didn't run until one thirty.

"Can I see?" Cassidy asked.

"May I see the trains," Agnes corrected her.

"May I see the trains?" Cassidy echoed.

Polly opened her car door. "Certainly. Let's take a walk around. We can't go inside, but we can look at them." She released Cassidy from her car seat while bemoaning the fact that it was easier to get in and out of a seat on a roller coaster than it was getting a child in and out of the car. "Leave your doll in the car, okay?"

"Okay," Cassidy agreed and climbed down and out. She ran over to Agnes and took the woman's hand, then turned back to Polly and held out her other hand.

"You two go on ahead," Polly said. "I'll be right there." She wanted pictures of these two. They didn't get out together very often and she wanted these memories for Cassidy when she got older. The two wandered over to one of the train cars on display and she smiled as Cassidy bombarded Agnes with questions, some as mundane as why parking stripes were painted white. Agnes had an answer for everything.

They'd walked to the far end of the parking lot and were heading around to look at the back of a train car when Polly ran to catch up to them. She passed a parked car and glanced inside. There was a strange lump in the passenger seat. If someone left their animal inside an enclosed car, she was going to be furious.

Agnes and Cassidy wandered off, unaware that she was no longer following them. Polly got closer to the vehicle and realized that what she was seeing was a man, slumped over in the seat.

She rapped on the window to get his attention.

"Not today," she muttered. "Not with these two here."

She reached for the car door and hesitated. No, they already had her fingerprints on file. She just needed to be careful. Using only the tips of her fingers, she tried the door and it came right open, releasing a smell she'd grown to know well. Polly slammed the door closed again and walked away, gulping in deep breaths of fresh air. That car was never going to be the same.

She already had her phone in her hand, so she swiped the call to a familiar number open.

"Good morning, Miss Giller. It's a beautiful day, but the minute I saw your number pop up, I knew you planned to wreck it for me. Where are you?"

"How did you know?"

"It's been long enough. Just about the time I begin to forget that this is what you do to me and I feel all light-hearted and fancy-free, you drag me back to reality," Aaron Merritt said. "I'll ask again. Where are you?"

"At the train depot."

"In Boone?"

"Yeah. A car has been parked here with someone in the front seat. It smells bad."

"Why did you open the door?"

"Because I felt the need to punish myself."

"One more question. Why are you at the depot?"

"I brought Agnes and Cassidy down to go to the bookstore and we needed to waste a little time before it opened." Polly couldn't believe all that had happened this morning and it wasn't even ten o'clock yet. This day could only get better.

"Polly?"

She spun around at the sound of Agnes's voice. "I'll be right there."

"What are you doing?"

"Would you take Cassidy for a walk down that way. I'll catch up in a minute."

Agnes frowned and then quickly reached to stop Cassidy from running toward her mother.

"Just go that way," Polly said. "I'll explain later."

"Am I about to experience a Polly-day?" Agnes asked.

"I'm afraid so."

"And I was so looking forward to going to the bookstore."

Polly chuckled and went back to the call. "Sorry. I don't want Cassidy near this yet."

"I understand. Well, you have your choice this morning. Me or Deputy Hudson. Who would you like to see first?"

"If I have a choice, I'll always choose Tab," Polly said.

Aaron laughed. "You're kinda mean. I'm telling my wife on you, but Tab will be on her way. She needs something exciting. She's tired of rousting drunks and handling break-ins."

"Tell her I'm here for her."

"Will do."

Polly put her phone in her pocket and strode to the other end of the parking lot where Agnes and Cassidy had found a bench to sit on.

"What did you find?" Agnes asked.

"Just a car with a bad smell."

"A really bad smell?"

Cassidy plugged her nose. "I smelled something bad over there." She pointed at the car.

"Sensitive little nose," Agnes said. "I didn't smell a thing. Are we waiting for the police?"

Polly nodded. "The sheriff's office. Have you met Deputy Hudson yet? She's a friend of mine."

"When would I have reason to meet a deputy? I'm a good person. I don't get into trouble and I don't stand around waving at them so they pay attention."

"You're missing out," Polly said. "You should try the whole waving thing sometime. You never know who might show up. Some of those deputies are kinda cute."

"Bet they're married. And when you have fifty years on them, it's not nearly as much fun." Agnes laughed. "Oh, what am I saying? I do enjoy a good ogling. Bellingwood has some attractive young men. I was a bit miffed when Doc Ogden passed me off to his partner. Not that Doctor Jackson isn't nice to look at, but that Ogden fella is drop dead hot. As in, I'd drop dead as long as he was there to perform CPR. Poor Hannibal would have an issue every week if I got a chance to stare at that man. And you had to bring in that tall drink of water to steal him from all us women. What were you thinking?"

"I had nothing to do with it. Those two did it all on their own," Polly said.

Cassidy looked up at her, then at Agnes. "I have to go to the bathroom."

"The museum is open now," Polly said. "We can take you inside."

Sirens wailed through town.

"I'll take her inside. You do your business. I left my tote bag in the car. Do you have any cash on you?"

Polly chuckled. "Sure?"

"We might buy a book in the gift shop. You're not broke, are you?"

"Agnes Hill, you are the most wonderful woman I've ever met." Polly handed her two twenties. "Have a party."

"Why don't you come get us when you're finished. I'd guess you want to handle this without any additional assistance from the peanut gallery."

"Thank you. I mean it. Thank you."

CHAPTER SIX

Glad that Agnes cared so much for her daughter, Polly watched her hustle Cassidy inside the building before emergency vehicles filled the parking lot. Polly wandered down the sidewalk along the depot and sat on a bench against the wall to wait. They were only moments away. As the first truck came in, she pointed at the car with the dead man inside. They all knew who she was. This scene was much too common for any of them to question whether she knew if it was a dead body or not.

People came out of their houses and a few came out of the depot, curious as to what was happening in their corner of the world. Once Tab arrived, Polly would tell her everything she knew and would be allowed to leave. She couldn't imagine facing this without being friends with folks in law enforcement.

Tab Hudson drove in and pulled up, then got out of her vehicle and sat down beside Polly. "Fancy meeting you here this morning."

"Aaron gave me the choice of you or him. I chose you."

"Thanks. Your cases are always interesting. What do you know?"

"Not much. We were wasting time until the bookstore opened."

"We?"

Polly gestured with her head toward the museum entrance. "Cassidy is inside with Agnes Hill."

"I haven't met her yet." Tab's eyes lit with glee. "You've told us so many stories, I feel like I know her. Did she see anything?"

"No. Sorry. She was on the other side of the train car when I realized what I was looking at."

"Any other cars in or out since you got here?"

"No. Nothing. But he's been in that car for a while."

Tab wrinkled her nose. "Fabulous. It's already warm this morning, so this won't be good."

"Not good," Polly said. "I didn't even realize what was going on until I got close. Whoever did this draped a blanket over him. It looked like laundry at first."

A young man wearing a t-shirt that said *Boone Sheriff's Department* on the back came over to them. "Deputy Hudson."

She stood. "Hey Alan, what do we have?"

"DB. He's ripe. Can't get time of death. That car cooked him. We'll take him back and send more information to you."

"Do you think he was killed here?"

"Don't know. He was definitely killed in the car, though."

"How?"

"Two shots. One to the temple and the other in the heart. Found both bullets. They wanted him dead."

"That's fast work," Polly said.

He grinned at her. "The bullets went through. One lodged in the seat. Saw it because he was slumped forward. The other was just above the seat belt feed." His grin grew wider. "Made Danny look for that one. I backed off to get a clean breath."

She nodded. "I didn't take time to look at anything. You'll find my prints on the door handle. As soon as I opened it and got a whiff of what was inside, I shut it and walked away."

"Good to know," he said. "Oh, Deputy. Here's this." Alan held out a wallet. "It was lying on the floor. There aren't any cards or cash inside, but his ID is there."

Tab flipped the wallet open. "Andrew Harrison. He's from Mason City. Wonder what he's got going on down here. Is that his car?"

Alan peered around the vehicles that had filled the lot. "Cerro Gordo plates. That's Mason City. When the body is out of the car, we'll doublecheck his registration."

"I'll run him," Tab said. "Anything else?"

"Hurry over," he said. "You don't want to miss this."

"Uh huh. I'm on it. Right now. See me hurrying along."

"Just saying. It's a treat. Nice to see you again, Ms. Giller."

Polly laughed. "Really?"

"It's always interesting. You know the guys from the office avoid you around town, don't you?"

"What? Why?"

"Because they're afraid you'll put 'em to work. We do our best to keep the body count down in the county, but you show up and everything changes."

"That doesn't make me feel very special."

Alan chuckled again. He was a good guy and she liked him. "We'll always take care of you. It's a good thing you're a nice lady. At least you have that going for you."

As he walked away, she scowled at Tab. "Great. They avoid me. I'm glad you're my friend."

"Might as well. I'm going to be spending time with you anyway. This way, I know you well enough to be confident you have nothing to do with the dead bodies you find."

"That's the only reason we're friends?"

"Now your paranoia is setting in. I need to talk to the manager. Want to go with me?"

"I think that's him right over there, staring at the excitement. He's probably wondering what this is going to do to his day."

"I'm going to ruin the start of it for him." With two fingers, Tab rubbed between her eyes. "It's hot. I have to spend the day talking to all of the neighbors and I'm going to have an annoyed manager on my hands. I haven't had enough coffee yet. Why couldn't you have found this in Bellingwood?"

"There's a nearly full cup of iced coffee from Sweet Beans in my car. Do you want it?"

Tab looked at her hopefully, then shook her head. "I can't steal your coffee."

"I'm healthy, I can get more and if it will help you do your thing, I'll gladly sacrifice it," Polly said.

"I hate to even admit how tempting your offer is."

"You go talk to the manager. I'll retrieve my coffee. If this is all you need from me, I'll gather Agnes and Cassidy and take them away. I promised them a bookstore and some lunch." She glanced at Tab. "Would you like me to bring lunch back for you?"

"No," Tab said with a laugh. "Thank you. I'll get lunch later. But I would love your coffee. I'll have to drink it down fast before I head over to the body. Do you see how I'm avoiding that?"

"I can't believe you aren't in there looking at every detail."

"I'll get the report. Alan and his team are meticulous. They don't need me hovering." A small cluster of people had come out from the depot and one man stepped forward when they approached. Polly was just as glad to not be part of that conversation.

As she opened her car door, she heard the man's upraised voice. "You don't think any of us had anything to do with that, do you?"

Tab's calm voice interrupted him and Polly shook her head. They would question everyone, but unless there was a good reason to suspect someone, no one in the sheriff's office automatically assumed guilt. It wasn't like a television show. These people did the work. She reached in and snagged the coffee cup and then sat down in the seat. Leaning over to open the glove compartment, she took out several napkins. Tab could at least rub Polly's germs off the lid of the cup.

"Cooties," she murmured to herself with a giggle. Why did those silly words get stuck in her head and show up at the strangest times? *Circle, circle, dot, dot. Now you have the cooties shot.* Her mind was bringing up the ridiculous now. Polly climbed back out of the car, glad she'd left the windows open when they stopped. The day was already steamy. Rattling the ice in the cup, she heard enough to know that the coffee was still cold.

Tab was jotting things down in the little notebook she carried, the group surrounding her all talking at the same time. She put her finger up, silencing most of them and then turned to say something to the manager. With a short nod, she dismissed them and headed for Polly.

"Did you find out anything?" Polly asked, holding out the coffee. She made a show of rubbing one of the napkins across the lip.

Tab took it from her, popped the lid off and handed that back. "See. Fixed it. No germs."

"Cooties," Polly said.

"I haven't heard that word in years," Tab said, rolling her eyes. She took a long drink. "Thank you for liking black coffee."

"I like the fun stuff too, but today required straight-up black gold."

"Are you sure?" Tab asked, pushing the cup toward Polly.

"I have plenty of time to get more. You're going to need it. What did your new friends tell you?"

"The car wasn't here when the last person left last night about seven. They didn't think anything of it being here this morning. Neighbors sometimes use the lot overnight, but they're good about being out by the time things get busy."

"Let me know if you need me," Polly said, a grin spreading across her lips.

"Hush, you. I figure that before I lose any sleep over this, you'll have found the link that ties it all together."

"Y'all should pay me."

"Nah. Instead, I steal your coffee. That seems fair." Tab took another drink, sighed and looked back at the scene around the car and took a third drink. "I'm not going to want this by the time I get over there."

"I can throw it away for you."

Tab creased her face into a frown and stuck out her lower lip. "That's just so wrong. One more. That way I will end up desperately needing the bathroom right when I'm in the middle of interviewing the neighbors." She took one last long drink and pushed the cup at Polly. "If that doesn't charge me up, nothing will. Thank you for coming to my rescue."

"You don't need me for anything else, right?"

"I've got the messy part. You take your friend and Cassidy out for a fun afternoon while I dig in and do my job."

Polly gave Tab a quick hug. "Thank you for coming when I call. You're the one who rescues me. If it costs a cup of coffee, I'm more than willing to pay."

Tab headed for the car and her cohorts while Polly headed for the main door to the museum. She dropped the coffee cup into a trash can and went inside.

Agnes and Cassidy were seated on another bench with a book open between them.

"Hey," Polly said.

Agnes smiled at her. "We found a book."

"About trains," Cassidy said.

"Would you like to go find some more books?" Polly asked. "Mrs. Hill wants to go to the bookstore."

Cassidy jumped down to the floor and handed the book up to Polly. "I love books."

"I know you do, honey."

"Are you sure you have time?" Agnes asked. "I can find another way down here tomorrow."

"We have plenty of time unless you have appointments that need to be kept. I was looking forward to lunch with you."

Agnes reached for Cassidy's hand. "Oh, stop your flirting. You already have my heart. And if you're looking to have my wrinkly old body, we should have a very different conversation. One that includes Henry."

Polly opened her mouth to say something, took in a breath, then closed it and shook her head. "No words." She took Cassidy's other hand and the three of them walked back outside.

Cassidy looked down at the activity at the other end of the parking lot, and recognized Tab standing beside Alan Dressen.

"Miss Hudson!" she yelled, yanking her hands from both Agnes and Polly. Cassidy ran toward Tab, and startled by her daughter's actions, Polly chased after her.

"Cassidy, stop," Polly called out. "Tab, stop her!"

In a flash, both Tab and Alan turned toward them and ran to the little girl. Tab reached down and snatched Cassidy up into her arms, no small feat. Even though Cassidy had trimmed down some, she was still a heavy little chunk of a thing.

"Miss Hudson." Cassidy threw her arms around Tab's neck.

"How are you today, Cassidy?" Tab asked as if nothing was happening behind her. "Alan Dressen, this is Cassidy, Polly's youngest daughter."

Polly caught up to them, a little out of breath, both from the chase and her fear that Cassidy would find herself enmeshed in the removal of the body from the car.

"It's nice to meet you, Cassidy," Alan said, patting the girl on the back. He smiled at Polly. "I'll leave you again. Still work to be done. You bring us such fun presents."

"I'm sorry, Tab," Polly said. "She saw you and started running. She's never done that before."

"Just glad you yelled at me. I'm never sorry to say hello to one of my favorite girls." Tab gave Cassidy a squeeze and put her back down on the ground. "I have to go back to work. Thank you for visiting me."

"Say good-bye to Miss Hudson, Cassidy," Polly said, taking the child's hand. Her heart raced as it still tried to catch up to what had just happened. Now was not the time to talk to Cassidy about running away from her. In a few minutes, when she was calm again, they'd have that conversation.

"Good-bye," Cassidy said, happy to leave with Polly. They walked back to the car.

Agnes bent over and took Cassidy's other hand. "You nearly gave me a fright, little girl. You shouldn't run away like that. I'm too old to catch up."

"I like Miss Hudson," Cassidy said, oblivious to what she'd done to Polly and Agnes. "She's nice."

"I'm sure she is," Agnes replied. "No running away, though. Hear me?"

Cassidy looked up at Polly, who nodded her agreement. "If you're holding our hands, you have to stay until you ask whether it's okay to leave us. Deal?"

"Deal," Cassidy agreed.

"Let's go look for some new books." Polly opened the back door and waited for Cassidy to climb up and into her seat. She glanced at Agnes who shook her head in surprise.

"I'm glad your friend caught her. How bad is it over there?"

"It isn't good from what they say. I don't know how deep into the mess Cassidy would have gotten, but she's never pulled away from me before. I'm thankful we were in a parking lot and not out on a street somewhere. That was terrifying."

"None of your other children ever did that?"

Polly thought back. It hadn't ever come up. The kids were safe enough back on Beech Street which ran in front of their home. They knew to look both ways before running across to the Waters' house. There was so little traffic there that they didn't have much to worry about. When the boys went to the swimming pool, they were always accompanied by someone older than them and were very conscientious about crossing the highway.

Even though the speed limit was thirty-five miles per hour, sometimes cars went whipping through town. Since Bellingwood had grown in the last few years, more and more cars traveled through, making that highway quite busy. There had been talk of putting a light at the Sycamore House corner, since the downtown area was only two blocks north, but no decision had been made yet. A traffic light would certainly slow traffic but putting one in was a reminder that Bellingwood was growing. That made it a huge decision for many people.

~~~

Polly leaned against Cassidy's bedroom door frame, wishing she had time to crawl into bed with the little girl for a nap. After they'd gone to the bookstore and out to lunch, all three were exhausted. Cassidy had fallen asleep on the drive home and though it offered an opportunity to talk about the morning, she and Agnes hadn't had much to say.

The boys were out at Elva's with Cat, Rebecca was at work, and Polly had let the dogs outside when she and Cassidy got home. She was worried that Cassidy might argue about a nap, but though there was always a test, it had been half-hearted. She'd had a huge morning. Hopefully she'd be down for a while.

Polly needed to spend a couple of hours in the office. They'd hired a designer to decorate the bed and breakfast and Polly had more ideas to send off to the woman. With the beautiful new building going up, they had all decided that a professional touch would be a good idea.

She'd talked to Lydia early on and wasn't surprised that her friend wanted nothing to do with decorating. It had been one thing to decorate an old existing home, but Lydia was intimidated by the big open spaces and the number of bedrooms. She didn't need that kind of stress in her life and after she admitted that to Polly, it was easy to move forward. Polly, Jeff, and Sal had interviewed three designers from the area and once they settled on one that they all thought could do the job, left it to Polly to work with her.

Loretta Nesbitt lived in Randall, just north of Story City. She'd grown up in small town Iowa and assured them she understood what it was they were looking for.

The first ideas that had arrived in Polly's inbox were splashy and polished. Though it fit the elegance of the house, it wasn't the look she wanted. If the next set of designs weren't close, it was going to be a long journey trying to bring them all together. While everyone wanted it to be beautiful, they also wanted a comfortable, homey, farmhouse feel.

Polly bent down and picked Leia up. The cat purred in her arms as they walked down the hall. She looked out the window to the back yard and groaned. They were having Shelly's reception this weekend. While the numbers wouldn't be big, Shelly was looking forward to this more than she'd looked forward to anything in the time Polly had known her.

Shelly's brothers would both be here and of course her father was taking time off work this week to come into town and help her prepare.

She wondered if Andrew had any extra days available this week to help here at the house. Polly started to make a mental note to ask him, then thought better of it and took out her phone. She sent him a text and put the phone back in her pocket. By that point, Leia was tired of being mashed in her arms and leapt to the floor.

"Sorry, little girl. I'm a terrible mom."

Then she realized she hadn't told Henry about her morning yet. How was she supposed to keep everything straight? And Lydia. She'd know as soon as Aaron got home from work. Polly needed to tell her that she was fine. It was nothing to worry about.

The man's name, Andrew Harrison, flitted through her mind. It was familiar to her for some reason. Where had she heard that name before?

Her mind was muddled from being tired. She didn't know if caffeine would help at this point or not, but maybe a few minutes on the porch outside the office with a tall glass of iced coffee and the warm sun would bring back her focus. If nothing else, a quick nap in the rocking chair wouldn't be the worst thing she could do today.

CHAPTER SEVEN

Thursday morning, Polly headed for Sycamore Inn. Agnes was at the Bell House with Cassidy. Cat and Andrea Waters had packed all of their kids, along with Rose Bright, into the Suburban and were on their way to Adventureland for the day. They'd invited Polly, but she was more than happy to refuse, you know, because she had to work.

Cassidy had been a little upset that she wasn't going until she discovered that Agnes would spend the morning with her. Polly was keeping that woman close even if she had to move her into the Bell House.

She hadn't been back to the hotel since Monday night and with everything that happened on Tuesday, the odd listening device placed in a room had been pushed out of her mind. Now that she was here again, she wondered if Chief Wallers had any more information about it. She hadn't heard anything from Tab Hudson about the murdered man she'd found in Boone either. Did these people not understand that she needed to be kept in the loop?

When she went inside, Kayla was at the front desk.

"Good morning," Polly said.

"Hi, Polly. We've been really busy this morning already and the coffee pot is empty. I'm sorry about that."

"Oh, honey, it's okay. I had two cups before I left the house. Don't do it just for me."

"There are people still in their rooms, so I should make another pot. How are you?" Kayla came around the counter and headed for the little dining area.

"I'm good. The boys are headed for Adventureland today with Cat and Mrs. Waters, so it was a little crazy getting everyone out of the house. The quiet here is nice."

"If you'd been here a half hour ago, it was crazy then, too, but I loved it. I get to meet people from all over the place. This morning, there was a lady here who lives in Alaska. I've never met anyone from Alaska before. I told Stephanie that I want to put a map up and stick pins in it whenever I meet people from interesting places."

"That's a great idea. Maybe someday you can put pins in it for all the interesting places you visit."

Kayla stopped what she was doing and turned on Polly. "Me? Go interesting places? Rebecca might do that, but I'll never be able to afford to travel like she does. I don't know if I even want to. It scares me."

"You visit fun places with Stephanie."

"I suppose." Kayla thought about that for a minute. "It's just that I feel so safe with her. She never makes me do anything that is really scary. And I don't think I'd like to be in an airplane. I'd be sick to my stomach the whole time."

Polly had to admit that flying wasn't her favorite thing to do, but she wasn't saying that out loud. "I think everyone gets scared the first time they fly. It's okay to admit it."

"That's just not my thing," Kayla said.

"Then if it's not your thing, that's okay, too." Polly headed back to the computer behind the counter and sat down. Everything was waiting for her, just like it was every Thursday morning.

June Livengood had cut back on her hours this summer since Kayla was available to work. Her Aunt April had gotten pneumonia a few months ago and was back home after a long hospitalization. June wasn't going to hear of putting her in a nursing home until it was absolutely necessary, so she'd rented a bed and put it in the living room. Henry, Skyler, Heath, and Hayden had gone over to help move things around in that tiny house to make it easier to care for the woman. A home health nurse came in regularly, but June hated leaving her mother alone with an invalid sister all the time. May Livengood could move around, but not easily. Everyone hoped that April would grow stronger and healthier over the summer, but June was pragmatic about it. Polly just wanted to make it better for her.

"Where's Skylar this morning?" she asked Kayla.

"He's in Boone. He should be back after lunch before all the check-ins start. Did you need him?"

"No, I was just curious. I haven't talked to you in a long time."

"I know, right?" Kayla said. "Everybody is always so busy and whenever we get together, it's like we have a million things to talk about. I can't believe we all have jobs. Do you ever miss being a little girl when you didn't have to work?"

Polly laughed. "All the time. But then I wouldn't know you and I wouldn't have my family and I wouldn't be married to Henry. I wouldn't give this life up either."

"Sometimes I wonder what it will be like if I ever get married and have a family. I want to marry someone nice like Henry or Skylar." She sat down on a chair beside Polly. "Sometimes I worry that I'll meet a bad man like my dad. I don't know what I'd do if that happened."

"You'd leave him if he ever hurt you. That's what you'd do," Polly said.

"But what if he didn't mean to."

Polly stopped typing and turned to Kayla, taking the girl's hands in hers. "Honey, any man that deliberately hurts you isn't worth it, even if he apologizes and says he will never do it again. If it was deliberate and he meant to hurt you, he needs help. Would you deliberately hurt anyone? Another friend? An animal? A child?"

"No!" Kayla said. "That would be awful."

"Then no one should ever hurt you. Ever. Not on purpose. And just so you know, it's not up to them to decide whether it was an accident or not. It's up to you." One of Polly's greatest fears with Kayla was that she wouldn't recognize an abuser. She was so innocent and caring. The poor girl would never believe that another person could deliberately hurt her, even after what she'd seen happen in her own home. Her father had been evil. That was obvious to everyone, but Polly knew that abusers could pass themselves off as the nicest people until it was too late. Kayla would be susceptible to that type of personality.

She reached forward and pulled Kayla into a hug. "I want you to meet a wonderful and loving man, too. I want you to have the happiest life, filled with friends and children and everything that you want."

"Rebecca and I are really different, aren't we?"

Polly nodded. "Yes, you are. I think that's what makes you such good friends. The two of you look at the world differently and you complement each other. I'm thankful you are in her life."

"She says she doesn't want to get married until she's at least in her thirties."

"Really." Polly hadn't heard that one yet. It didn't surprise her. Rebecca's dreams for her future were all over the place. "What does she say about having kids?"

"That if they never have babies, she'll adopt kids just like you did because there are so many out there that need a home. I want to do that too. Like maybe have a couple of kids and then adopt a bunch of them. Wouldn't that be fun? Mrs. Mikkels has a whole house full of kids and she's so happy. They all live in that big house and have all that land to run around. She said that someday they might get their own horse, but that Nate needed to make a lot more money then so she could quit working at the library and stay home and ride it all day."

"I don't think she'd enjoy doing that," Polly said with a laugh.

"She must have been joking."

"Probably."

"I think she likes working at the library. That wouldn't be a bad job either, except that you need to know so much about books. Do you know that I never read so many books before I met Andrew and Rebecca? They're always pushing another book at me."

"Do you like to read?"

"It's okay. Rebecca says that reading takes her to faraway places. I like to read about real people or at least made-up people in real places. I don't like those dragons or vampires or things like that. It's just too weird."

"That's the best part about reading. There is something for everyone and you certainly don't have to like what anyone else likes."

"I told Andrew that if he ever writes a book with vampires or dragons in it, I'd read that. Wouldn't it be cool if he became a famous author?"

"Even if he wasn't famous, it would be cool," Polly said.

"Sometimes I feel bad that I don't want to be famous like him and Rebecca. I just want to be happy."

"Honey, you are uniquely you. You are the only Kayla Armstrong in the whole wide world. Whatever you do with your life is what the world needs for you to do. You don't want to be Rebecca. She'll do that life just fine on her own. And you don't want to be Andrew. He's got that one covered. All you have to do is be Kayla. I love you just the way you are."

Kayla gave her a sweet smile. "Thank you. I love you, too. I talk about this all the time with Stephanie. She doesn't care what I do, but I think she wants me to go to college. Rebecca says I should go, just so I keep all my options open."

"They might be right," Polly said. "There are plenty of different types of college experiences. You and Stephanie can talk about everything and I'll bet you come up with a great plan."

"Maybe I'll meet my husband in college."

"Maybe."

The front door of the lobby opened, a man walked in, and strode to the counter.

"Excuse me," Kayla whispered and headed over to greet him.

Polly took a deep breath. Oh, she hoped that Kayla's life would turn out well. If Rebecca, Andrew, Skylar and Stephanie had anything to say about it, she'd be fine.

~~~

Polly sent a quick text to Agnes when she was finished, asking if she'd like anything from Sweet Beans. She'd spent so much time chatting with Kayla while she worked that she forgot to get a cup of coffee and she'd take any excuse to head to the coffee shop.

Agnes responded before she got out of the parking lot, so Polly stopped to read it.

"Nothing for us. But you have some visitors here. You might want to hurry home."

"Visitors? Who?"

"I'm not telling. Come home soon."

Polly frowned. That was odd. Lydia, Beryl, and Andy might visit, but they knew she worked at the hotel on Thursdays. Agnes wouldn't be coy about any of them showing up.

She hadn't seen Sal for a few days. With Mrs. Dobley occupied caring for Josie Riddle's children, it wouldn't be beyond Sal to bundle up her boys and bring them over to play at Polly's house. In fact, if this wasn't Sal and the boys, Polly needed to call her again and invite them to come for a morning.

That did it. She turned east and drove straight home. As she pulled into the driveway, she saw a car with Polk County plates parked on the street. Who did she know from Des Moines?

Then she looked at the front porch and a huge grin broke out on her face. She jumped out of the car, and even in the chaos of happy barking dogs welcoming her home, she took off at a run.

Ray Renaldi beat his brother to Polly and lifted her into the air.

"Let me in, old man. It's my turn," Jon said, pushing his older brother back. He crushed Polly to him. "It's good to see you, girl. Look at what you've done here. We're all proud of you."

"Mommy, look what the man made for me." Cassidy ran up to her, holding an origami hat in her hand.

Polly released Jon's hand and bent down. "Which one made this?"

"That one." Cassidy pointed at Ray, then lifted her shoulder and simpered. "I like him."

"So do I," Polly said. "I like them both very much." She took Cassidy's hand and walked with her to the front porch where Agnes sat in the porch swing, moving idly back and forth. "I see you met my friend, Agnes."

"It was good to finally meet her," Jon said, taking the empty spot beside the woman.

"Finally meet her?" Polly asked.

"I told you," Agnes said. "I'm well-known in international spy circles. These two boys have heard of me and my teams."

"You're kidding me, right?" Polly looked at Ray.

He shrugged. "We encounter all types of people in our work."

Polly frowned at him. "That wasn't an answer."

"It's all I've got."

"What are you doing in Bellingwood?"

"Business," Jon said, pushing the swing back and forth. When Cassidy stepped in front of him, he planted his foot and brought the swing to a stop. "Did you want to sit up here with us?"

She looked at Agnes, who nodded. "Yes, please."

Polly blinked. "Wow. All of those manners."

"We're working on them," Agnes said.

"This woman is a gem," Polly said, shaking her head. "Cassidy adores her. How long have you been in town?"

"We just got here. We wanted to stop and see you before we headed for the hotel. You do have room for us, don't you? From what I hear, even in this monstrosity of a castle, you don't have any extra bedrooms."

"Can you believe it?" Polly asked. "I'm so thankful for the hotel. We might have rooms available at Sycamore Inn. I'd need to check with Stephanie first, though."

"Your hotel would be perfect. We won't be in anyone's way," Ray said.

"You didn't tell me why you're here."

He shot a quick glance toward Cassidy, who was on Jon's lap, playing with her paper hat.

"How long are you staying, then?" Polly asked. She glared at him. "You will answer my questions sooner or later, trust me."

Jon laughed at them. "You know she's right about that. She's almost as bad as Mama when it comes to prying information out of us."

"How is your mother?"

"Mean as a snake and loving as a dove," Ray said. "We have a suitcase filled with things she's made for your kids."

"Like what?"

"You'll see." He aimed another knowing look at Cassidy. "She's declared war on the Renaldi clan. If one of the three of us doesn't produce offspring in the next year, she's cutting us all off."

"That sounds ominous," Polly said with a laugh. "Which one will fall into line?"

"Won't be Drea, that's for sure," Jon said. "She wants nothing to do with children. She told Mama that it's our fault, that we made her hate having siblings. I'm not sure what she's talking about. I was a good boy."

"Uh huh," Polly said. "I know you. Will it be you?"

Ray nodded. "He has been dating a nice girl. She's ready to get married, but he's dragging his feet. I told him that any girl who is willing to put up with his sorry behind this long is worth a big ring. Mama likes her just fine."

"That's one of the problems," Jon said. "I don't want those two ganging up on me."

"Give your mama the grandbabies," Agnes interjected. "I had to adopt Polly so that I had little ones around. Don't make your mother wait. How old are you, forty?"

Jon laughed. "Not quite, but getting there."

"Don't wait too long. You know what they say about aging sperm."

Jon and Ray gaped at the woman while Polly laughed aloud.

"More genetic problems in children crop up because of decrepit sperm. You're going to want to get on this," Agnes said.

"Best day ever," Ray said in a low tone to Polly. "Best day ever."

"Do you have plans for lunch?" Polly asked, eager to change the subject.

"I've been thinking about Joe's Diner since we got on the plane," Jon said. "Can we go up there?"

"We can go anywhere. We have several new restaurants in town."

"We saw construction going up on the east side coming into town. What's that?"

"It will be a new convenience store. More of the shops are filled uptown, and there's a little strip mall and big convenience store on the west side. Apartments are going in just south of that and houses have been popping up everywhere. We're putting a bed and breakfast up north of town, and do you remember Eliseo?"

"The fella that takes care of your horses?" Ray asked.

"His sister has stables just south of the B&B. There are so many changes."

"You'll have to take a ride with us and show us what's new."

"How long will you be in town?"

"As long as it takes," Jon said. He put his arm on the back of the swing and touched Agnes's shoulder. "Will you have lunch with us?"

"As long as you stop talking about sperm and babies," she said. "You'd embarrass me in front of my friends with that kind of talk in a public place. I don't know what you're thinking."

He blinked and looked at Polly.

"Welcome to my life," Polly said. "Let me take Cassidy in and we'll get ready to leave. Have you been inside the house yet?"

"We weren't allowed," Ray said, staring pointedly at Agnes. "She's a force to be reckoned with."

Agnes stood up, then pointed at the floor of the porch, indicating she wanted Jon to put Cassidy down. "I wanted to be certain you knew Miss Giller. People in our line of work can be cagey, you know. I'll take Miss Cassidy inside and make sure she goes to the bathroom. Anything else she needs before we leave?"

"That would be wonderful, thank you," Polly said.

73

"Now, I'm doing this so you three can talk about things that little ears shouldn't hear. But if you don't let me in on the secrets, I will be forced to rethink my attitude toward you boys. Got it?"

"Yes, ma'am," Jon said.

She led Cassidy in through the front door and once it closed, he and Ray burst into laughter.

"Where did you find her?" Ray asked.

"Face down in a yard," Polly replied.

"No way."

"Yeah. Cassidy saw her fall last April. I hauled her up and out of some broken down hedges and fell in love with the woman. She's like no one I've ever met before."

"You have that right. She's quite a character. Am I always going to wonder what's coming out of her mouth next?"

"Always," Polly said. "And you wouldn't want it any other way. Now, tell me why you're in Bellingwood."

"Andrew Harrison."

Polly looked at him. "The dead guy I found?"

"That's the one."

"How did you know he was dead? Why do you care?"

"Your sheriff's department ran a check on him and our system flagged it. Someone from our office needed to get involved. When we realized where it had happened, Jon and I fought for the chance to come out. We decided it was easier to just put both of us on the plane. Less bloody, you know."

"Who is Andrew Harrison and why does your company care that he died? Don't tell me he's an international spy."

Jon laughed out loud. "No, but his company contracts with us for security and protection. And it *is* an international company with ties to governments throughout Europe and Asia. Until we know why he was killed, we're in town."

Polly dropped into the swing. "International intrigue in Bellingwood? That's a bit much, don't you think? This is Iowa for heaven's sake."

"Your former governor is the ambassador to China. John Deere has plants all over the world. Rockwell Collins' Iowa City campus is blurred out on Google maps. I could go on and on, but those are just the obvious things that everyone knows," Jon said. "Iowa is no slouch when it comes to international dealings."

"But murder?"

He shrugged. "It doesn't always happen in DC, New York or LA. Bad guys travel to wherever they need to be."

She processed on that for a moment. "I know you're right. It's one thing for me to find dead bodies and know that the murder will make sense on a small-town scale. Big-time stuff like this feels out of place in Bellingwood."

"I hope you're right. It might be nothing more than a jealous husband," Ray said. "If that's so, we'll go home glad to have been able to see you again. I didn't want to say anything about Mama's gifts to your kids because she made a little doll for Cassidy. If you didn't want her to have it yet, I wasn't going to force it on you."

"She'd love it. That little girl loves gifts like that. She'll treat it like it came from royalty."

"It's just a rag doll. Mama wants her to love it to pieces. She's also been crocheting blankets for your four boys and for Cassidy. She has a quilt for Rebecca, another one for Heath and then she made a beautiful wedding quilt for Cat and Hayden."

"Wow," Polly said. "That's too much."

"She wants babies in her life," Ray said, elbowing Jon in the ribs. "If the babies she has to care for live in Iowa, she'll send things to Iowa. She wasn't finished with everything at Christmas and thought maybe she'd ship a package to you later, but we gave her a better choice. You know it feels like we all know your family. Mama watches your social media pages like a hawk, always telling us about the things you all are doing out here. She makes Drea tell her what you write about in emails over and over. She's awfully proud of you."

Polly felt tears come to her eyes. She chatted briefly with their mother once in a while, but didn't think much of it. "I had no idea."

"She wouldn't want you to think about it. She just loves watching over you."

CHAPTER EIGHT

Ray smiled across the table at Polly. "Drea and Mama tell us your stories all the time. It feels like we're already part of the family."

"Well, I know nothing about either of you," Polly said. "Jon, are you really in a long-term relationship? And the world is still spinning on its axis? What's her name?" She cut Cassidy's chicken tenders into bite size chunks and squirted ketchup onto the girl's plate.

"Look at you," Jon said, laughing out loud. "You are such a mom. Polly Giller, a mom. I can't get over that."

"She's a good mom, too," Agnes said. "One of the best. I'm proud of her."

Polly peered at the woman. "Thank you, Agnes."

"I'm just trying to impress the pretty boys, don't get too big of a head." She smiled and nodded at Polly, then grabbed Jon's forearm. "You didn't answer her question. It sounds like the two of you boys have a reputation out there in Beantown."

"Bigger than Boston," Polly said. "Everyone everywhere laments that these two won't settle down."

"I'm settling, I'm settling," Jon said. He took out his phone and swiped through several photos and then turned it for Polly to see. "Her name is Chloe Alberts. We've been dating for a few years now."

"A few years." Polly frowned as she thought. "Rebecca and Beryl didn't meet her when they were in Boston, did they?"

He shook his head. "No. She was in Atlanta that week. I remember thinking that I'd be in terrible trouble if she met your daughter and friend before she met you."

"That's right," Polly said. "And I was about to drag Rebecca out of her work and question her as to why she hadn't told me about Chloe."

"She's safe. She knew nothing."

"Marriage? Babies? The whole shebang?"

"If she'll have me."

Polly chuckled. "You've been together a few years and you haven't talked about marriage?"

"He didn't tell me until he'd been dating her for more than a year," Ray said. "And then he made me promise not to say anything to Mama until he was ready. That took another year."

"How did she take it?"

Jon rolled his eyes. "She's decided that Chloe is better for me than I am for her. I'm to straighten up and fly right, never to make life difficult for that girl. Whatever Chloe wants, I'm to ensure she has it. Yeah, Mama's happy."

"And Drea?" Polly asked. "Why didn't she tell me that you're serious about someone?"

"Did you ask her?" Jon asked.

"No, how would I have known?"

"You know Drea. If it isn't her story to tell, she says nothing."

Polly nodded. "That's right, but she knows I had a terrible crush on the two of you." She grinned at Ray. "You more than Jon."

"Hey," Jon said. "That's not fair. What was he going to do with you? He likes boys."

Agnes snapped her head toward the older brother. "You do, do you?"

Ray looked over at her. "Yes."

"Well, doesn't that just take it. About the time I finally decide there's a man who could take the place of my poor, dead husband, I discover that he's gay." She leaned across the table. "That's okay. All I want to do is look at you. We could be married on the sly. I'd gladly be your beard."

"Oh, dear lord," Ray said, snorting with laughter. "I love you, Agnes Hill."

Polly and Jon burst out in laughter until Cassidy joined in while patting Polly's arm. "What's funny?"

"Mrs. Hill is funny, Cassidy. She's flirting with Ray."

Cassidy beckoned Polly to come closer and whispered. "But she's old."

They all laughed again and Cassidy beamed, knowing she'd brought laughter, even if she didn't understand what she'd said.

"You know I have a million questions, right?" Polly asked.

Jon closed his eyes. "Of course you do. Go ahead, shoot."

"What does she do? Where is she from? Where did you meet? What made you fall for this one specifically? When is the wedding? How many children?" Polly ticked her fingers as she peppered him.

"That's impressive," Ray said. "It took us much longer to dig those answers out of him and I see him every day."

"He hasn't answered them yet," Agnes said, sitting forward, her meal forgotten. "These are two of the most interesting people you've brought to me yet, Polly. I like your life. Maybe I will move in to that big old house."

Ray gave Polly a questioning look.

"She keeps threatening. I keep offering and still," Polly said, "she likes her own little home."

Lucy came back to their table with dessert menus and placed them in front of Ray and Jon. "Are you interested in dessert today?"

"Ice cream," Cassidy said. Agnes coughed and the little girl turned to Polly. "May I? Please?"

Polly laughed out loud. "I'm going to have to say yes just for the wonderful manners you have. Agnes Hill, will you move in and work with the rest of my family?"

"Name the date," Agnes said. "I'll have to ask your boys to help me pack my things, but I'll move right in."

Polly gave her a look and Agnes shrugged. "I have to do something before my ghost grows stronger than me. Someday Aggie is going to take me off into the wild, blue yonder and I won't remember where I live."

"I don't think we're finished with this conversation," Polly said, a small frown creasing her forehead. She was never sure what to do with Agnes's conversations some days, but this one sounded more serious than usual. If she needed to make room in her home for the woman, she'd figure it out, but she couldn't imagine that Agnes was ready to give up her home.

"We are for today," Agnes said. "You have an interrogation to perform. That one needs to deliver some answers immediately."

"But first, dessert," Lucy said. "What about the rest of you? We have muffins and brownies from Sweet Beans, ice cream from the General Store and I think some of Sylvie's cheesecake is left."

"Nothing for me," Ray said, pushing his plate back. "This was wonderful."

Jon smiled. "I shouldn't. Gotta keep my trim figure, but a brownie in a dish of ice cream sounds terrific. Polly will you share it with me?"

"She's sharing ice cream with me, young man," Agnes said. "Unless you'd like to make it a double scoop and bring three spoons."

"The old bat isn't contagious, is she?" Jon asked Polly with a poker face.

She gasped and laughed. "Agnes, he understands you."

"Isn't that sweet. And no, I carry no known contagions. What you should be concerned about are those that haven't been discovered yet."

Lucy was laughing as the boys handed her their menus. "Two brownies and ice cream with three spoons and a bowl of ice cream for Cassidy. Does that sound right?"

DIANE GREENWOOD MUIR

Polly nodded. "Thank you for putting up with us. I'll get these boys out of your hair soon."

"It's good to see you two again," Lucy said. "And we're all glad that you're in town this time for something other than Polly's protection. I hope you stop in again."

"Thank you," Ray said, shaking his head. "This was not how I pictured my first day back in Bellingwood, but I haven't had so much fun in months."

"Back to you, Jon," Polly said. "Tell me more about Chloe."

"She's six years younger than me."

"Ah ha," Agnes said. "That's why you aren't panicked about children. Good for you."

He shook his head. "We met on a job. I was working security for her company. She's the vice president of sales and marketing for a biotech firm in the Boston area."

"Biotech?" Polly asked. "What do they do?"

"Mostly research into pharmaceuticals for rare genetic diseases. That's how they started. They've spread out into a multitude of other services across the spectrum. Chloe travels all over the country. It's a wonder we ever see each other, but we make it work. She's worth it."

"I wouldn't be surprised if she showed up in Iowa," Ray said. "When she heard that Jon was coming to see an old girlfriend, she suddenly became very interested in our trip."

"Did anyone tell her that I was married and that Jon and I were never an item?"

"I think all she might have heard from me was that Drea wouldn't let you two date because she didn't want to have to kill her brother. She's seen pictures of you." Ray grinned and tilted his head. "I might have saved a few to show her. You know, a beautiful woman is always good for a little jealousy."

"Great," Polly said.

"You should tell him thank you," Agnes said.

Polly frowned in confusion, then laughed. "Oh, for calling me beautiful. These two are schmoozers. I don't trust a single word out of their mouths."

"You are pretty, Mommy," Cassidy said.

"Thank you, sweetie. Now, Jon. Tell me why you finally fell for this one? You've played the field for a long, long time."

"I don't know," he said quietly, shaking his head. Jon reached out and put his hand on Polly's. "You know I adore you, right?"

"Sure?"

"Just want that to be clear. With Chloe, it was love at first sight. She's bright and articulate, self-confident and comfortable in her own skin. She needs me for nothing. She owns her own home, and takes care of an elderly grandmother who lives in an apartment down the street from her. She volunteers at an afterschool girls club and was ready to live her life alone if she didn't meet the right person. I was absolutely taken with her, so I asked her to have dinner with me. We talked about ridiculous things that night. Everything from baseball to science fiction novels. She likes them more than I do, but I'm not averse to reading."

"She has you reading novels?" Polly sat back, nearly bumping into Lucy who had arrived with their desserts. "Oh, I'm so sorry, Lucy."

"My fault. I should have expected you to throw yourself at me," Lucy said with a laugh. "I'm used to it. I know how to duck and weave."

~~~

Polly sat beside Cassidy as the little girl did her best to fall asleep. Jon and Ray had gone to check in at the hotel and would be back later. She'd taken Agnes home after lunch. They hadn't said anything more about her moving in. It was a conversation for a day when nothing else would distract them. Polly couldn't imagine giving up her independence, but then, she wasn't eighty-five and living alone either.

They would find room in the house if that was a decision they made together, but Polly wasn't sure if she and Henry were ready for a smart-mouthed, independent woman to live down the hall. It was one thing to have a house filled with kids. Cat and Hayden were growing into adulthood, but they still treated Polly and Henry with a lot of respect. Agnes had none of that and though it was fun to play, she didn't know if they could live like that.

"Mommy?" Cassidy whispered.

"Yes, honey."

"I'm not tired."

"I know. Just lie here quietly. I'm not going anywhere unless you fall asleep."

"I don't want to go to sleep. I had fun."

"It was a fun morning. All you have to do right now is close your eyes and think about all the fun things you did this morning. Okay?"

"But I'm not going to sleep. Are Ray and Jon coming back?"

"They sure are. They'll have dinner with us tonight so they can meet the whole family."

"I'm glad. They're nice men."

If nothing else, Polly was thankful that Cassidy was meeting nice men. She was thankful that all her kids were surrounded by good men. If you listened to the news, it felt like there was so much ugliness in homes and towns. Shelly Nelson had been caught up with the worst of what men would do. Cassidy's life had been on a trajectory to encounter those same types of people. Elijah and Noah had Roy Dunston to guide them, but until he'd shown up, they had nothing in the way of a strong role model. But here they all were, surrounded by people she knew and trusted. What a wonder.

Cassidy's breathing slowed and became steady as she finally drifted off to sleep. She'd be out for at least an hour, maybe more.

Polly waited until she was confident nothing would wake the little girl and gently moved off her bed, taking a moment to stand in the doorway to watch the sleeping child. She couldn't count the number of times she'd watched her children sleep. Their little faces looked almost cherubic. In those moments, she wondered how she would have ever lived without them. Then they woke up, tore through the house and she had moments of wondering what it might be to live as a single woman again.

She went downstairs and let the dogs back inside, then sat at the kitchen island and composed a text. She really did need to let Henry know what was happening. Things had moved so quickly this morning that she hadn't told him they were having guests for dinner.

"Jon and Ray Renaldi are in town. They'll be here for dinner." That ought to get his attention.

A few minutes passed before her phone rang. She'd already gotten up and was taking ground beef out of the freezer. She had been standing there, holding the frozen packages in her hand, trying to decide if there was time for the meat to thaw, when the ringtone made her jump. She dumped the packages back in and closed the freezer. It would be easier to go to the grocery store and buy fresh meat.

"Hi there," she said to Henry. "What's up?"

"I don't know. What's up with you?"

"You got my message."

"Why are the Renaldi brothers in town?"

"Something to do with that body I found the other day. Their company provides security for his company, so they're out here to find out if it was because of company business or something in his personal life."

"Interesting. How long will they be around?"

"Sounds like they're here until they get answers. Agnes, Cassidy, and I had lunch with them at the diner."

He laughed. "How did that go?"

"Agnes is a trip. She still insists that she has assassination and spy teams around the world and even had them in on the story. None of them gave it up, either. Henry, what if she really does?"

"Polly," he said, scolding her. "You have to be kidding. You don't believe it, do you?"

"Well, I didn't until today. She's been talking about this same thing for months. Who holds on to a gag for that long?"

"Maybe Agnes does."

"Henry, she also talked about moving in here with us again. She sounded more serious than ever before."

"Do you want her to move in?"

"I don't know. She's a bit much. I'm afraid I'd want to kill her after a week."

He laughed, though it sounded strained. "Maybe you need to find out if there is a reason she's pursuing this with you. Maybe it's financial, maybe she's worried about her health, or maybe she's afraid living by herself."

"I told her we needed to talk about it. There's too much going on right now, but I'll try to figure it out."

"What are you doing for dinner tonight? Do you want me to pick something up?"

"I thought we'd grill burgers and brats. I don't have any meat thawed, but when Cassidy gets up from her nap, we'll go to the store. I have potatoes, so I'll make up some potato casseroles and when Rebecca gets home, she'll help me cut things up for a salad."

"When are Cat and the boys supposed to be back?"

"Oh," Polly said with a sigh. "I forgot about that. They will be exhausted. Cat thought they'd be home by eight. I guess we don't have that many mouths to feed."

"Ray and Jon can spend time with them another night."

"That's a good idea. I might re-think supper. If we aren't feeding a horde, I might be able to make this work."

"Let me know what I can do."

"How are things going for you?"

"Good. I'm actually over at the Anderson's house."

"Right down the street?"

"Yeah, but I don't have time to come home and hug you." He giggled, something she rarely ever heard come from him. "A hug might turn into something else."

"That would be fine. Cassidy is sound asleep."

"I have the worst timing."

The back door opened and Rebecca came in, her face red and streaked with tears.

"Uh, Henry, I need to go. Rebecca just walked in."

"Is everything okay?"

"I don't know. I'll talk to you later."

"Let me know. I love you."

"I love you, too." Polly pushed the phone into her back pocket. "Honey, what's wrong? What happened?"

"Oh, Polly." Rebecca burst into tears as she rushed into Polly's arms. "I screwed up so bad. Deputy Bradford is on his way over."

Polly gulped. She held on to Rebecca as the girl cried, desperate to ask more questions, thankful that they were home alone today. "Come into the kitchen and tell me what's going on. Did something happen at work?"

Rebecca shook her head, while ugly snorting sounds came out of her mouth as she tried to gasp in enough air to speak. "No, not there." She closed her eyes and leaned her head back. "I'm such an idiot. It's all my fault. If I had just left it alone, nobody would have known. But Polly, I couldn't. I just couldn't." More tears flowed and she threw herself back into Polly's arms.

"Honey, if I'm going to be able to help you, you have to tell me what happened. Why is Deputy Bradford coming here?"

"Because I'm a minor and he can't interview me without a parent present."

"Interview you? Because of a crime?"

Rebecca dropped her chin to her chest. "It was just so stupid. It's all so damned stupid. And now, here I am, the one who has to talk to the cops. No one else is going to come forward. It's all on me. Why does this stuff happen to me?"

Polly moved Rebecca to one of the stools at the island and pushed gently so she'd sit down, then took the seat next to her. Putting her hands on Rebecca's knees, Polly turned the stool so they were face to face.

"You have to tell me exactly what happened. I want to hear it from you before Deputy Bradford knocks at our back door. Are you in trouble?"

"I think so."

"Is someone pressing charges against you?"

That brought more wailing and tears. Rebecca flung her arms to the top of the island and dropped her head into them as she sobbed and sobbed.

Polly took a long, slow deep breath. Emotions and tears were one thing. Dramatic episodes were another. She wasn't putting up with the second.

"Stop with the drama, Rebecca," she said calmly. "You need to tell me what's going on. I don't want to sit here and wait through another breakdown for you to come clean. Why is Deputy Bradford coming here? What are you accused of?"

"Shoplifting."

Polly sat back. "You stole something? From where?"

"It wasn't me, I swear. I didn't do it."

"Then why are you being accused of shoplifting?"

"I shouldn't tell you. I should just accept the consequences. It's no worse than what you did, right?"

"The police weren't involved when I did it. Luckily, my father had time to speak with the shop owner before she contacted them. But what I did has no bearing on what's going on today. Who accused you of shoplifting?"

Obiwan and Han barked just as the back doorbell rang.

"That's him," Rebecca said. "What am I going to do?"

"You'll tell the truth. I'd like to hear a full story out of you at some point." Polly got up and followed the dogs to the porch.

Bert Bradford stood at her door, his face solemn as she opened it. "Hi, Polly, can I come in?"

"Sure. Rebecca's in the kitchen."

"I'm sorry about this. I wish I didn't have to be here."

"Me, too," she said with a wan smile. "Let's figure out what's going on. Do I need to call Henry?"

"That's up to you."

"Give me a minute," she said and stepped into the foyer.

Henry answered her call right away. "What's wrong?"

"Bert Bradford is here. Something about shoplifting. Rebecca's been a dramatic mess since she walked in and I don't have any of the story. Do you have a few minutes?"

"I'd rather have come home to have fun with you, but I can make time. I'll be right there."

"Thank you, Henry."

CHAPTER NINE

Unsettled, Polly walked back into the kitchen to stony silence. Rebecca hadn't moved from her stool, and was doing everything possible to avoid looking at Officer Bradford. Bert, on the other hand, stood in the doorway to the mudroom, looking as if he wanted to be anywhere but here.

"I spoke with Henry. He's just down the street and will be here in a few minutes. Bert, can I get you a cup of coffee?"

"No, thank you," he said. "I'm fine."

"Come on in. Rebecca, would you go upstairs and make sure that Cassidy is still asleep? Why don't you wash your face before you come back down."

Rebecca shot her a look of relief and ran for the back stairway. The tension in the room dropped a thousand-fold.

"Come on in, Bert. Needless to say, she's freaked out."

"I understand," he said, walking over to the island. "This is difficult."

"I'd ask you to explain, but we might as well wait until Henry gets here. That way you don't have to tell us twice. Let's go into the dining room. It's more comfortable in there."

"I expected there to be more activity here with all of your kids," Bert said, taking a seat at the far end of the table.

"The boys are with Cat at Adventureland for the day. They won't be back until late."

"I haven't been there in years."

The sound of the dogs' nails on the kitchen floor scrabbling to the back door alerted Polly. "That has to be Henry. Are you sure you don't want something to drink?"

"A glass of cold water would be nice."

Polly nodded. This was so strange. Bert was usually in her house because something had happened to her. Now he was here because something happened involving one of her family members. She wasn't sure she liked being on this side of his attention.

Henry met her at the island. "What's up?"

"I'm not sure yet. Bert's in the dining room. Rebecca's upstairs composing herself. I'm getting him a glass of ice water. Do you want anything?"

"That sounds good. Thank you." Henry walked into the dining room. She was so thankful that he was here. Rebecca would be, too. The man was a calm, stabilizing force no matter the storm. She thought back to March when she'd found a potential employee dead on the floor of Mina Dendrade's new salon. He'd been upset that day. But then, his world was threatening to crush him and he didn't have much additional stamina.

Before she went back into the dining room, she sent a quick text to Rebecca. *"Henry's here. We're in the dining room. Come down soon."*

If Rebecca was anything like Polly, she'd avoid this confrontation as long as possible. One thing Polly had learned, only because of her age, was that dealing quickly with things like this meant that you could move on. All she could do was help her daughter get to the other side.

She carried the two glasses of water in and sat down. "Now, can you tell us what happened?" she asked Bert. "And what is Rebecca's involvement?"

He took a long drink of water, then placed the glass carefully on the table. "Several items were stolen from the General Store last Monday. There was a small group of high school kids there, but no one thought anything of it. They're your daughter's friends. It probably would have gone unnoticed, except that one of the items was a crystal candlestick that was one of a pair. The other hadn't been put out." He grinned. "You know that place. There is so much stuff around, there's never any extra space on the shelves. Anyway, a customer came in the next day and asked about them, wanting to give the set as a gift. There was no record of a sale."

The story was taking forever and Polly's nerves were fluttering. She just wanted him to get to the end of it and tell them why he was here.

"They still didn't think anything of it. You know how things get misplaced." He stopped for another drink of water. "Then today, Rebecca went back to the store. She tried to slip an envelope onto the counter beside the register with no one noticing, but another clerk saw it. She was busy at the time, but later opened the envelope and found money with this note." He pulled a piece of paper out and pushed it across the table.

Polly read the note, clearly in Rebecca's handwriting.

"I'm sorry about the things that were stolen. Here is the total amount, plus tax."

"So, they believe Rebecca stole from them and then four days later tried to pay for the items?" she asked.

"We aren't sure what to believe," he said. "That's why I'm here."

"They called the police rather than contacting us," she said, turning to Henry. "Nice."

"It's the right thing," Henry said calmly, putting his hand on her knee.

Because of the way the dogs were sitting, Polly knew Rebecca was in the kitchen, so she called out. "Rebecca, come in here, please."

With slow steps, Rebecca walked into the dining room. Her face wasn't quite as blotchy and red as it had been, but the poor girl would never be a pretty crier. Her face showed everything.

"Can you explain this note?" Polly asked her. "I recognize your handwriting."

"I wrote it," Rebecca said.

"And you put cash in the envelope," Henry prompted.

"I got paid today."

Of course. That made sense. "Why did you write this note?"

"Because what happened wasn't right."

Dragging information out of Rebecca was difficult when she didn't want to talk. This interview was going to be interminable if something didn't speed it up.

Henry sat forward and took Rebecca's hand. "No more stalling. Tell us. Tell Officer Bradford what happened. Why did you drop this off at the General Store?"

"Do I have to?" she asked. "Isn't it enough that the items were paid for? Why does anything else have to happen?"

"Did you steal those things?" Polly asked.

Rebecca looked at her with such shock and disbelief, Polly almost felt a physical assault. "No! I would never do that. I can't believe you'd even think I would steal. Isn't that why I'm working? So I can make enough money to buy things that I need?"

"Did someone else steal these items?" Bert asked. "One of your friends? Who are you covering for?"

Rebecca turned to Polly and then to Henry. "Please don't make me get anyone else in trouble. I'm not a thief, but I'm also not a tattletale."

"It's not that simple," Bert said. "While you're the focus, we know who was with you on Monday. If you didn't steal those items, we'll interview each of your friends. Someone is going to tell us who did this."

"You can't," she said, worry on her face. "Won't they just let it be since I paid for the things?"

"Think about it," Polly said. "If one of your friends shoplifted those items and got away with it, do you think they'll stop? Will they try again another time, hoping to get away with more?" Her heart sank as she realized that Rebecca's friends were people she cared for very much. If it was Andrew, Sylvie would be devastated. If Cilla did this, Andrea and Kirk wouldn't know what to do. She hoped that Kayla hadn't been downtown with them on Monday, but more than likely she was at the hotel.

Then Polly remembered Rebecca's fury when she got home from work on Monday and her conversation later in the gazebo with Cilla, Andrew, and Kayla.

She pursed her lips. "Come with me," she said, taking Rebecca's arm and leading her into the kitchen.

"I can't tell," Rebecca said. "It will never happen again."

"You can't be sure of that," Polly said. "Does this friend know you paid for her theft?"

Rebecca looked at the floor.

"Because she works there, right?"

"How did you know?" Rebecca asked, her eyes flashing.

"Because you were talking to your other friends about it in the gazebo the other night. Honey, if Libby is stealing from her own employer, she has a problem. Why did she do it?"

"I don't know. I just don't know. She was trying to show off that she could? I don't know why. She put the things in her purse behind the counter and told us to be quiet. Then she promised to put them back, but I know she didn't." Rebecca's eyes filled with tears again. "I thought I knew her. When I talked to her yesterday, I asked if she'd returned the things and she got really mad at me. Then she told me that they never noticed things like that because there was always so much stuff that got lost and broken."

"Do you think she admitted what she did after they called the police about you today?" Polly asked, putting her hand on Rebecca's back. "She's going to let you take the fall. Right?"

Rebecca nodded. "I guess so."

"Is that friendship?"

"We're supposed to cover for our friends," Rebecca said. "Even if they don't do it for us. I can't be the one to rat her out."

"Well, I can," Polly said.

"No, please."

"Honey, I am not going to allow you to take responsibility. If you had been the one to steal the items, Henry and I would be right there beside you as you faced the music. But not this, though you should have told someone when it happened."

"I really thought she would put them back. She said she would."

"Okay. You stay here. You don't have to be part of me getting your friend into trouble."

"I wish you wouldn't."

Polly stopped for a moment and took a breath. "Do you feel like I'm betraying your trust?"

Rebecca frowned. "I'm supposed to, right?"

"I don't know. How badly do you not want me to tell Bert about Libby?"

"I just want this to be over. She's going to know that I'm the one who told on her, even if you carry the news. She'll hate me forever."

Polly put her fingers under Rebecca's chin and lifted it so she'd look at her. "Honey, this is already the end of your relationship with Libby. Even if you didn't tell on her, she'd feel guilty about what she did to you. It might not be this week or even this summer, but pretty soon she won't be able to be around you. She'll be angry because you know something about her that no one else knows, something that makes her feel bad. That anger will fester until it becomes ugly. You might as well just get it out in the open and deal with it. She can be angry right now, but at least you'll see it coming."

"You think really weird about these things."

"I've been through a few of them," Polly said. "So, you or me?"

"I'll do it," Rebecca said. "I know you're right. But I want them to keep my money. At least I can do that for her."

"You have the biggest heart. I love you."

Bert and Henry watched them come back in.

Rebecca stepped up to the table. "I'm sorry for making this a bigger deal than it was. I really hate the idea of ratting out one of my friends, but Libby Francis took those things. She works at the General Store and tried to show off that she could steal something while we were there. I thought she was going to put everything back, but when I asked her, she got mad at me. That's when I decided to pay for the things myself. I couldn't live with the idea that they didn't have that money just because she was trying to prove she could get away with stealing."

"Your other friends saw her take those things?"

Rebecca huffed out a sigh. "Please don't drag them into it, too. Everybody just feels so gross about it. I don't want the money back, but Polly's right. I'll bet Libby tries it again. She even kind of hinted at it when I talked to her yesterday. I just don't want to be there when it happens." She looked at Henry. "And Polly was right when she said that Libby was going to let me get in trouble for this. She's probably the one who turned me in. I'll bet she saw me slip that envelope onto the counter."

Bert gave Polly a slight nod when Rebecca wasn't looking and it was all Polly could do not to growl in frustration.

"Do you believe me?" Rebecca asked him.

He hesitated, then nodded. "I do. I wish you would have told someone about this the day it happened, but I understand. It isn't easy to watch a friend do something wrong. You always hope for the best."

Henry walked Bert to the back door and then returned to the kitchen where Polly and Rebecca stood. "Well, that was some excitement. I don't want to go through that again."

"I'm sorry," Rebecca said.

"I wasn't thinking about you." He let out a small chuckle. "I fear we have four boys who will bring home more trouble than I'm prepared to deal with. How are you doing?"

"Okay. Would it be all right if I went back to work?"

"What does Mr. Greene think you're doing?"

Rebecca glanced up at the clock. "Oh well, no big deal. I'm supposed to go back later anyway. He knows what happened. I told him. And I called Beryl. She knows I'm not coming up this afternoon."

"You really like him, don't you," Polly said.

"He's so easy to talk to. It's like he's seen everything and done everything. I should text him." Rebecca took out her phone, looked at it and turned back to them. "I don't know if it matters, but Andrew told me I should tell you guys about this whole thing on Monday. Then you went over to the hotel that night and you found the body the next morning and the whole week just went to hell. I didn't want to make things worse."

Polly blinked.

"Sorry," Rebecca said. "Let me send this text." She walked to the glass doors at the back of the kitchen and typed into her phone.

Polly smiled at Henry. "Thank you for coming home. It was nice having you here. She needed you."

"She needed you, but I'm glad I was close. What do you want to do about this?"

"If she doesn't get the money back, I want to replace it."

He frowned. "Might be a better lesson if you didn't. We'll make it up to her another time. If Rebecca makes decisions, she needs to be okay with the follow-through. How much do you think it was?"

"I'd guess it was about thirty dollars."

"She can afford that lesson. She's the one who insisted she didn't want it back. Don't take that away from her."

"You're right," Polly said. "Thank you." She reached up and kissed his cheek. "Go on back to work. I'll try to keep the rest of our toes out of the fire before you come home."

"I'm heading up to the B&B after this. I'll be there the rest of the day. Give my girl a hug."

She glanced back at Rebecca, who was talking on her phone. "Will do. I love you."

He smiled, then bent to rub Han's head and left.

"Henry's gone?" Rebecca asked.

"Yeah. Had to go back to work. Did you talk to Mr. Greene?"

"He's glad I told the truth. Said I was building character." Rebecca grimaced. "Character sucks."

"Language."

"Sorry. Thanks for being there with me today."

"I'll always be there," Polly said. "And whenever Henry can be there, he will, too."

"I don't know how I'm ever going to face Libby again."

"Honey, you have it all wrong."

"What?"

"You're the wrong person to be worrying about it. She should be concerned with having to face you. You didn't do anything wrong. In fact, you're the hero. You tried to cover for her. You tried to do the right thing. In all of it, Libby is the one who made bad choices."

"What if she lies to Officer Bradford and tells him that she saw me steal those things?"

Polly sighed. "Why don't we wait and see. If we have to cross that bridge, we will do it together. This is why it's good to be honest about things up front. The truth is, if Cilla and Andrew saw her steal, they'll tell the truth, right?"

"That's right." Rebecca's eyes lit with relief. "They'll stand up for me."

"Exactly. She was foolish enough to show off in front of all of you. If she lies to get you in trouble, your friends won't let her get away with it either." Polly grinned. "Speaking of friends, you will never believe who is coming to dinner tonight."

"I won't be here," Rebecca whine. "Remember? I have to work until eight o'clock."

Polly laughed out loud. "Well, doesn't that just take the cake. Nobody is going to be home for dinner. Then I shouldn't tell you a thing. They'll still be here tomorrow. Maybe I'll make you wait."

"That's not fair."

"Fair, shmair. I'm a terrible mom."

"No, you're not. You're the best mom ever. That's what I tell everyone." Rebecca flipped Polly's hair. "And you have cool young-mom hair. You're like the best, coolest mom in the whole world. Who's in Bellingwood?"

"Absolutely no squealing," Polly said. "Promise?"

"Come on!" Rebecca said.

"Ray and Jon Renaldi."

Rebecca stopped moving, then she waved her hand in front of her face. "The two hottest men in the world? They're here? In

Bellingwood?" She dramatically flung the back of her hand to her forehead. "I'll swoon! I can't wait for Cilla to meet them. She's just going to die. She's literally going to die."

"Literally, figuratively, but yeah."

"Why are they in Iowa?"

"Something to do with the dead guy I found in Boone. They provide security for his company."

"What was his name?"

Polly thought a moment, then she said, "I just remembered where I know that name from."

"What name?"

"The dead guy. I don't believe it. Just a second." She took her phone out and dialed a familiar number.

"Bellingwood Police. How may I direct your call?"

"Mindy? This is Polly Giller."

The dispatcher hesitated. "Is everything okay, Polly. I just heard from Bert. He left your house, right?"

"Oh, yeah. That's all over and done with. Is Ken around?"

Mindy laughed. "It's always something with you, isn't it? He's in the office. Just a minute."

When she put Polly on hold, Polly shook her head. "I should have just called his cell."

"What's going on?" Rebecca whispered.

"Polly? Do you have something else to tell me?" Ken Wallers asked, coming on to the call.

"Did you hear that I found a dead body in Boone on Tuesday?"

"Yeah. I heard something about it. What's up?"

"His name is on the list."

"What list?"

"The list of names that Skylar gave us. He'd stayed in the hotel in the room that had the bug in it. I couldn't figure out why I knew the name when Deputy Hudson showed me his driver's license. It just hit me. You and Sheriff Merritt are going to be working together again, right?"

He chuckled. "It's a good thing the two of us are friends. I'll give him a call."

"So, uhhh, do you remember when the serial killer was in Bellingwood with my old boyfriend?" she asked.

"Yeah?"

"Well, the two guys who came into town to give me protection are back. You're going to want to meet them."

"Okay?" he drew out. "Why?"

"They're going to be involved in this case, too. Their security company is involved with all of this."

"It's just never easy with you, is it, Polly?"

"I'm not going to apologize. Their names are Jon and Ray Renaldi."

"This is turning into a bigger deal than I expected," he said. "I'll get in touch with Aaron. Tell your friends we'll want to meet them. I don't want them in the way."

Polly took a breath. "They're good guys, Ken."

"I'm sure they are. We'll talk later."

She ended the call and sighed. "I should have kept my mouth shut."

"It's not like he wouldn't find out, right?" Rebecca asked.

"Yeah, but it wouldn't have had to come from me."

"It sucks telling on your friends, doesn't it."

Polly glared at her. "Language again."

"Sorry."

CHAPTER TEN

That Friday morning, Polly was up early. Andrew was coming over to spend the day with the boys and help get things ready for Shelly's celebration party Saturday afternoon.

She had given Ray and Jon Renaldi the option of coming over for a small family dinner last night or going out. They chose to do neither and spend the evening at the hotel. There would be plenty of time for them to meet everyone.

Cat and the boys were home by eight o'clock and the kids didn't know whether to fall asleep or babble incessantly about their wonderful day. They were exhausted.

Rebecca got home not long after. She and Cilla sat out on the front porch talking until nearly eleven. The girl was loyal and knowing that she'd gotten Libby into trouble was difficult. Now she was worried about what would happen this fall when they got back to school. But she'd get through it; she always did.

Her phone buzzed with a text before Polly had stepped out of her bedroom. Henry was already gone. She wondered what he needed.

"Hey, you up yet?" Sal sent.

"Absolutely. Big day of cleaning here at the estate. Shelly's party is tomorrow."

"We'll be there. Do you need any help today?"

Polly squinted at her screen. What a strange question. *"I think we have it under control, but if you want to come over, I'll find something for you to do."*

"Great. I'm going to hit Sweet Beans. I'll bring breakfast for everyone and coffee for you."

"Okay," Polly sent back. *"You okay?"*

"Yes."

She waited for more, but that was the end of Sal's communication. Well, hmmm. Then Polly wondered if Sal knew that Jon and Ray were in town. She'd know in a half hour.

Cassidy peeked out her door when Polly walked past. "Can I get up now?"

"Sure, honey," Polly said. "Did you sleep well?"

Cassidy nodded. She came out wearing a pair of blue plaid shorts and a bright purple and yellow t-shirt. She had green socks on and her pink tennis shoes.

"You look ready for a fun day," Polly said.

"Is Andrew coming over?"

She'd paid attention last night when Polly and Henry talked about the day today. What Polly hadn't realized was that Cassidy might have a crush on Andrew. He was wonderful to her, letting her choose when to play with her brothers and when to sit out. He always encouraged her to do whatever she could do. No wonder there was a bit of love there.

"You bet. Is that why you dressed up?"

Cassidy preened.

"You look wonderful," Polly said. "Nice job." There would be a day that they would deal with whether or not her outfits matched, but today wasn't that day. As long as Cassidy saw beauty in all the colors, Polly would encourage her.

"Shh," Polly said as they headed on down the hallway. "We're going to let the boys sleep in if they want."

Cassidy picked up her feet to tiptoe past Caleb and JaRon's

door. The dogs had already left the boys' rooms and were still outside. Once summer arrived, Henry let them out when he got up They were content to play and lie around in the sunshine until Polly got downstairs.

That was going to be her job today. It wasn't one she enjoyed, but she knew it was necessary. Picking up after her big dog and her medium-sized dog was no fun. She thought about asking Andrew if he'd like to make some extra cash, but the way he complained about cleaning his own yard, she just plain didn't want to hear it. For the kids to have fun in the back yard, she spent a few minutes every day cleaning things up. But today it seemed important to double check and make sure that no special bombs would be uncovered when they had guests here tomorrow.

Cat was already in the kitchen when she and Cassidy got downstairs.

"Good morning," Polly said. "I didn't expect to see you out of bed yet."

Cat yawned. "The sun really took it out of me yesterday, but Hayden was processing on something this morning and would not shut ..." she stopped and looked at Cassidy. "He wouldn't be quiet. I finally decided to give up and come downstairs. We have a lot to do today and I wanted to map out a plan."

"A plan, huh?" Polly laughed. "I kinda thought we'd clean until we dropped."

"Or that. I started coffee and was trying to figure out what to do for breakfast."

"Sal will be here in a half hour," Polly said. "She's bringing breakfast for everyone. I don't know what it will be, but at least it will be something."

"That would be awesome. I was thinking that Andrew and the boys could clean up the back yard. Pick up toys and put things away. Then we need to work in the kitchen and dining room to make sure this is all cleared out."

Polly looked around. No matter how hard they tried, this room collected everything that came into the house. At least the dining room was generally safe from everyone's stuff, but not this place.

Books and toys, empty boxes, trash that hadn't made it into the trash bins.

"Where did that skein of yarn come from?" she asked.

Cat chuckled. "We were making hair for a paper doll that Caleb created. I picked it up at the General Store. I thought I told them to take that to the basement." Her eyes widened. "Oh, I'll bet you want to take Shelly's family on a tour through the tunnel. We need to work on that today, too. I hope we have enough totes down there to stow all of the toys."

"We're going to make this as clean as we can and then we're going to not worry about it," Polly said.

"I'm not sure how to work that way," Cat said with a laugh. "Mama would turn into a drill instructor on cleaning days. Nothing was left undone. Especially if there was the faintest possibility that we might see a guest within the next ten days."

"I expect the boys to be relatively neat and clean for company, but I can't do the tyrant thing," Polly said. "Cassidy and I will tackle the living room and library this morning. We're going to walk the yard looking for dog poop after lunch."

"Dog poop," Cassidy said with a giggle. She'd parked herself on the floor under the counter of the island, one of the safest places in the room when her family started moving as fast as they did. That way she could be part of everything. She hated missing out.

The back doorbell rang and before Polly or Cat could get there, it opened. "Hey, Polly, it's me. Can I let the dogs in?"

Andrew's voice had changed this last year. It wasn't quite as deep as his brother's, but it was different.

"Sure," she said, stepping back as Obiwan and Han came dashing into the kitchen. They knew where Henry left their breakfast and ran right to it.

"Sal's right behind me." He held out a box. "This is for everyone for breakfast. I told her I'd bring it with me."

"You're a good kid, no matter what they say." Polly took it from him. "Come on in. The boys are still in bed. So is Rebecca, for that matter."

"She won't get up for a long time," he said. "She hates mornings." Then he lifted his upper lip in a mock snarl. "So do I, but every time I think I get to sleep in, someone wants me to do something."

"Poor Andrew. We'll wake her up once we start cleaning. Thanks for coming over."

"No problem. What am I doing today? The foyer?"

"You and the boys are going to start in the back yard, the shed and tunnel and the basement. Hayden's mowing early tomorrow morning and I want everything clear so he doesn't have to stop," Cat said.

"Got it." Andrew sighed and turned to Polly. "I just got done cleaning up Padme's poop. If you give me a couple of bags, I'll do that too. I might as well. Figure it's my lot in life. Eliseo says it isn't as bad as horse poop, but still."

Polly hugged him. "You're my hero. I'll give you money, lots of money."

He shrugged. "You're already paying me plenty. It's okay."

She glanced at the door as Sal came up the steps.

"Can I come in without knocking?" Sal asked, opening the door.

"Hello there! Come in. Where are your boys?"

"Home with Mrs. Dobley. We invited Josie's two to come over and play. I couldn't believe it, but Mrs. Dobley says she'll have fun with them. Four! What is that crazy woman thinking?"

"She must love them."

Sal held out a travel cup. "I used one of mine this morning. I swear it's clean."

"Thank you," Polly said. "You're awesome. So, what's up?"

"I missed you and I know you're going to be working hard all day to get ready for the party. I thought I'd help if you'd let me."

Polly took in her friend's *cleaning* outfit. It was less splashy than usual, but still. Sal wore a sharply pressed blue blouse over a pair of denim shorts and clean blue tennies on her feet.

"We're going to get dirty," Polly said.

"I'm ready. Where do we start?"

"Breakfast first. What did you bring?"

"Mom made up a whole box of stuff," Andrew said. "We have breakfast sandwiches and muffins, cinnamon rolls, everything."

"What would you like, Cassidy?" Polly asked, bending down to help the girl stand up.

Sal giggled when she caught sight of Cassidy's outfit. "I want to have that much style," she said. "It's fantastic." She tapped Cassidy's nose. "Girlfriend, you look amazing today."

"Thank you," Cassidy said. She climbed up onto a stool.

"She really does," Sal said quietly. "She's losing some of that weight."

Polly nodded. "I just want her to be healthy. The poor thing has to run to keep up with all of us. Her brothers never slow down. One of these days her short little legs will sprout and we'll all be left behind. So why are you really here?"

"Can't a friend offer to help another friend when that friend is doing something special for somebody else?"

"Yes, a friend can do that, but it's never happened before so I'm suspicious."

Sal cackled. "I need to talk to you about a couple of things with the foundation. Jeff and I met yesterday, and we have a few proposals we'd like to take to the board. I want to make sure that you approve before we move on anything."

"When's the next board meeting?"

"July fourteenth," Sal said with exasperation. "Don't you read your emails?"

"Yeah, but I forget until the week before when my calendar sends me a reminder."

"You're useless. We only have a couple of weeks and I need time to pull things together if you think we should go ahead with these ideas."

Polly plucked one of Sylvie's chocolate muffins out of the box. "We're heading to the office for a few minutes," she said to Cat. "It isn't anything private, so don't worry about interrupting if you need me. Then I'll start cleaning."

Cat nodded, her mouth full of a cinnamon roll.

"Guess who's in town?" Polly asked as the two of them walked down the hall.

"I have no idea."

"Go on. Guess. Why would I ask you to do that if I didn't think you couldn't figure it out?"

Sal frowned and shook her head. "Context?"

"You and me. That's all the context you need."

"You and me, Bellingwood or you and me, Boston?"

Polly lifted a shoulder.

"Not Bunny."

"Oh lord, no. I would have called you last night and told you to come over and help me deal with her. Much more fun than that."

"I don't know," Sal said with another shrug. "Jon and Ray Renaldi."

"That's it!" Polly said. "They showed up yesterday."

"Shut up. They did not. I was just tossing it out there. Why are they in Bellingwood? Aren't they like big-time promoters or something with the Bruins? What does that have to do with Bellingwood?"

Polly pointed at a chair and Sal sat down as she took her seat behind the desk. She took a long drink of the iced coffee and smiled. "I love that stuff."

"I know you do," Sal said with a laugh. "You're so easy to please. Tell me why Jon and Ray are here."

"They don't do sports promotion; they have a security company that takes care of large corporations around the world. The guy who died on Tuesday works for one of their clients. They're afraid that it has something to do with some nefarious problem, so they're here to help the investigation along."

"That will make Aaron happy," Sal said flatly.

"He likes them a lot. Don't forget, they rescued me from Joey Delancy … twice."

"That's true. Did they tell you they were coming?"

"No. They just showed up. I came home from working at the hotel and they were on my front porch. Agnes Hill was here with Cassidy and she wouldn't let them inside the house."

Sal giggled. "I can see it. She might be little and she might be old, but I'll bet she can be scary as hell. How long will they be in town? I'd love to see them."

"Until they figure out why the guy was killed, I guess," Polly said. "Jon's dating someone. It sounds serious."

"No way. I thought he'd never get married."

"I don't know why Drea hasn't told me about her yet. Her name is Chloe and she sounds great. Even his mother likes her. So, tell me about your plans."

Sal reached down and picked up her purse, then took out a tablet. She swiped a few times and put it on the desk in front of Polly. "We have four things we'd like to put on the table for the next two years. The first is to re-build the playground at the elementary school. It badly needs to be updated. As Jeff and I talked, we realized that there are several families with disabled children in town, so we're going to investigate accessible playground equipment."

"Yeah," Polly said. "Why wouldn't we?"

"You once talked about putting in a sprinkler park downtown. You know, in that empty space between the hardware store and the empty building. We'd like to put that out for bid."

"I'm sorry I haven't done more with that. There just never seems to be enough time."

"Well, we're going to get it started. Then, we want to discuss seeding new businesses. Jeff and others from the Chamber have a list of people interested in putting small businesses in town, but they're looking for investment dollars. I think we need to discuss these. We'll look at their business plans and bring the ones we feel have potential back to the board."

"I don't understand," Polly said. "These are all great ideas. Why wouldn't I be on board with them?"

"Those are the easy ones," Sal said. "The next one is going to require us to raise funds if we move forward with it."

"Okay, what?"

"We want to build an indoor / outdoor recreation center. A swimming pool, basketball courts, pickleball courts, volleyball, a bigger ice rink for hockey, maybe more baseball fields. It all depends on how much money we can raise and what we can find for a location. Bellingwood needs something like this."

Polly sat back. "Umm, wow. That's a huge undertaking. Are we really ready for that?"

"We believe it will take a couple of years just to get underway with plans and fundraising. We won't begin anything until we have at a minimum fifty percent of the funds in hand. This is a very long-term project."

"Okay, say we get this built. Who will manage it? Who will maintain it? Are you planning to sell memberships? That kind of defeats the fundraising for a community project, but otherwise how will you pay for all of that?"

Sal grinned. "I told Jeff you'd move right past the initial concerns to long term plans."

"Oh," Polly said sheepishly. "Sorry."

"No, it's okay. I don't have all the answers yet, but I know that we need to have at least some of them before we consider presenting this idea to the board. It might not be ready on the fourteenth."

"It wouldn't hurt to at least put it out there and let people think about it," Polly said. "When I think about those types of facilities, I think about the YMCA. They have huge amounts of national funds behind them. I've seen other types of facilities attached to bars and bowling alleys. This feels different than that."

"It is. Maybe we start small. We purchase land and put up some courts. We'll have a ten-year-plan in place for continued growth and building, based on numbers. Think of it more like a community center. There are a few in Iowa that are doing exactly what we'd like to see happen."

"I'm still not sure how you plan to manage this. If we want it to be successful there will have to be a great deal of marketing. People don't just show up to play volleyball out of the blue."

Sal nodded.

"I don't mean to be negative," Polly said. "I opened Sycamore House without a clue as to what I was doing."

"Then you hired Jeff."

Polly grinned. "And he's going to work on this project, too. I should trust the two of you more. Either of you could make this happen. The two of you together will be a powerhouse."

"This is why I wanted to talk to you first," Sal said. "These questions will all come up when we lay out the idea. If you're on board, you'll be a positive voice when everyone else panics. The thing is, we don't expect to do this right away. We want to begin planning now, but it will take years to come together."

"There is no reason not to," Polly said. "Bellingwood won't stop growing. You can count on momentum to carry some of this."

"I don't want to count on anything but our hard work," Sal said. "Have you heard any more from the designer about the rooms at the B&B?"

"Not yet. She said she would have something back to me next week before the holiday. I guess that will be in time for the board meeting, too."

"No hints? The last ideas were wild. I couldn't believe she hadn't listened to us when we described what we wanted."

"I described what we wanted," Polly said, "but she was watching you. The style she chose was exactly like you. Elegant, flashy, bright, and bold. Once I brought her back to earth and showed her a more comfortable farmhouse style of design, she latched right on to it. Apparently, that's a big deal these days. It will be good. I have confidence."

"I'm glad you do. If the B&B is successful, we have so much more we can do."

"If?" Polly asked. "What do you mean, if? It *will* be successful. Jeff turned Sycamore House upside down in just over a year. I wouldn't be able to do half the things I'm doing in Bellingwood if he hadn't happened into my life. Before we know it, the B&B will be turning people away until we finish more rooms."

"I love the way you think," Sal said. "So should we clean? Where are we going first?"

"If your mother could see you now, she'd pass out from the shock."

"What? I clean my own house. I'm good at it, too. The only thing I'm terrible at is cooking. And that's only because I don't care."

"I know." She was right. Sal's house was quite clean. She'd always been like that, well, except for the first year or two of college when the two slobs shared a dorm room. "We're responsible for the living room and the library this morning."

"That's easy stuff. Where are the dust rags and the vacuum?"

"I'll bring everything right in. I can't believe you're doing this."

Sal grinned. "Someday I'm going to ask you to do something awful and remind you of this day."

CHAPTER ELEVEN

Having Andrew eat lunch with them was a huge treat for Polly's boys. They spent most of the meal vying for his attention and he ate it up.

Her phone rang while they were in the middle of eating lunch. She ignored it, having left it in the kitchen on the charger. Unless she was expecting a call, no one messed with mealtimes. However, with as strange a week as she'd been having, she worried. Then she got mad at herself for worrying. The argument was an old one and she'd gone over it many times in the last few years. Just because she had a cell phone didn't give anyone permission to scream for her attention whenever the whim hit them.

"Oh," Andrew said. "I didn't tell you."

"Tell me what?"

"You are never going to believe what Jason did."

She chuckled. "How bad is it?"

"Mom is freaking out. He bought a motorcycle."

Every single cell in Polly's body clenched up. She couldn't move. "He did what?"

"Yeah. That was Mom's reaction, too. He didn't even tell her. He just did it. He says he got a really good deal on it and he'll save a ton of gas money going back and forth to Boone."

"Did he sell his car?" She felt her mouth dry out as she tried to breathe. Poor Sylvie.

"No. He told me that while the weather is good, I can drive it. Then when it gets cold, I'll have to go back to riding with someone else unless I have my own car by then."

"I'll bet your Mom loves that, too."

"Not so much." Andrew chuckled. "Eliseo is cool with it. There's some work they need to do on the motorcycle so Jason can ride it and Mom's making him take a class at the community college. You know he doesn't have to since he's nineteen, but she told him that he wasn't living with us if he didn't."

"Good for her," Polly said.

"Eliseo said he'd take the class with Jason. He said I should take it, too."

She blinked. The idea of Andrew on a motorcycle might put even Polly in an early grave. "Are you going to do that?"

"I don't know. Eliseo thinks Mom should take the class with us. That way she'd know what Jason knows and he couldn't get anything over on her. And heck, maybe she'd even like riding."

"Oh yeah," Polly said, sarcasm lacing her tone. "I can totally see that."

"I want to get a motorcycle," Elijah said, standing up from his seat at the table in his excitement. "When I get my driver's license, can I?"

"No," Polly said and turned back to Andrew. "Are you all really taking the course as a family?"

"Eliseo and Mom are still talking about it. She's so mad at Jason right now they aren't talking. He's nineteen. He should be able to make his own decisions, shouldn't he?"

She nodded absently. "When did he buy this thing?"

"He bought it last weekend," Andrew said, trying to hide a grin. "He didn't tell Mom until last night at dinner. You should have heard the fight at our house."

Polly took in the five little faces who were drinking this whole story up. Cat was doing her best to not react, but a huge smile creased her lips.

"Have you ridden a motorcycle?" Polly asked Cat.

The young woman nodded. "Daddy has a Harley. He loves it. Mama even likes riding with him."

"Your mother?" Polly asked. She wasn't sure why she was so surprised. Cat's mother was such a nice, quiet little woman.

"Hard to believe, isn't it," Cat said. "They used to ride a lot more than they do now. She says they're getting too old. I think she's afraid she won't be able to pick herself up off the concrete if they go over."

"They've gone over?"

"Sure," Cat said. "That's why they wear leather. Dad's really safe. All of us have ridden with him. Dom and Nic are saving up to get bikes and Julian can't be bothered with it. Dad will make sure they have all the safety training, but they've been listening to him harp about it their entire lives. He'll kill them if they do anything stupid."

"Effective training method," Polly said with a grin.

"Mama wants one of those nice Gold Wings. She told Dad she'd ride more if he sold the Harley and got something that was comfortable."

"Your mother," Polly said, shaking her head. "On a Harley. I'd like to see that."

Cat laughed out loud. "I have pictures on my computer somewhere. They're kinda cute."

Polly turned to Andrew and stuck her finger in his face. "You will never put my daughter on the back of a motorcycle."

He pulled back with a grin. "What if she puts me on the back of one?"

"Ohhh," Polly said. Her upper lip curled of its own accord. "That wouldn't surprise me at all. I should call your mother and make sure she knows that she'll get through this."

"That's what Eliseo told her. Both he and Jason promised that it will all be done right. She didn't want to hear it, though."

"She wanted to know before Jason bought the motorcycle," Polly said. "That way she would have had some input."

He shook his head. "She would have tried to talk him out of it. He said it was one of those *ask forgiveness instead of permission* things. She said that she wasn't forgiving him. Eliseo said she didn't mean it. She told Eliseo to shut up or he'd be sleeping on the couch."

Polly started to snicker, then burst into laughter. "What did Eliseo say to that?"

"That she didn't mean that either and he loved her, and that Jason was an adult and she had to let him make adult decisions."

"I'll bet that went over well."

"Yeah, she told Jason that if he wanted to make adult decisions, maybe he should find his own place to live. That's when Jason walked out."

"Oh, no," Polly said.

"He didn't get very far. Eliseo sent me after him. Sometimes Jason is a lot like Dad. He gets really stubborn and then he gets mad. He was mad and said some nasty things to me."

"I'm sorry."

"It was okay. I knew he was just mad. What was he going to do, punch me? We're brothers. We've already been there, done that. At least he said all those bad things to me when we were outside and Mom didn't have to hear them. When he finally calmed down, he admitted he didn't have anywhere to go unless he went to sleep at the barn."

It hurt Polly to realize that she and Jason had spent so little time together these last few years that his first thought was to go to the barn rather than come here. But the truth was, the years that he spent with her, they'd been at Sycamore House and at the barn. Jason had never become comfortable here at the Bell House.

"I miss your brother," she said.

"He kinda mentioned that last night, too. Whenever anything really bad ever happened before between him and Mom, you were always there to talk to. He's right. Even now, you kinda show up when we need you, like you did last summer."

"Rachel called me to come over to Sycamore House last summer to talk to you, you know," Polly said.

"Yeah, but you came and you took me home. I guess that's what I did for Jason. I just had to make him stay until he quit being so mad."

"You're a good kid." Polly glanced around the table. "Okay. Everyone pick up your plates and take them to the kitchen. We aren't finished cleaning yet."

"Aw, come on," Elijah said. "This is fun."

"Talking about someone else is always fun," Polly said. "It isn't productive, but it's fun. A couple of things, though. Whatever you hear at this table about other people stays at this table. I don't want you talking to Mrs. Donovan or Jason or Mr. Aquila about any of this. Do you understand me? Andrew was telling me about his experience last night. If you turn around and talk about it, it becomes gossip and you're only carrying stories because you want to see what kind of reaction you'll get. Am I clear?"

"I still want a motorcycle," Elijah said.

"When you turn thirty-five, you can make your own decisions. Until then, you're my kid and I tell you what to do." Polly gave him a quick hug as he walked past her into the kitchen. "And nobody leaves the kitchen until it's straightened back up," she called out.

"What are we working on this afternoon?" Cat asked.

They'd gotten more done this morning than Polly expected. The back yard looked great, except for the mowing Hayden would do tomorrow morning. She and Sal hadn't worked together in years and she'd forgotten how things went with that dynamo. They were through the living room, bathroom, library, family room, and dining room by eleven o'clock. Swept, vacuumed, dusted, and picked up. There were baskets of items on the steps in the foyer, but otherwise, the place looked great.

"I want the boys to carry the baskets upstairs and put whatever is in them where they belong," Polly said. "If you want to take them ..." She lifted her eyebrows and gestured with her head toward the west. "I'd be okay with that."

"Are you sure?" Cat asked. "It would be good for them to have some play time. They worked hard this morning."

"It's up to you."

Cat nodded. "Boys, how about going to the swimming pool this afternoon?"

Caleb and JaRon had just come back into the dining room and both boys lit up. JaRon bounced. "We're done working?"

"For today," Polly said. "You each need to carry a basket upstairs and put things in the rooms where they belong. If you really don't know, leave them in the basket on the hallway floor."

"I'll help," Cat said. "We'll do that and then head out. What are you doing?"

"Andrew and I will finish up the bathrooms."

Andrew groaned. "Seriously? I wasn't the bad Donovan. Jason was."

"I'll tell your mother you have a pass on the next mistake you make."

"We get to go swimming. We get to go swimming." Caleb and JaRon sang out into the kitchen where their brothers were finishing with cleanup.

She heard Noah groan. "Do I have to?"

In a moment he was standing in front of her. "Can I go to the barn instead? Eliseo said it was okay any time I wanted to go over there." The swimming pool was right across the street from Sycamore House.

Polly reached out and took his hand. "You haven't wanted to go swimming very often this summer. Something up?"

"I'd just rather go to the barn." But as he said it, he looked away.

"Let me call Eliseo to make sure he isn't busy with something else," she said. "You just have to pay attention to when Cat wants to come home, okay?"

"I usually just call Eliseo when we're ready to leave the pool," Cat said. "It's easy."

~~~

"The bathrooms are pretty clean already," Polly said after the boys had left with Cat. She'd put Cassidy down for a nap. There had been some tears when the little girl begged to go swimming. She knew better, but that didn't stop her from trying. And Cassidy was exhausted. She'd chased Sal and Polly around the house, up and down the stairs, helping whenever Polly could give her a small task.

Throughout lunch, Cassidy barely said a word, just ate her sandwich and watched the activity around her. Since she'd started talking, she rarely missed a chance to make herself heard. That alerted Polly to how tired she was.

Wearing her kids out until they fell into bed at night was the one way Polly could assure herself a good night's sleep. With so many adults and neighbor kids around as well as all the baseball and soccer games, there was always something for the boys to be doing. She was thankful to have Cat, Hayden and Heath living here to help her and Henry come up with ideas to keep those active boys moving during the day.

One thing Polly hated hearing from anyone in her family was that they were bored. The boys had learned that lesson early. She didn't care if they sat still, but they couldn't complain about it. If even a hint of the word came out of someone's mouth, they were all put to work. She shook her head as she realized they hadn't even tapped the wellspring of excitement in the attic. One of these days she needed to get up there and find out what they had going on. It just seemed so overwhelming, Polly continued to avoid those stairs and today was not the day to think about it.

Andrew looked at the cleaning bucket in her hand. She'd put it together this spring once all four of her boys had been inducted into the bathroom cleaning hall of fame. He put his hand out. "That for me?"

"Just wipe down countertops and scrub out the sinks. I promise you don't have to do toilets."

"It's no big deal. I've cleaned 'em before."

Polly's phone rang again. She'd completely forgotten to check it in the craziness of getting the boys out the door with Cat and putting Cassidy to bed.

"Really, it's just this one off the kitchen. When you're done in there, I want to doublecheck the foyer. We need to sweep the patio off, too. I forgot about that."

"I got it," Andrew said. He took the bucket and headed for the bathroom while Polly went for her phone.

"Hello?"

"Hey, Polly. Are you busy this afternoon?" Ray asked.

"I'm cleaning the house. We're having a celebration for a friend tomorrow afternoon. What's up?"

"Jon and I are headed to Boone to meet with Sheriff Merritt. I wondered if you wanted to go with us, but if you're busy ..."

"Did you call earlier?"

"No. Wasn't me. This just came up."

"I'm sorry, Ray. I don't dare. Have you talked to the Bellingwood Police Chief yet?"

"No, why?"

"I might have gotten you and Jon into trouble with him. I'm so sorry. I'm used to everyone getting along and not worrying about stepping on each other's toes. I'm not sure he was happy with a couple of private security guys getting in his way."

"You know that's the last thing we're going to do."

"I know that. You know that, but Chief Wallers doesn't know you yet." She bit her tongue as she tried to stop herself from telling him about the dead guy staying at the hotel. It wasn't fair. If she hadn't talked to Ken yesterday, she would have told Ray and Jon everything. The thing was, not giving people the information they needed always meant that they weren't able to make necessary connections. She'd wait until they talked to Aaron. Or maybe she'd call Aaron and see how he felt about it.

"You got quiet," Ray said. "Something going on?"

"No, just walking through things in my head. Sorry. You guys need to get in front of Chief Wallers, too."

"I'll speak to the sheriff. He's got a deputy who's in charge of the investigation? Hunter? Hudson?"

"Tab Hudson."

"Tab. That's right. That's why I went to Hunter. Blond surfer guy from the movies."

"Hot blond surfer guy," Polly said. "I remember him. She's not blond and I don't think she's ever surfed, but she's a good friend of mine. She can come off kind of severe at first, but all you have to do is tell her funny stories about me and she'll lap it right up."

He chuckled. "We have a few of those."

"I'm sorry about dinner last night. I think everyone will be around tonight. Would you like to come over? It will be casual. Maybe even just pizza. We're all going to be exhausted."

"We don't have to intrude on your Friday evening."

"Intrude? I don't think so. I can hardly wait for you to meet my family. The boys will love you. Rebecca still hasn't finished swooning and Henry's looking forward to seeing you again. Maybe six thirty or so?"

"Can we bring wine or beer? Jon wants to check out that Secret Woods place back here. Is it any good?"

"It's wonderful. If you want to pick up a couple of bottles, that would be fine. In fact, Deputy Hudson lives with the owner."

"No kidding. Polly, you live in a small, small world here. Everyone is connected."

"That's just the way it is in the Midwest," she said. "Don't dress up or anything. We'll be in shorts and t-shirts."

"Thanks, Polly. I'll tell Jon and we'll make an appointment with your police chief. No worries. We don't want to cause anyone any stress."

"Thanks, Ray." As soon as Polly ended the call, she swiped through to call Aaron. When she looked at her phone, she realized the missed call had come from Shelly. She'd handle that in a minute.

"Please, please, please tell me that you haven't called with another dead body. I can't take another one this week," Aaron said.

"No, not this time. I should have gone through your switchboard. Have you talked to Ken today?"

"Yeah, what about?"

"Did he tell you I recognized the name of the man who was killed from the list of people who stayed in the room where they found that listening device?"

"That's what he was trying to say," Aaron said. "We got interrupted. He said he was going to fax us a list of names. He said something about the hotel, but I didn't get the whole story. Okay. Makes more sense now. Tab and I are going up to meet with him on Monday."

"Ray and Jon are coming down to meet with you ..."

"In just a little bit," he said. "That was a surprise."

"I know. So, uhhh, Ken got a little testy when I told him who they were and why they were here."

Aaron chuckled. "Two big-time, big-city security professionals showing up in Bellingwood, Iowa? Of course he did. I'll take care of it. He just needs to know how much these boys mean to us. They won every lottery in my book by keeping you safe."

"I didn't tell them about that guy staying at the hotel. They need to know."

"Got it," Aaron said. "I'll take care of it. We'll all be fast friends in no time."

Polly relaxed. She hadn't realized how much Ken's reaction had bothered her. The last thing she needed was to make anyone in the law enforcement community angry. Every time she turned around, someone in her family needed them. "Thank you. They're going to be in town for a while. Would you and Lydia like to come over for dinner sometime next week? We'll ask Beryl and the Speceks, too."

"You know who to talk to," he said. "I don't make plans; I just follow orders."

"I love you, Aaron Merritt. Thanks for keeping an eye on me."

"I do it for love, Polly," he said with a laugh. "They couldn't pay me enough."

When she finished talking to him, she sent a quick text to Henry that she'd invited Ray and Jon to dinner and that they were having pizza. Before she called Shelly, she sent the same text to

118

Heath, Cat, and Hayden. Heath responded right away that he would be out with his girlfriend, Ella Evans. It felt like those two were going to be a lifelong couple. The boys liked her; she was willing to play games outside with them. Evidently, she'd played softball in high school and could hit like nobody's business. She and Heath went to the kids' ball games, something that flabbergasted both Polly and Henry. But spending time together was spending time together. Ella's younger brother, Barrett, had given up on trying to get Rebecca's attention, though he spent time with the entire group that hung out together.

"Hey, Andrew?"

"Yeah?" He came out of the bathroom wearing a pair of yellow rubber gloves.

"What are you doing?"

"Just scrubbing the toilet. Figured it needed it."

"Uh, okay. Sorry."

"No worries. What's up?"

"Is Barrett Evans dating anyone?"

"Not Rebecca. I can tell you that."

She snorted at his response. "I get that."

"Yeah. He was kinda interested in Libby Francis." He shook his head. "Don't know how that's going to work out now, though. Barrett's mom is kind of a hardass."

Polly blinked. "Marnie Evans? She's the nicest lady."

"Sure, if you're an adult or a client at the vet clinic. She puts up with less from her kids than my mom does."

"I have never seen her like that."

"Oh, she's nice and all. She just won't put up with anybody's crap. She calls it as she sees it and doesn't shy away from anything. By the way, I didn't want to say anything when everyone was here, but Rebecca said you and Henry were really cool about, you know, everything."

"Rebecca didn't do anything wrong."

"I know. But you believed her when she told you what happened. And then you didn't force her to tell on Libby, you just talked her through everything. Like you always did with me."

"And then I make you both clean toilets."

"It's our lot in life." He drooped his shoulders, then stood up. "Anyway, she said you were great, and I told her that's just who you were." With that, he turned and went back into the bathroom, leaving Polly standing there, almost speechless.

"I love that kid," she whispered to herself.

CHAPTER TWELVE

"Fed and watered," Rebecca said.

Polly peered at her. "What?"

"Everyone has been fed and watered. I've covered the dishes and emptied the trash cans. Is it okay if I go over to Cilla's?"

Polly looked around the back yard at Shelly Nelson's friends and family. Rebecca had been gracious for the last two hours; no one would miss her. "Sure. I appreciate your help this afternoon."

"I'm not being rude, am I? I mean, I'm really proud of Shelly for coming this far and getting her life together, but ..." Rebecca sighed. "You really don't care?"

"I really don't care."

With a sigh of relief, Rebecca went into the kitchen through the glass doors.

The party had been very nice. Shelly's father and brothers were good people who, after a year and a half, were finally comfortable around the girl who had spent five years of her life in pure and utter hell. Mike Nelson, Shelly's father still watched her like a hawk. Maybe he was afraid that she'd be lost to him again, or maybe he was just thankful she was back in his life.

Her oldest brother, Matthew, had come over with a friend of his from Marshalltown and the other brother, Jason, was here with his wife, Margo, and their two children, Dean and Delia. Dean was JaRon's age and Delia was two and a half years old, too small to really play with the older kids. Her mother kept a pretty close eye on her anyway. Shelly's brothers didn't interact with anyone else at the party, but then Polly didn't really expect them to. They found a spot in the gazebo and hunkered in. It had been years since they'd lived in Bellingwood and most of the people who were here today had come into town after they'd left.

Marta was in the gazebo with the other woman who regularly worked in the bakery, Rita Smithson. They'd given up trying to talk to the brothers. It had been entertaining to watch. Marta was not to be denied, but even she finally gave up.

"What are you doing?" Sylvie asked. "Observing the crowd?"

Polly smiled. "I haven't had a chance to talk to you. Are you avoiding me?"

Sylvie laughed. "I just got here. I knew that once I sat down, I'd have to explain things and it was going to take time."

"Are you speaking to your son yet?"

"Andrew said he told you everything." She sighed. "Nope. We aren't talking yet. Mostly because we haven't been in the same house at the same time. Polly, that boy infuriated me. What in the hell was he thinking?"

"I don't know. That he's actually the independent young man that you raised him to be?"

Sylvie flashed a mock snarl at her. "Don't you be sassing me, young lady. I'm the mama here."

"I know. You're right. Will you forgive me?"

"Eliseo told me that the bigger deal I make out of this, the more rebellious it will make Jason. He thinks it's just a phase and that if I let Jason work it out, it will be over before too long."

"Sounds about right," Polly said, sitting back. She reached for the glass of iced tea on the table beside her, pulling her hand back when she bumped it wrong and nearly knocked it to the ground.

Sylvie handed it to her. "Klutz."

"I can't help myself. You know that Jason is going to want to buy a horse or two of his own one of these days," Polly said. "He'll have to sacrifice something to make that happen. If he gets tired of the motorcycle, he'll sell it for cash to supply his equine habit."

"I nearly kicked him out of the house," Sylvie said. "I can't believe Andrew stopped that mistake from happening. I don't want to be that mom."

"He's going to have to move out one of these days."

"But not until he finishes the vet tech program. I promised him that. It's only another year. Polly, I was so mad. I haven't been that out of control since I kicked Anthony out."

"Jason scared you with this," Polly said.

"Yeah. He did. And it really made me angry that he did it without talking to me first."

"Do I have to say it?"

"What?" Sylvie asked. "That he's an adult and will do a lot of things without asking my permission?"

"He already is, Sylvie. Just like you raised him. He's making decisions on his own. This happened to be one that you disagreed with."

"Oh, now you're really pissing me off."

Polly chuckled. "Because I'm right or because I'm crossing boundaries."

"Because you're right."

"If you were comfortable riding a motorcycle, this never would have come up."

"But you don't think he should have one, do you?"

"It's not my decision. Will I let my boys have motorcycles?" Polly closed her eyes and shuddered. "Henry and I talked about it last night when we were in bed. I want to tell you that I'd be open minded and after they proved to me that they could be responsible and would follow every safety guideline and ride the safest ones, I'd be okay. That would be a lie. I don't know what I'll do. Will they be able to ride while they're young enough for me to say? Nope. But at age nineteen, I'd hope that we had given them enough sense that they make good decisions."

"That's rude," Sylvie said, sticking her tongue out. "It terrifies me that I didn't do my job with those boys."

"Well, you did. They've had some hiccups, but you can't protect them from everything. They don't live in a bubble and you can't helicopter their lives. You didn't when they were younger, why start now?"

"I'm going to have to apologize to that stupid boy."

"You know," Polly said with a laugh. "It occurs to me he knew he would draw your wrath when he went ahead and did it without talking to you. He just wanted to have the bike in hand so you couldn't talk him out of it."

"You're right. That's exactly why he did it that way. And I saw through his behavior immediately which is what made me so angry." Sylvie took a long breath. "I need to not get wound up about this again." She waved at Eliseo. "He's so worried about me. It's pretty funny. He and Andrew think we should take the motorcycle course as a family."

"That isn't a bad idea. That way you'd know more. It would help you handle this better and it wouldn't hurt to have Andrew learn. You know that at some point he'll be on that thing."

"No," Sylvie said. "Just. No. I want them to be in elementary school again. This young adulthood thing is going to put me in an institution."

Sal came over and dropped into another lawn chair. "What are you two deep in conversation about?"

Sylvie looked at Polly, then at Sal. "Jason has a motorcycle. I'm not cool with it."

"What is it with men?" Sal asked. "Mark says he's always dreamed of having one."

"Is he going to get one?" Polly asked.

"I don't know. It's his money. I told him he better have a big ole life insurance policy with me as the beneficiary because I'll be cashing it in, hiring a cute pool boy, and living the life of leisure."

Polly laughed out loud. "That's one way to handle it."

"You don't have a pool, though," Sylvie said.

Sal shrugged. "So?"

"We should get going," Mark said, coming over to them.

"I just sat down," she replied. "Are you in a hurry to go home?"

He waggled his eyebrows. "Maybe not home. Mrs. Dobley doesn't expect us until seven-thirty or eight."

"Why, Mr. Ogden, are you inviting me to go parking with you?"

Polly and Sylvie burst out laughing.

"Surely we can talk Polly into renting us a hotel room for an hour."

Polly put her fingers in her ears. "Nah, nah, nah. I don't hear a thing. I don't know a thing. Make it stop. Make it stop."

"You can use my house," Sylvie said. "Just strip the sheets off the bed when you're done."

Polly tilted her head and stared. "That's just weird. They have a perfectly good house of their own with sheets on a bed that is comfortable to them. Mark can hold his horses until the kids are asleep. Right? Right."

"You prude," Mark said. "I need to run over to Ames and pick something up from the vet school. A buddy is holding it for me. Do you mind, Sal?"

"You could leave me here."

He sagged. "I could. Do you want me to come back for you or will you get a ride home?"

Sal flashed Polly a grin. "I'm kidding. I can think of nothing more romantic than driving to Ames to pick up smelly medicine for stinky cows. My life is so sublime."

"Or ridiculous," Mark said.

She gave him her hand and he pulled her up. "Let me tell Shelly we're leaving. This was a nice party, Polly. It was sweet of you to do this for her."

"I didn't do anything except clean my house." Polly laughed. "Oh wait, you helped with that. The rest of this is all Shelly and her dad."

"You have such a nice back yard. It's made for parties like this." Sal walked over to where Shelly was sitting with more of the girls from the coffee shop.

She stood when Sal approached and after a quick hug, Sal waved at Polly and walked out with Mark.

"I thought there would be more people here today," Sylvie said.

"Shelly didn't want a lot of people. Just her family and the people she knows from work. Mr. and Mrs. Worth were here earlier, but he wasn't feeling well, so Nora wanted to take him home. I don't think they're comfortable with people they don't know."

"They take such good care of Shelly and Lissa," Sylvie said. "What a wonderful find that apartment was. First, Stephanie and Kayla found a home there and now Shelly. I don't think Lissa is going to be in town much longer. She's talking about moving to some place in Minnesota with a high school friend."

Lissa Keenan had been Polly's waitress at a restaurant in Ames last fall and had lost her job and her apartment in one evening. She took Polly up on a free room at the hotel, and once she landed in Bellingwood, got a job at the coffee shop and bakery, then moved with Shelly into the apartment above Nora and Orville Worth's home. As nice as the girl was, she hadn't made an effort to become part of the community, no matter how hard people tried.

"I hope she can find her place," Polly said.

"Shelly doesn't say much, but I think she'll be happier without her around. Lissa isn't much for making friends and I guess she just hangs out in her room all the time. They don't cook together or watch television together. Nothing. It's been good financially for them to share the rent and I think they've both saved a little money, but Shelly is looking for a bigger life. Lissa just wants to do what she's always done, nothing more."

"I don't even understand that behavior," Polly said. "But I get it that people aren't all Type-A personalities."

"You're kind of a Type-A plus," Sylvie said with a laugh. "You wear the rest of us out while we try to keep up with you."

"Have you heard anything from Camille?" Polly asked. "Is her mother okay?"

"She called yesterday, worried about the coffee shop. I told her to stop worrying. Josie had things under control, and this morning, Skylar came back and filled in. It's nice having him in town." Sylvie laughed. "He has so much fun behind the counter. Women must have heard he was back, because for a while he was swamped with his old regulars. He charmed them, flirted with them, and sold a whole lot of coffee and baked goods. I miss having him up there, too. He's always laughing."

"You can't have him back. I need him at the hotel."

Sylvie leaned forward. "So, the dead guy you found? He stayed at the hotel? And that's why the Renaldi brothers are in town? You know it's all the gossip, don't you?"

"Not surprising," Polly said with a laugh. "When men that hot come into town, everyone talks."

"It's just not that, it's the whole thing. I heard someone say that it's like international intrigue. A hired killer was here to take him out because he was carrying secrets about high-tech weapons."

Polly laughed so hard she snorted, then she stopped. "I don't actually know any of that. I don't know what the guy did. All Jon and Ray told me was that they were hired by his company. I wonder what his company does?"

"Makes high tech weapons," Sylvie said. "Hello. We're in the know up there at the coffee shop."

"That can't be right. This is Bellingwood, for heaven's sake. No one in town deals with international weapons buyers. Come on."

"All I'm telling you is what I heard."

"Heard from who?"

Sylvie smiled. "Well, let's see. There was a whole chain of people involved in this one."

"Oh dear."

"You miss out on all the good gossip when you stay at home, you know."

Polly looked up and waved good-bye to several of the baristas who were leaving. Shelly came over to her and Sylvie and sat down.

"Thank you for doing this, Polly. It was perfect."

"I'm so proud of you. It was nice to meet your family today, too."

Shelly looked over at the gazebo. "I don't really know my brothers anymore. It's kind of weird. Dad thought that we'd be friends again, but I tried to tell him we never really were. Jas and Matt weren't around much after Mom died. They kinda treat me like I'm breakable."

"That will get better with time," Sylvie said. "I'm glad they came today. Sorry I didn't get here earlier. Eliseo put a gift on the table for you."

"You didn't have to do that," Shelly said. "This wasn't about presents. I should be giving all of you presents for everything you've done for me. Marta has invited all of us to go out to lunch at Davey's tomorrow before they go home. She asked if I wanted to come over and spend the night with her so I can keep celebrating."

"That's so nice."

"I love her. I don't know what I'd have done without her." Shelly caught herself. "Without any of you."

"Marta is pretty wonderful," Polly said.

"Dad and I will help clean up before we leave."

"There isn't much to do. We just need to gather your things and the extra food."

"You made such a beautiful cake, Sylvie. Thank you. It made me cry."

"Oh, honey. People should do beautiful things for you. You deserve it," Sylvie said.

Mike Nelson walked over with little Delia in his arms. "Margo is wondering where we've lost Dean to."

Polly stood up. "I saw them go into the shed, which means they're in the tunnel or playing with Legos in the basement. I can look for them."

Noah and Elijah had taken a few minutes at the beginning of the party and then escaped over to the Waters' house. Caleb and JaRon were fine with entertaining a new friend, especially after Polly bribed them with the promise of new Star Wars Legos sets. The older boys would have stuck around for that, but they were just as happy to leave.

She went inside and headed for the basement steps, listening for the sound of boys playing. Dean was a quiet boy and he'd liked the idea of playing with Legos. They'd been up and down several times. Every kid liked playing in a tunnel. Margo hadn't been too excited, but Shelly dragged her brothers down so they could see the whole thing.

"Boys?" she said, going into the playroom. She laughed. There were towers of Legos everywhere. "What are you doing?"

"We were making a castle, but then we made the towers," JaRon said. "Look." He stood and ran into one, crashing it to the ground. Caleb got up and crashed into another and young Dean followed suit.

"Dean's parents are getting ready to leave," Polly said.

"No," Dean whined. "I'm not ready."

She watched Caleb and JaRon's faces. They were ready to do something more active, she could tell.

"Maybe you'll have to ask your mom for Legos," Polly said.

"I have lots of Legos," he said proudly. "I just don't have anyone to play with."

"You can either go out through the tunnel or upstairs into the house. Your choice." She wasn't going to try to cajole him. He wasn't her child and her boys had been really good to play with him for so long today.

"Let's go through the tunnel," Caleb said. "Come on." He took JaRon's hand and they waited for Dean to join them. The little boy kicked at another tower, and after it crashed to the floor, he sullenly followed them out and into the tunnel.

Polly waited at the doorway until she saw them pass through into the basement of the little shed, then pulled the door shut. She grinned and kicked at the last tower of bricks, giggling as it fell to the ground. "Mama Margo is going to have fun with that spoiled little boy as he grows up," she said to herself. "And I owe my boys a big thank you." She flipped off the light and went back upstairs.

By the time she got outside, Dean was already whining and complaining to his parents about having to leave the toys behind. She wasn't surprised to hear Margo tell him that they would stop somewhere and buy him a new toy. Yeah, that's it. Encourage his bad behavior.

~~~

"I want to sleep in tomorrow morning," Polly said as she got into the passenger seat of the Suburban later that evening. Caleb and Jaron, Noah and Elijah were already buckled into their seats.

"Really?"

"What I want isn't what I'm going to get, but I still want it."

They were on their way to Agnes Hill's house to pick Cassidy up and take the kids to Ames for dinner. She was exhausted and wanted nothing more than to crash, but her family had been spread out all day today and the kids were ready to do something … anything other than sit in the house for the evening.

Rebecca was with Cilla, Heath and Ella were out together, and Hayden and Cat had been gone all afternoon since they didn't need to take care of the kids. They'd be home any time now and would enjoy the quiet of the house to themselves.

Last night's dinner with Jon and Ray had been a lot of fun. The four boys were thrilled to have two more people to entertain with their stories and hi-jinx. Henry started a batch of homemade ice cream when he got home. By the time they were ready to wind down after a few games of volleyball, they'd been entertained as the Renaldis told tales on Polly.

Once the kids were in bed, she and Henry stayed up talking with Jon and Ray, while drinking way too much wine. It had been wonderful to relax and spend time with her friends.

This morning she'd been up early, a little hungover, but nothing she couldn't manage through. Especially since Hayden started mowing at eight thirty.

Shelly and her father showed up just after noon, which was what she'd called about the day before. They'd brought a few decorations for tables and helped put things up out in the gazebo. Shelly had given Polly and Henry a beautiful hand-blown glass vase filled with colorful daisies.

"I'm thinking wings and burgers tonight. How does that sound?" Polly asked the boys.

"Wings!" Elijah shouted.

"I want a hamburger," JaRon said.

"You boys can have whatever you'd like. I'm very proud of you. Thank you for playing with Dean."

"He was kinda mean," Caleb said. "I told him we didn't say bad things to each other."

"What did he say?"

"He said that I was stupid because I didn't make my tower like his. He told us that he had more Legos than we did and that his were better."

"That's not true, is it?" JaRon asked.

"It doesn't matter whether it's true or not," Henry said. "You each have the Lego bricks that you need to play the way that you want to play. One isn't better than the other."

"He said that his dad was going to build a bigger tunnel than our tunnel."

"Did he," Polly said, grinning at Henry. "Well, when it's finished, maybe they'll invite us over to go through it."

JaRon groaned. "I don't want to go."

"Me neither," Caleb said.

"We have the best boys in the world," Polly said to Henry, reaching out to take his hand. "They were saints this afternoon."

"Bribery will get you everywhere. Are we shopping for more Legos tonight?"

"Do you mind?"

He chuckled. "After what it sounds like they went through, not at all."

She'd much rather buy toys for her kids when they behaved well than when they whined.

CHAPTER THIRTEEN

Rising up on her toes, Polly gave Henry a quick kiss. "Thanks."

"You need an evening with the girls. We've got this." He smiled down at Cassidy, who was holding his hand. "Don't we, Cass."

She nodded and then pulled on his hand. "Dolly house."

Cassidy hadn't played much with the doll house that Heath and Henry had built for her last Christmas, and she also hadn't had Henry's undivided attention in quite a while. The house resided in a corner of the foyer, which also made it difficult for her to play. If the boys were in there, they were throwing balls or chasing each other, and none of them wanted to sit in front of a doll house. If they weren't in the foyer, she had no interest in playing by herself. Tonight, Henry had offered to do anything she wanted while Polly met her friends at Pizzazz. Playing with the dollhouse was at the top of her list.

The boys were still outside, except for Noah, who was curled up with a book in the overstuffed chair they'd added to the library. Polly wasn't even sure what he was reading these days. He moved through books as fast as Andrew did and the two boys loved discussing what he should read next.

Heath was home this evening, much to everyone's joy. He and Hayden were playing ball with the boys while Cat was upstairs soaking in Polly and Henry's jacuzzi bathtub. She didn't do it often, but whenever Polly offered, Cat took the opportunity. Everyone should, just because it was so amazing.

Rebecca was at the hotel with Cilla and Kayla. The big basement room that Henry and Skylar had redone last summer was the perfect place for a sleepover and Rebecca hadn't had time to talk to Kayla since things fell apart with Libby.

There had been no more communication between the two girls, but as gossip always went, Rebecca heard the rest of the story from others who knew both girls.

Libby tried to deny everything until her mother found more items that she'd taken from the General Store, as well as things she'd pilfered from several other stores in town. Libby's parents were devastated. They had enough money to purchase things she needed and even things she wanted, so why she felt the need to shoplift, no one could imagine.

The money Rebecca had offered was returned to her, and Libby's mother set about making restitution around town. Rumor was, they talked about leaving Bellingwood because of this, but Libby's father wanted nothing to do with that. Someone said that he'd talked of dumping her in jail for a weekend just to teach her a lesson. Rebecca was certain that Libby wouldn't be returning to school in Boone. The embarrassment would be too great.

Polly desperately wanted to call Mrs. Francis and tell her about Alistair Greyson. He was a good man and great with kids of all ages. She hoped that Libby would find her way to him, and that rather than ignore the problem, the family would find a way to move through it. Libby was a bright, energetic and sweet girl. Whatever she had going on needed to be dealt with so she could have a future.

Polly parked in front of Sweet Beans which was across the street from Pizzazz. She hadn't gotten a chance to be there enough this last week. That would have to change tomorrow morning. She grinned, took out her phone and sent a text to Ray Renaldi.

"Any plans tomorrow morning? How about coffee at my favorite coffee shop?"

"Starbucks in Ames?" he asked, adding a smiley face.

"Not in this lifetime. What time is good for you? I'll probably have Cassidy with me."

"We're meeting with Sheriff Merritt and Chief Wallers at eight o'clock. Is nine thirty too late?"

"Sounds great. I can't wait to hear how it goes."

She smiled. At least now she had a good reason to be there in the morning.

It had been a while since she and her friends had come to Pizzazz for pizza on a Sunday evening, but Sylvie had asked about it before leaving Shelly's party yesterday. Polly sent out texts to Sal and Joss and was surprised to hear back from both of them that they couldn't wait.

While she crossed the street, Polly looked for any of her friends' vehicles, but didn't see anything. She opened the front door and Joss waved at her from the table in the back where they always sat. The place was as busy as usual. It had been a while since they'd come up on a Sunday evening, so she was glad their table was available. As she headed that way, she heard laughter and turned to see who it was only to find Jon and Ray at a table on the far side of the restaurant.

"There you are," she said. "Have you eaten?"

Jon stood up and gave her a quick hug. "We just got here. Are you picking pizza up again for your family?"

"No. I'm meeting friends. You should join us." Then she stopped. "I think. Let me ask if there's anything they want to discuss in private. It's kind of our weekly wrap-up whenever we're all available."

"We're just fine on our own," Ray said. He'd stood when Jon released her, gave her a hug and sat back down. "What else is good here, other than their pizza?"

"Everything. I don't think I told you Friday night that the owner, Dylan Foster, is Sal's brother-in-law. Dylan's wife and Sal's husband are sister and brother."

Ray shook his head. "What is it with you people in Iowa? Everyone is connected."

"It's awesome, isn't it?"

"The Renaldi boys are in the building!" Sal Ogden strode across the restaurant, garnering everyone's attention.

"Sal Kahane, as I live and breathe. How's our favorite Beantown girl doing in the middle of corn country? You look amazing." Jon was the first one out of his seat.

"If I wasn't married to the best-looking man this side of the Mississippi, I'd make a play for you," Sal said, kissing his cheek. "You're a sight for sore eyes. What did you bring me from home?"

Jon reached over and grabbed his brother's arm. "Here. You can have Ray."

She lifted up on tiptoes to kiss Ray's cheek. Sal was tall, but he towered over everyone.

"What will you do with me?" he asked. "Evidently, I'm yours now."

"Oh my," she said, swooning into his arms. "Whatever I want."

By now the whole restaurant was staring at the scene unfolding, some in shock, some with laughter. Polly was grinning from ear to ear.

"Have you ordered dinner yet?" Sal asked.

"We were just asking Polly what was good here. She served us their pizza the other night."

"You have to come back and sit at our table." Sal waved at Dylan behind the counter. "Hey, Dylan, we're moving these two back with us. That okay?"

He nodded and waved.

She grabbed up their glasses and menus, then said, "Get the rest. You're coming with us."

When they glanced at Polly, she shrugged. "I guess you're coming with us. I don't remember whether you met Joss and Sylvie. They'll be joining us. Joss is already back there."

Sal slithered through the tables, followed by Ray, then Jon, who were doing their best to be inconspicuous. Polly could have told them that was impossible whenever Sal was in the room.

"Joss Mikkels, this is Ray Renaldi and his brother, Jon," Sal said.

"Don't get up," Ray said when Joss tried to stand. He put his hand out. "You work at the library, right?"

She wrinkled her forehead. "Yeah? How did you know that?"

"Your husband is a pharmacist and you adopted five children before you had your own baby," Jon said, stepping forward to shake her hand.

"That's a little creepy," she said with a hesitant smile. "I know who you are, but not that much detail."

Jon laughed as he sat beside her. "Our mother is entranced with everything Polly does and everyone she knows in Bellingwood. It's like her own personal novel or something. She talks about you all as if you are her friends. Whenever we're there for dinner, she tells another story of someone who lives here. Whether it's stories that Drea tells her after talking to Polly, or something she sees on Polly's social media, she is never so happy as when she spends a few moments in Bellingwood."

Joss chuckled. "That's wonderful. Sounds like she needs grandchildren."

Ray had taken a seat across from Jon. "That's our boy's responsibility. He has a couple of years before Mama gets involved."

"Involved?"

"Don't even ask," Jon said. "None of us want to know what she'll do. It will probably involve garlic, pasta and a great deal of wailing and gnashing of teeth, but after that, there will be grandchildren."

"Tell me you have a woman who is ready to be part of that deal," Sal said. She'd sat down next to Ray and was leaning against his arm.

"I do," Jon said. "Speaking of that, what are you doing for the holiday, Polly?"

"We're having a big backyard cookout," Polly said. "Will you two still be in town?"

"I hope so. Chloe is flying out on Wednesday. I can't wait for you to meet her."

She took in a quick breath and her eyes lit up. "That's wonderful! Can you talk Drea into flying out, too?"

Ray huffed a laugh. "We didn't even think of that. I'll give her a call."

"Won't your mother be lonely?" Joss asked.

He shook his head. "If you're asking whether she'd fly to Iowa, there's no way. She has plenty of family and friends who keep her busy when we're out of town."

"They're out of town a lot," Polly said. "Mama Renaldi has never been one to sit around and wait for her boys to show up. But when they're available, they'd better be at her dinner table."

"Or else," Jon added.

"I can't wait to meet Chloe."

"We were going to talk to you about it tomorrow morning at coffee," Jon said, "but this is much better."

Polly felt a hand on her shoulder and looked up at Sylvie. She moved to the chair at the end of the table, letting Sylvie sit down by Sal. "We made a party."

"Hi there," Sylvie said shyly. "You wouldn't remember me."

"Oh, I remember you," Ray said. "You have those wonderful boys, Jason and Andrew, and you can cook like nobody's business. You run the bakery now?"

She nodded as she sat down. "Wonderful boys is a question mark these days, but that's me. I'm surprised you remember.

Joss sat forward. "They were just telling us how much their mother knows about Polly's world here in Bellingwood."

"Really," Sylvie said. "Like what?"

Jon laughed. "Like everything. Let's see. She loves the pictures of your son with the big horses. And you're dating Eliseo? The guy who works at Sycamore House? And Andrew is back with Rebecca, right?"

Sylvie laughed out loud. "Hmmm, I didn't realize there was so much information about us out there."

"It isn't like he knows your bra size or how often you have sex," Sal said.

"No, that's you," Ray replied.

She sat straight up and looked at him. "Excuse me?"

He cackled. "I'm kidding. But I assumed. Was I right? You do have two little boys and Mama says that you and your husband are the most gorgeous things she's ever seen. She also said that the way you look at each other tells her that your marriage is going to be just fine."

"Oh, dear heavens," Sylvie said with a laugh. "That's just crazy. Does she know everyone in Bellingwood?"

"I wouldn't be surprised," Jon said.

"Tell us about the murder victim," Sal said. "I hear that he held military secrets and worked for an international weapons dealer."

Jon raised his eyebrows. "That's what you heard, eh? I suppose that's as good a story as any."

"It isn't true?" she asked.

Ray put his hands out, palms up. "True. Not true. It's not ours to discuss."

"But you take care of security for his company. We don't even know what that company is," Sal protested. "We're your friends. Surely you can tell us something. Anything. Inquiring minds are desperate to know."

"That bright little mind of yours is going to have to focus on something other than our investigation," Ray said.

"But Polly always tells us what's going on when she's involved in a murder. And she's always involved in murder. In fact, she's involved in this one. So you tell Polly and she'll tell us."

"I don't know anything," Polly said. "Nobody's talking and I hate it." Then she pursed her lips. "No, that isn't true. This has been quite relaxing, not knowing anything."

"Aren't you curious?" Joss asked her.

"Yes, but if there's nothing I can do about it, then there's nothing I can do. I'm just going to sit back and enjoy spending time with my friends tonight."

"That means you'll get on solving this thing tomorrow, right?" Sal asked.

Polly shook her head. "Hey, I thought you were going to call Tab and invite her to come up."

Sal nodded. "I did, but she and JJ are doing something at Secret Woods. I swear, she is way busy with him now that they live together."

"I shipped three cases of their wines back to the office," Ray said. "I was impressed. We'll give Mama a few bottles. You know she'll only drink one of them so she knows what it tastes like. The other bottles will be given a place of honor in her wine rack. Just because they're from Bellingwood."

"She does understand that I would be glad to ship her as much wine as she wants," Polly said. "Right?"

"No, these will be treasured by her. We're expected to pick up mugs from the coffee shop for her and then I need to beg you for a t-shirt from Sycamore House," Ray said. "She even tried to send money out with me."

"I just love her."

"You need to come back to Boston one of these days," he said. "She misses you."

Polly nodded. "Maybe when Jon finally gets married."

Jon frowned. "We're getting married in Hawaii, didn't I tell you that?"

"No, you're not," she said with a scowl. "Your mother would kill you dead."

"You got me there. No, it will be a big thing. Chloe's family is big, too, but they have no idea what is coming their way."

"Have you set a date?"

He sat back in shock. "Are you kidding? I haven't even put a ring on her finger yet. We just started discussing the possibility after the first of the year."

"How long have you been dating?" Joss asked.

He slid her a glance. "Not you, too."

"No, I don't know. How would I know? I wasn't being mean."

"Three years," he muttered into his glass.

"I see. Well, you wouldn't want to hurry, especially at your age." Joss kept looking down, but a wicked grin crossed her lips.

"My age? My age?" he protested. "I'm younger than Polly."

"Not by much," Polly said.

"Iowa is a tough town. First, Mrs. Hill tells me my sperm is getting too old and now your friends are picking on me. Maybe we can find a judge to marry us next weekend."

"Not out here, you don't," Polly said. "I do not want your mother to make her first trip to Iowa intent on murdering me because I stole her wedding."

"Wait. Agnes Hill told you that you had old sperm?" Sylvie asked. "That lady doesn't shy away from anything."

"No, she doesn't," Polly said. "I never know quite what to make of her." She waved at Dylan, who had glanced their way a couple of times. "I'm starving. We need to order. Do you two know what you want?"

Ray grabbed up a menu. "I suppose you already know."

"We always have the same thing," Joss said. "Since we're together so rarely these days like this, it's nice to fall back on something familiar."

Sylvie nodded. "I'm having a beer tonight. Maybe two. Maybe even three. If I can't drive, will you take me home, Polly?"

"Still bad at your house?"

"Not really bad. Just silent. Eliseo and Andrew don't know quite what to do with us. Jason slinks in and out in a hurry and avoids me whenever he's there. I'm going to have to trap him one of these days, but I knew he had a million things going on this weekend."

Joss frowned. "What's going on?"

"I can't believe you haven't heard," Sylvie said. "I made plenty of noise about it. Jason bought a motorcycle."

"Fun," she said. "He'll have a great time. I used to date a boy that had one. We went everywhere on that thing. It was awesome."

"Your mother was okay with it?" Sylvie asked.

Joss shrugged. "I don't know. We were safe. She didn't say much."

"I'm not handling this very well."

"You know your son is a good kid, don't you?" Joss asked her.

Sylvie nodded, then shook her head. "I know he is. I ... I don't

140

know. It's just nothing I was prepared to deal with. When they put that baby in your arms, someone should let you know that there will never be a moment in the rest of your damned life when you aren't thinking about those stupid kids. Worrying about them and wondering if they need you." Tears spurted from her eyes. "And so instead of telling him how much I love him, I yelled and screamed and pushed him away. I'm a terrible mother."

Polly put her arm around Sylvie's shoulders. "Jason understands that you yelled and screamed because you love him so much."

Jon sat forward. "Our mother yells and screams as a matter of course. If she didn't, we'd think she was really angry with us."

They all looked up when Dylan approached the table. "I'm so sorry. One of our servers had to take his mother to the hospital and we're short-handed. I didn't mean to make you wait." He put two baskets of cheese bread down on the table. "This is on me and so is dessert. Anything you want."

"Do you need me to help you?" Sal asked, standing up. "I can wait tables."

He laughed and waved for her to sit back down. "We're doing okay. Things have already started clearing out. I knew you guys wouldn't hate me forever. You won't, will you?"

"We might," Jon said. "We don't know you."

"Oh, but yes you do," Sal said. "Unless your mother's storytelling ways have missed Polly's regular Sunday night trips to the local pizza place."

"Wait," Ray said. "You're married to the dance teacher, right?" He nodded. "Of course. And she's the sister to the gorgeous doctor. That's what you were telling me."

Dylan shook his head. "I've missed something."

"Their mother is a wonderful woman," Polly said. "She loves me and I adore her. She's fallen in love with Bellingwood and everyone that I talk about here. No need to worry. I don't think she'll stalk any of us."

"I'm not worried. Well, not too worried. Do you want your regular?"

Polly looked around at her friends and they all nodded. Jon and Ray placed orders for sandwiches, and Sylvie ordered her beer.

After Dylan left them, Ray smiled. "Maybe we should stop telling everyone that we know their business, Jon."

"I don't know. It's kind of fun to watch their reactions."

CHAPTER FOURTEEN

Opening the front door of Sweet Beans the next morning, Polly took it all in. She hoped to never tire of moments like this. Josie Riddle waved at her from the front counter.

"How was your weekend with Gavin's family?" Polly asked when she got to the counter.

"It was good. The kids love seeing their grandparents, and they have so many cousins on that side."

"You were just visiting?"

Josie shook her head. "One of his nieces had a solo in church and her brother read scripture. You know how it is with big families. Small events bring everyone together. They barely need a reason."

Polly smiled, though she had no idea what living in a large family was like. Until now. She blinked as it occurred to her that someday there would be grandkids running around the Bell House, traipsing through the tunnel, and begging Grandpa Henry to take them to the shop. She had to stop before tears ran down her face. "Are you going back for the Fourth?"

"Are you okay? Did I say something?"

Polly brushed aside a tear that had escaped her eye. "Sometimes I'm just a dope. I don't come from a big family."

"Neither do I," Josie said. "Gavin has enough family for you and me and everyone."

"I was thinking about how my kids would have that big family to come home to. I love what we have now, but that will be fun."

"Gavin and I talked about this a lot when we were first married," Josie said. "He just assumed that we'd have four or five kids. That's what his family did. He was surprised when I kinda freaked out. We compromised with two or three. If we have another one, I'll be fine, but after that? Fixing it."

Polly laughed. "Huh. My friends all want big families. You know Joss Mikkels, right?"

Josie smiled. "She's the librarian. I love her. She's so good with the kiddos over there. Doesn't she have a bunch of children?"

"She adopted five and then had one of her own."

"I can't even," Josie said. Then she looked up, stopped talking and her mouth dropped open, just a little bit, but it was open.

Polly turned to see who had come in. She'd heard the bell clang but hadn't thought a thing of it.

"Close your mouth," she whispered.

"Who are they? I've never seen them in town before."

Jon Renaldi swept Polly into his arms for a hug. "Good morning, gorgeous."

"Stop it, you dog," Polly said. "Josie, this is Jon and Ray Renaldi. Jon is the hound dog, here. They're old friends of mine from when I lived in Boston. Guys, this is Josie Riddle. She's the assistant manager here at the coffee shop and her husband, Gavin, works for Henry as his supervisor."

"See, Ray?" Jon said. "Everybody out here is connected. I've never seen anything like it."

Ray put his hand out and Josie shook it. "Don't mind him. He's a hick. I can't take him anywhere."

"Do you need breakfast or just coffee?" Polly asked.

"After what we've been through, I could eat my way from here to the moon," Jon said, "but yes to coffee and tell me what's good."

"Sylvie is our baker," Polly said. "Anything you see in there will be wonderful."

"Then I want that blueberry Danish and one of those ..." He tapped on the glass of the display case. "I'll have a lemon poppyseed muffin."

Ray shook his head. "Some of us don't have a girlfriend and need to keep in tip top shape."

"I work out," Jon said with just a hint of whine in his voice. "You know I can still take you."

"Any time. Any place," Ray said. "I'll be there and kick your ..."

"Boys," Polly scolded. "You're in public and there are children here." She pointed down at Cassidy, who was looking up at the two men with adoring eyes. Though Cassidy was five years old, she had missed so much of her early development, especially when it came to affection. She craved whatever people would give her. She had so much growing up yet to do.

"I should have said hello to you first, Cassidy." Ray knelt down and, when she put her arms out, he scooped her up and settled her on his forearm.

Polly shook her head. That man was strong. She'd always known it and she'd always appreciated it. Sometimes it was just nice to be reminded of how much strength he had.

"Coffee for you, too?" Josie asked

"Black. Make it a large. You got this, Jon?"

"You go sit," Jon said. "I'll bring it over."

Polly gave Josie a small wave. "Thanks. I'll talk to you later." She followed Ray to a table along the window on the west side of the building. The patio was open and several people had gathered outside with their coffee.

"This really is a nice shop," Ray said as he put Cassidy down into a chair that Polly pulled out. "Does she need a booster?"

"I'll be right back with it." Polly put her coffee down along with a glass of juice for Cassidy. As she walked back with the booster seat, she stopped to watch Ray talking to the little girl. Cassidy was animated and he listened intently.

"He's good with kids," Jon said, coming up beside her. "If I could figure out how to let him have any that I manage to produce, I'd do it. He needs a family of his own."

"Will he ever settle down?" Polly asked, slowing to walk with him.

Jon shrugged. "If the right person comes along, but Ray isn't looking. I wonder sometimes if he doesn't believe he deserves love. You know, Dad was never okay with the idea of someone being gay. I don't think he ever knew about Ray. That's just not something that's appropriate in a macho family like ours. Mama loves him no matter what, but he worries that if he were to commit to a relationship, it would be too real for her. She'd still love him, but it would put a strain on things."

"In this day and age?"

"Mama doesn't come from this day and age. And neither do the rest of the people in our family. Oh, the younger generations would accept him, but even some of them would make a big deal out of it and want him to get all socially progressive. He just wants to live a quiet life."

"You're a good brother. I'm glad you understand all that," Polly said. She picked up the pace and they got to the table when Cassidy flung her arms around Ray's neck and said, "I love you, Uncle Ray."

"What did you say to get that response?" Polly asked, putting the booster into a seat. She looked up at Ray and saw tears in his eyes.

"I just told her how pretty she looked in her dress today. She's a sweetie."

"You're such a softie. Here, Cass, let's get you settled."

Cassidy clung to Ray. "I want to sit here."

Holding back the sigh she wanted to release out loud, Polly moved the booster to the chair beside Ray. "Sounds like your morning was interesting."

"It does?" Jon asked. "Why?"

She laughed. "Because you said so."

"Oh, that was because of Ray's obsession with rundown shacks and gravel roads. We had to check out every one of them."

"You'd still be driving if he was obsessed with those things," Polly said. "No, really. How did the meeting go?"

"Sheriff Merritt calmed your police chief down before we even got there. That part of it went well. Honestly, Polly. How do these law enforcement agencies even exist without you working for them? If you hadn't put that name on the list together with the dead guy, they never would have made the connection."

"Sure they would. Aaron and Ken have lunch together every week. I know for a fact that they compare open cases. Especially something as big as a murder and as odd as a listening device."

Jon pushed Ray's coffee in front of him. "Once you pointed out the connection, it helped them combine forces. When Chief Wallers realized we wanted nothing more than to do whatever it takes to help him close the case, he was fine. Your friend, Deputy Hudson is smart. She's asking good questions."

"Like what?"

"Like why we're here and how we found out about the murder so quickly."

"Those seem obvious."

"There were a few other things we discussed," Ray said. He had his arm on the back of Cassidy's chair, ready to jump whenever she wanted a drink of her juice. Polly shook her head. That little girl had just found her mark.

Cassidy turned toward the front of the building where there were tables made for children, along with some toys and shelves of children's books. "Will you take me to the play area?" she asked politely.

"Wow," Polly said, nearly under her breath. "She has him well in hand."

"Leave your juice here," Ray said. "Let's see what we can find."

Jon chuckled. "That's adorable."

"Tell me what I should know about this," Polly said. "Why are you guys here? I've been trying to be patient, hoping that you'll just tell me. If I have to get pointed with you, I will."

"Ray and I discussed it. We know about you. We also know that you won't talk about it to anyone."

"Unless I need to tell Tab or Aaron."

"Exactly. We aren't hiding anything. They already know that Andrew Harrison worked for a software company based in Kansas City. He was meeting with companies in Ames when he spent the night in Bellingwood. We aren't sure why he chose this hotel, but he'd made reservations here a week before the trip."

"Someone could have seen his itinerary."

"We're working on who had access."

"What does the software company do? What type of industry are they in?"

"They develop security protocols and software for many different types of companies. In fact, our company uses them."

"What types of companies did Andrew Harrison work with?"

"See, that's the smart question. He works with banks in Iowa, Nebraska, Minnesota, and Illinois."

"Big banks like Wells Fargo or First National?"

"Now, that's another good question. He has small accounts throughout the Midwest."

"So, if someone could get access to him, they could whittle money away? Is that what you're thinking?"

"We don't know. The software company has multiple layers of security and they haven't seen anything that looks like it's out of place. Since his murder last Tuesday, they've been digging through everything."

"He's a software guy?"

"One of their top developers. His death created a rather large hole. They're scrambling to find someone who is as qualified as Harrison."

Polly's mind was spinning as she considered possibilities. The whole thing felt too big for Bellingwood.

"What are you thinking?" Jon asked.

"Nothing much." She chuckled. "That's not true. I figure for every idea that pops in my head, you've already got it and three others on the table. I don't know anything about that business. Nothing. I haven't even considered security software for Sycamore Enterprises. Who wants to dig into our records?"

"We've asked two people to come up from Kansas City to look at your logs," Jon said.

"You what? Why?"

"Because somehow the murderer knew where he was staying and discovered what room he'd been assigned. That piece of information wasn't on his itinerary. They got into that room before he arrived and replaced the clock with their own. They accessed it through your network."

"I assumed that since it was wireless, they had someone nearby to pick up the signal."

"Nope, they used your network. We figured that much out. You have another friend down at the sheriff's office that's a bit of a computer whiz. She uncovered that."

"Anita Banks," Polly said. "Why didn't anyone tell me?"

"It just happened this morning when we all started putting things together."

"She figured it out that fast?"

He chuckled. "She called your hotel manager. After he checked with Mr. Lindsay at Sycamore House, we were given access."

Polly pulled her phone out to see if she had any missed calls or texts. There was nothing. "I can't believe no one thought to inform me. That will change." Then it hit her. Today was Jeff's day off. He wouldn't have any issue with the sheriff's office checking the network, especially after the concern over finding a listening device last week. And it wouldn't occur to him that she didn't already know. "I need to be on the list of people to call when something strange happens at Sycamore House. At least Skylar called me before he brought in the police when they found that thing. I should be glad of that. So, now you're bringing in more people to dig through our system?"

"We hope this team will learn a great deal more. Miss Banks. Anita, right?"

She nodded.

"She's asked to be allowed to work with them, to observe what they do and how they do it. Our guys love to show off. It should be fun."

"Do Skylar and Jeff know that more people are coming to look at our network?"

He shook his head. "No. We told the sheriff that we'd discuss it with you and make plans from there. They'll be in late tonight, so we need to make reservations at the hotel. Plans are for them to start tomorrow morning. It shouldn't take long. They hope to be back on the road by noon."

"Wow," Polly said.

"They might find nothing. We just need to start somewhere."

"Does this rule out a domestic thing, then?"

"We won't rule anything out. It seems convoluted for a wife or lover to go to the trouble of planting a listening device in his hotel room."

"Sure." Polly watched Cassidy and Ray absently as she considered what Jon was telling her. "The company hasn't gotten any job applications this week, have they?"

He shot his head toward her. "What?"

"I just wondered if someone killed him knowing that it would create an opening in the organization. One they could fill."

"That's good thinking. I'll double check. Of course, no one will be hired without extensive security checks."

"They'd think of that, if it's what happened."

"You've been watching too much television."

Polly grinned at him. "Reading books, Jon Renaldi. That's where all the good ideas come from. Books, not television." She pointed at Cassidy. "Once that little one came into my life, my television viewing time tanked. Since last fall I haven't seen anything other than the little bits of sports that Henry watches in our bedroom. The kids mostly watch movies. I think the only reason we have television access in the house is for the older kids. Cat and Hayden use it to unwind at night and I find Heath downstairs after everyone else has gone to bed."

"You're so good with those boys. I don't know if I'd have the discipline to keep them away from television and tablets."

"It's not about discipline." She shrugged. "Okay, I suppose it is on some level. Each of them have had to deal with different learning issues and anger problems. I'd rather fight with them about watching television than hear from their teachers that they refuse to concentrate or focus, that they zone out during class, on and on. It's easier for me than most because I have the older kids in the house to help. We divide and conquer during the week. Most parents don't have that. I have a lot of freedom. My boys started out with such awful backgrounds, I wanted to make sure that we did everything possible to create success. Since I won't let them have access, Henry and I are careful to not spend time messing with our phones either. Unless we're using them to communicate, we put them away. When the boys see Henry on his tablet, they know that he's working. Now, I will sit down in the office and chat with your mother and mess around on social media, but they don't have to know everything. Right?"

"Did you ever think you'd have this many kids in your life?"

"Not at all. It just kind of happened. Henry and I went through the foster parent certification process, but once Caleb and JaRon came into the household, we couldn't add more, especially if they were going to be temporary. I don't have it in my heart to let kids go once they've become part of the family."

"When will you adopt the last three?"

"They're still working to get parental rights revoked. As soon as the paperwork for that is finished, we'll move toward adoption. I'm waiting with Cassidy so that we can adopt all three at the same time."

"They're all siblings? That's just crazy. I know Mama told me so, but when you see them, it's hard to believe."

"They all have the same mother. Three different fathers."

"You're a good person, Polly."

"You'd do the same in the same situation. Don't tell me you wouldn't. The truth is, I couldn't have brought this many children into my house without Henry. I wouldn't have moved into the Bell House if Hayden and Heath weren't part of the family. Without them and without that big house, I don't know if I'd have ever considered fostering Caleb and JaRon. Rebecca was always going to be mine. Elijah and Noah are here because Henry's college friend, Roy Dunston, knew that we'd take care of them. Once I met them, I knew that I wanted them to be my sons."

"They're the ones who went back to Chicago and lived with someone else, right? Then they showed up as your Christmas gift?"

She smiled. "I can hardly believe Henry managed to pull that one off. What an incredible surprise."

"I can hardly believe you and he found each other." Jon took her hand. "You know that I always loved you, right?"

"But not that way."

"I thought that maybe someday when I finally got tired of being a player, I'd find you and beg you to ignore my sister and marry me."

Polly looked at him. Her crush had always been on Ray, but since he was gay, she knew better than to ever think they'd be together. Jon had been like a brother. Maybe it was because Drea made such a stink about them never being together. Not because she didn't want Polly as a sister-in-law, but because she didn't think much of the way Jon treated the women he dated.

"You're awfully quiet. You didn't see me that way?"

"Drea would have killed you."

He nodded. "I was disgusting. I know that. I knew it then, but I was having fun. You haven't answered my question."

"I never did, Jon. Maybe I could have if things had been different, but they weren't. You were my brother. I trusted you to be there when I needed you and you always were. I'm so thankful for that."

"I am too. Henry is a great guy. I don't think there is anyone on earth more perfect for you than him. I can't wait for you to meet Chloe. I hope you love her."

"I can't imagine why I wouldn't."

"You know it makes me nervous."

"What? Me meeting your girlfriend? Why?"

"Because I care what you think. She's going to be part of our lives forever. You're my family. What if you think she's a mean, snobby, uptight witch?"

"Is she?"

He frowned in surprise. "No."

"Then I won't think that of her. If she loves you, Jon, that's all that matters."

He nodded. "I suppose. I really want you to like her, though."

Polly took her hand away from him and then patted his arm. "I'm sure I will. You have nothing to worry about."

CHAPTER FIFTEEN

"Marie invited me and Cassidy to have lunch at her house," Polly said. "If I called, she'd meet us downtown somewhere instead. I know she'd love to see you."

Jon looked at his empty plate and then at her. "Lunch? After I ate that?"

"Ray didn't eat anything."

"That's his problem."

Ray shook his head. "Both of us have work to do this afternoon. So far, this trip has felt more like a vacation than a work trip."

"He is such a downer, but he's right," Jon said. "My inbox climbed over three hundred this morning and that's after I've weeded out the trash and spam. If I don't manage some of these things, I'm going to be in trouble. I have seven to eight hours ahead of me this afternoon."

"Did you hear back from Allegheny Systems?" Ray asked.

Jon nodded. "They want to discuss the contract, but it's a go. I'll fly up in two weeks after Jeremy has had time to dig in. He's leaving on Monday."

"Good." Ray grinned at Polly. "The two of us are rarely in the same place at the same time. We discuss most of our clients first thing in the morning."

"Video calls?" she asked.

"If I'm decent," Jon said. "Ray thinks that four thirty is a great time to start the day. He doesn't understand that some of us have lives and those lives don't like being awakened because he's already started drinking coffee."

"Only on Tuesdays," Ray said. "Our clients in the UK and Europe prefer to have conversations when they're in their offices."

Polly shook her head. "I told Marie we'd be there by eleven thirty. If you have that much work, we probably won't see you tonight, right?"

"Not tonight," Jon said. "Tomorrow's Tuesday."

"You know that means it's three thirty in the morning here in Iowa, right?"

He flashed his eyes to his brother. "I'm in hell. Everyone tells me that Iowa is heaven. They're wrong."

"Can we help you get Cassidy and your things to the car?" Ray asked.

"Thanks. I can do it."

"We're going that way." Ray reached down and pulled Cassidy up and into his arms. "Polly tells me you're going to visit your grandmother."

"And Molly," Cassidy said. "She's my friend."

"The daughter of the girl who works for Henry," Polly added.

Jon laughed. "Oh, we know. Her father was a friend of your dad and he asked for your help finding her when she ran away from home. Colorado, right? Her mother won't have anything to do with her and she had a baby while she was living with you. Wasn't she chained ..."

Ray hushed him and gestured with his head to Cassidy.

"Sorry," Jon said. "How am I ever going to get used to having small children around? I never know when to keep my mouth shut."

"You figure it out fast," Polly said. "If you don't, they repeat things at the worst possible times. This one was mute for the most part when she moved in and sometimes I didn't even realize what I was saying. After she began talking, one day I heard her tell Marie that smoking was a disgusting habit. She used those exact words. I'd had that conversation with Rebecca about one of her classmates three months before the words came out of her mouth. I don't even remember Cassidy being in the room. Back then, she used to hover near me and sit silently until I noticed her. I often wonder how much she took in during that time and when it's going to come popping out of her mouth."

"After the first baby, Chloe and I are moving to Bellingwood to learn from you."

Polly chuckled. "I'm not great with babies. Come see me after they turn four years old. Sal, on the other hand, is wonderful."

Jon looked at her, his eyes wide in wonder. "Who in the world could have imagined that? You've met her mother. Where did she ever learn to be a mommy?"

"When did you meet her mother?" Polly asked. "Sal kept her away from normal people as much as possible."

"That's right. You'd moved back to Iowa by then. We provided security for a fundraising event she was involved with."

"Lila Kahane was in charge of a fundraising event large enough to hire you?"

"She was just part of the committee. In fact, if I remember right, she was the one who initiated contact with us, though. But that woman is not loving and kind."

"Her husband is a good man," Polly said. "I really like him."

"He'd have to be to stay married to her this long."

"He also works long hours."

Jon nodded. "That could have something to do with her behavior, too."

"What are you going to do about you and Chloe having careers that involve so much travel? You work as hard as anyone."

"So does she," he said. "We're still trying to figure it all out. The thing is, what we have right now is perfect. We don't get stressed about the times we're apart, and we enjoy the times we're together. It frightens both of us that will change when we're married. I don't want her to feel as if she can't do the job she loves when we have children."

"You two will work it out. And beware," Polly said with a smile. "Children make you want to change. You don't think you will right up until the point they're in your life."

"That scares us, too," he said. "We like our lives. I know that sounds selfish, but I don't want to change things just because we procreate."

Polly hugged him and waved at Ray who was walking around outside the coffee shop with Cassidy. "I know this makes no sense to you today, but you need to be patient and let things happen as they will. You've lived most of your life that way, why change now?"

"Because it's bigger than me, now," he said, frowning at her. "This involves Chloe and then our children. Dear lord, Polly, I'm talking about a family. Me."

"Couples do it every day. I don't want to take away from what you're feeling, but you can't let your worries take over. If someone had told me when I was considering this move back to Iowa that I would have guardianship of seven kids from age four to age twenty, plus a husband, in-laws, friends with babies, and the responsibility for employees and multiple businesses, I would have crawled into a hole and never come out. Don't overthink it. Let it happen naturally. One day you might be as happy as I am."

"You are happy, right?"

She leaned up and kissed his cheek. "More than I can express."

"You know I can't talk to anyone about this. I hate saddling Chloe with my fears. Ray thinks I'm being dramatic and Drea tells me that I should do whatever makes me happy. It isn't just about my happiness."

"Oh, Jon," Polly said. "You can always talk to me."

"You have so many people here who need you."

"I have time for you."

"Maybe I just needed to get to Bellingwood and see your face again. I feel like I've turned into a whiny little boy, worrying about my future."

"Maybe a little." She swatted at his arm. "Come on, Jon. You've been single and fancy free for as long as I've known you. It makes sense that you're worried about a change this big. As long as you and Chloe are in it together, you'll be fine."

He laughed. "Mama would say *from your lips to God's ears*."

Polly walked through the door he held open and heard Cassidy's giggle. Ray chased her around the corner of the coffee shop and the little girl ran to Polly, screaming in joy.

"You are so good with her, Ray," Polly said. "Thank you."

"I figure you were straightening my brother out. He needs to be whipped into shape. The boy won't listen to me, that's for sure."

"You never say anything worth listening to," Jon said. He knelt in front of Cassidy. "I'll see you later, Cassidy."

For some reason, Cassidy lowered her eyes and backed up.

Jon looked at Polly, fear flitting across his face.

She shrugged. "You never can tell. Cassidy, let's get into the car. It's time to go see Molly and Grandma."

Cassidy spun, looking for Ray. "You put me in the car," she said, holding up her arms.

"On it." He swung her up and headed for the car.

"What did I do?" Jon asked. "I'm a failure. How do I fix that?"

"You quit worrying about it for now," Polly said. "Ray has an easy way about him. He's not trying to impress anyone, and he's not worried about whether he'll make a good dad. He's just Ray. You be Jon. That's all that matters."

"You really don't hold back sometimes."

"Nope. Got no time for that. You go get your work done, talk to your girlfriend tonight and we'll see about getting together tomorrow." She raised her voice so Ray could hear. "Did either of you talk to Drea about coming out?"

Ray stood up from being bent over in her back seat. "She can't come. Another time."

"That's too bad." Polly hugged Jon again. "Stop worrying so much. If you can't change what's coming at you, it's time to get on board and enjoy the ride."

"Choo choo," he said glumly.

~~~

Polly wandered into the Sturtz workshop after having lunch with Marie, Jessie, Molly, Bill, and Cassidy. She was leaving Cassidy for the afternoon so she could spend time with Edna Dahlman at Sycamore House. They usually met on Monday mornings, but Edna had taken the morning off to pick her daughter and granddaughter up from the airport in Des Moines. They were spending two weeks with her and she'd been ecstatic.

Polly and Jeff had tried to insist she take more time, but Edna wasn't ready to take two full weeks away from work, and besides, her daughter would be exhausted after traveling today, so coming in to work was Edna's preference.

Polly waved at Doug Shaffer and pointed back to the piano workshop where she'd met so many interesting people last week. She was fascinated by the work they were planning to do and wanted to check in as often as possible. She'd intended to be back before this, but there had been too many other things going on.

Passing into the well-insulated room was always a relief. Even if she did wear ear protection, the rumbling in that shop would always be present.

"Polly," Len said. "How are you? I didn't expect to see you today."

"I'm just here for a minute. Had lunch with Marie. She's watching Cassidy this afternoon."

"Look who we have here," one of the men said.

Polly cringed. She couldn't remember his name. She put her hand out. "I'm not checking up on you, I'm just here to see what's been happening."

He shook her hand. "Roy Eslick. Brandon Fortney, and Haley Ferguson."

"I'm so terrible with names. I'll try to do better next time."

"You heard their names once," Haley said from a work bench where she was working on the felt of the hammers. "How could you possibly remember?"

Parts and pieces of the piano were spread all over the room, but there were hand-sketched charts lying beside nearly all of the pieces.

"Worried about how we'll put it back together?" Brandon Fortney asked.

"I wouldn't necessarily call it worried, but I'll admit to being curious."

He pointed at a laptop computer and Polly saw herself on the screen. "Errr, what?"

"We record everything when we're moving parts around. Not only do we have written records that follow each piece, if we are worried that we've forgotten something, we can check the video."

"Is it recording now?"

He shook his head. "The camera is on, but it isn't recording."

"That's what you think," Roy said. "I don't trust those things. I hang a piece of paper over the camera on my laptop. I don't need the government recording my life at home."

"They aren't doing that," Brandon said.

Haley laughed. "You never know. Better to be safe than sorry."

"We heard about you, Miss Giller," Roy said.

"Polly. Call me Polly. You're digging around in the belly of my piano. That puts us on a first name basis, don't you think? What did you hear about me?"

"You found that poor man's body down in Boone. Heard he'd been shut up inside a car on a hot day. Bet that stunk to high heaven."

She chuckled and shook her head, then gulped when the memory of the smell washed across her. "Yeah. It smelled pretty bad."

"Who do you think killed him? Rumor is, it was a professional hit man from Chicago."

"That's the rumor, is it?"

"Yeah and you brought special investigators in from Boston to catch him before he kills anyone else."

"There's always a little bit of truth in rumors, isn't there," Polly said. "I have friends from Boston who are here. His company hired theirs a long time ago. They probably would have sent some minor tech guy out, but I practically grew up with these boys, so they took the opportunity to visit."

"Len says they saved your life a couple of times," Haley said. She'd turned around to watch the conversation. "You were being stalked by a serial killer? How is that even real in a little town like Bellingwood?"

"My question exactly," Polly said.

"Was the guy's name really Andrew Harrison?"

Polly had to think at Brandon's question. "The serial killer?"

"No, the man whose body you found last week. Andrew Harrison. Right?"

"Yes. Sorry, my mind had gone off on another track. Why?"

"I knew him. Well, mostly, I know his wife." Brandon grinned at Roy. "You remember her. Dorie Harrison? The pianist? I've tuned pianos for a bunch of her concerts. She. Is. Hot."

"That's the man?" Roy asked, a slow grin growing on his lips. "She is more than hot. She's ..." He fanned himself. "Va Va Voom."

"Who says that?" Haley asked. "What are you, ninety?"

"Hate to say it, Haley, but even you would be impressed with her beauty," Brandon said. "She's kind of a tough customer, but once you figure out what she wants with the piano, she leaves you alone to do your work."

Roy shook his head. "I haven't done too many of her concerts. She likes the young boys." He winked at Brandon. "You're still young. How did you manage to hook up with the likes of her?"

"Danny Reynolds used to tune her pianos," Brandon said. "Then he got that bad case of hepatitis about five years ago and couldn't work. When it happened, it was last minute and I was in town. She liked what I did, so just kept asking for me. It's a good gig. I travel a lot for it."

"Does she flirt with you?" Haley asked, her voice a taunt.

Brandon shrugged and looked down. "A little. It's just her way. I kinda think she has to because she gets so snotty and mean. It's her way of making up. She gets way worked up before a performance. You just have to get out of her way."

"Did her husband travel with her?" Polly asked.

"Sometimes. She didn't like it much when he was around. It was like she needed to be in her own little world and didn't have time to be thinking about anyone else's needs, you know? Being on stage is hard work, trying to make sure you don't make a mistake and playing music that certainly isn't easy. But that's her pre-concert jitters. Once she hits the stage and sits at the piano, it's like she turns into a completely different person." Brandon smiled. "Her face turns almost angelic when she gets into the music. Unless it's a dark piece. You can see her transform before your eyes as her fingers play the first notes. Her whole body tells the story to her adoring audiences."

"Sounds like someone's got the hots for the lady," Roy said. "She's a grieving widow now."

"Yeah. She had a bunch of concerts coming up. I wonder what that's going to do to her." He frowned. "I'm supposed to be in Omaha with her on Saturday and I haven't heard that she canceled it. That's weird. I'd have assumed she would."

"Do they have kids?" Polly asked.

Brandon looked up and huffed. "I don't even know. I've never seen any at her concerts, but that doesn't mean much. She couldn't handle them if they were there. Dorie ..."

"Dorie?" Roy asked. "Not Mrs. Harrison."

"She told me to call her Dorie," Brandon retorted.

"Does she know you have a girlfriend?"

"Yeah. What of it."

Roy raised an eyebrow. "Nothing. Just asking. You were about to say something?"

" I don't remember," Brandon said. "She's got a lot to deal with, her husband murdered and all. I should send her an email. I didn't put that together until just now."

Polly absolutely adored young clueless men. Okay, that wasn't true. They mostly drove her batty, but they were certainly entertaining to watch.

Haley picked right up on it. "Seriously, Brandon. You work for this woman. You think she's hot. You hear that a man died who has the same name as her husband and it takes you longer than a week to put it all together?"

"I would have if she'd canceled her concerts," he said, a touch of whine in his voice. "Come on. I can't help it. I've been busy here with this piano. I knew I didn't have another job for her until Saturday."

"He's still young," Roy said. "These things take a few years to sink in."

"You mean, like life?" Haley asked and turned back to her work.

Polly looked at Len and grinned. "I should probably get going now that I stirred everyone up. Sorry about that."

He chuckled. "I know this about you. We needed the break. Sometimes we forget there is life going on outside these walls."

"It's kind of cool seeing the piano spread out like this. Elijah asked if you would mind him returning to spend more time here."

"We'd love it," Roy piped up. "He's a good kid. Curious and willing to be helpful. Not enough pianists understand how their instruments work."

"Not like other musicians," Brandon said. "String players know how to tune their instruments and replace strings. Reed players know what different sounds will come from different types of reeds. They keep a close eye on the keypads and wipe out the inside of their instruments regularly. Vocalists know their instruments better than anyone. But pianists? They want to walk in, sit down and have the instrument work perfectly."

"Because they can't carry it with them," Roy said. "Give 'em a break, bud."

Brandon looked at him, perplexed. "I heard you complaining about the same thing just last week. Why is it okay for you ..."

"Whatever. You're still young. Read the room, boy. Read the room."

Haley's back shook as she laughed.

"Keep 'em out of trouble, Len," Polly said as she headed for the door. "Thanks for the entertainment, all. And thanks for working on my piano."

When she got out to her car, she opened her phone and made a quick call.

"Sycamore House. How may I direct your call?"

"Hey, Kristen. This is Polly. If I run to Sweet Beans before I come over to meet with Edna, would you like me to pick something up for you?"

"Really?" Kristen asked. "That would be awesome."

"Wait. Tell you what. Ask everyone what they want. If Scott and Eliseo are around, make sure to ask them. Call Sweet Beans and place your order. I'll pick it all up."

"You're the best boss ever."

"Remember that when Jeff starts saying terrible things about me," Polly said.

"I'll trip him so he goes splat."

Polly laughed. "Perfect. Call in the order and I'll see you in a bit."

CHAPTER SIXTEEN

After Polly finished with Edna, she still had time before Marie expected her to retrieve Cassidy, so she headed for the barn. Noah was here this afternoon and she loved seeing him with the animals. After his initial terror at being around the big Percherons, he'd made a decision to not let them frighten him. Once he pushed aside his fear, he discovered how much he loved the horses. When his brothers were swimming at the community pool, he begged to be here. How could she possibly deny him that?

Noah was getting taller, but his legs were outgrowing the rest of his body and that made him awkward. Just like Eliseo, he discovered that being with the horses meant there was no judgment. They didn't care what he looked like or that he felt like a lumbering giant among short people. They only cared that he was one of their humans.

She walked through the first pen and into the open door at the front of the barn. "Hello!"

Jason Donovan came out of one of the back stalls. "Hi, Polly. What are you doing here today?"

"Checking on Noah, if I have to be honest. Where is he?"

Jason grinned. "He and Eliseo are picking sweet corn. Since Thursday is the Fourth, they're planning a big Farmer's Market Wednesday. We're pulling out all the stops."

"Oh." Polly was disappointed, but at least Noah was busy. It also meant he'd be exhausted when he got home. "How long until they come back in, do you think?"

He glanced up at the big clock on the wall. "They'll be out another hour at least, but don't worry. Noah has his hat on and Eliseo has plenty of water."

"I wasn't worried. How are you doing?"

Jason shook his head. "I'm okay. You talked to Mom, right?"

"I did. A couple of times. Are things any better at your house?"

"Not really. I know we have to figure out how to get past this, but it's way awkward. We both said some mean things to each other."

"I guess it stinks turning into an adult and still having to live with your mom."

"It's not so bad. Eliseo and I've talked a lot. She's just worried and he's right. She wants me to grow up, but she doesn't want to stop telling me how to live my life. He says it's because she's already experienced so many things and doesn't want me to make mistakes like she did. But I don't think this is a mistake. I want to save money and gas is getting expensive. I can drive that motorcycle for a lot less than my car."

"Really?" Polly asked. "How much will you save every week?"

"I'll get twice the mileage on the motorcycle as I do in that car."

"And how much work do you have to put into it before it's drivable?"

He shook his head. "It's already fine. Eliseo wants me to have it checked out before I ride it anywhere, just to make sure. The guy I bought it from took good care of it. He had to sell it because he and his wife just had their third kid and he needed the cash."

"I understand that," Polly said with a smile. "You kids are expensive. How long do you think you'll be mad at your mom?"

"It's already gone on too long, but I don't know what to say to get past this."

166

"How about *I love you and I'm sorry*?"

"I do love her, but I'm not sorry for getting the motorcycle. She can't just yell at me every time I do something she's scared of and then expect me to break down and obey her."

Sylvie did expect her boys to fall into line without much of a fight. She'd trained them for years that they were her sons and were to act like it. She didn't put up with much pushback. That they had a backbone at all was testament to the fact that she did it with love and respect.

"You're not ready to be friends with her yet, are you?"

He sagged onto one of the benches, still clutching a handful of leather tack. "I am. It just makes me mad that she won't let me grow up."

Polly smiled and sat down across from him. "Here's the deal. She never will. No matter how old you are, your mother will still tell you what to do and expect that you listen to her and obey."

"That's not fair."

"You know what I say about things being fair," Polly said. "It might not feel fair, but Jason, she's your mother. She taught you how to poop in the potty. She held your hand when you were scared to go to Kindergarten. She sat beside you when you were sick as a dog. She waited with you when you got your driver's permit and then your license. She let you drive away in her car by yourself. Your mother doesn't stop being your mother overnight because you turned one year older."

"I know that, but we've been working on me becoming an adult for years. She's the one who taught me to be independent and think for myself."

"And she prayed you would never think differently than she does, even when she knows that's not possible. You know, Dad used to do the same thing. He was always telling me what to do. It felt like he thought I was too dumb or naïve to make a good decision without his input. I'd been flying back and forth to Boston for a couple of years and suddenly he was telling me to be sure to arrive at the airport early enough to have time to check in and get to the gate. When I moved out of the dormitory into my own apartment, he had an opinion about every neighborhood and apartment I visited, even though I was the one who lived in Boston. When I bought my second car, he couldn't help himself. He told me what kind of extras I needed to have, how much I should spend on insurance and then he checked up on me to make sure I paid the sales tax. Uh, Dad, do you think I've lost my mind? I'm a responsible adult."

"Did you ever say anything to him?"

She laughed. "Oh yeah. We had a huge fight when I was looking for my apartment. I just felt like he had no idea what my life was like. He didn't know that I had grown up and could make my own decisions. He was clear out here in Iowa and didn't understand what things were like in a big city. I insulted his intelligence and his wisdom. He yelled at me and called me a spoiled brat and a self-centered baby. It was a very bad conversation. And the worst thing was we were thirteen hundred miles apart and couldn't see each other face to face to fix it."

"What did you do?"

"I fumed and kicked things. Then I took a walk. Then I told Sal what a stupid, awful man he was. Then she told me I was acting like a child. That didn't go over well with me either. I stomped out again and suddenly I remembered something my mother told me when I was a little girl. She told me that if more than one person told me something about myself, I might want to pay attention. At the time I was upset because a teacher told me I talked too much in class. Then my PE teacher told me the same thing. I tried to convince Mom that they had it in for me. She thought I might want to reconsider my behavior. But when Dad and Sal called me a baby, it hit me that some of this might be my problem.

"I found a tree, sat down and blew my nose. Crying, you know. I thought through the whole thing. Yes, Dad was wrong about some of what he'd told me because he didn't know the area. But he was right when he tried to get me to see how important it was to be safe and to check prices for offstreet parking and other things like that. I apologized to Sal and then I kicked her out so I could call Dad and apologize to him. Not because I wanted to do things my way, but because I'd been selfish and acted like a child. When you wanted your mother to treat you as an adult, did you act like an adult?"

Jason closed his eyes and took in a breath. "No."

"Parents make us crazy, but if we want them to see us as grownups, we can't throw tantrums because they believe differently than us. I expect different behavior from Heath than I expect from Elijah. They have ten years between them. If Heath mouthed off every time I told him what I thought about his actions, his behavior, or whatever, I'd be very disappointed that he was still acting like Elijah does in the same types of conversations."

"But you don't just tell him that he's wrong and expect him to turn around and make a completely different decision."

"He hasn't gone out and bought a motorcycle without talking to us," Polly said, a tiny smile on her face.

"But if I'd talked to her, she would have said no and then the guy would have sold it to someone else."

"So?"

"Well, I wouldn't have gotten it."

"So?"

"I wanted that motorcycle. It was a great deal."

"Was that great deal really worth a huge fight and three or four days of not talking to your mom?"

"Yes," he said, nodding effusively. "Absolutely."

"Oh. Okay." Polly sat still, waiting for him to think through it.

It didn't take long. He let out a frustrated sigh. "Maybe not. But it isn't right that I should ask her permission."

"No, but you could have had the discussion first. You do understand that it looks like you were trying to hide it from her because you didn't trust your own decision making."

"No, I didn't trust that she'd believe I could make the right decision."

"Really?" Polly asked. "Wow. It's like this was the first time the two of you had ever gone through anything difficult."

"What?"

"You not trusting her. You and she have never been through anything difficult where she might have proven herself to you."

"Yes, we have," he protested, then realized what she was saying. "Oh. I see. Man, I really screwed this up."

"You both did."

He looked up at her, just a little bit of hopefulness in his eyes. "Both of us?"

"Your mom knows that she went over the top."

"Do you think she'll be ready to talk to me?"

"She was ready on Friday."

"I wasn't."

"I get that. And one other thing, Jason. You can always talk to me. Don't make me come down to the barn to find you."

"I thought you were looking for Noah."

"You're right, but I knew you'd be here. I saw your car."

"It's just that ..." He looked at her, pleading for her to understand.

"That life has taken us on separate paths, and we haven't found a good way to connect like we used to."

"Yeah. I've got so much going on and you have that big family. You have enough to deal with. You don't need me."

"Making bad assumptions again, sweet boy," she said. "Don't assume your Mom won't trust you and never assume that I'm too busy to talk to one of my favorite people."

Polly frowned and scooted back so she could lean against the wall. "Maybe I do need to hire a person to keep the house clean and manage my life. This is the second time today I've had to tell someone that I have time for them. You never used to worry about that, you just showed up in my office when things were tough."

"It would be a lot easier to get to you if you weren't clear over on the other end of town."

"I miss being in the middle of the action here, too," Polly said. "I don't know what my family would do if I wasn't home."

"You'd be here. What do you have there that you can't have here?"

"A bed so I can take a nap in the middle of the day," she said with a laugh. "You've given me something to think about, though."

"I did?"

She nodded. "I don't have to be home while the kids are in school. Right now, I travel to meet with everybody when I have business to handle. Once Cassidy starts school this fall, maybe I will change things." Polly stood and walked over to sit beside him. "I do miss seeing you. You really are one of my very favorite people."

"Would you ever ride on the back of my motorcycle?"

"Will you have an extra helmet?"

His eyes lit up and he nodded. "Of course. Does that mean you will?"

"It means I might. No scrape marks on the body of that thing, though. I want to see a clean, unmarked paint job. Got it?"

Jason put his arm around her shoulder. "I'll try."

"Do or do not. There is no try."

~~~

Noah and Eliseo were going to be out longer than Polly wanted to wait, so she headed back up to the main house. Since this was a holiday week, the place was empty. Mondays were quiet since Stephanie and Jeff were gone, but there was usually a class or two, or even a lunch meeting upstairs. Not this week. She headed for the office and dropped into a seat in front of Kristen's desk.

Kristen looked up from her computer. "Well, hello there."

"Weird question," Polly said. "I could probably get this from the system, but how often are those rooms in the addition rented?"

"The upstairs rooms are rented sometimes when there is a big wedding reception. That's turned into a nice add-on for the bride and groom. We offer a package with champagne or wine from Secret Woods and other gifts from shops around town. They can either buy it with a breakfast pastry basket or a coupon if they'd rather go up to Sweet Beans."

"What about the two rooms on the main floor?"

Kristen gave a small shrug. "We've already pulled the bed out of the back room. It's usually used as another meeting room. People like looking out over the creek and the gardens. Jeff and Eliseo are talking about putting a patio outside. Don't you think that would be nice?"

"It would be," Polly agreed. "And the other one?"

"If we have overflow with a wedding party. Sometimes."

"We aren't bringing in a lot of artists and people like that who want to stay for a month?"

Kristen shook her head. "Jeff says that we're sending those type of people up to the B&B once it's open. It was a fun idea, but this place is so busy all the time now, people don't get the same kind of privacy and quiet they did when you were living here. Why are you asking?"

Polly chuckled. "You know, it feels like this is information I should already have."

"Yeah," Kristen said. "A lot of things happen around here during the day."

"Exactly. I'm missing out and I don't much like it."

Kristen sat up straighter in her chair. "You're thinking of coming back to work here? Really?"

"I don't know," Polly said. "I won't do anything until this fall when Cassidy is in school, but it would be a good idea."

"Jeff and Stephanie have been talking about turning the classroom space across the hall into more offices. Do you want something there?"

Polly looked out the door of the office. They'd already changed things around quite a bit, moving the conference room so Edna had an office. The thing was, Polly wasn't looking forward to a small cubicle. She missed her big office with windows that looked out on the parking lot. If she couldn't have that, being able to look out the window and see the horses would be enough.

"Don't say anything to Jeff or Stephanie. I want to talk to him to get a feel for what he thinks before I make a decision."

"How am I supposed to keep this to myself?" Kristen asked. "It would be awesome. You're fun to have around." She leaned forward. "I know Jeff misses you. He doesn't act like it, but sometimes he talks to Stephanie about things and mentions that he wishes you were here because you'd have good input."

Polly nodded. Pulling her family together had been the most important thing she'd done these last few years, but they were more stable now and she could afford to release some of her worries about them. Heath would be a junior this fall. Wow, so would Rebecca. She'd have a car, so Polly wouldn't need to worry about getting her to the bus on time. The boys and Cassidy would all be at the elementary school and Sycamore House was as close to them as the Bell House.

The only problem would be maintaining that big house. She did a lot during the day and it was never enough. She needed to have this conversation with Henry. He'd tried to talk her into hiring help since the day they moved into the monstrosity.

What would it be like to walk into a clean home every afternoon? The dogs would miss her. What in the world? She'd miss them.

She stood up. "Mum's the word, Kristen. You have to promise me."

Kristen pulled the zipper across her lips and scowled. "If I have to. This is good news, though. I hope you do it."

"Hello, Ms. Giller."

Polly looked up at the huge mountain of a man who had walked into the office. She stood and shook his hand. Scott Luther had been working here since April and everyone liked him. Jeff told her over and over that he'd been a good find.

"You look like you're hot," Polly said.

"Working out back in the gardens. We only have two days until the biggest Farmer's Market we'll see this year. Gotta make the place look nice. Good thing we aren't busy inside." He took a bandanna from his back pocket and wiped his forehead. "Just came in to check if you heard about that part for the mower."

Kristen handed him a note. "Pick it up anytime tomorrow morning. They're open at seven."

"I'll get it before I come up to work, then," he said. "Thank you. I'd best get back to it. Gonna stop in and see what Miss Rachel has for us in the refrigerator. She's always making up something cool and sweet to drink." He smiled at Polly. "I know I say this whenever we talk, but thanks for the job. This is a good place to work." With that he turned and left, walking toward the kitchen.

"He's a nice man," Kristen said. "If you can believe it, Eliseo is even more laid back having the extra help here. I know he doesn't like working inside the building. Scott does as much as he can so Eliseo doesn't have to."

"I'm glad. That's good to hear." Polly walked to the door and turned back. "No talking."

"Got it," Kristen said. "I promise."

CHAPTER SEVENTEEN

Grinning when she realized who was calling her name, Polly turned away from the front door of Sycamore House and stopped to wait. "Doug Randall. I miss you. What are you doing home in the middle of the day?"

"I took the week off. Well, you know, just three days. Thursday and Friday are holidays. Mom wanted help with her gardens. She's bringing a bunch of arrangements and plants up for the Farmer's Market on Wednesday."

"You're a good son. Sounds like this is going to be huge."

"It was such a good idea. This place is always busy on Wednesday afternoons and evenings now. Rachel says that more and more people want to participate. Mom can't do it every week, but she paid for a table for this one."

"I'm glad. How are you?"

"Good. Do you have a minute?"

Marie would keep Cassidy until Polly showed up. She knew how random Polly's life could get and it wasn't like anyone would forget where Cassidy was. "I have time for you. What's going on?"

He sighed. "I don't know."

Polly hooked his arm with hers and walked toward the kitchen. No one was in there, so they'd have privacy. "Talk to me."

"Billy's been on me to schedule a meeting with you and Henry."

"About what? Would you like to re-work the apartment?"

"No, but that will be part of this conversation. I feel really weird about this, but instead of sitting around doing nothing, I need to move forward."

"You do?" Polly smiled as she sat down at the long table along the back wall. It made her happy that this table was still here after all these years. She'd had so many conversations and meals here while looking out the window. The first time she'd sat at this table, old rusted out playground equipment littered the yard. Now, Eliseo had beautiful gardens out there, lush and green, pregnant with vegetables that he and his friends picked throughout the growing season.

"What do you mean?" Doug asked.

"I love you very much, Doug, but you always seemed to be satisfied with whatever life handed you. Are you finally going to do something proactive?"

He chuckled. "Never change, Polly. Please, never change."

"What do you mean?"

"Thump me right over the head before the conversation even gets started."

"Oh. Sorry. I should be more circumspect. Why don't you tell me what's going on before I give you any more trouble. What's going on? Are you planning to finally ask Anita to marry you?"

He looked at her in shock. "You know about that?"

"Has it happened yet?"

"No." Doug slumped onto the bench across the table from her.

"Do you have a ring?"

He shook his head. "Not yet. You know she's really rich, right?"

"So?"

"So, how am I supposed to pick out a ring that won't embarrass her? I can't afford anything like what her family could give her."

"Does Anita want a big, fancy ring?"

"She hasn't said. But she deserves something nice. I mean, all the guys she grew up with would be able to buy her a big ring."

"Seems like she's with you and not with them. Anita knows you can't afford a big ring. If she wants a fancy ring, she'll buy it for herself."

"But she shouldn't have to," Doug said, taken aback. "That's my job."

"No, your job is to buy a ring that means something to the two of you, not a big fancy ring that will put you in debt for years." Polly held her hand out. "Look at that ring. Tell me what you think Henry spent on it."

He frowned and shrugged. "I don't know. A lot. That's a nice diamond."

"He spent about five hundred dollars."

"That ring is worth way more than that. What?"

"It's my mother's engagement ring. Henry had it cleaned, resized, and replaced one of the little diamonds on the side. This ring means more to me than any big diamond thing we would have found at a jewelry store. Buy a ring she loves and that you can afford. The most important thing is that you tell her how much you love her and want to spend your life with her. That's what you want, right?"

"I think so."

Polly leaned in to catch his eye. "You think so?"

"Okay, there's this thing."

Her heart sank. She hated hearing about *things*. Especially if they were things that were going to make her think less of someone. She held her breath, waiting for the big reveal.

"I don't want her to think I'm marrying her for her money. It scares me that I waited too long. If I'd just gone ahead and asked her before Christmas, it wouldn't have been a big deal because I had no idea about all her money. But now that I know, I'm afraid her family and everybody else who knows will think that I'm some kind of gold digger."

"Yeah. I don't think that's a worry. We all know you and we know you aren't like that. Anita knows that too."

"But okay, there's more."

"You're killing me, Doug. Spill it. All of it."

"Well, this is why I wanted to talk to you and Henry. Did you know that Billy is going to go to school and get his certification to be an electrician?"

"I didn't," she said. "Are you planning to do the same thing?"

"No. Billy told me that I can't."

She chuckled. "Why not?"

"Because he says that I don't want to be an electrician for the rest of my life. He says I'm too smart."

"Huh," she said raising her eyebrows. "He's right, but what's going on?"

"He loves the work. I didn't know anyone could love that work, but he really likes it. He wants to own his own company. Jerry told him to go for it. He and Rachel are saving money to buy a house and they want a family and all of that."

"Are you planning to work for Billy someday?"

Doug shook his head. "No. When he told me that I didn't want to do this for the rest of my life, I realized he was right. Yeah. I can do it, but my favorite thing is talking to the people we work for. I like listening to them and hearing about their lives and all of that. So, we're talking one night up at the Alehouse and when he asked what I wanted to do, I told him I wanted to own a place like that."

"Like the Alehouse?" Polly perked up. This was new.

"Yeah, but not really. This is why I wanted to talk to you and Henry. Because you know about the real estate in town and businesses and all of that. I haven't even talked to Anita about this yet. What if I bought one of those old buildings and renovated the bottom into a kind of bar and arcade? Make it retro so that it's got all the old nineteen-eighties games. And then do a setup where I host game nights with computer games and even some of those new card and board games. Like we used to do at Sycamore House. And then, I could turn the upstairs into a home for me and Anita. Okay, that's everything. What do you think?"

It was a terrible time for Polly's nose to start itching, but while she rubbed it, she took the moment to think.

"It's a terrible idea. I'm glad you're the only person I told," Doug said. "Even if I don't like it, I can still work for Jerry and maybe someday for Billy."

"No, no, no," Polly said. "My nose itched. That's all. I believe anyone who wants to own a business should give it a shot. How would you pay for it? Will you borrow money from your parents? Is your credit good enough to take out a loan? Would they co-sign it?" Then she stopped and slowly nodded. "Oh, I see. This is why you're worried about Anita. If you do this and you're married to her, you have access to her money."

"And I don't want anyone to think that's the reason I'm marrying her." He gave her a small smile. "I have money saved, you know."

"A lot?"

"I suppose. Not like Anita's kind of money. Not even like your kind of money, but if I had to put a down payment on a house, I could. It isn't like I've had a lot of things to spend it on these last five years."

"You mean, like a ring or something crazy like that."

"Whatever. I've kinda liked having a nest egg, just in case something happens. If I buy a ring ..."

"You'll have a fiancé and then maybe a wife, who, by the way, also brings home a salary making it possible for the two of you to rebuild that nest egg."

"I'm not thinking about this right at all, am I?"

She let out a breath. "What you are screwing up the most is that you're talking to me and not Anita. Doug, do you love her?"

He looked up at the ceiling and over at the sink, then back up to the ceiling and down at the table.

"What in the world, Doug? It's a simple question."

"I just don't talk about this stuff. Yeah. I love her. I'm stupid for her. If she told me to crawl across gravel to ask her to marry me, I'd do it. There. You happy?"

"More than I was a few minutes ago. The way you act, it's as if you are bored with the idea of love. Come on, you can do better than that."

"It's just not the way I was brought up."

"I know better than that, too. Your mother tells you that she loves you."

"But Dad doesn't. He thinks that if you say it too often it makes it less important, so he never says it. I heard him tell Mom once that she should know he loves her because of what he does around the house."

"Well, let me tell you, Doug Randall. You can never say the words often enough. People are desperate to hear them. When is the last time you told Anita you loved her?"

He coughed.

"Does she say it to you?"

"Yeah. And I try to say it back. But sometimes it's awkward."

"The more you say it, the less awkward it will become. But that's neither here nor there. That's for the two of you to figure out, though if I ever hear her wonder about your love for her, I'm coming for you."

He smiled. "Okay."

"First things first. Talk to Anita. Do it soon. Tell her about your dreams. Tell her that you want to be her husband. From what I've heard, she's close to asking you to marry her."

"That would be easier."

"Don't choose a path because it's easy. Make it worthwhile. The two of you will have that memory for the rest of your lives. Whether it's a conversation that you have together or you get down on one knee or Anita presents you with an engagement ring, it will be a memory. Make it a good one."

"Do you think Eliseo or Jason would hook up the horses for us?"

"You want to ask her to marry you on a carriage ride?"

"Wouldn't that be romantic?"

"Have the two of you ever been in that carriage?"

"No, but we walk down and talk to the horses in the evenings. Eliseo gave me a bag with treats for them. He keeps it full for us."

"Really. I had no idea. If you asked him, he'd gladly help you pull that off."

"What about buying a building downtown. Would you and Henry be willing to help me with that?"

"No," she said. "We won't."

His face collapsed in grief. "You won't? Okay. I get it. It's too much. I'm so sorry I bothered you with it."

"Doug, I'm sorry. I didn't mean for you to fall apart. I was being cute, and it didn't go quite the way I planned. We will not help *you* with this, but we will help you and Anita. The two of you have to do this together. I don't want to get deep into this without her being involved."

"Oh, I thought I'd crossed some line with you."

"I'm sorry. That was mean of me. After you and Anita discuss this, then Henry and I would love to sit down with you. While we wait for that to happen, I want you to take a look at the empty buildings in town. We still have a bunch on the main street. There are also plenty of buildings on the side streets that would be good for what you're thinking."

"It would be more fun on Washington."

She smiled. "It would be a lot of fun. You and Anita need to put together a business plan ..."

Doug gasped. "A business plan? I don't even know what that is. How do I make a business plan?"

"Go online. There are templates and sample plans out there. This is going to take research. Especially if you're planning to borrow money."

"Research?"

"Find out all you can about businesses like you're considering. Do they exist? Are they successful? Research what is happening in Bellingwood. You'll want details like population growth and age demographics. What age group will your bar aim at? Are you in direct competition with other bars in town? How will you market the place? What other types of activities will you provide?"

"Where do I find that stuff?"

"Talk to Jeff Lindsay. He'll be an amazing resource." She shook her head. "Every time I have a bright idea, I talk to Henry first, but then I talk to Jeff. He's the one who takes it from an idea to a practical business. Henry and I will help you through a great deal, but Jeff should be involved. The other person to talk to would be Sal Ogden. Since she's gotten involved with the Sycamore Foundation, she's spent a great deal of time learning about Bellingwood. And Nan Stallings. She's put together marketing plans for businesses in town. Ask her to give you a quick overview. You'll want to pay these people for their help."

"This is bigger than I thought."

"You could have just bought a building and applied for a liquor license and hoped for the best," Polly said. "But if you want it to be successful, you'll want to put in the time and research. And trust me, if Anita's family finds out that you invested that kind of time, they'll be impressed."

"That can't hurt. Her mother doesn't like me very much. She thinks I'm a red-neck hick."

"Opening a bar won't help that image."

He grimaced. "This is probably a bad idea."

"Stop that, Doug. If it's something that you'd like to do, grab the dream. If it falls apart, you move on from there and try something else. Just don't let anyone like Anita's mother or your own crazy fears stop you from trying."

"Anita says that to me all the time."

"She does?"

"Well, not that exactly, but she says that I could do anything if I wasn't scared about failing."

"She's right. She knows you well. Are you ready to do more than passively live your life?"

He blinked. "And, she's back."

"Now that I know what's been going on up there in your mind, I have enough information to be dangerous. You have a lot of work ahead of you. If you aren't ready to dig in, you're going to be miserable."

"You don't run away from hard work."

"No," she said, "but I grew up on a farm. Dad may not have had me out working in the fields, but I never had time to sit around and twiddle my thumbs. Then it was college and my job at the library was amazing, but it was hard work. I needed to be successful so I could afford to live out in the Boston area."

"Then you moved here and went crazy. People wonder if you ever sleep."

"I sleep very well," Polly said. "Usually I'm so exhausted, I can't help it."

"How long do you think it will be before I can open my bar?" Doug asked. He was trying hard to be a grownup, but he was still so young.

Polly took a long look at him. The yearning in his eyes for acceptance and approval was still there after all these years. Somewhere along the line, he'd lost the playful orneriness she'd seen when they first met. He shouldn't be this worried about his life. He deserved so much more than what he was doing right now. It was a meager existence. Afraid to show Anita how much he loved her, afraid to move out and do something risky, afraid that people would judge him for all of it.

"I don't know right now, but it will come. I promise. Talk to Anita. Do it sooner rather than later. Doug, you are so ready to move forward, but your fear of these conversations is stopping you."

"Sometimes I wish you were back in your old apartment. I felt better just knowing you were there to talk to if I needed you. Even if it was just a quick conversation in the morning before work or at the end of the day when we used to grill out. Do you remember those nights? That was so much fun. The dogs would play in the back yard and we'd just talk."

She put her arm out on the table, reaching across. When he hesitated, she nodded. He took her hand. "Doug, I love you to pieces. I want you to be happy. Whatever I can do to make that happen, I will."

He rubbed the top of her hand with his thumb, his eyes focused on the movement. Then he looked up. "I guess I love you, too."

"You guess?" she asked with a smile.

He looked her in the eyes. "I love you, too."

"Talk to Anita when she gets home tonight. Take a walk down to the horses. She needs to be part of this. If I know her, she is desperate to be part of your life. She loves you very much."

Nodding, he looked back at their hands on the table, then pulled his away. "Okay. I'll do it."

~~~

Cassidy had jabbered about her afternoon most of the way home from Marie's house, but when Polly pulled into the driveway, the little girl was nodding off.

"Honey, we're home."

"Home?" Cassidy asked, her confusion apparent.

"Were you having a dream?"

"I was on a cloud. It took me to ..." Cassidy frowned. "I don't remember."

"That's okay. Let's go inside. I need to think about what to make for supper."

"Can we have sketti?"

"Spaghetti?" Polly asked. "Try it again. Say it slow. Spa-get-ti." This was one of the words she worked on with all the kids. It was amazing the twisted variations they came up with.

Cassidy pursed her lips, then said, "Ska-get-ti."

"One more time. Say spa."

"Spa."

"Do you hear the difference?"

Cassidy pulled at the belt in her car seat. "Can we go in?"

"Okay. Just try it."

"Spa-get-ti."

"Perfect. Hold on. I'll let you out." Polly got out and opened the door, then opened Cassidy's door so she could get out of the car. The dogs came tearing around from the back yard to see them, barking and yapping in joy.

Han chased Cassidy to the side door. Obiwan started after them, then turned back to Polly and sat down beside her. She put her hand on his head and rubbed it absently. "Obiwan, I'm

184

pooped. I say that I want to get back to Sycamore House so that I can be there for all the action, but at the end of a day like this when I've done nothing but talk to my friends about their lives, I'm tired. They wear me out."

He nuzzled the palm of her hand with his nose.

"You're right. It's a good tired. I miss spending time with them. But did they all have to hit me on the same day?"

He let out a soft bark and walked to the side door, slow enough that she caught up to him. When she hit the first step, he ran on up, stood in front of the door and barked again.

"You're good for me, Obiwan. You keep me sane." Polly leaned down and ruffled the hair on the back of his neck, then hugged him close. "I love you, just in case anyone asks."

CHAPTER EIGHTEEN

No sooner had Polly put her hand on the door handle, than she heard her name from across the street.

"Polly!"

She turned and headed back down the steps.

"Polly!" Andrea called again.

"Coming! What's up."

Andrea had run across the street and met Polly in the driveway. "Do you have a few minutes?"

Polly glanced back at her house. She really needed to be thinking about supper. "I suppose. I just sent Cassidy inside, though. I have to tell Cat that she's there and I'm not."

"It will only take a few minutes. I promise. You aren't going to believe who is sitting in my house."

"Unless it's the murderer and he or she is ready to make a full confession, I have no idea."

"The what?" She shook her head in confusion. "You haven't solved that one yet? What a slacker."

Polly laughed. "It's only been a week." She took out her phone and made a call.

"Polly?" Cat asked.

"I'm outside. Cassidy just came in. I need a few minutes to go over to Andrea's house. You're there, right?" The Suburban was in the driveway. Where else would Cat be?

"I have her. The boys and I are in the kitchen cooking dinner."

"You're kidding me."

"They wanted tacos. I told them that unless they helped, we were having raw octopus."

"Look at you, working their little brains. Thank you. I'll be home soon."

"No worries. We're fine."

Polly ended the call. "Not my favorite, but at least I'm not cooking."

"What?"

"Tacos. The kids love them. Oh well. Now, what's going on at your house?"

"Come on over. I couldn't believe it when they showed up. And they won't go home without talking to you."

"Who are they?"

Andrea rolled her eyes. "Just come on."

They stopped in the middle of the street when Polly grabbed Andrea's arm. "Don't do this to me. I can't take any kind of a surprise today."

"Been a rough one?"

"Not so rough, but definitely intense. Tell me."

"Mary and Libby Francis."

Polly turned to go back home. "I don't want to deal with them."

"You're kidding, right?"

"Yeah," Polly said, sighing in frustration. "I am. I don't run away from these things. Why are they at your house?"

"They wanted my help bringing you to the table."

"To the table?"

Andrea grinned. "Those are my words, but they want to talk to you."

"What about Rebecca?"

"They figure that without you, Rebecca is off the table."

"You need food, don't you, Andrea," Polly said.

"I know!"

"How long have they been here?"

"Only about twenty minutes."

"That's why you're chasing me down instead of calling me."

"I saw you leave earlier today with Cassidy. The two of you aren't usually gone this long. Polly, this is the most convoluted thing I've ever experienced. Talk about chasing your tail. Why they couldn't just call you and ask to meet, I don't know."

Polly tugged on Andrea's arm before they went up the front steps, pulling her in close. "They are kind of weird. Why can't everyone be normal like us?"

"What a boring place we'd live in if that were true."

"With you and me?" Polly asked. "Not likely. Come on." She went in the front door as Andrea held it open.

Mary and Libby Francis were seated at the dining room table.

The house was in chaos and would be until construction was finished on the room they were adding to the back. Everything had been moved out of the way and since Andrea's family was so big, there was just no place to put things. Henry had thought he'd have things finished by the end of June, but life got in the way sometimes. The walls were up and windows were in. Drywall was going up tomorrow and they were finishing the deck in the next few weeks.

Mary Francis stood up when Polly walked in. "Thank you for coming over," she gushed. "I didn't know how else to talk to you."

Polly nodded. "I wish you would have called. I'd have made time. What's up?"

"Libby feels awful about what happened last week."

Libby looked as if she wanted to be anywhere else but here, but she didn't look as if she felt awful. She looked more like she wished her mother would fall in a deep, dark hole. The girl avoided Polly's eyes, her arms were crossed and an ugly scowl filled her normally pretty face.

"Libby?" Mary said. "I know you want to say something to Polly."

When all eyes turned to her, Libby muttered something unintelligible.

"See," Mary said. "We feel terrible."

Polly glanced at Andrea. Was the woman delusional? Andrea shrugged.

"Okay, thank you," Polly said.

"I want the girls to be friends again. Rebecca is so important to Libby. She's helped her make so many friends in high school. And Cilla, too," Mary said, putting her hand out to touch Andrea's arm. "Those girls are all so tight."

"Mary, can I speak to you outside?" Polly asked.

Andrea shot her a look. Polly sent one back, chuckling inside. She should know Polly well enough by now to realize no one was getting away with this. But the confrontation wasn't going to happen in front of Libby. Polly needed to find out if Mary was truly nuts or just trying to cover for her daughter's bad behavior.

"About what?" Mary asked, but she followed Polly as they headed out the front door.

Polly led her down the front stairs and a few steps away from the house. "What's going on, Mary? Your daughter doesn't want to be here. She doesn't want to fix her friendship with Rebecca and she doesn't look like she feels terrible."

"Yes, she does," Mary insisted, her eyes filling with tears. "She's a mess."

"I understand that. She got caught. But Mary, she set Rebecca up to take the fall. No, that isn't the worst of it. She accused Rebecca of stealing from the General Store when in fact, she'd done it herself. Who does that to a friend?"

"You don't understand." Mary crumpled in on herself and tears flowed freely.

"That's right. I don't understand. What's going on?"

"I can't," the woman said so quietly that Polly barely heard her.

"Can you give me a hint?" Polly put her arm around Mary's shoulders. "Did you at least tell Andrea?"

Mary looked up in surprise. "Oh, no. I can't tell her. I can't tell anyone."

"You have to. Does it have to do with Libby stealing things?"

"It's not her fault."

"Has she done this in the past or is it new behavior?" Polly asked, trying to figure out what in the world was going on.

"She's never done anything like this before." Mary shrugged away from Polly and walked over toward her car. "It's my fault."

"How is her stealing things your fault?"

"Because ... because. Oh, I just can't talk about it."

"Mary, you need to talk to someone. Has anyone recommended Libby meet with Alistair Greyson?"

Mary peered at her, a frown on her face. "The man who ran the hotel?"

"He's a certified counselor. He's worked with kids most of his career and he's very good." Grey had spent time with all four of her boys and they loved him. She could directly attribute much of Caleb's growth this last year to the work Grey did to help him come to terms with his anger and his past.

"I don't know if Don would go for that." The woman broke down into tears again. "I don't know what to do."

"What to do with what?" Polly asked.

"He wants a divorce. We have to move out. He says it's his house and we have to find somewhere else to live. He doesn't want the kids to live with him. He's met another woman who has her own children, so his own family has to go. What kind of man did I marry, Polly?" Mary slid down the side of her car to the ground so fast that Polly couldn't catch her.

"Oh, Mary, I'm so sorry," Polly said, kneeling in front of her. "How can I help you?"

"I don't know. He left two weeks ago and told me that we had until the first of August to find another place. He'll pay for rent for a year, but by then, he says I have to find a job and start paying for things on my own."

If that didn't explain Libby's recent behavior, nothing would. She was desperate to reach out to her father. Polly's heart broke for the girl.

"Mary, look at me," Polly said.

The woman looked up, her eyes suffused with tears.

"You need a good lawyer. You need to lean on your support system."

"Don is my support system," Mary said. "Don and the kids. Everything I do is for them."

"You have me. You have Andrea. We'll be here for you. But let me tell you right now, Don can't get away with kicking you out of the house. He doesn't get to make decisions for your future. The minute he asked you for a divorce, he gave up any right to tell you what to do. From here on out, you don't listen to him, you don't talk to him, you don't obey him. Do you know any lawyers?"

"Only Darrin Cloake. He takes care of everything for the farm."

"He's Don's lawyer, right?"

"Yeah."

"You won't use him. What about Al Dempsey?" Al was a friend of Henry's and if he didn't do this type of law, he'd know someone who did.

Mary shook her head.

"We'll call him tomorrow. No more decisions until you've talked to someone who will represent you. How long have you known about this?"

Mary dropped her head. "Since school was out. I tried to hide it from the kids, but when he moved out last week, I was the one who had to explain why. I don't understand why he doesn't even want to be with them anymore. What kind of man does that?"

"I don't know," Polly said. "I can't imagine."

"They love their father. He isn't playful or fun, but he's always been decent to them. I can't tell them that he doesn't care if he ever sees them again. It's going to destroy Libby. She's spent her entire life trying to get his attention. Every time he acknowledges her, she beams."

Polly felt bile rise in her throat. That kind of person made her ill. He knew how much that little girl wanted him to love her and it was disgusting that he made her work so hard for it.

"You and your kids really need to talk to Grey," she said.

"I can't afford that."

"Yeah, your lawyer can make sure that's part of the settlement. Don can pay for it. He screwed 'em up, he can pay a counselor to help them get past this."

"I don't know what to do next. I feel so lost."

Polly put her hand out and Mary took it, using her as leverage to stand. "What you're going to do is take care of your family. Tomorrow, I will help you contact Al Dempsey and line up a good, strong lawyer. Then, we'll contact Grey. After that, we'll look for a place for you to live and then, Mary Francis, you're going to discover what a strong, wonderful woman you are. You are more than Don Francis's wife and you have friends who will stand beside you while you get through this."

"I don't think I can."

"Not by yourself, you can't, but you aren't by yourself any longer. Right here you have two of the strongest women I know in Bellingwood."

When Mary didn't act as if she understood, Polly smiled. "I'm talking about me and Andrea Waters. I'm glad you came here today, even if things haven't gone quite the way you planned. Either one of us is a force to be reckoned with, but the two of us together? There isn't much stronger than that. We'll help you navigate your way through this. Life isn't over for you, Mary. Your kids need you. They need to know that it is possible to come out on the other side of something this awful and still be a whole and healthy person."

Mary shook her head. "I'm not so sure I can do it. I'm not strong like you two are."

"Sure you are," Polly said. "It might not feel like it today and it might not feel like it in a month, but you are. You are still here and you're still trying to teach your daughter to do the right thing. Are you feeding your kids breakfast in the mornings?"

"Yes," Mary said, confused.

"That means you're getting out of bed and pulling yourself together in order to care for them."

"No one else will. I have to."

"Exactly. Even if taking care of them is the only reason you hold it together, it's enough for now. We won't let you down. Your only responsibility is to hold on to your kids."

"I can do that. I've always done that."

"That's enough. Let's go in and talk to Libby and Andrea."

~~~

"You've been quiet all evening," Henry said. He was in his chair in the bedroom while Polly stood at the sink in the bathroom, washing her face.

She stuck her head out. "I've been waiting all day for this moment. It felt like a whole week happened in eight hours. Thank goodness Cat took care of dinner. I'd have done it, but it might have been peanut butter sandwiches."

"No jelly?"

"Who knows?" She chuckled as she came out into the bedroom. "It's so good to be at this point. How was your day?"

"Pretty normal for a Monday, which is boring stuff. Your day sounds more interesting. Was it?"

"Let's see." She grinned at him. "Yes."

"Yes, what?"

"Yes, it was more interesting."

He waited a beat for her to add more commentary, but she slipped between the sheets and fluffed her pillow.

"That's all you're going to say?"

"Okay fine." Polly yawned. "Jon is nervous about getting married and having children, one of the guys who is working on our piano knows the wife of the murdered man. Jason is trying to grow up, Doug wants our help putting together a business downtown and is nervous about getting married. Oh, and Don Francis wants a divorce. He's told his wife she has until August first to move out of their house with the children. He's not interested in being part of their lives any longer. Evidently, he's found someone else who has her own children and he'll be moving them into the farmhouse."

"That's all?" he asked. "Sounds like you had a slow day."

"I know. Wait. One more. I'm ready to hire someone to take care of this place so I can go back to work at Sycamore House during the day."

He sat straight up. "You what?"

"With all that I just unloaded on you and that's what gets a reaction?"

"That's the biggest news you delivered. The rest is everyone else's problem."

"The rest is stuff I have to help handle, but yeah, you won't need to be involved with anything but Doug's plans."

"I don't even know where to start. You want to hire someone? To do what part?"

"Clean, mostly. And I don't want this person to be responsible for the kids' rooms. They still get to do that, but to help us keep up with laundry and do the vacuuming and sweeping, the dusting and windows. You know, the stuff I'm terrible at anyway, but if I'm not here, I'll never get it managed."

"Because you want to go back to Sycamore House? That's fantastic."

"I'm tired of having to pack up and go somewhere if I want to meet with people. It used to be that they could drop in. Sycamore House is much closer to all the action than living clear on this end of town. Beryl and Lydia never just stop in. Sal never just drops over. If I want to see anyone, I have to go to the coffee shop and hope that we run into each other. I'm missing out on creative business conversations with Jeff, as well as with Jeff and Sal concerning the Foundation. There are so many things happening over there that I don't get an opportunity to be involved with because quick decisions get made and I am too far away to consult. Today I realized that Jason was falling apart over this whole motorcycle fight with his mother and if I had an office there, he would have stopped in to talk to me. I miss him. Doug Randall was so glad to see me that he dragged me off to the kitchen over there so we could talk. And that's a whole big thing I want to discuss with you sometime. Not tonight, though."

"Where do you plan to find room for your office?"

"I talked to Kristen today to find out how much is happening in the addition. Not much, as it turns out." She gave him a sheepish look. "I should probably have known that. Anyway, they're using the back room on the main floor as a conference and meeting room. I'd like to take over the front room. This evening I've been thinking about it. I'd have my desk and then I'd like a nice comfortable setup with couches and chairs. Those rooms are huge. I could have a small table, too. Then, if I can talk you into it, I'd have you build more cabinets and shelves for me. Then I could put my Star Wars stuff back up."

Henry laughed. "Focus on what's important. That room would work as an office."

"And I'd be close to the horses again. I could watch them all day and go down to the barn whenever I like. I miss them."

"I know you do. And I know you miss the excitement of being around people during the day. You haven't complained once about having to be here all the time."

"I wouldn't have had it any other way. The kids needed me close while they grew comfortable with their new lives. Cassidy will be in school this fall, so I won't worry about what she does during the day. It feels like a perfect opportunity."

"Do you have someone in mind to do the work around here?"

"Not yet, but if we start looking now, something will come up. It always does. You're okay with this?"

He frowned at her. "Polly, I have been trying to talk you into hiring someone to help you in this big old place since we moved in. You have too much going on in your life to be saddled with cleaning up after all of us."

"But ..."

"But, nothing," he said, interrupting her. "I know you've relied on Cat to help, but still, the two of you should be able to do the things you want to do, not work to wrangle the rest of your family to help clean. You spend too much time worrying about this house. You have better things to do. Both of you do."

"Will you marry me, sweet prince?"

Henry laughed. "I'm sorry, I'm already married to a most

wonderful woman. A woman who doesn't always understand how important she is to me."

Polly scooted over on the bed, then climbed out and slipped into his lap. "Mary Francis was a wreck today because her jerk of a husband never saw how lucky he was."

"I'm not that stupid."

"No, you aren't. Does your friend, Al, do divorce stuff?"

"Al Dempsey?"

"Yeah. I told her I would help her with this."

"Of course you did."

Polly slapped her forehead. "I forgot. I need to be at Sycamore house tomorrow morning. Jon and Ray have some computer whiz-kids coming in to look at our networks and see if they can pull any data from them."

"What kind of data?"

"Anything from the days that Harrison guy was staying at the hotel. I don't think we have a system robust enough to have anything they can find, but you never know. Jeff and I need to discuss more security on that system. If their people can help us, we need to do better."

"Hard to believe we live in that kind of a world. This is Bellingwood, for heaven's sake."

"That's what I say." She smiled. "I suspect Anita will be there. The two of us need to talk, too."

"Don't be setting Doug up."

"Doug needs to be set up. He wants to put a bar and arcade downtown. Maybe buy a building and renovate it, as well as renovate the upstairs so they can live there."

"Doug Randall? The kid who hasn't ever grown up?"

"I think he's ready."

"You did have a day." Henry pushed her off his lap. "Since you spent time solving everyone else's problems, maybe you could solve one of mine."

"Sure. How can I help you?"

He pointed to the bed. "Let's discuss it under the covers."

"Oh," she said. "I'm good at that kind of problem."

CHAPTER NINETEEN

Everyone was finally up, fed and moving Tuesday morning, but it had taken long enough that Polly was late to the early morning meeting the security company was having with Jeff, Skylar, Jon, and Ray. She'd hoped to have time to get coffee at Sweet Beans, but instead, she tore out of the house for the hotel.

June Livingstone was alone in the lobby when she got there. She pointed at the front door and said, "They went that-a-way."

"Did they find anything?" Polly asked.

"Not that I could tell, but there was a whole bunch of techno-babble speak going on and I wasn't part of the conversation."

"How's your aunt doing?"

June shook her head and sighed. "Not great. We keep hoping that she'll get a second wind, but I'm afraid the poor thing has had too much wind knocked out of her. Mother does her best, trying to stay positive about it all, but she's worried. If Aunt April dies, Mother will be so lonely. They pick on each other like nobody's business, but they are each other's best friend."

"I'm so sorry. Would it be okay if Cassidy and I brought dinner to you this weekend? I know she'd love to see you."

June's eyes lit up. "That's just the sweetest thing. People are always telling me to call them if I need anything. I don't know what I need. I just need to get from one day to the next, but yes, Mother would love to see little Cassidy. To be honest, so would I."

"I'll call you first, but plan on us showing up Saturday afternoon with something fun."

"You're a dear."

"I appreciate you, June. And yes, of course, call if you need anything, but I know better. You never will."

"You're right. I'm not about to bother someone else with my problems. We've gotten through difficult times before, we'll get through them now."

Polly left, her heart heavy. June had once joked about her life beginning after her mother and aunt passed away, but that woman loved those two old ladies, and her life would change drastically when they were gone.

She headed for Sycamore House, frustrated at having missed the action at the hotel. Jon had told her the two people from Kansas City wouldn't spend a lot of time here, but this was crazy. She pulled into the parking lot and ran inside, grateful that it seemed like they were just beginning to gather in the office.

Jeff looked up when she came in. "Finally," he said. "Life of leisure, eh?"

"I know. I'm such a bad person. Have they found anything?"

"Nothing yet, but they're going back to put together a proposal for our systems. Especially once we add the B&B to our properties."

"Properties." Polly shook her head. "You make it sound like a huge management corporation."

He lifted his eyebrows. "I hate to freak you out, Polly, but it is growing into a big management corporation. We're going to be unstoppable one of these days."

"Okay, great." She smiled at Jon and Ray, who had settled into Jeff's office with two very young people. They looked to be no older than Jason or Heath. "They're so young," Polly whispered.

"It's killing me. I'm barely thirty and they look young to me."

"While you're here, Polly," Kristen said, holding up a stack of paper. "Would you check these over? I want to give them to Edna this morning so we can get June's paperwork finished up."

Polly took the papers and sat down in front of her desk. She looked up at Jeff. "You and I need to have a conversation before I leave."

"Am I in trouble?" he asked.

She waggled her eyebrows as Anita Banks walked in the door to the office.

"I know I'm late," Anita said. "I tried to get here earlier, but Sheriff Merritt had me on another job first thing this morning. I thought I could finish it faster, but ..." She took a breath. "... I'm late and I didn't want to miss this. I want to see what they're doing."

Jeff gestured for her to follow him and they went into his office.

Polly flipped through the papers and then stopped. "What's this?" she asked, laying a bill in front of Kristen.

"Pest Control? Isn't that the company we use out at the hotel?"

Polly nodded. "Yes, but I just approved a bill for them last week." She picked the invoice up and checked the date, a flash of an idea running through her mind. "Bring up the hotel's guest list and find Andrew Harrison's name."

"What's going on?" Kristen asked.

"It seems odd. Why was pest control there a second time? Jeff?"

He came back out.

"Did Skylar say something about there being a problem at the hotel with mice or bugs?"

"Not at all. We take care of it every month. No big deal."

"He would have said something to you if there was an extra call, yes?"

"Absolutely. What's going on?"

Kristen held her hand out for the invoice in Polly's hand. "Same date as Harrison's check-in," she said. Then she pointed at the time stamp on the invoice. "That says five-thirty. He was there after normal hours."

"Can I borrow your phone?" Polly asked, reaching. Kristen

turned it around and pushed it toward Polly. She dialed the toll-free number on the invoice and waited, punching numbers until she finally got to someone in customer service.

"Yes, this is Polly Giller from Sycamore Enterprises and I have a question about an invoice."

"Invoice number, please."

Polly rattled it off and said, "He was there after hours and none of my people requested this call."

"Someone must have requested the call," the young woman insisted. "The system automatically spits out an invoice when our technicians complete their work. Let me see if I can find more information for you."

Handing her phone to Jeff, she said, "Dial Skylar, would you? I have a weird feeling about this."

"Why am I not surprised?" he said, shaking his head.

The customer service representative came back and said, "That's odd. We don't have a record of who requested this service. It should have been on the invoice."

Polly scanned the invoice and recognized the technician's name — the same person who had done their work for the last two years. "Tell me how this works. How does the system generate an invoice?"

"Each vehicle carries a tablet log. Whenever the technician makes a stop, the GPS records their arrival and departure times, sending that information to us. If it is a personal stop, the technician marks it, and the system moves it through a different process."

"How long was he at the hotel that evening?" Polly asked.

"It wasn't long at all, which is why you were only billed for the minimum hourly call."

"How long?"

"Twenty minutes."

"I'm surprised that he logged this service call," Polly said to Kristen. "That seems foolish."

"What do you mean?" the young woman asked.

"Oh, sorry. Nothing."

"All service calls must be logged. Our vehicles are equipped with GPS tracking devices. If a technician's logs and tracking don't match, they are fined. Each week they mark any personal travel and that is deleted from their paycheck."

"I see. Well, that explains it."

"I have Skylar," Jeff said. "What was your question for him?"

"Did you ask if he'd requested an additional call?" Polly asked.

Jeff nodded. "He says that he didn't."

"Ma'am, if you are disputing the invoice, I'll need to set up a claim request."

"No, that's okay. That isn't what this is about. Thank you for your time." Polly hung up without waiting for more questions and put her hand out for her cell phone. "Sky?"

"Yeah, Polly. What's going on?"

"How well do you know this Steve Robertson who does our pest control?"

"I don't know. Pretty good, I guess. We always talk when he comes in and I see him at the Alehouse sometimes."

"He lives in Bellingwood?"

"Yeah. Up north on Polk Street in a little house. He used to have a roommate, but I think that guy moved out in March. Not married or anything. Something wrong?"

"I hope not. I'll let you know."

She ended the call and sat back. "Something's wrong."

Ray came out of Jeff's office. "We aren't finding anything on the network." He took one look at her face and said, "What's up?"

"Yeah. You wanna take a ride with me?"

Jeff turned his head slowly back and forth between the two of them. "Don't do it. I know what's going to happen. You don't want to see this."

"See what?" Ray asked, furrowing his brow.

"Don't say I didn't warn you."

"It's probably nothing," Polly said. "Can you leave your brother here and come with me?"

Ray poked his head back in the office. "I'm going out with Polly. We'll be back in a few."

As they walked out of the building to her car, he took her arm. "What's going on?"

"Sometimes things go together in my head and I've learned to follow my instincts."

"This sounds ominous."

"It could be."

"Should we call the sheriff?"

Polly laughed as she got into the driver's side of the car. "We could, but if it's nothing, I'd have pulled them away from whatever it is they should be doing. If it turns out to be something, then at least I've got a real reason to call them."

"So why am I along? For the ride?"

"Because sometimes I'm a chicken and I want a big strong boy beside me when I knock on a strange man's door. If he has a roommate and there is no problem, I don't want to be the only one who is trying to come up with a good reason for being there."

"Jeff seems to think you're going to find something awful."

"He's only been with me a couple of times when I found a body and the last one freaked him out. I've never seen him so frightened."

"He doesn't seem like the type to let things bother him."

"Evidently, dead bodies are what push him over the edge. Stephanie had to yell at him and tell him to straighten up that day. He was embarrassing himself."

"None of us understand why you are so comfortable with it."

She let out a strained giggle. "I'm not sure that I'd call it comfortable, but what am I supposed to do? I'd rather it was me than someone else."

"Why not let it be someone else?"

"Think about Jeff," she said. "If you were to ask him today to describe one of his worst life experiences, he'd tell you about that day." She pointed north. "It was just on a gravel road up there. His imagination worked overtime and he was horrified. I'd rather it was me than a family member. They don't need that memory. I'd rather it was me than some poor postal clerk or delivery driver. They see enough strange things during their days."

"But why you?"

"Why not me? It isn't as if I'm going to break or fall apart. I have the strength to handle it. I'm able to separate myself from the event. It's not pleasant, but it isn't nightmare-inducing."

"You aren't the same Polly who lived in Boston."

"No, I'm not," she said with a smile, turning left onto Polk Street. "Look. There's the van. Kinda weird that it's still parked at home at this hour of the morning, don't you think?"

"You're certain of this, aren't you." Ray shook his head. "I don't think I want to go inside."

Polly pulled in behind the pest control van and turned to look at Ray. "That's fine, then. You stay here. I'll go be the big strong girl while you quiver in your boots."

He chuckled. "You aren't very nice."

"Not the same Polly who lived in Boston, remember?"

"Let's do this." He took two deep breaths, then opened the car door. "Stay behind me."

"Because a dead body is going to rise up and suck my neck? No vampires in my world."

"Because if he's dead and someone killed him, they might still be around." He stopped her in the driveway. "Why exactly do you believe he's dead?"

"Because I think he was hired to plant that clock in the room. No one would question why a pest control van was parked at the hotel. Even if our night guy saw it, he wouldn't ask any questions. It wouldn't even occur to him that it was out of the ordinary."

"But why would the murderer hire someone instead of just buying a uniform?"

She looked at him. "Who knows why? Maybe it's his brother. Maybe Steve was drinking at the Alehouse and someone asked if he wanted to make extra money. Maybe the murderer knows something about him and extorted him. All I know is that he wasn't supposed to be at the hotel on the night that Andrew Harrison checked in. And I know that his truck shouldn't be parked at his house at nine thirty on a weekday morning."

"Unless he's on vacation."

"So, he'll answer the door and you can tell everyone that I've lost my marbles."

"You don't believe that, though, do you?"

"Nope. Are you ready for this?"

"You know that if he was killed in the last twenty-four hours, that means the murderer might still be in town."

"I'm counting on that," Polly said. "We have to find him and I'm not about to traipse all over kingdom-come to look for him."

"Or her," Ray said. He patted his hip. "Damn it."

"What?"

"I'm not carrying."

"Are you usually?"

"When I'm on the job. Yes."

She chuckled. "He's already dead. We're safe."

"Murderer still in town. Remember?"

"Uh huh." Polly was already walking toward the front door, her phone in her hand.

"What are you planning to do with that phone? Bonk the murderer in the head?" Ray asked, his voice low.

"Call Aaron," she said in a normal tone. "Ray. I promise you. He's either answering the door or I'm going to walk in and find another body."

"You're awfully cavalier."

"It's because you're here. You make me feel safe."

"Mama will never believe this."

"Yeah, maybe you don't tell her that I walked into this one. I'm afraid she might fly to Iowa just to swat me."

When Polly knocked on the front door, both of them sucked in a breath as it opened at her touch.

"See," she said. "Told you."

"What's his name?"

"Steve Robertson."

Ray poked his head inside the door. "Mr. Robertson? Are you here? We're from Sycamore House and would like to talk to you. Hello?"

"It's me, Mr. Robertson. Polly Giller. Are you here?"

They waited a few moments and Polly nudged the door open a little further with her hip. "Is anyone here?" she called out. "Mr. Robertson?"

"Polly, we need to call the sheriff," Ray said. "I'm not comfortable with this."

She nodded. "You're right." She took one step inside the front door and peered around the wall of the tiny foyer into the living room. "You're absolutely right."

"You didn't," he said flatly.

Polly stepped back out onto the stoop and turned her phone face up, swiping until she landed on the phone number she was looking for. She turned on the speaker and nodded at Ray.

"Now, you're just showing off," he said.

"Your fault. I've spent years trying to impress you and here is where we've ended up."

The call connected and Aaron said, "Polly, I know where you're supposed to be. Why aren't you there?"

"Because I had a hunch?" she said. "Will you buy that?"

"A hunch about what?"

"About the extra pest control bill that showed up in our office."

"Pest control bill. I'm confused."

"It's Polly," Ray said. "You shouldn't be."

"Who's that with you?"

"It's me, Sheriff Merritt. Ray Renaldi. Polly made a quick connection about something while we were at the office and dragged me out to find a dead body with her."

"Bellingwood probably needs someone other than Polly to show visitors around town. But then, you've been down this road with her before. You really saw a pest control bill and decided someone was dead because of it?"

"It's the technician. Steve Robertson," Polly said.

"Steve's dead? Damn it. What happened? Where are you?"

"You know him?"

"Sure. He's taken care of our house for years. We have a problem with mice and Lydia won't get a cat. How is he involved?"

"I don't know that. All I know is that I'm at his house and he's been shot. He's sitting in a recliner in his living room."

"You went in?"

"The door was open. I stepped inside and saw him. Ray tried to make me stop, but ..."

Aaron huffed. "Like that will happen. Sit tight. We'll be there as soon as I make some calls. Steve Robertson? He's the last person I would have expected to be involved in this mess. He's just a normal guy. Steve Robertson." His voice faded as he set the phone down and then ended the call.

"It will be a few minutes," Polly said. "Do you want to wait here on the stoop or sit in the car?"

He looked at the open front door. "Not here."

She smiled and leaned against him. "I know this was fast and totally nuts, but thanks for coming with me."

"This makes me want to move to Bellingwood and follow you everywhere you go."

"It doesn't happen every day. Most of my life is boring. I make sure the kids are fed and watered, I listen to my friends tell me about their lives, I do my work, I live a normal, wonderful life."

"Until you don't." Ray went around the front and got back into the passenger seat of her car.

"Until I don't. But even then, I try not to let it turn my life inside out. I find a body, then I call Aaron, and his people take care of the details."

"Still," he said. "This is a lot. I don't know how Henry does it."

"He's a good man."

"Yes, he is."

"What about you?" she asked. "Jon told me about Chloe. Is there anyone in your life that helps you escape from reality?"

He smiled. "That's a good way to put it, but no, not right now. It's just too difficult."

"Too difficult to love someone?"

"Too difficult to handle the ups and downs of finding someone, learning to trust and then figuring out how to integrate them into my family and help them understand the work we do."

"I never expected Jon would be able to do that, but he has."

"He was lucky. Really lucky. If Chloe weren't as independent and strong-willed as she is, they'd never have gotten this far. No way was Jon going to put up with a mousy, quiet, pretty girl."

"That's who he usually dated, though."

"Exactly. He'd date them once or twice and get bored. Until Chloe came along, no one could hold his interest longer than that. She's never going to be boring. Kinda like you."

Polly laughed and pointed at the front door of the house. "This is the exception. I really am boring."

"I don't believe that for a moment."

"It's going to be hard for you when Jon gets married," she said quietly.

He heaved a sigh. "Probably. Things have already changed now that they're together. But I'd rather he was happy than hanging around with me." He put his finger up as she opened her mouth to speak. "You can't fix my relationship status. I don't want anyone to fix it. I'm very happy. I enjoy my work and I like my life. When Jon and Chloe start having children, I'll enjoy being an uncle. I wish I could make people understand that I'm okay and don't need to have them messing in my personal life."

"I get it," she said. "It felt like the whole world was pushing me to marry Henry. It didn't matter that I wasn't ready. As long as they thought it should happen, I didn't really have a say."

"Luckily that turned out well for you."

"It turned out wonderfully. If you ever decide to settle down, you'll find the right person."

A look that Polly would have taken for sadness passed across his face, but was gone as soon as it was there.

"Are you okay?" she asked.

"Sure, why?"

"I don't know. Just thought I saw something in your eyes."

He shrugged. "Nothing."

"You found someone, didn't you."

"It didn't work out."

Polly took his arm. "What happened?"

"He wasn't ready to be in a relationship."

"Oh, Ray. I'm sorry. How long were you together?"

"I don't know. Eight months or so."

"And it was serious?"

"I thought so. Everybody thought so, but then one night he told me that it was over. He couldn't do it. I wasn't about to beg, so I let him go."

"Do you ever see him?"

"He moved away."

"Oh, honey, I'm sorry."

"But that isn't why I'm still single. I'm not pining away for him. I'd dropped a lot of balls at work while we were together and Jon had to cover for me. That's not who I am. If I'm ever with someone again, they'll know exactly how important my work is. I'm not sacrificing parts of my life because they demand that I become someone they can be with."

"Really? That's what he expected?"

"He never said, but yeah. Jon told me he was glad the guy moved on because otherwise, he was going to have to confront me. I'm not in a hurry to head down that path again."

They both looked up as emergency vehicles poured into the neighborhood.

"Time to put on our professional faces," Polly said. She reached over and gave him a quick hug. "I love you, Ray."

"Thanks. I love you, too. I'm fine. I really am. I've had plenty of time to get over it. But I don't talk about it very often, so yeah, there's that."

CHAPTER TWENTY

Sycamore House was much quieter when Polly and Ray got back. The pair from the security company in Kansas City was already gone. They hadn't found anything more than what Anita knew would be there ... which was nothing.

Anita was still in the office talking to Kristen and Rachel. She'd been thrilled to meet the security consultants. For her, every encounter was an opportunity to learn.

Ray hadn't said another word about his life and Polly didn't press.

She walked into the main office with him and all faces turned to look at them.

"You did it again," Jeff said.

"How did you know?" she asked.

Anita put her hand up. "Me. I know everything." She laughed. "Aaron called and asked me to meet him up there when they're finished with the body. There are several computers and some other tech he wants me to look at."

"Our guys should have stayed," Ray said. "They might be able to help."

Jon shook his head. "Maybe, but they were impressed with Miss Banks, here. Landry said she was as good as anyone he knew and if she ever wanted a job, they'd hire her. I don't think you realize what you're worth," he said to Anita. "Forensic techs at your skill level aren't easily found."

"Thanks," she said with a demure smile. "That's nice of you to say. I enjoy my job and I'm not looking to leave this area."

"We'd hire you," Ray said. "You could stay in Iowa and travel for us. You'd see the world."

"From the inside of a jet and tiny little computer rooms," Anita replied. "I'll have more opportunities to travel and actually see the world if I stay here. And besides, where would Polly be without me?"

Polly pushed at Ray's shoulder. "Yeah. Leave my girl alone. You don't get to fly out to Iowa every five years and attempt to poach my friends."

"Just putting it out there. Jon, I want to get back to the hotel and ask more questions about this Steve Robertson. How did he not show up on our radar?"

Jon nodded. "I'm sorry we disrupted your morning for nothing. I'd hoped for more."

"It's fine," Jeff said. He reached out to shake Jon's hand. "You've given me enough information to put together a presentation for expanding our systems. I had no way of knowing how hard we've been pushing our current system."

Polly raised her eyebrows. "What does that mean?"

"The businesses are growing, the system needs to grow," Jeff said. "We'll talk."

She chuckled. "We have a lot to talk about. I'll be right back." Walking out of the office with Jon and Ray, she stopped at the main door. "Are you two busy tonight? Would you like to come over for dinner?"

The two brothers looked at each other and shrugged.

"Sure," Jon said. "We don't have any other plans."

"I'd hope not. If you have other friends in Iowa that I don't know about, I'll be annoyed with you."

"No one but you, my love," Ray said, giving her a hug. "What time?"

"Let's say six thirty. It will be casual again. I pulled steaks out of the freezer last night. We'll put those on the grill."

"Nothing like a steak in the Midwest," Jon said. "I'm there."

"When does Chloe get in?"

He smiled. "Tomorrow afternoon. I'm heading to Des Moines to pick her up. Don't know if Ray is going with me. Are you, bro?"

Ray shook his head. "I'll let you meet your lady love on your own. Unless you need backup. I have plenty of work to do."

"We may not get back until late," Jon said.

"We'll take care of him," Polly said, still holding on to Ray.

He laughed. "I'm a big boy. I can take care of myself."

"Whatever," she said. "Thursday will be a big day. There's a parade and the downtown area will be filled with activities."

"Fireworks?" Jon asked.

"Later that evening. We go up to the ballfields. It's a big party."

Ray gave her a squeeze. "We'll see you tonight."

"Thanks for going with me this morning."

He shook his head. "I'll never understand you."

"Don't even try, bro. Don't even try," Jon said.

Polly held the door for them and smiled. It was nice to see them and to finally realize that, though she loved them dearly, the infatuation she'd had for both men when she was younger was long gone. It really did feel like she had two brothers in Jon and Ray. They'd always be there if she needed them and she would always love them.

Anita and Rachel waved as they passed her while heading for the kitchen.

"Anita," Polly said. "Just a sec."

Rachel went on to the kitchen and Anita turned to Polly. "What's up?"

Suddenly, Polly panicked. She didn't want to betray Doug's trust in her. What was she thinking? "Uhhh, so, whatever happened with all of those wedding plans? Anything? I know you were talking about the Bell House." Well, that was lame.

Anita smiled. "I know Doug talked to you yesterday. We had a long discussion about our future last night."

Polly closed her eyes and sighed in relief. "Thank goodness. I walked into this and realized I had no good way to back out of it. How did that go?"

"Really well," Anita said. "I wish he had said something to me a long time ago, but that isn't his way. I already knew about his hope to open an arcade thing downtown. He told Billy, who tells Rachel everything. But I wasn't about to let Doug know that. I acted all surprised."

"Good for you," Polly said with a grin.

"The thing is, I have enough money to pay for the building, the renovation, and whatever he needs for startup," Anita said. "I'd be glad to give it to him. It's not like spending that money will change my life." She shrugged. "Well, I suppose it would. Especially if I'm going to live there, but you know what I mean. The money is no big deal and what I know of Bellingwood is that it really won't cost that much. Those buildings aren't expensive. At least not like buying something in and around Boston. That's just stupid money. This is stupid-cheap."

"What did that conversation do to Doug?" Polly asked.

"Freaked him out a little. He's such a good person." Anita huffed a laugh. "That's the thing that I can't make Mother understand. Grammy gets it. She said so the first time she met him, though she was a little surprised that I hadn't found someone who was as driven as Daddy and the rest of my family. Doug is definitely not a pushy go-getter."

"No, he isn't, but he's steady and trustworthy. If he starts something, he'll finish it."

"We talked about a lot of different ways he can do this. I'd rather not have him borrow money if he can help it. Especially if we're going to get married."

"If?"

Anita rolled her eyes. "That boy is enough to make me crazy. He talks like we're going to spend our lives together and then he does nothing about it. It's like the idea of being married terrifies him, but he's perfectly comfortable making a lifetime commitment. I'm the one who should be leery of marriage. My parents are wackadoos. His parents have a wonderful, loving, normal relationship."

"You've learned a lot about Doug in the last few years," Polly said. "Has he ever done anything normal?"

"No," Anita said with a laugh. "Not even once. You're right. This whole thing is certainly teaching me to be patient. He'll figure it out and surprise me one of these days. But we had the best talk last night that we've had in a long time. Whatever you said to get him off his keister worked. Thank you."

"Doug was the one who tracked me down. He wanted to talk. He wants to move forward. He's allowed himself to become a sloth, reacting to what the world hands him rather than standing up and taking what he wants and needs. He's much too young to be that person."

"No one should ever be that person." Anita shrugged. "I probably haven't helped. Maybe I make it too easy for him. It never occurred to me that he wanted to be something other than what he is. Once Rachel told me that he was thinking about doing something more with his life, I should have pushed. But sometimes I worry that if I push, he'll bolt."

"More likely, he'll fall down on the ground, his legs and arms rigid out in front of him."

Anita peered at her. "Like a fainting goat?"

"Exactly," Polly said, laughing. "That sounds like Doug, don't you think?"

"It really does. It's a perfect description. Are you and Henry willing to be part of this project if we decide to do it?"

Polly smiled when Anita included herself in the project. "I spoke to Henry last night. It sounds like fun."

"You gave Doug quite a bit of homework. He told me what you were looking for."

"If he's willing to put in the work on preparation, it will say a lot about how much he'll invest in the business," Polly said.

"That's what I told him. We'll make it happen."

Anita surprised Polly with a hug. "Thank you. You pushed him and that motivates me to keep encouraging him. Doug Randall will no longer be known as my own personal sloth. He'll be an upstanding contributor to Bellingwood society before we know it."

"Don't get all crazy," Polly said.

"I told Rachel I'd help her load up the van before I have to head up to Mr. Robertson's house. Thanks, Polly."

"You're welcome." Polly turned back to the main office. This was why she loved being here. Right smack dab in the middle of people and fun and excitement.

She walked back into the office and pointed at Jeff's closed door. "Is he in there?"

"Are you talking to him now?" Kristen asked.

"Yeah. I supposed I'd better. Wouldn't want you to explode."

Stephanie came to the door of her office. "Hi, Polly. It's been a while. How are things with Rebecca? I know last week was rough for her. I should have called."

"We're good." Polly took a quick breath. "I need to make a quick phone call. Sorry. You just reminded me that I promised to help someone this morning. Things got out of hand."

"Dead bodies?" Kristen asked. "I'd guess so."

Edna had come to her office door. "Is that true? You really found a dead body? Just because of an invoice for pest control?"

Stephanie grinned. "She makes the weirdest connections and before you know it, she's off solving murders. We've learned to stay out of her way."

"This happens often?"

Polly shook her head. "I can't believe you haven't heard rumors about me. It happens more often than one might think."

"I'm not much for gossip," Edna said. "When people start talking about other people, I tune them out."

"See," Polly said, pointing at Edna. "That's the way you should live your lives." She smiled. "It's the way I should live my life. Excuse me, all. I really do need to make a phone call. I'll be back in a minute."

She walked into the hallway and realized people were meeting in the classroom across from the office, so she went on out into the addition. Stepping outside into the warm and humid air, she took out her phone and swiped through to Mary Francis's number.

"Hello?" Mary said hesitantly.

"Mary, this is Polly Giller. I told you I would help you this morning and I'm sorry to be calling this late. The morning ran away with me."

"That's okay. I don't think I'm ready to deal with any of this right now. I appreciate your offer, but you shouldn't worry about me."

Polly had been afraid of this. If she were face to face with Mary, the woman's fears wouldn't have a chance to overwhelm her. "Mary, you need a good lawyer. Otherwise your husband will take advantage of you. He already has. I hate to press, but are you sure?"

"It's just so much," Mary said. "I don't know how I can do it all. I've never had to face anything like this in my life."

"That's why you have friends."

"I don't have any that aren't friends with Don, too. I know they'll side with him."

"You have me. You have Andrea. And trust me, once your friends understand what he's doing to you, they won't be very happy with your husband. What he's doing is wrong."

"I'm so scared."

Polly wanted to tuck this woman under her wings and protect her. "I wish I could take that fear away. All I can do is offer to help you get through this. Henry's friend, Al Dempsey, is willing to talk to you. If he can't take this on, there are others in his firm who will."

"Do I know his family?" Mary asked.

"Maybe. The Dempseys farm outside of Bellingwood."

"That means they'll find out about me. I'm so ashamed."

"I understand this is difficult, but Mary, people are going to know something is going on when you move out. They're going to know when Don moves this other family into the house." Just saying those words made Polly want to be sick. What was this man thinking? "It won't be as bad as you're imagining. More people than you realize will support you. And you have nothing to be ashamed about."

"They're going to talk about us," Mary said. "The last thing I ever wanted was to be part of the rumor mill."

"As someone who lives there on a regular basis, it's not the worst thing that can happen," Polly said. "Would you like to make the appointment with Al, or would you like me to set up a time."

"Will you go with me?"

"If that's what you want."

"I don't know if I can do this alone."

"Then I will go with you."

"Should I take Libby?"

"Maybe not for the first meeting. You probably have some hard things you'll need to tell Al. After that, it's up to you as to whether she's part of this."

"I don't want them to be part of anything. I want to protect them from all of it, but I can't." Mary began crying, heart wrenching sobs that didn't seem like they'd ever end. Polly could do nothing but let her go. The sound of her crying was too loud to speak over.

After what seemed like several hours, but was only moments, Mary lurched herself to a stop, breathing deeply in and out. "I ... I ... I ... I'm sorry," she got out.

"It's okay," Polly said gently. "It's really okay."

"I don't have anyone to talk to." Mary's words were punctuated with short breaths as she worked to bring herself under control.

"I'm here for you."

"You're busy, but thank you."

"Mary, I'm not too busy." Polly bit her upper lip. "Do you have plans for Thursday?"

"No, we might go up to see the fireworks, but nothing else."

"Why don't you bring your family to our place Thursday after one o'clock. We're having a big thing in the back yard. There will be plenty of food and games for the kids."

"You don't want us there," Mary said.

"I wouldn't have invited you if I didn't." Polly wasn't certain if that was true, but at some level it was.

"Rebecca won't want to have Libby at her house. Not now."

"Rebecca isn't that petty." Another half-truth, but Polly would make sure that Rebecca had plenty of opportunity to talk about it before anything happened. "She and Libby have been friends for a long time. Neither girl wants this mess to last forever. Come over. Andrea and her family will be there. The back yard will be filled with kids and we'll have a great time."

"We'll think about it. Thank you. And thank you for reaching out to your lawyer friend. When do you think the appointment will be?"

"He won't be available until next week. I'll talk to him this afternoon and get back to you. Do you have any days when you can't go?"

"No. I have nothing. Thank you, Polly." Mary abruptly hung up and left Polly standing there holding her phone to her ear.

"Well, that was weird. What have I done?" Polly chuckled as she headed back inside. If her family wasn't used to her rescues by now, they never would be.

Jeff was talking to someone in the hallway when she opened the door. He looked up and gave her a quick wave, then pointed at a bench. Okay. She could wait a minute.

It didn't take that long. He came over, but before he could sit down, she was up. "Walk and talk."

"Where are we going?"

"To the addition."

"No bodies, right? You had your fill this morning, haven't you? How bad was it?"

"Not so bad. I knew he was there."

"How? How did you know, Polly? Do you have any idea how crazed this stuff makes me? I'm so glad we aren't married."

"Well, that would be awkward," she said with a laugh. "If it makes you this crazy, then what I'm about to address with you might be hard to swallow."

"Oh," he said, worry in his tone. "Now what?"

Polly opened the door to the front room on the lower level of the addition. "I want this room."

He frowned. "What for? Are we hosting someone this week for you?"

"Nope. For me. I want to come back to work."

Jeff laughed out loud. "You what? You work all the time."

"I want an office again. Here at Sycamore House. I'm done with my exile. It's time to come home."

He'd walked through the room to stand in front of one of the tall windows. Turning back to her, he said, "You're serious, aren't you."

"I am. This is where I want my office."

"It would be perfect for you. Close enough to be part of the daily activities, far enough away that you can do whatever you want. You can look out and see your horses. It's not a bad idea."

"I know you rent the upper rooms to brides and grooms ..."

Jeff put his hand up, stopping her. "It's not that often and I'm glad to move all of that to the hotel or the B&B. This is suddenly a really interesting discussion."

"Why?"

"Because we have so much more that we need to do here. Moving you, me, Edna, and Stephanie into these rooms makes sense. Would Henry consider ripping out the walls of the current office space and creating smaller offices over there?"

"I'm sure he would."

"Not now, it's just a thought rumbling around in my head."

"Always something going on up there."

"This is a good idea. I'm glad you're coming back. We need you. I'm uncomfortable calling you over here whenever we need to discuss something."

"I'm glad to be here."

"I understand that, but having you nearby will make things much more fun." He gave her a smile. "Or interesting. I'm not sure how much fun I'll have if you find bodies in our nooks and crannies."

"I don't intend to do that."

"Whatever. You'll certainly liven up the joint. I miss having your friends show up on a whim. They're always entertaining."

"Sweet Beans might go out of business if I'm not up there every day," she said with a laugh.

"I'm certain you'll find many reasons to visit them. When do you want to start? What should we be looking at for you?"

"Not until after school begins."

He nodded in understanding. "Cassidy."

"Yes. One of the reasons I want my office out here is so the kids won't be in people's way if they come over after school." She pointed at the front corner of the room. "I'll create a sitting area there with toys and games. I won't stay until five o'clock every day since I'm not ready to give up my afternoons with them. That time is too important."

"We'll work you to death right up until you leave, then," he said. "I'll have Eliseo and Scott move this furniture out so you can bring in what you'd like. This is a good idea, Polly. We need you."

"I need this place, too. It's my home as much as the Bell House is my family's home."

"Can I tell the staff?"

"Absolutely. Kristen knows already. I had a flash of insight with her yesterday and made her promise to keep it quiet until we'd talked."

"That's impressive. She usually isn't that circumspect."

"I begged."

He chuckled. "Good to know. I'll keep that in mind. Welcome home, Polly."

CHAPTER TWENTY-ONE

In case her day hadn't been strange enough already, as Polly went out the front door of Sycamore House, a familiar Jeep screeched its tires as it pulled into the lot. Lydia sped toward her and lurched to a stop in front of the building, startling Polly, who had stayed on the sidewalk when she saw what was happening.

"Quick, get in the back," Beryl said after rolling down her car window. She was dressed in a wildly colored flowy blouse and jeans and wore over-sized sunglasses and a big-brimmed straw hat, decorated with flowers and a big ribbon tied into a bow on the side.

"What?"

"Don't ask questions. Get in. Subterfuge and all that. Move it, move it, move it."

Polly chuckled, opened the back door and climbed in behind Beryl. Before she had time to pull the door closed, Lydia tore out of the parking lot and headed north, back into town.

"What's going on?" Polly asked. "Is everything okay?"

"No time to talk. We're kidnapping someone," Beryl said.

"Who?"

Lydia was shaking with laughter. "You, you silly girl. Who else?"

"Me? Why are you kidnapping me?"

Beryl turned to look at her. "Because you've been incognito these last few weeks and we don't want anyone to know that we could find you so easily."

"Where are you taking me?"

"Lunch. Now, no more questions. We don't want the fuzz to find out what we've done."

"The fuzz? I left him earlier this morning. He was busy."

"We know all about it," Beryl said. She pulled her hat down over her face while turning in her seat. "We're undercover."

"What does that mean?"

"It means we're investigating a disappearance."

"I'm afraid to ask," Polly said.

Beryl took her phone out, swiped it several times and began to recite. "Missing. One Polly Giller. Age. Forty."

"Not yet," Polly protested. "Don't rush me."

"Age. Not quite forty. Last seen herding kittens, dogs, children, and dead bodies. Her friends ask that anyone who sees her call the local constabulary to report the sighting. Do not attempt to restrain her. She is a sly one and captivity will only serve to cause her to bolt for parts unknown and unseen."

"You're a nut," Polly said.

"Hush. We're on the case."

"Where are you taking me?"

Beryl lifted the front of her hat. "For a kidnap victim, you insist on asking far too many questions. Didn't I tell you to hush?"

Polly zipped her lips shut, then she said. "Will you feed me? I'm starving."

Swatting at Lydia, Beryl shook her head. "This one will not hush. Shall we stuff food in that mouth?"

"Sounds like the best idea you've had all day," Lydia said. "How does Sweet Beans sound? Andy is already there, and Sylvie said she'd come out and join us. We called Cat and she assured us that she had things well in hand for the next hour or so."

Polly breathed a sigh of relief. She hadn't intended to leave Cat with the children for quite so long this morning. "Thank you."

"We know where your heart is," Beryl said. She tossed another wildly decorated hat into Polly's lap. "Put that on. You need a disguise. We don't want anyone to recognize you. They might make an attempt to spirit you away. We can't have that now that we finally discovered your whereabouts."

"No big sunglasses?" Polly asked.

Beryl tossed a pair of those into the back seat. "Thought you could get one over on me, didn't you? I don't go anywhere without my cheap gas station glasses. I even bring extras for my friends. Are you ready to go in?"

There was nothing Polly could do except follow along, so she put on the glasses and hat as Lydia parked down the street from the coffee shop. Before she opened her door, Beryl was already there, holding a hand out. Polly took it and laughed when Lydia came up on her other side. The two women each took a side, looping her arms into theirs.

"Not gonna let me go?" Polly asked.

"We finally have you; you're stuck with us," Lydia said.

"I can see this coming from Beryl, but you're pushing the edge of your own crazy, aren't you, Lydia?"

Lydia cackled, tipping her hat. "I've been forced to spend extra amounts of time with the crazy lady because you've been so busy. It's rubbing off. And now you are out there chasing down murder victims. I haven't had a chance to talk to you since you found the first one. Aaron asked me to keep you off the streets. He's having a hard time keeping up with you."

Polly laughed until she snorted. "He didn't."

"Yeah," Lydia said plainly. "He did. That was the phone call this morning that spurred this little get-together. We're saving my husband from more of your antics. I like my pumpkin-buns happy. I'll do whatever it takes."

Beryl went through the front door first, dragging Polly behind her. "We're over here. Keep quiet. We don't want to spook the natives."

Polly looked where Beryl was pointing and saw Sylvie and Andy at a table, both wearing big floppy hats and sunglasses. She laughed. "If my life wasn't perfect before, it certainly is now."

As they walked toward the table, Beryl danced around Polly, her eyes dancing around the coffee shop. "No one is looking at you. No one sees you. It's safe. You're safe."

Lydia pulled out a chair beside Sylvie. Beryl pushed Polly into it, then sat down, dragging her chair up next to Polly's. "I've got your back. No one will even know you're here."

"I don't know if I've been kidnapped or I'm in protective custody," Polly said.

"Neither do any of us," Andy commented. "How long do I have to wear this silly hat? I can't see anything with these glasses on."

Beryl whipped her own hat off her head and flung it at Andy. "You are the worst silly-maker in the world. How are you even my friend?"

Andy looked at her in shock. "I feel like a fool, sitting here in this crazy getup. Everyone is staring at us."

"So what?" Beryl asked. "It isn't like the whole town doesn't know that you're my friend."

Everyone else slid their hats and sunglasses quietly off and an uncomfortable silence settled at the table.

"I'm sorry," Andy said, letting out a loud sigh. "You know how I am. Now, look what I did. I made this fun lunch with Polly awkward." She picked up Beryl's hat and set it on her head. "Please, forgive me."

"Only if you buy me a cookie. Not just any cookie. It has to be the grandest, most expensive cookie in the place. How much will that cost her, Sylvie?"

Sylvie glanced back and forth between the two of them. "Cookies are inexpensive. Maybe she should buy us a pie. Marta made a strawberry rhubarb pie this morning. Does everyone like that?"

"That sounds acceptable." Beryl hugged Polly before moving her own chair back to its place at the table. "Pie it is. Maybe two. I need to take one home so that I can do self-care this evening."

Lydia snorted. "Have we kissed and made up?"

"Not yet," Beryl said. She stood, walked around to Andy, grabbed the woman's shoulders and planted a sloppy kiss right on her lips. "There. I feel so much better."

Andy wiped at her lips and threw her head back in laughter. "I can hardly wait to tell Len that someone else kissed my lips today. Now I have to decide whether it will be more interesting if I don't tell him who it was or if I tell him it was a girl."

"I kissed a girl and I liked it," Beryl sang, dancing back to her chair. "Miss Polly, you get to have anything you like today. We're buying." She cackled. "Do you like the way I did that? I brought her to her own restaurant and offered to pay. I'm a generous soul."

"We're paying," Lydia said. "For everyone. We don't want Sweet Beans going out of business because the owners and managers give away their food. So, how gory was the dead body this morning?"

"Lydia," Andy scolded. "Let us at least eat our lunch before you dig into death and destruction."

"I'm sorry, but Andy, how do you ever live with those grandkids of yours? Surely, they say worse things than all of this. They puke, poop, spit up, eat boogers, play in dirt and mud, on and on."

"Not as much now as they used to. They're good kids."

"Lily-white pansies," Beryl muttered. "At least when they visit Grandma."

"No, they aren't," Andy said. "I'm not that bad. It's just that we're in public."

"*Public* doesn't give a hoot in hell about us. Every person in this place has been entertained. They'll go home or back to work with stories of a group of crazy ladies who are having more fun than they are. You should be proud to be part of that group."

"I am, I am. I said I'm sorry." Andy looked at Polly. "Len says you've been over to the shop a couple of times. Did you freak out when you saw your piano in pieces?"

"Nah," Polly said. "I haven't spent any time with the thing, so I have no personal attachment. If he'd done this after I'd owned it for twenty years, things might have been different, but right now, it's exciting to see how the pieces fit together. I'm looking forward to the day I bring it home."

"We're going to expect a recital," Lydia said. "You'll have to play it."

Polly slowly turned, shock filling her face. "Uhhh, no. I don't think so."

"Come on," Beryl said. "Winkle, Winkle?"

"I'm sorry, what?"

Beryl cackled. "You heard me."

"Yeah, don't know that one," Polly said. "A fun recital would be a good idea. I'll talk to Jeanie Dykstra when we know more about timing. She'd probably love not having to clean her house for the next one."

"You should do something bigger than that," Andy said. "Imagine having a talented pianist in your home for an evening. You know, like in the old days. You could have a *salon*."

"We could all wear our bustles and carry parasols," Beryl said. "Cucumber sandwiches and petit fours."

"I'd be fine with fancy food and drink, but no bustles or parasols." Polly leaned forward, looking straight at Andy. "Maybe Len would play for us some evening."

A slow smile crossed Andy's face. "He warned me that you were going to tell on him."

"What?" Lydia asked.

Polly grinned. "Len Specek once wanted to be a jazz pianist. He played before he married his first wife. Are you going to get him a piano now, Andy?"

"You bet I am," she said coyly. "He doesn't want me to, but now that I know that about him, I have to, don't you think? He deserves to have that joy back in his life after all these years." Her eyes filled with tears. "Do you know he used to sneak into the church basement and play when no one was around? He hasn't done it in a while, but when Pastor Boehm was here, he once caught Len and invited him to show up whenever he wanted to. Why did he never tell me?"

225

"Sounds like his first wife wasn't keen on his artistic side," Polly said. "But now that you know, he can find it again."

"I told him that he could either buy a new one or if he found something he wanted to restore, I'd gladly go that route, too."

Beryl hadn't said a word. When Lydia poked her, she said, "What?"

"Nothing? You have nothing to say?"

"I'm just in shock that anyone would give up their creative side for so long. We *must* have an old-fashioned *salon* at Polly's, and Len will play. Lydia, you'll make the food, I'll bring the wine. It will be a celebration of the return of the artist."

Polly pointed at the front counter. "Speaking of food and drink. I'm starving. Can we get this party started?"

Andy was the first to stand. "I really am sorry about being a party pooper. Sometimes I just can't stop my mouth."

"I thought that was Beryl's problem." Sylvie stood and took Andy's arm. "Let's go look at the pies."

When they got to the front counter, Camille gave them a tired smile. "Hello, ladies. It looks like you're having quite the party."

"We snuck Polly out of her life." Beryl leaned forward to draw Camille into the conspiracy. "She's incognito."

"Or kidnapped," Polly said. "They can't decide. How is your mother?"

Camille closed her eyes and breathed in slowly. "She's in good hands."

"What does that mean?"

"She's at University Hospital. They're going to do a balloon stent tomorrow."

"And you're here?"

"I'm going back over tonight to be with her. I just wanted to come in for a day. Josie has been a trooper, but she can't work every day of the week. I feel awful asking her to do everything."

Sylvie frowned. "I didn't even think to ask this morning."

"You were insane back there," Camille said with a smile. "Everyone is ordering baked goodies for their parties on Thursday."

"Are we keeping you from something?" Beryl asked Sylvie. "I didn't mean to intrude in your work."

"I can take lunch. I have enough good help. Everyone is working this week," Sylvie said. "This is me taking care of myself. I needed a dose of Beryl's craziness. But Camille, let me know if I can help you."

"We have it covered," Camille said. "I called Skylar and he's going to double up some shifts at the hotel so that he's available, too. We're okay."

"Let me make our lunch, then," Sylvie said.

Camille laughed. "I have plenty of help today. Josie made sure to schedule extra people all week. She's been wonderful."

"If you need someone to drive you to Omaha or anything like that," Lydia said, "let me know. I understand how difficult it is to care for a sick person and try to do your job. Especially when the job is nearly three hours away."

"Thank you so much," Camille said. "I have vacation time and Jeff is wonderful. He offered to stand behind the counter, but I'm afraid he'd get frustrated and end up giving everything away. Honestly, it feels good to be here and normal for a few hours. Mama has plenty of people around to keep her occupied today and I was ready for a break."

"A break would have been walking around the zoo," Polly said. "Not driving back to Bellingwood so you can get up early and serve coffee all day."

Camille smiled. "You have no idea how peaceful this is. I know everyone, they've been generous and caring when they ask about Mama, and all I have to focus on is serving them. It's been a nice interlude. I'll go back to the insanity tonight and then suffer through a family who feels like every single family member should be in the waiting room during surgery. I've warned the nurses that they will be overrun but I don't think they fully understand what I meant." She chuckled. "There could be upwards of fifty or sixty people there. And the chapel? Oh, it will be complete chaos. They'll not have ever seen a prayer service like my family can bring. Those doctors in the operating suite won't know what hit them when this group gets down on their knees. Mama will be in fine hands."

Lydia reached across the counter and touched Camille's hand. "We'll be praying too."

"Thank you. All right, what can we fix for you today?"

"Enough of the emotional stuff?" Beryl asked.

Camille laughed. "I'm glad I was here today. I would have hated to miss out on this much excitement."

Beryl preened. "Look. We're her excitement."

They placed their orders and headed back to the table.

"That poor girl," Lydia said. "Do you see how tired she is? I wish I could help her."

Polly nodded. "I need to reach out to Skylar. June Livengood's aunt is in bad shape and I know he's been letting her have extra time off. He's going to run himself ragged if he's working here and at the hotel."

"He's young," Sylvie said. "If it were a problem, Stephanie would have said something. She's as protective of him as she is of Kayla."

"I just never saw those two together. He's so ..." Lydia's voice drifted off as she tried to come up with a comparison.

"Cute? Skinny? What are you implying?" Beryl asked.

Lydia frowned. "Not that. He's worldly. All hip and up on the contemporary lingo. Stephanie was sheltered. At least that's the way she seems to me." She looked at Polly for affirmation.

Polly nodded. "She was. She probably still is. They're good for each other. She settles him and he stirs her up. That girl was desperate to live a bigger life, to go places and do things that she could only dream about when she was stuck in the house with that horrible man for a father."

"Now she's so busy she doesn't have time," Sylvie said. "But I did hear her tell Jeff about a trip she's planning to Chicago with Kayla just before school starts."

"Good for them," Polly said. "I'm glad they're doing that. Both girls need to get out and experience more of the world. Beryl, are you ready for your trip with Rebecca?"

Beryl and Rebecca were planning to go to the Pacific Northwest during the first week of August. Her agent had set up meetings with several galleries and clients, but the two looked forward to sight-seeing as well. Rebecca had been hesitant to ask for time off since Reuben counted on her, but he'd been horrified that she might miss out on a great opportunity.

"I haven't started packing, if that's what you mean," Beryl said.

"Tell me you don't pack a month before a trip."

"You don't pack a month before a trip."

Polly shook her head in disgust. "You're a weird woman."

"I'm obedient."

Everyone laughed out loud at that.

"We have a few minutes before our food comes," Lydia said. "With Andy's permission, I'd like to ask Polly a few questions about the murdered men she's found this last week."

Andy shrugged.

"There's not much to tell," Polly said. "I know there's a connection between them."

Lydia nodded. "Aaron said as much. But what?"

"I have an idea that it's something about that clock thingie that was spying on the dead man, Andrew Harrison," Polly said. "Steve Robertson installed it for the murderer. That's the only thing that makes sense. No one would have paid any attention to him going into a room." She looked around. "You all know that Jon and Ray Renaldi are in town, don't you?"

Beryl back-handed Polly's arm. "I heard that and I'm quite disappointed in you."

"Why?" Polly asked, rubbing where she'd been hit. "What did I do?"

"You haven't invited us over to spend time with those gorgeous young men. Are you keeping them all to yourself?"

"Jon is engaged and Ray is gay. How is that going to do you any good?"

Beryl sneered at her. "It's not like I want to ravage them. They'd be too weak for me anyway. I need a man with a lifetime of experience. But I wouldn't mind an hour or two of watching them walk and talk and move around. Come on, a woman has to have her eye candy."

"Women have been protesting that type of behavior for decades and you think it's appropriate to gawk at good-looking young men?" Lydia asked.

"I won't gawk. I won't wolf-whistle. I won't make a scene. I just like to look. They're pretty." Beryl let out a growl that purred in her throat. "Verrrry pretty."

"She's not wrong," Lydia said.

Polly laughed. "No, she isn't. We're horrible. Objectifying those poor young men."

"The young one is really getting engaged?" Andy asked. "Have you met his fiancé?"

"She'll be at the party on Thursday."

Beryl let out a wolf-whistle that time. The others at the table all looked around to see who might be watching them. Of course, the whistle caught the attention of the entire coffee shop. "They're coming to your party? I need to re-think my wardrobe for the day. Maybe I'll bring a few clothing changes. That way, they won't recognize me each time they meet me. Lydia, we're going to need to bring out the additional identities I've tucked away in the safe."

"Got it," Lydia said. "Operation Beryl-on-the-hunt."

Beryl leaned across and stuck her finger in Andy's face. "That's how you play the game."

"I said I was sorry," Andy protested. She stood up and crossed her arms, then said loudly enough to be heard throughout the coffee shop, "Attention, everyone."

Beryl gasped. "What are you doing?"

"I am a fuddy duddy and rained on Beryl Watson's parade when she arrived here today. I'd like to announce to you all that I'm very sorry and can be as crazy as her." Andy promptly sat back down. She bent over and came back up with the hat and sunglasses in place. "I have to wear these now. I just embarrassed myself."

"You embarrassed me," Beryl said, her eyes wide. "But that was impressive."

Gayla Livingstone approached the table carrying a tray with their food. She was giggling as she handed over their plates. "You ladies really know how to party. Do you have bottles of wine under the table or something?"

"That would have been a grand idea," Beryl said. "I'm afraid that this level of silly behavior is completely alcohol-free. I didn't know Miss Andy had it in her."

"I don't," Andy muttered. "My head hurts."

Sylvie rubbed Andy's back. "You're fine. Everyone knows you and Beryl are best friends. A little crazy-cakes is expected."

"I'm the good girl," Andy protested. "She's the crazy one."

"We can throw that dogma out with the bathwater," Beryl said.

Gayla put a plate in front of Polly. "You all are so much fun. I want to be you when I grow up."

"Start now," Beryl said. "That way people will never expect you to be normal."

CHAPTER TWENTY-TWO

"So, I don't understand how the murderer even found Steve Robertson," Ray mused.

Henry nodded. "Unless it was someone local. Everyone knew Steve."

"You think we have a professional killer living in Bellingwood?" Polly asked, dropping her tone so the kids wouldn't hear. The boys had begged to put up their tent in the back yard. Sleeping outside was one of their favorite summer activities. If they left the door to the little shed open, everyone had access to the basement, including the dogs. Obiwan and Han generally slept outside with the boys which gave Polly and Henry another level of comfort. The truth was, they were probably on their own for only three or four hours. Heath was a night owl, staying out late with Ella most nights and checking on them when he got home. Henry was generally up and moving by five o'clock. Polly also discovered that when the boys slept outside, she wasn't the only one who woke up to check on them. Hayden had pointed at his bleary-eyed wife a couple of mornings. She'd gotten up throughout the night to wander down to the kitchen and make sure everything was as she'd left it when she went to bed.

At Polly's question about the professional killer, Ray shook his head. "I just don't know. We haven't found anything that suggests someone is trying to access bank security using Andrew Harrison's credentials and there haven't been any odd applications for his position. The security company is keeping a tight rein on everything they're doing. Nothing."

"Do you think it's personal?" Henry asked.

Polly sat forward in her chair. They were on the patio outside the kitchen doors, a warm breeze moving through the yard. "Did I tell you that his wife is a pianist? One of the men working on my piano at the shop tunes pianos for her when she tours. He told me that she hadn't cancelled a concert she has coming up this weekend. You'd think they would let her out of the contract due to her husband's murder."

"Maybe she's cancelled everything by now and your friend just didn't know when you talked."

"I suppose."

Jon chuckled. "Don't you think that if she was behind the murder, she would at least have tried to make it look like she wasn't?"

"By cancelling things?" Henry asked.

Jon nodded. "And making a show of her deep grief. From what we've heard, she's not terribly sad that he's dead."

"Was he a bad man?" Polly frowned. "What's going on there?"

"I don't think he was necessarily a bad person, though we're just digging into his home life now."

She blinked at him. "You're what? You and Jon are sitting here on patio. I don't see much digging."

Jon laughed out loud. "She has us there. Ray has an appointment to meet with the wife tomorrow morning."

"Mason City, here I come," Ray said. "Is there anything fun to see up there?"

"That's the home of Meredith Willson," Henry said.

Ray looked confused and Jon said, "No way. You're kidding."

"You have no idea what he's talking about, do you?" Polly said.

"It sounded like I should," Jon said with a laugh. "Who is Meredith Willson?"

"He wrote the musical *The Music Man*. You know, *Seventy-six Trombones*? *Ya Got Trouble Right Here in River City*? *Pickalittle, Talkalittle*? *The Wells Fargo Wagon*? Come on, surely you know this," Polly said.

Jon peered at her. "Sing a few of them. Maybe that would help."

She opened her mouth and Henry waved her off. "He's teasing you."

"Brat. He also wrote *It's Beginning to Look A Lot Like Christmas*. So there." She stuck her tongue out at him.

"If you have a few extra minutes, Clear Lake is close to Mason City and you can go see the Surf Ballroom, where Buddy Holly had his last show before the plane crash," Henry said.

Jon shook his head. "That was a little before our time."

"It's a little before my time, too," Henry said, scowling at him. "But it's part of our history."

Polly stuck her tongue out again. "So there. Nothing like having to come to Iowa to learn about the history of music. Good heavens."

"I didn't know Willson wrote that Christmas song," Henry said.

Jon pointed at her. "See. So there."

She laughed. "I only knew because we sang it in high school choir. The director was a huge Meredith Willson fan."

The lights came on in the kitchen, startling them all as the evening had begun to wane. Polly turned around as Rebecca flung the sliding glass doors open.

"I can't believe you invited that bitch to come to our house," she said, her face filled with rage. "Do you ever even give a thought to anyone but yourself? How could you do this to me? Trust me, I won't be around. At least I have a car now so I can leave. What were you thinking, Polly? I just don't even know."

Henry was out of his chair and crossing the patio before Rebecca had finished speaking. She saw him coming, slammed the door shut again and stomped off.

"Whoa," Jon said. "You raise 'em with passion, that's for sure."

Polly rolled her eyes. "Sorry about that. I should go in and deal with her."

"No," Henry said, his hand on the door handle. "I don't know what she's talking about yet, but she's going to sit and stew on this one for a while. She can just freakin' wait for you to talk to her. While she's waiting, which bathroom do you want cleaned?"

"The kids' bathroom would be awesome," Polly said with a laugh.

He was inside in a flash and Polly was still laughing when she turned back to her two stunned friends. "That's our punishment for mouthy kids. They clean bathrooms."

"No way," Jon said.

She nodded. "It started with Rebecca when we were still at Sycamore House. She made me so angry one evening. I didn't want to yell and scream and I needed something for her to do that would give her time to settle down, be enough of a punishment for her to remember and get her out of my face while I calmed down. I sent her into the bathroom and told her to start cleaning. Now, the kids all know that if they can't speak respectfully, or choose to make bad decisions, they clean bathrooms. It's lightened up my cleaning load quite a lot. And no slap-dash jobs are allowed. They either do it well or they do it again."

Jon sighed and looked at his brother. "That would have been easier than Mama and the back of the hairbrush."

"You got that once," Ray said. "And you deserved every single lick she gave you. I can't believe you stole her car. You were only twelve. And then you talked back to her when the police brought you home after you planted it in the Russo's front yard."

Polly burst out in laughter. "You did not."

"I was young and stupid. It's my only defense," Jon said. "I spent the entire summer landscaping that yard. All I did was tear up a corner, but was that what I fixed? Oh no. I spent every Saturday following old Mr. Russo around while he told me where he wanted me to move these plants and put those bushes. I mowed and trimmed and worked my fingers to the bone."

"Was stealing the car worth it?"

He shrugged. "Not really. I only wanted to go down to the market and pick up a new Superman comic. Mama told me I had to wait until she'd take me that weekend, but I just knew they'd be all gone by then. And you know what? They were."

"Isn't it weird the things we remember?" Polly asked.

"I haven't thought about that in years. But man, that Superman comic was important to me."

"Do you even still have all those comics?" Ray asked his brother.

Jon shrugged. "They're in boxes in Mama's attic. She keeps telling me that I should move my things out, but every time I try to schedule a time to do it, she comes up with something else for me to do."

"Maybe when you start bringing babies for her to hold, she'll release your belongings," Polly said.

With a laugh, Jon said, "You think she's holding them hostage?"

Henry came back out and dragged his hand across Polly's shoulders as he walked past her to his chair. "She's scrubbing and feeling a little chagrined that she made a scene in front of our guests. You talked to Libby's mother?"

Polly nodded. "I told you I was going to. That poor woman is a wreck. And obviously, so is Libby. Can you imagine your family falling apart around you while your mother acts as if nothing is wrong? The girl is desperate for attention and I'd guess a small part of her hoped her father would bail her out of this whole thing and realize how important he is to the family. Mary is so tied up about it that she can't see her way past the loss. That August first deadline is looming, but she thinks if she ignores it, maybe the whole thing will go away. Libby's thefts just brought everything out into the open."

"Which makes it a good thing?" Henry asked.

"It certainly exposed their problems, giving Andrea and me an opportunity to help them. Tomorrow, I'll call Al Dempsey and make an appointment for next week. Andrea is looking at apartments and rental homes and checking into moving companies. If we can pull this off, Don Francis will pay for everything, and we'll make the move as easy as possible on Mary and her kids. That jackass won't get away with this behavior. Not when Polly and Andrea are on the case."

"Andrea?" Jon asked, emphasizing the second syllable of the name. "Pronounced like my sister's name? I rarely hear that."

Polly nodded. "I couldn't believe it when she moved in across the street." She pointed down past the cemetery. "My friend, Andy, lives down that way. She's just a normal Andrea. Do you ever find that people with the same name all show up at the same time in your life?"

"We have three Rays in the office right now. One of them is a girl, but you really have to concentrate so you make sure the right one is paying attention."

"And four Joes," Ray said. "It's like we fell in love with the name and made sure everyone was using it." He looked at his watch. "We should go. I want to do some work before I sleep tonight. I'm going to be on the road by six tomorrow morning."

Laughter and giggling came from the tent that had been set up in front of the porch outside Polly and Henry's office.

"They're having fun," Jon said.

"When Heath is with them, they feel like they've won the lottery," Henry said. "He's not around that much now that he has a girlfriend, so they know how important it is to enjoy the time he gives them."

"You have a wonderful family," Ray said.

Polly lifted her eyes upward. "Even the sweetheart who is upstairs cleaning the bathroom. She hasn't had to do that for several months. I guess it was due." She stood and backed up while Ray stood beside her. "Thanks for spending time with us. I'm glad our kids have gotten to know you two. It feels like my family is whole now."

Ray hugged her. "We're the fortunate ones to have the two of you accept us like you have. It means the world to me."

"Me too," Jon said. "We won't see you until Thursday, right?"

"You're heading to Des Moines to get Chloe tomorrow?" Polly said.

He smiled. "I'm looking forward to seeing her again."

"You two talk every day and video chat every night," Ray said with a dramatic eye roll.

"It's not the same," Polly said, slipping her arm around Henry's waist. "We did video chat when you were in Arizona. I was glad for it, but I was even more glad when you were in Bellingwood."

"She wasn't ready to admit it, but she loved me," Henry said with a grin.

They walked around the side of the house with the two men and stood at the steps while Ray and Jon left.

"I don't want to deal with her," Polly said to Henry.

"She'll be fine. It probably was a bit of a surprise."

"I was going to talk to her. We just haven't had time yet."

He pulled her close. "Whether or not you had an opportunity to talk to her about this is beside the point. That she thought she could speak to you like that in front of guests, disrespecting you in front of your friends? Oh no, that won't fly."

"The best thing about raising kids with you is that you always have my back," Polly said, walking up the steps to the door.

"We're a team. You're rarely wrong." He held the door and gave her a grin.

"You are so smart," she said, laughing. Polly lifted up and kissed him. "That is definitely the way to my heart."

"I wasn't aiming for your heart."

"All right. There too. Do you want to drag Cassidy out of the tent? She's not sleeping out there with the boys tonight."

He nodded. "Does she need a bath?"

"It depends on how easily she comes inside with you. If she struggles and throws a fit, we'll put her in a warm bath to help her relax. Otherwise, that can wait until tomorrow."

They never knew with Cassidy and had plenty of experience managing through her chaotic emotions. Summer break had been a good experience for the little girl. She had grown more comfortable with her brothers and learned to be part of a big family who rarely sat still. Polly wanted to ensure that she had as much social interaction as possible before school started this fall.

As Henry headed for the office, she dragged her feet across the kitchen, not wanting to go upstairs. Cat and Hayden were out this evening with friends from Ames, so the upstairs would be all hers if Rebecca decided they needed to have a shouting match. It didn't happen very often, but when it did, things got loud quickly and then just as fast, were calm again. It was a wonder that children ever made it to adulthood. At least Rebecca would have a strong foundation on which to build her own family.

Polly headed down the hallway. Now that she was here, it was better to just get on it and deal with this. She strode to the bathroom and said, "Rebecca?"

When she didn't get a response, she frowned and pushed the door open. Rebecca jumped and yanked earbuds out of her ears.

"You scared the hell out of me."

"Wow. Language," Polly said.

"Whatever. You scared me. My mouth just reported what my heart felt."

"When I say, *Wow, language,* your response should be *sorry.*"

Rebecca shrugged. "I'll probably end up with a second bathroom before this is over anyway. Might as well make it worth my time."

And Henry thought she'd be contrite.

"Do you want to talk about it?"

"Why should I? You didn't ask me if it was okay to invite my arch enemy to our party on Thursday. It isn't like you're going to uninvite her. I'll just find a way to be somewhere else."

"First of all, no you won't. Secondly, you know full well that I don't ask your permission to invite people to our home."

"Why not? I have to."

"You want responsibility for paying the bills now?"

Rebecca shrugged and bent back to the toilet.

"How did you find out? I was going to talk to you about this later after Jon and Ray were gone."

"Libby texted me," Rebecca said, flashing a look at Polly. "She had the audacity to text me. So, my enemy tells me that she's showing up in two days and my own mother can't be bothered."

"You know what it's been like today," Polly said. "When things were quiet, you and I would have talked about this. You know me better than that. I wouldn't spring something like Libby's arrival on you without a conversation."

"I had to hear it from her via text," Rebecca said, her voice rising. "From her."

Polly leaned against the door frame. "If your phone had been in its charger like it was supposed to be, you wouldn't have seen it until much later. Did you think about that one?"

Rebecca didn't say anything.

"I'm more than happy to have the conversation with you when you decide to be a decent human being. Are you ready for that?"

"I'm going to be in trouble. I'm going to clean bathrooms. I'm going to apologize. Yada, yada, yada. My life in a nutshell."

"Pretty big nutshell," Polly said. "I really am having a hard time feeling sorry for you, but I can almost guarantee that when you hear what I have to say, you'll feel bad enough to apologize and send a different kind of text to Libby."

"I haven't sent one back. I was in shock that you did that to me. Then Henry took my phone away."

Henry was such a smart man, even if he didn't read Rebecca well sometimes.

Polly walked in, dropped the lid on the toilet seat and pointed at it. "Sit. You're going to listen to me. Then we can discuss."

Rebecca dropped the rag onto the pile of dirty towels she'd pushed into a corner. She was nearly finished. The bathrooms were pretty clean these days. She sat down, planted her elbows on her knees and her head in her hands. "Go ahead."

"Libby's father is divorcing her mother. He's given them until the first of August to find a new place to live. After that, he's moving a new woman and her children into the house. He's told his family that he's not interested in being their father because the other family needs him more than they do." Polly stood in silence to let Rebecca process what she'd said. Even saying the words brought an oppressive feeling to the room. How could he do this?

Rebecca didn't move. Moments passed. Polly stood in silence.

"I'm the worst friend in the world," Rebecca said quietly. "I knew something was wrong, but when she accused me of stealing, all I could think about was myself. It didn't occur to me that she was living in a hell in her own mind and that's why she was so different. Libby would never have done that before. Why can't I ever put myself in someone else's shoes?"

When she looked up, her face was stricken with grief. "She needed us and I was focused on punishing her, I didn't even think about why she'd done it in the first place. Does Cilla know?"

Polly lifted a shoulder. "I'm not sure. Mary and Libby were at their house yesterday. Mary is trying to figure this out."

"Where are they going to go? He's just kicking them out? After all these years? Libby loves her bedroom and they have that great pool. We're always out there. And her dogs. What will they do with the dogs? Polly, we have to help them."

"We are," Polly said with a smile. "Andrea and I are on it. I'm taking Mary to meet with a lawyer next week ..."

Rebecca interrupted. "Good. I hope they slam that man with everything. Make him pay."

"Andrea is working on finding a place for them to live and ways to help them move. We're going to be there to give them as much support as possible. And that's why I invited them to join us on Thursday. It's also why I didn't want to tell you until I could explain what was going on. This isn't something I wanted to talk about in front of the boys."

"I'm so sorry," Rebecca said. "I knew I was going to have to apologize, but wow, I'm just the worst." She laughed. "You know, in Sunday School, we talked about sackcloth and ashes. I know it's a horrible analogy, but I feel like that's how I should dress for a couple of days. I deserve it."

"You're fine. We all jump to conclusions. I had no idea this was going on and the last person I wanted to speak to yesterday was Mary Francis. But at least I wasn't mean to her."

Rebecca looked around the room. "Every time I jump to a conclusion, one more bathroom gets cleaned. It's like I'm Tinkerclean, the fairy."

"The boys are going to love having a clean bathroom."

"Yeah, and none of them had to do the work." Rebecca stood and crossed to Polly. "I am sorry for the way I spoke to you. That was so rude."

"Yep. You really made Henry angry."

Rebecca's eyes grew wide. "I couldn't believe it when he came after me. I knew I was in trouble, but I couldn't shut it down. He's scary even when I know he'd never hurt me."

"He never would."

They heard Cassidy chattering as she and Henry came down the hall.

"I didn't think she'd come in quietly tonight," Rebecca whispered. "She was having so much fun in the tent when I went out there earlier."

"Sometimes we take our luck when we get it," Polly said. "Are you nearly finished?"

"Just have to wipe the mirror. I'll take the towels down and start the load."

Polly gave her a hug. "I love you, my girl with the big heart."

"Now if I could just control my big mouth."

CHAPTER TWENTY-THREE

"Honey, Mrs. Hill won't be here for a while," Polly said to an impatient Cassidy. "Why don't we take a walk before she arrives."

Cassidy had been bouncing all over this morning. She could hardly wait for Agnes to arrive.

"Where we go?" Cassidy asked.

Polly raised her eyebrows. "Slow down, sweetie. Ask me the question again."

"Where are we going?" Cassidy asked, putting space between each word.

"Good job. I want to walk down to see Mr. Heller. He's been very busy this week and I'd like to invite him to come to our party tomorrow."

Cassidy clapped her hands. Polly was grateful that Charlie Heller, the caretaker for the cemetery behind their property, was such a gracious man. The kids found reasons to go through the gate and hedges to visit him as often as possible. Cassidy rarely went by herself, but even she enjoyed their walks through the peaceful grounds. Charlie had put her in the little cart one afternoon while he was clearing out old flower arrangements after

Memorial Day and drove her around while Polly talked to Andy on Andy's back porch. The girl had been enchanted with the trip and had gathered the dying posies into bunches around her.

Heath rousted the boys early this morning before he left for work, tasking them with moving the tent to another section of the yard. They were in charge of bringing their sleeping bags and pillows into the basement every morning. Sleeping outside in the tent kept their rooms clean longer than usual, but the basement had become a catch-all for everything they wanted to play with at night. Flashlights, lanterns, snack buckets, games, canteens of water. Everything came inside, and much to the boys' chagrin, the first time someone complained about not finding what they needed for the next night of camping, all four were relegated to the lower level until things were cleaned and organized. Polly had purchased so many large tubs this last year to collect the junk her kids amassed; she was sure they'd run out of storage space soon. Henry and Heath built shelves to store the tubs, but she hated that those would fill up and never be looked at again. She couldn't think about it today.

Right now, the four boys were upstairs getting ready for a day out at Elva Johnson's house. Nat, Lara, and Abby Waters were going out, too. There would be horseback riding, picnics, volleyball and pickleball, playing with goats and any other stray livestock that Elva managed to latch on to. Her family would all be at Polly's tomorrow, so while Polly and Cat prepared for the party, Elva offered to take care of the kids.

Polly had lost count of how many people had been invited. The parade started at ten thirty in the morning, and fireworks weren't scheduled to begin before dusk at nine thirty, so between those two events, Polly and Henry planned on a regular flow of people in and out of their neighborhood and back yard.

Rebecca asked permission to take over the front porch for her friends. She and Andrew had put together a large music playlist and they were going to rock the porch. Polly didn't care as long as she helped with setup today and cleanup when things wound down.

She'd hoped to say goodbye to the boys before Cat took them out to the Johnson's house, but Cassidy was tugging at her to go. They would have to live with the attention they had received at breakfast. Tales of spooky sounds and strange lights, stories of dreams that felt like reality, tattling on each other about talking too much or leaving the tent when Heath was asleep filled the time spent in the dining room. Every time they were outside, they had fun.

"We'll be back before Mrs. Hill is here," Polly said to Cat. "Tell the boys to be good and to call if they need us."

Cat nodded from the kitchen sink. "Will do. I won't be gone long. Do you have a plan for today?"

"Not really. We'll set up games in the foyer and drag tables and chairs up from the basement of the shed. Then I want to start shaping hamburgers and making homemade ice cream."

She wanted to freeze several batches of ice cream today, knowing that there wouldn't be enough time to freeze the amount they'd need for everyone tomorrow. Even with two freezers going all day tomorrow, it wouldn't be enough.

"Do you have the ice cream recipe somewhere?" Cat asked. "Other than in your head? I can never remember the proportions."

Polly pointed at the cupboards. "Taped on the inside of one of those. I can't either. Would you make sure we have enough chocolate chips and brown sugar to make cookies, too?"

"With everyone bringing something?" Cat asked, her eyes wide.

"Yeah," Polly said with a laugh. "Andrew begged. I couldn't resist him. They'll be easy. Andrea is coming over after lunch to help with whatever we have left to do."

"She'll remember the cornhole games, right?"

"I don't know. If not, she'll get them later. I can't worry about that. Okay, Cassidy and I are out of here. I'll see you when you get back." Polly opened the sliding door and waited for Cassidy to bounce down the steps. When Obiwan and Han looked at her piteously, she shook her head. "You can come, too. Charlie loves you boys best of all."

The dogs followed Cassidy to the back gate and all three waited for Polly to arrive. When she unlatched it, they bolted for the hedge separating the two properties and pushed through. Polly and Cassidy walked around to the sidewalk and followed it into the cemetery. She didn't even bother with leashes any longer. The dogs knew where to find Charlie and would wait patiently for Polly to show up. Charlie gave them a treat apiece when they got to him and had another waiting if they stayed in place until Polly got there.

This morning, he was out on his Gator, pulling the cart behind him. Cassidy pulled at Polly's hand. "I want to ride. Please?"

Charlie saw the dogs first and turned to look for Polly, then waved. He pointed at the cart and headed their way.

"Good morning," Polly called out when he was still a fair distance away.

"Hello to you. And to you, Miss Cassidy. Would you consider riding with me back to the shed? I don't think Obiwan and Han will wait much longer for us."

Cassidy ran to the cart, then stopped and looked back for permission. Polly hurried over and helped her daughter up and into the cart. "Go ahead. I'll be there soon."

"You ride, too," Cassidy said, patting the wooden floor.

"I'll walk. You have fun."

Charlie Heller was gruff and a stickler for proper behavior in his domain, but when it came to kids and dogs, he was a huge teddy bear. Her brood would never see his gruff side unless they were disrespectful of the people whose graves he cared for. But, because he wanted them to be comfortable here, he told them stories about the people behind the names. He'd been here for years and had come to hear stories from family members and friends. She kept encouraging him to write those stories out, knowing it would be quite a treasure, but he insisted he had no time for that. Maybe when he was too old to do the work, he'd finally do something with it.

Obiwan and Han were lying in the sun beside the caretaker's shed when she finally got to them. It was already warm this morning. The dogs would find a soft spot in the air conditioning when they got back to the house and not show their faces until absolutely necessary. She chuckled at the thought of her four grimy little boys coming home from a day playing outside with the animals at Elva's house. Maybe she should have waited to make Rebecca clean their bathroom.

"Haven't had a chance to talk at 'cha since you found that man in Boone," Charlie said. "Quite the thing. Hear ya found young Steve Robertson yesterday morning. Now, we all know that they're connected. Have ya figgered out how yet?"

She shook her head. "Still working on it."

Charlie stepped in close and lowered his voice. "Got a buddy who lives up Mason City way. Rumor is that Andrew Harrison ran drugs."

"What?" Polly asked. "What kind of drugs?"

"You know. The upper-class kind. They're makin' a big deal out of it on the news and all. Opioids or some such. Anyway. Pills. He has a high-class clientele in the Midwest because of the people he works with. His wife is in on it too. You know, she's a piano player. Does all of this touring. I think he's got a brother or maybe it's her brother. Anyway, the brother is a doctor and there's this whole crowd of them that hired those two ta transport the pills to clients." He shrugged. "It's just kinda a rumor."

"That's a pretty specific rumor," Polly said. "And hard to believe."

"I was gonna come talk to you about it, but it's been busy around here. I know you're friends with the sheriff. He'd look into it without making a big deal, yeah?"

"He would. I'll talk to him and tell him what you said. They didn't find any pills on the man."

"Prolly because the killer took 'em," Charlie said.

"So why was Steve Robertson killed?" If she had the old guy talking, she'd take whatever he could tell her.

"Heard there was a spy thing, a recording device in the room at the hotel," Charlie said. "Did Steve put it in there?"

Polly chuckled. "You hear a lot of things, Charlie Heller."

"No one pays much attention to me. It's like I'm part of the landscape. I listen and file it all away, just in case it might be necessary. So, was that what Steve did?"

"I suspect so."

"Bet'cha he heard something he wasn't supposed to have heard. Steve wasn't no dummie. He had a bunch of computers in his basement. He'd know how to listen in, even if he wasn't supposed to."

She hadn't heard anything about Steve's computers from Tab or from Aaron, but then she probably wouldn't.

"How would your buddy up north know about this, but the police have no idea?" Polly asked.

"They don't prolly run in the same crowd."

"What crowd would that be?"

He gave her a sly grin. "The crowd that has enough money to hide their faults from law enforcement."

"And he's your friend?"

"Enough of a friend that when something hits the news about his territory, I can make a quick call. I figgered that if he knew something, he'd tell me, just to brag. If he didn't know nothing, he'd tell me that, too."

"What does this buddy do for a living?"

"Nothing I'm going to tell you. You spend way too much time with those men in uniform."

"You know that if I talk to Sheriff Merritt about this, he's going to ask more questions."

"I like the sheriff a lot," Charlie said. "He can ask me any question he likes. I'll tell him what I think he needs to know. He doesn't need to know who my friend is. If they can't uncover the information they need without dragging my buddy into the investigation, they ain't worth much, now, are they?"

Polly's mind was a-whirl with this. It might be that Tab and Aaron were already on the trail of drugs. They wouldn't necessarily tell her what was going on unless she directly asked the right question. She needed to call Ray. He'd be upset that Andrew Harrison had managed to stay under the radar, but from what she read in the newspapers, this opioid problem was hiding in plain sight.

"What else do you know about this?" Polly asked Charlie, a knowing smile on her face. "You aren't finished with the story yet, are you?"

"I thought I was."

"Where would the murderer have hooked up with Steve?"

"That boy spent way too much time in the bars, and he liked to brag about being in rich people's houses around here. How they trusted him with their security codes. He'd tell anyone who listened about his big-time accounts. The boy trapped mice and killed bugs, for God's sake. He was desperate for attention."

"Henry says everyone knows him."

"Because he talks to anyone who will listen." Charlie pointed off to the left. "His mama is right over there, God rest her soul. She would have slapped his mouth quiet by now if she was still living. His daddy, on the other hand might be spending eternity next to a God-fearing woman, but he was a nasty one. Heard he beat Steve with the buckle of a belt every night whether the boy deserved it or not. That poor kid was always looking to impress the old man. Then he started acting out just because he knew he'd get a beating. He deserved better than to get shot in the head, but he didn't have much of a life."

"Did he have any friends in town?"

Charlie shrugged. "You could call 'em that. Steve was more of a hanger-on, even in high school. He was smart about computers and stuff, so they used him. You wouldn't know his buddies since they're from Boone. Let's see, what were those last names. One of them, his dad was on the city council. Kept him out of lots of trouble."

"Even from Aaron?" Polly asked.

"It wasn't nothing that was so bad the sheriff couldn't let it go. Especially if he wanted to keep his job. Wright. Yeah. That was the last name. The other was another friend of his. Burrell or somethin' like that. Give the sheriff those two names and he'll know right where to go."

"Did Steve do most of his drinking in Boone?"

"Nah. He was a local boy. Those friends of his weren't much impressed with his pest control job, even if he could get into rich people's houses. See, the only vehicle he had was that van and the company kept a good eye on it with that GPS thing. Steve tried to detach it once and they were down here and on him like white on rice. Heard him telling the crowd at the bar that it kept him honest. He could get in, but the company kept a good record and they always knew where he was. Guess that was a good thing. At least his friends couldn't talk him into stealing."

"No, just planting a Wi-Fi device," Polly said.

"How did you ever figger out it was him?"

"The company billed us because his van logged him in at the hotel and he didn't think to tell them it wasn't a call."

"Oh, that was a mistake."

"Charlie, I came down to invite you to our party tomorrow afternoon. The back yard is going to be full of people and I'd love to have you come."

"Fancy dress up affair?" he asked.

"Not at all. As comfortable and casual as you can get. We're going to have plenty of food. Henry's setting up horseshoes between the hedge and the fence."

"That's a good idea. Should-a thought of that long time ago."

"He said the exact same thing. Kids will be playing volleyball and other games. It's just food and conversation. From the sounds of it, that's right up your alley. You might learn all sorts of things."

"Oh, come on, now," he said. The man blushed. "I sound like a gossip. I just listen and if it's important I tell someone."

"I appreciate you telling me this. Aaron or Deputy Hudson might stop by to see you later today."

"I'll be here. Tell your sheriff friend to send the pretty deputy. I like her. She's a smart one."

"And pretty, too."

"You know, Miss Polly. Every woman has something beautiful about her. Some of 'em you have to look a little harder, but it's there for the finding. Sometimes when it's all over their face, you discover their hearts ain't so pretty. The perfect ones are like you. Pretty on the inside and the outside. Your Henry is a lucky man."

"Thank you, Charlie." She gave him a hug, causing him to blush even deeper. "Now, I need to get Cassidy back to the house. Mrs. Hill is coming to spend the day with her."

He frowned. "I've heard her talk about this Mrs. Hill, but I don't 'spect I've met the woman yet. She lives in Bellingwood?"

Polly pointed south and west. "In a small brick house over there. She doesn't have family in town and she's from Boone. She and her husband used to own a buffet there about thirty or forty years ago."

"I remember that place. Used to eat there a lot. Good food. Will she be at the party tomorrow?"

Polly chuckled and lifted her eyebrows. "Yes. Would you like me to introduce you to her?"

"Stop that. It's just not often that I don't know someone in town."

"I'll be sure to fix that tomorrow, then. You'll be there?"

"After the parade?"

"Any time after that. Thank you."

"I didn't do nothing. Good to see you, though. Would ya like me to give your little girl a ride back up to the hedge? Those short little legs of hers take a long time to get anywhere."

Polly looked over at Cassidy, lying on the beautiful grass between the dogs. She'd taken a few of the dead flowers out of the cart and had strung them together like Rebecca taught her with the dandelions in their own yard. "Are you ready to go back, sweetie? Mrs. Hill will be there soon."

Cassidy jumped up and ran over to them. "Do you like my necklace?"

"That's very nice," Polly said. "Tell Mr. Heller thank you for the candy and the flowers."

"Thank you," Cassidy said, wrapping her arms around his legs.

He frowned at Polly, tears in his eyes. "Your kids are too nice to me."

"You deserve it. Come on, Cass. Time to walk."

Cassidy looked longingly at Mr. Heller's cart, but took Polly's hand. The two dogs waited a few moments, just to make sure they were really leaving and sauntered along beside Polly.

When she got back inside the fence and made sure the gate was latched, the dogs ran for the house. Cassidy skipped along the yard while Polly took her phone out. Her first call was going to be to Ray, who more than likely didn't have enough information for the conversation he was about to have with Dorie Harrison.

CHAPTER TWENTY-FOUR

Andrea Waters jumped up from the counter and scrubbed her hands on the dishtowel she'd tucked into the waistband of her shorts when the back doorbell rang. "I'll get it."

"Thanks." Polly's hands were deep in the kitchen sink as she was washing the can and paddles for the first ice cream maker. Andrea was packing ice cream into containers for the freezer, a sticky business to say the least. One more batch in each ice cream maker and they'd have a good start for tomorrow.

"Hey, Polly," Tab Hudson said as she came in. She looked around the kitchen. "Wow. You have food everywhere. How many people are going to be here tomorrow?"

Polly shook her head. "I have no idea at this point. We've invited everyone we know. You and JJ are coming, right?"

"Of course. I'm making Mom's baked beans, but I think I need to buy more ingredients and make at least a double batch."

"Don't worry," Poly said. "Even if I've invited the whole world, they're all bringing food. We'll have plenty."

Tab chuckled. "Wouldn't be a party at Polly's house if there wasn't too much food."

"Exactly. What are you doing this afternoon?"

"Just finished talking with Mr. Heller. He's such a character." Tab sat down on one of the stools. When she reached out for a chocolate chip cookie, Andrea slapped her hand away.

"Bad deputy," Andrea said.

Tab laughed out loud. "Bad deputy wants a cookie. Bad deputy is going to have one and if you aren't nice to her, bad deputy will handcuff you to the countertop."

"Third person conversations are always so interesting," Andrea said. She pointed to the ice cream she was packing up. "Would you like a dish of this to go with your warm cookie?"

"Hey," Polly said. "What if we run out tomorrow?"

"Thought you said there would be plenty," Tab retorted. "But no, thank you. One cookie is all I need. Maybe two."

"Milk?" Polly asked, pointing at the refrigerator.

"Man, twisting my arm. Might as well go all out. Yes, please."

"What did you learn from Mr. Heller?" Andrea asked, carrying containers to the freezer on the back porch.

Polly nodded. "She knows about my conversation with him this morning."

"I wish he would have said something to us before about this Andrew Harrison," Tab said. "I don't know if we could have stopped Steve Robertson's murder, but maybe."

"He didn't get any of that information until after Harrison was killed. And even then, he thought it was just rumor. Why would he believe that you didn't know about it?" Polly asked.

"You're right. It's just frustrating. This changes our entire investigation. First it's about banking security ..."

"It still might be," Andrea interrupted. "Who's to say that some of his best clients aren't working at those banks? It's a great connection. Hah. Your systems security salesman is your best supplier for drugs. I like it."

"We don't," Tab said. "We're bringing DCI in and if this crosses state lines, that means the FBI will get involved. Do you see what you did here, Polly?"

Polly took a step back. "Me? I didn't do anything."

"Let's see. You found two dead bodies, brought in outside security consultants, talked to a crypt-keeper who gave you a big stinking clue and you try to tell me you didn't do anything?"

"It's not my fault." Polly stuck out her lower lip.

Tab looked sideways at Andrea. "It's never her fault."

"I wouldn't want it to be my fault either," Andrea said with a laugh. "Thank goodness my only job is to live across the street from her."

"What about those guys who Mr. Heller said were friends with Steve Robertson? Do you think they have any idea who he might have been in contact with?" Polly asked.

"Do you mean who might have killed him?"

"Yeah."

With a grin, Tab picked up a cookie. "You do understand I just now finished talking to him. We haven't interviewed anyone else. I'd have to be in Boone to do that and it's much more fun to be in your kitchen eating fresh chocolate chip cookies."

"Nobody has come forward to talk to you about Steve's death?" Polly asked. "He didn't have any friends who were worried about him?"

"Not that we've found. But then we didn't have your connection to the local gossips either. Mr. Heller gave me names to check. How does that old man get all this information anyway?"

Polly chuckled and nodded her head to gesture at the upper level. "Agnes is like that, too. These older people sit quietly in the background and no one notices them. They're invisible, so they hear everything. I think old Charlie must spend a lot of time at the bars. Bet'cha he barely drinks enough to get a buzz, but he hears everything. Best spies ever."

Cat came inside through the sliding glass doors, her face red and dripping with sweat. "I just hauled up the chairs from the lower level of the shed. We don't have to worry about that."

"I was going to help you," Polly protested.

"No problem. I needed the workout. When Hayden gets home, I'll have him help me bring up the tables."

"Justin will bring our grill over when he gets home this afternoon," Andrea said. "I asked him to pick up an extra propane tank, just in case."

Polly's eyes shot to the ceiling. "Thank you. I need to remind Henry to pick up an extra one. He said he was going to but hasn't done it yet."

"I need to go out," Cat said. "I can get it."

"Do you mind?"

"Not at all. In fact, since Cassidy and Agnes are upstairs, I'll just do it now. What time does Mrs. Hill need to go home?"

"I have no idea," Polly said. "She brought a big bag of goodies with her today. She plans to be here as long as we need her."

"How do you land on these people?" Andrea asked. "They fall into your life and take care of you." She pointed at Cat. "Like her. You have a built-in nanny because you rescued a kid off the street and embraced his older brother. How does that even work?"

Cat laughed. "That's a great question. I fell in love with a man and before I knew what happened, I'd fallen in love with this big family and begged them to let me work here. Craziest thing I've ever done."

"All I know is that one of these days Cat and Hayden are going to want their independence and I'm going to be lost," Polly said. "Until then, I'll work her fingers to the bone."

Snatching a cookie as she walked past the island, Cat headed for the door. "I'll be back in less than a half hour. Do you need anything else?"

"We're good," Andrea said, looking at Polly and Tab for affirmation. They both nodded.

After Cat was gone, Tab said, "She's amazing."

"I know," Polly agreed. "I dread the day she leaves me for her own life."

"This is her own life," Andrea said. "Give her some credit for being smart enough to make good decisions. Who knows, she may never leave you."

Polly rolled her eyes. "That would just mean more babies in this house. They can move out when that starts happening."

Tab took out her phone and they heard it buzzing. She swiped through things and then held up a photograph to Polly. "Recognize either of them?"

Polly leaned across the island, but couldn't get close enough to see the pictures, so she walked around. "No, should I?"

"It's the two men that Mr. Heller told me were friends of Steve Robertson. I just wondered if you'd seen them in town. At the hotel. At the scene of either of the murders."

"You're kidding, right?" Polly asked.

"Look, you're the one who pulled Steve Robertson out of the air. Then, Charlie Heller tells you about an opioid ring out of the blue."

"He didn't call it that."

"No, but his buddy, whoever that is, just happened to mention to Mr. Heller, the day before you just happen to show up down there, that he just happened to hear a rumor about a dead guy that you just happened to find."

"And his wife," Polly said.

The two women laughed out loud.

"Is this how things usually work with her?" Andrea asked Tab.

Tab sneaked her fingers over and took another cookie. No one said a word. "Sometimes it's more subtle than this, but yeah. Polly finds bodies and then clues fall into her lap. If I didn't know her so well, I'd think she was a master criminal, planning out the details of an impossible life. I'll be honest, I was more than a little curious about her when Sheriff Merritt first put me on the job. I was there when she and Henry found his uncle in the ditch, but that one was understandable. They were looking for him after that big storm. What was another one? Oh yeah, that lady whose husband ran the bank. Cindy Rothenfuss or something. I couldn't believe Polly wasn't involved. How in the world did she keep finding all those clues?"

Andrea shook her head. "I don't know that story."

"Mean lady. Dead in a cornfield. She had an affair with a bank clerk and he killed her," Polly said, matter-of-factly.

"How many stories are there?" Andrea asked.

Polly shrugged. "Fewer than the stars in the sky and more than the fingers on my hands."

"Enigmatic. Nice," Andrea said. "Someone should write these down. Your grandkids will want to know about your life before they arrived on the scene. Give them context for your insanity."

"I should take off," Tab said. "Lots of work ahead now that Polly's gotten involved." She grabbed two more cookies.

"It's not my fault." Polly took a napkin from the holder and handed it over. "You make it sound like I do this on purpose."

"That's downright mean of me," Tab said. "If you see your friend, Ray, before he contacts us, tell him not to wait too long. We want to hear what he found out when he talked to the widow. He hasn't called you yet, has he?"

Polly shook her head. "I'd have told you."

The doorbell rang again.

"I'll get it," Andrea called out, jumping to her feet.

"I'm right here," Polly said. "I'll get it."

She turned the corner onto the porch and laughed out loud. "Look who's here, Tab."

Ray Renaldi stood at the back door with a dark-haired woman who wore too much makeup and was dressed all in black.

"With a friend. Huh."

She opened the door. "Come on in. Don't mind the mess in the kitchen. We're getting things ready for tomorrow's party."

"Polly," Ray said. "This is Dorie Harrison."

Why not?

"I'm sorry for your loss, Mrs. Harrison," Polly said. "Please come in."

As the woman entered the kitchen, Polly shot a look at Ray. He smiled back at her and gave a slight shrug. However, when he walked into the kitchen, he turned and sent the same confused look to Polly and mouthed, "Deputy Hudson?"

Polly grinned, then said, "Mrs. Harrison, this is Deputy Hudson. She's investigating your husband's murder."

"We've spoken on the phone," Tab said, putting her hand out. "It's nice to meet you. What finally brings you to Bellingwood?"

"I'm actually on my way to Boone with Mr. Renaldi." The woman rolled the *r* in Ray's last name. "He insisted that I ride down with him to speak with you. There really was no resisting him. But before we take me to the sheriff's office, *I* insisted that he bring me to meet his friend, Polly."

Polly glanced at Andrea and at her friend's smirk, realized she had to be thinking the same thing. She'd rolled his name, but none of the other words that began with the letter *r*. She gave Andrea a mock glare and turned back to the conversation.

"What was your purpose for coming to the sheriff's office?" Tab asked patiently.

"Why, to admit my part in Andrew's activities, of course. I was aware that he was involved in something illicit, but until this came about, I had no idea to what extent."

"You knew about the drugs?"

Mrs. Harrison made a show of humility, dropping her eyes and sighing loudly. Polly recognized the dramatic behavior since her daughter did it on a regular basis.

"I'm ashamed to admit that I did. It was a horrifying discovery, but what is a wife to do? I'm expected to protect him in all things, am I not? He was such a good man, otherwise."

"I see," Tab said. "When did you discover that he was selling these pills?"

"It's been three or four years now. He has ..." She pursed her lips. "I'm sorry. He *had* a large client base. All over the Midwest." Turning to bat her eyes at Ray, she said, "Everywhere that he had an account, he established a new territory. It brought in a great deal of money."

"And that didn't trouble you?"

"Why would it trouble me? His clients are brilliant, highly educated wealthy men and women. If they choose to access medication through Andrew because their doctors are too uptight to care for them, who am I to question that? They are adults and can make their own decisions. I'm not their keeper."

Behind the woman, Ray spun his index finger, lifting it to the sky. Tab saw the gesture and took in a breath.

"Mrs. Harrison, I'll be glad to take you the rest of the way to Boone."

"I'd much rather go down with Mr. Renaldi." She rolled the *r* again. "His company is contracted to provide security for us."

"No, Mrs. Harrison. Just for your husband. I told you to contact your lawyer," Ray said. "And if Deputy Hudson is offering to take you to Boone, I'm glad to release you into her custody."

"Custody," the woman cried out. "What do you mean by that? I'm not being arrested, am I? For what?"

Tab put a hand out to placate her. "This is much better. I can take you in through the back doors and no one will know that you are there. We aren't placing you under arrest. You were planning to come in and speak to us, right?"

"Well, yes, but this feels official."

"It's better this way," Ray said. "You do need to contact your lawyer. My company does not provide security and services to family members unless requested to do so by our client."

"But Andrew would want you to do just that."

"He's not here to request it. Please go with Deputy Hudson and call your lawyer."

Tab took the woman's arm and then handed her the two cookies. "Polly just made these. They're still warm."

"I don't want your damned cookies," Mrs. Harrison said, batting them to the floor. She flailed about, causing everyone except Tab to back away. Even Ray took a step back, giving Tab a slight bow.

When Mrs. Harrison managed to land a solid hit to Tab's midsection, Tab took it in stride, swiping the arm behind the woman. In a flash, she had the other arm behind her as well and gripping the two wrists together, pulled out a pair of handcuffs and snapped them in place.

"You probably shouldn't have gotten physical with a deputy," Ray said. "Especially with this deputy. It's going to be less pleasant from here on out."

"But I've done nothing," Mrs. Harrison cried. "You can't do this to me."

Tab took her by the arm and led her out to the porch. Ray moved to open the door for her. "Need anything else from me?"

"Your report."

"It will be in your email before the end of the day," he said. "Not much there. I heard from Polly about the drugs, asked a few questions and surprise, surprise, she thought it would be better to admit it up front than to deny it. Of course, she started the day out high as a kite. You'll find a nice supply in her purse."

"She doesn't have permission to search my purse," Mrs. Harrison said.

"We'll talk about that when we get to Boone," Tab said. "How are you a concert pianist if you're this out of control? I don't understand that at all."

"I'm always in control."

"I see."

After Tab and Mrs. Harrison were gone, Ray came back into the kitchen.

"That was interesting."

"What in the world?" Polly asked. She went past him to the pantry to get her broom and dustpan. "Did she really ask to come here to meet me?"

"It was the only way I could get her into the car. I wasn't certain that I'd bring her into your house until I saw the deputy's car outside. At that point it was all about the entertainment."

Andrea howled with laughter. "I wonder what it's like to put up with her at a concert venue."

"I'll never understand how she can use drugs like that and still focus to play," Polly said.

Ray took the broom from her. "I don't think she's been using that long from what she said. There was something about a back injury last year."

"Charlie mentioned that she might have family members who were getting the drugs for her husband."

"A brother, a sister, and an uncle," Ray said. "I'll leave that to the police to figure out. I just wanted to get her down here. I'm not at all interested in being part of the investigation."

"How did you find out about her relatives?"

"She wanted to tell me about everyone else. I believe she thought that if she could deflect attention from herself, she wouldn't be involved. You know, talk loud enough, accuse everyone else and then stand in the middle of the chaos like she's an innocent party. The problem is, she's known everything, been glad to live like a queen from the money that has rolled in, and even helped her husband make connections with doctors, nurses, and pharmacists. She's deep into it."

"Tab said that the FBI would be getting involved."

"Absolutely. And that means Jon and I will be busy for a few months trying to coordinate with them and Andrew Harrison's clients. More than a few of those will be part of this."

"Does that mean you'll be visiting the Midwest more often?" Andrea asked.

He shrugged. "Polly might get tired of us." He held out the dustpan and Polly took it from him.

She walked out to the mudroom with it and dumped it in a trash bin. "I'd love to have you and Jon around more often." When she went back in, she took the broom from him and returned the items to the pantry. "Tab was kind of impressive with that woman. I love seeing her in action."

He nodded. "I watched her tense her stomach muscles. She saw it coming and took the blow. I wouldn't want to fight her in a dark alley."

"I can't believe you didn't step in," Andrea remarked.

"Nope. Deputy Hudson knew exactly what she was doing and didn't need me to be involved. If she'd given me a signal, I'd have stepped in. She was in complete control."

Polly sidled up to him and gave him a quick hug. "You know that's one of the reasons I love you, right?"

"What do you mean?"

"You could be a big ole macho Italian strong-arm, but you're not. You're smart, respectful, and thoughtful."

"All while being a big ole macho Italian strong-arm," Andrea said.

He had the grace to blush, but laughed and said, "Aw shucks, ladies."

"You just slaughtered your macho strong-arm rep there." Polly went back around to the sink and turned the ice cream cans right side up. "Do you think she had anything to do with her husband's murder?"

"I don't think so," Ray said. "I could be wrong, but she seemed genuinely sorrowful at his loss. There wasn't any playacting around that, though there was about everything else she did. That woman is definitely an excellent performer."

"Then who would have killed him? And who was spying on him? What did he do on this trip that was different than any other trip?"

CHAPTER TWENTY-FIVE

Rather than one small float, Jeff had gone all out for the Independence Day parade this year. Everyone was involved. Eliseo drove his team of Nat and Nan and had Polly's boys with him in the wagon. She and Jason rode Demi and Daisy in front of Eliseo's team, while Henry pulled up the rear with his T-Bird.

Jeff had ordered an immense banner with *Sycamore Enterprises* spelled out along with pictures of their various locations. He even had a beautiful architectural sketch of the new B&B. Kayla, Rebecca, Andrew, and Cilla preceded everyone carrying the banner. Jeff had also ordered a nice magnetic sign for Sturtz Construction and Henry agreed to put it on his T-bird, but only for the duration of the parade. She couldn't believe he'd allowed that. The funniest thing was that Agnes Hill and Cassidy were riding in the car with Henry. He'd be ready for a very stiff drink by the end of this morning.

Fire trucks and emergency vehicles, police cars, and even Tab and Aaron in their sheriff's vehicles were part of the parade. Reuben and Judy Greene had borrowed Bill Sturtz's pickup truck and decorated the bed with a huge iron flag that Reuben had made sitting amidst a garden of potted trees and plants. They sat in the back while Bill and Marie rode in front.

Mark Ogden and Sal were in his pickup truck. She had her dachshunds with her, but the bed was just fun. Dr. Jackson and Marnie Evans, Mark's partner and assistant were back there with a goat and the pot-bellied pig from Elva Johnson's farm.

Behind him was Elva and her kids riding horses and carrying a banner for Bellingwood Stables. Elva had finally settled on the name and was proud to show it off.

The library had put together a float that looked like an old bookmobile, and even the pharmacy had a float. They'd created an old-fashioned apothecary and the staff was giving out colorful stick candies.

Businesses throughout town had spent the last month designing and building floats for the day. They were ready for the celebration.

Rachel, Sylvie, and the crews from Sycamore Catering and Sweet Beans were part of the action on the street, handing out candy and coffee coupons.

As they waited for the parade to start, Polly turned to Jason. "How are things at your house?"

"Better," he said. "We talked. Mom still doesn't like the motorcycle, but at least she listened to me."

"I'm glad. Where's Mel?"

He pointed toward the front. "She's walking with her dad beside the bank's car. They're handing out some kind of commemorative coin."

"Who's driving the bank car?" Polly asked.

Jason peered at her. "The new president and his wife. Damon Morrissey is his name, I think. Mel's dad doesn't like him much. And his wife is a total bi ..."

Polly cut him off with a look.

"Sorry," he said. "She's like this prima donna who doesn't think her ..." He stopped and laughed. "I need to clean up my mouth. Both of them act like they're doing Bellingwood some kind of favor by being here. Denny doesn't think they'll be in town very long. She hates it here and he keeps trying to move up. The thing is, he's useless. Denny says that he's always late and he takes off early. When he's there, he doesn't want to talk to anybody. He makes Denny do all the work. That's who I think should be the president, but I'm no one."

"That's weird," Polly said. She'd heard rumors that the new president was a jerk. Jeff didn't like him, but he worked with others at the bank, so didn't have occasion to spend much time with the man. Henry hadn't said much, choosing to do the same — work with nearly anyone else.

"And he's been taking weird days off. No notice. Just calls in and says he's not going to be there. All he has to do is schedule vacation, but he just won't show up. He told Denny that it's personal time, not vacation time."

Polly frowned. "How often does this happen?"

"Well, it's been getting worse according to Denny. He didn't come to work a couple of days last week and he didn't answer his phone. He didn't show up on Monday this week either. I know that because Denny was supposed to have vacation all this week and he had to go in to work. When he finally reached Morrissey, the guy told him that he could have the rest of this week and all next week off to make up for it and he wouldn't mark it as vacation time."

The bank in Bellingwood had been through some rough times the last few years, starting with Cindy Rothenfuss. While her husband had been the bank president at the time, she and one of the tellers had siphoned money away. Her husband left town after it was over, though he'd been cleared of any wrongdoing. They'd gone through temporary management changes and everyone hoped that Damon Morrissey would be a stable force. The town's biggest worry was that the bank would close. While there was one other bank in town, people weren't comfortable with change.

Before she could spend much more time thinking about it, the parade in front of them moved.

Jason started to laugh.

"What?" she asked.

"Eliseo and I are going to have to come back up here with scoops when this is over."

She turned back to see Daisy lift her tail. "It never fails, does it? I remember when I was in a parade in high school. I was in the marching band and I swear to high heaven, every horse in the county was in front of us. You should have seen us dodging those piles. The director had ordered us to keep our lines straight, but there was no way. The worst thing was when we were playing our instruments and had our eyes on the music in front of us."

"Don't tell me you stepped in it."

"Not me, but the guy playing the tuba did. He was furious and you should have heard the bloops and blurps coming out of his instrument." Polly cackled like a fiend. "That was the worst."

"There's no avoiding it unless we put those bags under their tails. Eliseo says that one parade a year isn't enough to train them to that. So, we'll clean up the streets. It's my favorite thing."

Polly laughed as they turned onto Washington Street, the main street through town. The library on her right looked wonderful with its flags flying high. Washington Street was filled with throngs of people. Okay, throngs might be an exaggeration, but there were more people than she'd ever seen at one of these parades.

"Look at that," Rebecca yelled, turning around to them. "This is so cool." She waved at friends along the way.

It was hard to believe this was her life. Polly had never dreamed she would be living like this when she marched along a parade route with her band in high school. How could she? That felt like a lifetime ago. She turned in her saddle to look at the wagon behind her. Noah was sitting beside Eliseo in the front, proud as could be. She gave him a wave and he beamed. Caleb, JaRon and Elijah were hanging off the sides of the wagon, waving at people along the route. She caught Elijah's eye and he waved like mad at her. Young Polly would never have thought that she could love four little boys so much.

When she'd been in high school, Polly wasn't one of those girls who looked forward to getting married and having children. It was never a priority. Even throughout college, when her friends were starting that chapter of their lives, it held no interest for her. When people bugged her, she tried hard not to be offended that her decision to live a different type of life seemed unacceptable to them. Once, when she'd asked her dad why he wasn't pressing her, he told her that it was her life. If children would be part of it, she'd be a wonderful mother. If they weren't, she'd be wonderful at whatever she chose to do. He'd have loved knowing these kids and wouldn't have questioned for a moment that she and Henry chose to do this instead of what the world expected of them.

The parade wound through town and ended in the parking lot of the elementary school. Before they took the horses back to the barn, Jason rode over to talk to his girlfriend, Mel, and her father. Polly followed, realizing that the flashy convertible with the bank's banner was parked beside them.

She jumped down from Demi and led him over. "I see you all the time," she said to Denny Divelbiss, "but I didn't realize you were Mel's father. I'm glad to put that together." She put out her hand.

He smiled. "I guess I've always known who you were, Ms. Giller." He tapped the elbow of a man who had his back to them. "Damon, excuse me."

When the man turned to them, Polly wasn't terribly surprised to see a drawn face with bloodshot eyes. He was a handsome man in his late thirties. Dark hair, dark complexion, about five-foot-ten. He wore a well-cut linen suit and wiped sweat from his face with a white cloth handkerchief.

"Yes?" He asked Denny impatiently.

"I just wanted to introduce you to Polly Giller. She and her husband own Sycamore Enterprises."

"Nice to meet you."

Polly was desperately trying to remove the glove from her right hand, while holding Demi's reins, but it wasn't necessary. He didn't put his hand out to shake hers.

"It's nice to meet you. I'm sorry I haven't made an effort yet," Polly said. "You look awfully hot. Are you okay?"

"Fine. I wish we wouldn't have had to do this today. I had better things to do, but I was informed it's tradition."

"Have you been sick?"

He stepped back, bumping into his car. "Why do you ask that?"

"Just wondering. You look warm. I thought your wife was riding with you."

Denny smiled. "She got out earlier. It was probably too warm for her."

"She has her own vehicle," Damon Morrissey said. "I let her out so she could walk to it and go on home."

"Been a wild week in Bellingwood and Boone," Polly said. She touched Denny's arm. "You know, with the murders. I hear they think that someone local killed those two men."

After a quick glance at Morrissey for his reaction, she bit her lip and continued. "The man whose body was found in Boone worked with banks around the region. I'm surprised you didn't know him."

Denny frowned and looked at Damon. "Was that the security system guy who comes in regularly? I guess I didn't put that together. You spend more time with him than anyone else and you never did introduce me to him. Did you know him well?"

"No," Damon said shortly. "Excuse me, I need to go home and check on my wife." He opened the door and put his foot on the floor of his car.

"But you two are together every month. You always leave for lunch with him," Denny protested. "I wish I'd known that was who was killed. Why didn't you say something?"

The parking lot was filled with cars and people milling about, talking about activities during the rest of the day. There was no way that Damon would be able to get his car out of the lot. He suddenly realized that and stepped back out of his car and slammed the door shut.

"I need some air," he said, waving his arms to push Denny and Polly away.

"Maybe I should call 9-1-1," Polly said. "You look like you're having an attack of some kind." She took out her phone.

"No, just leave me alone," he said and pushed, sending her into a truck behind her. He shoved at Demi, who stood firm. The horse didn't have a lot of space. Without paying any attention to where he was walking, Damon kept moving and before Polly could open her mouth to stop him, he slipped in the pile of horse manure that Demi had just dropped. His slick leather shoes gave him no purchase and without even a peep, he ended up on the ground. No one moved. A look of shock crossed everyone's face, even those who hadn't been part of the conversation.

Denny reacted first and strode over to offer his hand, only to pull it back when Damon planted his own hand right in the middle of the manure in an attempt to stand up.

"Just a second," Polly said. She got into his car and opened the glove compartment where every good driver kept extra napkins.

"Get out of there," Damon said, then sank in on himself as Polly saw a gun lying atop a stack of napkins.

Using a napkin, she picked up the gun. She'd seen enough television to give it a quick sniff. It had been shot recently. That was all she could tell about it. She gently set it down on the passenger car seat and got back out of the car, handing Denny the rest of the napkins.

Jason looked across Demi at her. "Should Mel ride him back to the barn for you?"

"You know what's about to happen, don't you?" she asked.

"All hell's going to break loose."

Mel frowned. "What does that mean?"

Jason shook his head. "Polly thinks Damon Morrissey killed those two men."

Her eyes grew wide. "He did?" She ran over to where her father had given the napkins to Damon Morrissey. A few paper napkins weren't going to clean up the mess he'd made of himself. "Dad?"

Denny shrugged and let out a long breath. "Go on with Jason, honey. I'll tell you what happened."

"You know about this?"

He frowned. "No. I mean, I'll give you the scoop on what's about to happen. Why would you think I knew?"

"He's your boss."

"Not really. He's just *a* boss. And not a very good one at that."

Damon tried to scramble up. Polly stepped in front of him and with a slight push to his shoulder, sent him back to the ground. "It will be better for you if you sit still."

"I am not sitting in horseshit," he said.

"You'll be in jail soon. I understand they have showers and nice clean jumpsuits there."

"You think you're so smart."

"Why did you do it?" Polly asked, drawing her phone out of her pocket.

"Do what?"

"Why did you kill Andrew Harrison?"

"Who says I did?"

"The gun in your glove compartment."

He turned and looked back at the car, then scooted away from the pile of horse manure, his hands and his butt leaving a trail as he moved. She wasn't worried. He was just trying to get away from it; he wasn't trying to escape.

"I don't know about any gun."

"So, it won't have your fingerprints on it and it won't be the gun that killed Andrew Harrison and Steve Robertson?"

She dialed Tab's number and laughed, knowing that it was mean of her to call Aaron when she had a body, but Tab when she had the murderer.

"Polly, where are you?" Tab asked. "I'm meeting JJ at the winery and then we're coming over. Do you need something?"

"To turn a murderer over to you."

"No way."

"Bank president. Damon Morrissey. He hasn't told me why, but you're going to want to bring a couple of buckets of water with you. He fell in a Percheron-sized pile of horse crap and can't seem to get out of it."

"Wait. He what?"

"Yeah. Don't bring your car over. Who do you dislike the most in your office?"

Tab laughed. "He's covered in horse crap? How did you do that?"

"He did it. Well, Demi helped. Oh, and I found his gun in the glove compartment."

"Are you freakin' kidding me? How do you do this?"

"I just talk to people."

With a huff and then a sigh, Tab asked, "Where are you?"

"We're in the elementary school parking lot. There's quite a crowd. This might have been more entertaining than the parade."

"Things were so quiet this morning," Tab said with a sigh. "I should have known something was up. My car was all clean and fancy for the parade and now this."

"Tell me you have a tarp or something for just these types of situations."

"But he's going to stink up the back seat. It's not fair. Did he tell you why he killed them?"

"Why did you kill Andrew Harrison?" Polly asked Damon again. "In fact, tell me why you had Steve Robertson install a spy cam."

"Getting a little dirt on Harrison," Damon said. "He told me he was meeting a girl there. And then he told me that he was going to quit selling to me, so I needed to find another dealer. He's been taking care of me since before I moved to Bellingwood. He couldn't just cut me off like that. I figured that if I had proof of him cheating on his wife, he'd leave things as they were."

Polly nodded. "And then you killed him after you had the video?"

"There was no video. She never showed up. I met him the next day and tried to talk him out of leaving again. He got angry and told me to go to hell. I killed him and took what he had. Should last me until I can find someone else."

"Steve Robertson?" Polly prodded. She couldn't believe this jerk just admitted to murder without so much as a second thought. The world was upside-down sometimes.

"Idiot. Tried to blackmail me. Not the brightest bulb in the box. When Harrison turned up dead, Steve realized I might have had something to do with it. I should have just given him the money and told him to leave town. All he wanted was twenty-five thousand."

"He would have talked," Polly said. "Everybody always does. Even you."

She heard short blurps of the siren and when she turned, people moved out of the way. Tab drove up to them and got out of her car. She rubbed her hand across the hood. "So clean. So very, very clean."

Polly swiped the call closed and put the phone back in her pocket. "Gun is on the front seat of his car. I picked it up with napkins. Didn't touch anything but the car itself.

"We have your prints on file," Tab said. She knelt down. "Damon Morrissey, I don't want to touch you, but I'm placing you under arrest for the murders of Andrew Harrison and Steve Robertson. You have the right to remain silent. Anything you say can and will be used against you in a court of law. You have the right to an attorney. If you cannot afford an attorney, one will be provided for you. Do you understand these rights?"

He nodded, sighed, and rolled his eyes all at the same time. "Call my wife," he said to Denny Divelbiss. "Tell her to call our attorney."

"No," Denny said. "I'm pretty sure I no longer work for you and the last thing I want to do is get involved. You can call her when you get to Boone."

"Wha ... what?" Damon sputtered. "I'll have your job."

"I don't think you'll even have yours when they're finished with you," Denny said.

Tab grimaced and closed her eyes as her body shuddered. "I do not want to do this."

"Maybe this will help." Ray Renaldi came up from behind the car with a large beach towel.

"Where'd you come from?" Polly asked. "And with this?"

"We were walking back to your house when we saw the excitement. Heard what happened and I knocked on a door. A very nice lady told me she had an ugly beach towel that she was planning to take to the humane society, so I gave her ten bucks and brought it with me. Small town Iowa is awesome. Why don't I stand this one up and you can put cuffs on him," he offered Tab.

She chuckled. "I will gladly take you up on that. I have a tarp in the trunk. My beautiful clean car. My flashy clean uniform. It's just not fair."

CHAPTER TWENTY-SIX

Demi was on the way back to the barn with Jason and Mel, making Polly much later than she'd intended. As much as she loved those moments with Demi, brushing him down and turning him out, she just plain didn't have time today. She still wasn't sure how many people would be coming to her house today. Things were as ready as they would ever be, but she'd intended to grab a quick shower and hug on her kiddos before the afternoon's festivities exploded.

"Slow down, Polly," Ray said.

She slowed her pace. They were walking home together from the parking lot. "Sorry. My mind started racing, so my feet followed along."

"Are you okay?"

"What do you mean?"

"With everything that happened back there?"

"You mean the arrogant jerk falling into a pile of horse crap and admitting to murdering two people because he's a drugged out self-entitled idiot? Yeah, I'm fine with that."

"You sound a little hot under the collar."

Polly took Ray's hand. "I hate that people think they can get away with taking advantage of others. Whether it's because they have more money, more education, a better job, whatever the case might be. No one gets to flaunt their power, especially when it destroys lives."

"You could say that Andrew Harrison destroyed lives by supplying those drugs."

"Yes, you could and if I'd have had the opportunity to put him away for doing that, I would have. But murder? No. And poor Steve Robertson. He was so willing to do anything to get attention and the money to feel like he was important. But in Morrissey's eyes, he was worthless, too. Just someone else to be eliminated. And ten to one, he truly believes his lawyer and his money will get him out of these charges."

"Then the next few months will be quite a surprise for him."

"I hope so." She smiled up at him. "Thanks for showing up. Where's your brother?"

"Probably at your house by now. He and Chloe were downtown watching the parade."

"I didn't see him."

Ray shrugged. "Who knows. He was there. Your family and businesses are quite impressive. I'm glad I had the chance to be part of this today. Polly, we are so proud of you."

"It's nothing," she said, tipping her head down.

"It's everything. You are amazing. This was fun."

They turned the corner onto Beech Street and Polly groaned. Cars were parked everywhere and people were heading in to her yard. "I'm late."

"You're fine. You have friends and family who know where you were and what you were doing."

"Yeah, But I wanted a shower and a chance to sit down and think for a few minutes before the day got moving."

"Take those few minutes. We have your back."

"I'm just whining. I'll be fine. Tomorrow I'll be sad that it's all over and my house is silent again."

"Your house will never be silent."

She chuckled. "You speak truth."

"Polly! There you are." Josie and Gavin Riddle came around the corner on the other end of Beech Street with their two little ones.

Polly waved at them. "He works for Henry and she works at the coffee shop," she said quietly to Ray.

He squeezed her hand. "You don't have to tell me about everyone who is here today. I'm good with just accepting that you know them, and they are part of your world."

"It's going to feel weird to not introduce you."

"Then let me leave you here and head inside. Do you need me to take care of anything?"

"You've already done more than enough. Just make sure I meet Chloe."

"Got it." Ray crossed the street as she met up with Josie and Gavin.

"How are you?" Polly looked down at their kids. "Did you see the parade?"

"You were on a big horse," Josie's son, Freddie, said.

"I was. His name is Demi. Someday maybe your Mom and Dad can take you to the barn to meet my horses."

He looked up at his parents. Josie smiled. "We'll do that. I heard a rumor that you solved the mystery today."

Polly glanced down at the kids. "Yeah. Right there in the horse poop."

"I thought they were kidding," Gavin said. "The bank president? That was unexpected."

"That's what I thought," Polly said. They walked into her yard and she smiled at the evolving chaos. Rebecca and her friends had taken over the front porch. The kids were under strict orders to not take people inside the house. Showing them where they could find a bathroom was one thing, but bedrooms were off limits. They were all expected to be outside with the party.

"There will be quite a few kids here today," Polly said. "You and Gavin do what you want, but if you catch one of mine, they'll be glad to show CJ and Freddie around."

Josie smiled and nodded. "We'll see. Where should we put

this?" She was carrying a couple of grocery bags and Gavin had a casserole dish in a sling.

"Just through there is the back yard," Polly said. "Tables are set up. It will be crazy. You'll fit right in." She waited a moment for them to make their way and headed for the front porch. "Hey there, everything good here?"

Rebecca leaned back in the porch swing. "All good. It wasn't quite as much walking as the parades in Boone, but it was still hot. We should have a lemonade stand. We'd make a ton of money."

"I think you misunderstand what the day is about," Polly said with a laugh.

"No, it would be for a charity or something. We'd raise hundreds of dollars."

"Another time. Not today. Besides, we don't have ingredients to make that much lemonade."

"It was just a thought. Did you really push the president of the bank into horse poop? Everybody is talking about it."

Polly shrugged. "Maybe. I didn't want him to get away."

"He was the murderer? Why?"

"And this, kids," Polly said dramatically, "is why you don't do drugs. Bad things tend to happen to you. You fall into horse poop while wearing your fancy linen suit and a lady who should know better won't let you get up until the cops arrive."

"Your mom does the best stuff," Dierdre Adams said. She looked different today. More relaxed and less sullen. It also helped that she'd toned the goth look way down. She was still dressed in black, but her makeup wasn't quite as harsh and she'd softened the spiky hair on top of her head.

"I'm heading around back," Polly said. "Is Henry here?"

"He and a bunch of guys are hanging at the grill," Andrew said. "He called Eliseo and he's bringing our grill over. Jason's helping."

"Really? They don't need to do that. We can cook things on the indoor grill in the kitchen." She took off at a trot and caught up to Leroy Forster who was coming in with Ben Bowen and his wife, Amanda. The two men worked for Henry and she'd known them from the days she was living out of boxes at Sycamore House.

"There's the star of the hour," Leroy said.

She'd been afraid of this big man for years. He was brusque, loud and didn't care what he said. But the day he'd called to tell her that Henry had been in a terrible car accident, she'd discovered what a soft-hearted man he really was.

"Because I can ride a horse or throw a party?" Polly asked with a grin.

"Heard you took down the president of the bank. Never liked that man," Leroy said. "Shoulda known he was up to something shady."

"I wasn't expecting murder, though," Polly said. "It's good to see you here. I need to catch Henry before he starts bringing grills in from all over town."

"We could have loaded ours up," Amanda Bowen said. "You should have called."

"That's the thing," Polly said. "We don't need them. Men and their cooking gear. I'll talk to you later." She smiled at them and wove her way through their friends to the patio where Henry, Kirk Waters, Jeff Lindsay, and Bill Sturtz were standing.

"Polly!" Bill said. He pulled her into a side hug. "We wondered if the police were going to ever let you go."

"Me too," she replied. "Tab did not want to take that man back to Boone in her clean car."

"You really pushed him into horse crap?"

"I did not. He fell in it. When he tried to get up, I might have given him a little push to keep him in place, but I didn't push him in the first time."

"She has an answer for everything. I'm glad you married this one, son," Bill said.

"You mean out of his thousands of choices?" Polly asked. She winked at Henry.

"That's exactly what I mean. They were beating down the door to get to him."

Henry laughed. "Eliseo and Jason are bringing over another grill."

"Why? We can use the one inside."

He pointed at a small table that had been set up. "We got more meat than we expected. Mom and Aunt Betty marinated pounds and pounds of chicken. We've already started grilling those."

"Oh," Polly said. "Okay. We still could have used the one in the kitchen."

"I'd rather just stay out here. Eliseo was more than willing. As soon as they finish with the Percherons, they'll run home and get it. You okay?"

"I'm good. Do you know Denny Divelbiss?"

He nodded. "Sure. Mel's dad. He's a good guy. Why?"

"Well, he was part of this whole thing at the elementary school. I invited him to come over. He didn't have any other plans."

"That's great. We should have just invited the whole town."

She turned back toward the entrance to the back yard and saw Lydia, Beryl, Andy, and Len come in followed by Joss, Nate, their nanny, Traci, and all six kids. Elva Johnson and her crew walked in with them. Before she turned back to Henry, she saw Marta, Shelly, and Shelly's father, Mike, come in with Nora and Orville Worth, the couple who owned the house where Shelly lived.

"I think we have most of the town here," Polly said. "I really want to get inside and change into shorts. Can you hold down the fort a little longer?"

Henry gestured out over the yard. "Everyone is taking good care of themselves. All we need to do is announce when they can start eating and the party will be off and running."

"Another fifteen or twenty minutes," Polly said. "Give more people time to get here. We're just getting started."

He caught her arm as she walked past to go up the steps into the kitchen.

"What?"

"I love you, you know."

"I love you, too. What's this about?"

"Everything. All of these people. Our kids have friends, we have friends, we have a wonderful place to host parties, and you find dead bodies and their murderers. There's no shortage of entertainment with you around."

"Now you're being rotten."

"Maybe." Henry leaned in and kissed her. "Go change your clothes. Nothing will happen until you come back."

"Be sure it doesn't. I don't want to miss anything."

Polly ran in and scooted up the back steps, nearly crashing into Hayden and Cat who were about to come down.

"Sorry," Cat said, her face flushed.

"No problem. Everything okay?"

Cat bit her lip. "Yeah. It's fine."

"What?" Polly asked. "You look like you've seen a ghost. Talk to me."

Cat and Hayden looked at each other, then she burst out. "I think I'm pregnant."

Polly grabbed the girl into her arms. "Congratulations. That's fantastic."

When Cat gave her a half-hearted hug, Polly pulled back. "It is fantastic, isn't it?"

"It's too early," Cat said. "This was not in the plans. We were supposed to be finished with school and I'd have at least a year or so in my job and Hayden would have a good job before we even thought about having babies."

Polly pulled her back into a hug. "Honey, you have to let go of your best-laid plans. You have each other. You have us and you have a life inside you that will change the world."

"What?" Cat asked.

"Trust me. Babies change your world and children have so much potential. You never know. Today is a day for excitement and joy. You don't have to do any of this alone. You'll be fine. I promise."

Hayden was beaming and couldn't stop touching his wife.

"You're happy about this, aren't you, Hayden?" Polly asked.

"I just want her and the baby to be healthy. Everything else is just a matter of getting through it. At least she's doing her student teaching this fall."

"Exactly," Polly said. She reached up and touched Cat's cheek, brushing aside tears that had started to fall. "I know it's scary, and since you weren't planning for it, you haven't given it any thought, but you have an immense family who will surround the three of you with so much love."

"I don't want to tell anyone else yet," Cat said.

"That's fine. I love you two so much," Polly said. She felt her own tears threaten. "I can't believe that you're going to bring more life into this family." Then she frowned. "I'm too young to be a grandma."

Hayden laughed and even Cat grinned at her. "Too bad. Maybe we'll teach the baby to call you Granny Giller, just for fun."

"That sounds awful, but whatever I'm called, I am absolutely thrilled. Anything that you think can't be dealt with, we'll figure out." Polly hugged Cat a third time. "I'm so happy. What a wonderful thing to know today."

"We heard about your morning," Hayden said. "That's crazy."

"It definitely is. Okay, you go downstairs. I need to make a quick change. Thank you for telling me."

Cat nodded. "Thank you. I'm so scared."

"You get to be scared," Polly said. "We'll be there whenever it's too much." She watched them walk down the steps and tears broke through as she turned to head for her bedroom. Life never stopped moving forward. Just about the time she thought things might settle down, another little one was about to enter her home. At least she hoped they would feel confident about this being their home. Until they were ready to move out, she was happy to have them here.

Polly felt much better in her shorts, tank top and sandals. When she walked past the open door to the foyer, she heard voices and went out onto the landing. Not seeing anyone, she wandered down the steps and grinned when she found Jon and a cute young woman standing in the center doorway to the hall.

"Hello," she said.

"I was just showing Chloe around," Jon said apologetically. "I hope that's okay."

"Of course it is." Polly strode up to the two of them and put her hand out. "I'm Polly."

"You are!" the young woman said. She was all of about five foot nothing and had the sweetest face with bright blue eyes. Polly couldn't believe this woman was the powerhouse that Jon had described, but looks could be deceiving. "I'm Chloe. Jon is terrible at introductions. You have a wonderful home here. I can't believe you live in this big place."

"You haven't met her family," Jon said. "She needs a place this big for everyone."

"I keep hearing about them. I guess I hadn't put it all together. Thank you, Ms. Giller, for allowing us to join you today."

"It's Polly and I'm glad to meet you. Hearing that Jon had finally found the woman of his dreams was a wonderful surprise."

"I don't know if I'm that ..."

He interrupted. "You are. I promise."

Chloe laughed. "You're sweet, but you might change your mind someday and I don't want your dreams to become nightmares."

"Let me tell you, Chloe," Polly said. "If this one has introduced you as the woman of his dreams, that means he's never planning to change his mind. You wouldn't have made it to the first meeting with his mother if you were just a fling."

Jon shook his head. "This is not what I wanted to talk about today."

"When did you want to talk about it?" Chloe asked.

"Never would be fine with me."

"How much of the house have you seen?" Polly asked.

"I think the whole main floor. Is that right?" She turned to Jon, who nodded. "He brought me in through the tunnel. That is fun! What a great place for kids to play. In fact, this whole town is like the perfect place to raise kids. I have some clients who grew up in Iowa and they always talk about their childhoods with longing that I don't see in a lot of other people. You moved back from Boston, right?"

Polly nodded. "I lived in Iowa until I went to college, but then, yes, I moved back."

"Because of family?"

"No. I'm an only child and my family is gone. I just wanted to be where I could breathe again."

"I understand that," Chloe said. "Especially if you knew that kind of life before moving into the city. I don't know what I'd do without all the excitement. Knowing that there is always something to do no matter what time of day it is. I love the crush of people and knowing that I'm just one little part of something so vibrant and big."

"I loved that too," Polly said. "It's why I stayed so long. Isn't it wonderful that we have both options and everything in between? No matter what you love, you can find it."

Chloe smiled. "We should let Polly get to her party. It was nice to meet you."

"How long are you staying in town?"

"Now that you wrapped everything up so neatly," Jon said, "we plan to fly out on Saturday."

"You'll be here tomorrow?"

He nodded.

"Then come over tomorrow evening. We'll relax and get to know each other without scores of people around us."

Chloe looked at Jon, who shrugged. "Are you sure? Won't you need to recover?"

"I can do that any time. I'd rather spend time with you," Polly said.

Jon nodded. "We'll be here." He guided Chloe back into the hallway and they headed for the kitchen.

Polly went out on the front porch and found even more kids there than when she got home earlier. Libby Francis was sitting by herself at the far end of the porch. Polly turned to Rebecca. "We're starting lunch soon. You all can go to the back yard any time."

"Cool," Andrew said. "I'm starving. Eliseo and Jason just got here."

"Great. Rebecca, can I talk to you inside?"

Rebecca looked at Kayla and Cilla, gave them an eye roll and followed Polly into the foyer. "I tried to talk to her," she said when the door closed.

"To Libby? She's not having it?"

"She told me that her life was none of my business and that I'd already done enough to ruin it, so I should just back off. She's only here because her mother made her come."

"You're going to let her get away with that?" Polly grinned at her daughter.

"What do you mean? I tried. If she wants to sulk, that's not my problem."

"I know it's hard to believe, but it *is* your problem."

"No," Rebecca said sternly. "It is not. She dug her own hole and doesn't want a hand to get up out of it. Not my problem. I have other friends to think about."

"If Cilla were in this much hurt because of things she had no control over, would you behave the same way? If Kayla quit talking to you because of all she had to deal with, you'd be okay with that?"

"That's different."

"No, it's not different. You are strong and healthy. You have a family who loves you and friends who want to be with you. When you have everything in the world going for you, you also have a responsibility to care for people who need you to lift them up. Libby needs you whether either of you want to admit it."

Rebecca lifted her lip in a mock snarl. "You don't make it easy to be your daughter."

"If you weren't such a wonderful person, I would never expect this of you."

"Maybe I should work on being rotten. This is hard stuff."

Polly nodded and pulled Rebecca close. "Life is made of hard stuff. Libby didn't wander off into the back yard when she got here, she stayed close to you. She could have gone back to her car, but she didn't. That girl desperately wants you to help her fix this. She doesn't know how to do it on her own. Help her. You have it in you."

"I hate it when you're right," Rebecca said. "Does that mean because I have a good life, I have to take care of everybody else?"

"Not everybody else. Henry and I will pick up the slack when we can, but when someone has been your friend and needs you to support them, yeah, you're up."

"Sometimes I wish I didn't have friends that needed me."

"Trust me, that feeling is going to be part of your life forever, but you're better with them."

"How do I do this?"

"Just sit down and talk to her. Don't talk about anything stressful. Laugh about me and the man in horse poop. Talk about your cats. Tell her something funny about your brothers. She knows what it's like to have younger siblings. Tell her about cleaning toilets. Whatever it takes, just talk to her."

"I can talk. I do that really well."

"Yes, you do. You are a master."

Rebecca looked up at her. "Should I be offended by that?"

"Your choice. I love you, sweet girl."

"I love you too. Not sure if I love that you expect so much of me, but I still love you."

"I don't expect anything of you that I'm not confident you can do."

Rebecca stepped back. "Okay. I'll do it. If you're wrong about me, you're cleaning the next bathroom."

"I promise."

~~~

Polly slung her leg across Henry's as she snuggled up to him later that night. He turned toward her. "Long day."

"But it was a good one when all was said and done. The fireworks were fun. I love watching those boys. Cassidy didn't know whether to fall asleep or throw her arms up in glee."

"Agnes is so good with her. I was afraid she might fall asleep too, and I'd have to carry both of them to the car."

"They were pretty cute." Polly kissed his cheek. "Thanks for all you did today. I get an idea for a party that blows up and becomes the biggest get-together the town has ever seen and you go with the flow, making sure we feed everyone and keep them happy."

"We have a mess to clean up tomorrow."

"That's tomorrow," Polly said. "Tonight I'm just glad for a good day."

"When do you have to go down to the sheriff's office to finish giving your statement?"

"If I can get out of here tomorrow afternoon, I'll run down. Can you believe it was Damon Morrissey? That bank is going to be in so much trouble."

"Second time something has happened with one of its employees." He squeezed her tight. "They need you on the hiring committee."

"Nope. Don't want that responsibility. Cat's pregnant."

Silence fell over their bedroom and then Henry breathed. "Umm, wow?"

"She doesn't want to talk about it yet. The poor girl was taken off guard by the whole thing. Hayden's thrilled, but she's worried about how their life plan has been tossed out the window."

"She's lived here with you long enough, she should have learned that plans are simply recommendations."

"Cat will get there."

"When ..." he started.

Polly put up her hand. "I didn't ask any questions. Next winter or spring, I'd guess."

"They won't try to move out, will they? They're more than welcome to stay until after Hayden graduates."

"We'll have those conversations when she's ready for them. They need to settle down about the whole thing first."

Henry caressed her cheek. "At least she has you to be normal and sane."

"About a baby? I don't think so. Those things terrify me."

"You're so funny," he said with a laugh. "You're going to be a grandma."

"And you a grandpa. Don't get cute with me."

"I'll be a great grandpa. This is going to be entertaining. Speaking of entertaining, did you see Mary Francis talking to Reuben and Judy Greene?"

Polly frowned. "No. What were they talking about?"

"According to Uncle Dick, Reuben talked to her about coming into the gallery this fall to work for him."

"What? How did he even know?"

"I'm sure Mom told them. She's paid attention to all that has happened with Libby because Rebecca was involved."

Polly often forgot how small Bellingwood truly was. "That makes sense. Well, that would be wonderful. Rebecca was great with Libby after a little encouragement."

"I was surprised to see them all together. She's a good kid."

"Rebecca?"

"Yeah. Good for her."

"Tell her that, would you? She isn't sure about the whole taking care of people who need it thing, especially after they've made your life hell, but she'll get there."

"She has a pretty good role model."

"I dump bad men in horse crap."

He laughed out loud. "Best story of the day, I just have to say. There was no one at the party today who liked that guy. If they could have given you an award they would have."

"I don't know," Polly said, dropping her head to his shoulder. "He's smart, educated, good-looking, had a good job and still got caught up in drugs and murder. I worry about my friends and my family. It's too easy to get your hands on that stuff."

"I know. We all do. Your family is lucky to have you love them, though. You'll kick their behinds if they get themselves into something like that."

"You're right, there," she said. "I talked to Jon's Chloe today and got to thinking about how thankful I am that I moved to Bellingwood."

"A lot of us are," he said, his hand rubbing down her back. "Very happy."

She put her finger on his lips and brushed it down his chin and neck. "I wouldn't have wanted to miss out on these moments for anything."

THANK YOU FOR READING!

I'm so glad you enjoy these stories about Polly Giller and her friends. There are many ways to stay in touch with Diane and the Bellingwood community.

You can find more details about Sycamore House and Bellingwood at the website: http://nammynools.com/. Be sure to sign up for the monthly newsletter so you don't miss anything.

Join the Bellingwood Facebook page:
https://www.facebook.com/pollygiller
for news about upcoming books, conversations while I'm writing and you're reading, and a continued look at life in a small town.

Diane Greenwood Muir's Amazon Author Page is a great place to watch for new releases.

Follow Diane on Twitter at twitter.com/nammynools for regular updates and notifications.

Recipes and decorating ideas found in the books can often be found on Pinterest at: http://pinterest.com/nammynools/

And, if you are looking for Sycamore House swag, check out Polly's CafePress store: http://www.cafepress.com/sycamorehouse

CPSIA information can be obtained
at www.ICGtesting.com
Printed in the USA
LVHW041615290819
629407LV00011B/582/P